THICKER
Than
WATER ₃

Also by Takerra Allen

Thicker than Water

Still Thicker than Water

THICKER
Than
WATER₃

TAKERRA
ALLEN

Kensington Publishing Corp.

http://www.kensingtonbooks.com

DAFINA BOOKS are published by

Kensington Publishing Corp.
119 West 40th Street
New York, NY 10018

All Kensington Titles, Imprints, and Distributed Lines are available at special quantity discounts for bulk purchases for sales promotions, premiums, fund-raising, and educational or institutional use. Special book excerpts or customized printings can also be created to fit specific needs. For details, write or phone the office of the Kensington special sales manager: Kensington Publishing Corp., 119 West 40th Street, New York, NY 10018, attn: Special Sales Department, Phone: 1-800-221-2647.

Dafina and the Dafina logo Reg. U.S. Pat. & TM Off.

ISBN-13: 978-1-61773-624-7
ISBN-10: 1-61773-624-4
First Kensington Mass Market Edition: October 2015

eISBN-13: 978-1-61773-625-4
eISBN-10: 1-61773-625-2
First Kensington Electronic Edition: October 2015

10 9 8 7 6 5 4 3 2 1

Printed in the United States of America

Acknowledgments

God—You are the man. You are the truth. To you be the Glory. Journey, Mommy loves you. Everything I do is for you. Jaielyn, the sweetest, most beautiful stepdaughter ever. Love you. Barry, so glad to have you as my husband. I love you. Mommy, it's getting a little easier. But I still miss you, every single day. Daddy, thank you. I'm so proud to have you as my father. Dee, I'm so lucky to have you holding me down in both aspects of my life—in business and as a great friend. We're doing it! Kiss my babies. My sisters, N'neka and Leslie. My brothers, Corey, Billy, Landon, Malik, and Joe, love all you guys. Pac, they can picture me rollin' now. I owe it to you. Nana, I miss you every day and I love you. The best aunts ever, Les and Barbara. Carol Floys, my fairy godmother. Ms. Brenda and Jennifer and the Roman and Mobley family. Love you guys. All of my family that I adore—cousins, nieces, nephews, etc., I love you guys so much. To my luvs, my adoring and incredibly patient readers, I love you guys so much. You are my fuel, my purpose, and I am so grateful for you all. Thank you so much for your support up until this point. I am just a girl from Jersey who started writing and you guys started reading, and it's all because of you that the rest of the world is paying a little attention now. I hope I keep you guys forever. Kensington/Dafina, thank you.

SO . . . this is it. The closing of a saga. The end of an era. I want to thank the cast of the *Thicker than Water* series for everything you have done for me. Books like *Heaven's Hell* and *Restricted* may have made the magazines and award shows, but you put me on the map with the readers. So to me, you guys are the truth for that. (Sorry Heaven, G, Jordin, and Julez :/) I can't believe this is it. I can't believe that I won't have you guys to fall back on, characters that the world has fallen in love with, the ones I can always come back to and peek in on their lives, write it up and know that they will love it because you guys are so authentic. But I promised you guys would go out with a bang, didn't I? Sasha, thank you for being my beautiful leading lady, and for showing the readers your naïveté and your flaws, even when it made them want to wring your neck. Thank you for doing it again in this one. Chauncey, thank you for showing the world that real dudes do mess up, do stupid things, and don't always make sense. But they can still be irresistible. Respect, thank you for letting me introduce you to the readers. I know you don't like to be looked in on like that. But they had to see it to believe it. Kim, I know you're gone. But thank you for blessing me with your charisma while I could. You set an ill foundation in TTW, and two books later, your memory still lives on. Neli, thank you for being my disturbed, broken-winged bird. You took a lot of hate from these readers. Jayde, you happily picked up that hate. Thank you for being a perfect villain. Someone's gotta be the bad guy, right? Tatum, thank you for being real. As real as the girls that walk by me every day. A little tough, a little weak, a little happy, a little sad, and I appreciate you letting these people look into your life to see that. And thank you for playing my star . . . one . . . last . . . time.

Prologue

"Have you ever felt so alone and then looked in the mirror, and realized you probably hate yourself more than everyone else does?"

—Neli, *Thicker than Water*

"I'm Adriana . . . What's your name?"

"Lola . . ."

"Nice to meet you, Lola." Adriana smiled, extending her dainty hand to the brown-skinned, Coca-Cola-bottle-shaped woman next to her.

Lola continued to file her nails as if she didn't see the gesture.

"So . . . what nursing school did you graduate from?" Adriana probed.

". . . I went to Emory."

"So did I! What hospital did you work at before this?"

Before attempting to reply, the newest nurse subtly rolled her eyes at the hyper girl's chatter. Adriana reminded Lola of a less cute version of Lucy Liu. And she *knew* that Adriana was not her real name. What Asian was named Adriana?

"This is my first position. . . ."

Lola was nervous by the silence that followed.

"Your first . . . ? Really . . . ? They put you on ER your first day?" Adriana held a confused facial expression. "Wow, have you been trained? Did you even consult with any of the doctors?"

"Damn, you ask a lot of fucking questions!" Lola snapped, losing her cool and immediately regretting it.

Before Adriana could even recover from the harsh response, a young girl on a gurney covered in blood came whizzing by their desk, pushed quickly by EMT workers.

"It's that time, people . . . We need a doctor, now! This woman's been shot!"

Lola and Adriana immediately ran from behind the Emergency counter anxious to assist.

Oh my God! She's so young, Adriana thought to herself. *And she's really pretty.*

Lola was lost in her own thoughts.

She's so bloody. . . . Goodness, am I going to be able to do this?

Adriana took control and wheeled the wounded young girl into one of the nearest rooms.

"The doctor's already been paged!" she let Lola know, feeling like this could be a shock on someone's first day. "That's normal procedure. We have to start the IV and check the vitals, her airways, her pulse, all of that."

Just then the doctor entered and immediately approached the victim.

"She's losing a lot of blood! We have to stop this bleeding!"

"You! Start the IV," he ordered, pointing at Adriana; however, Lola already had it in her hands.

"I'm already doing that," she answered meekly. Two

other nurses who had entered with the doctor began to tend to the bleeding and Adriana decided to check the young woman's vitals.

"No, you go check her belongings! See if we can get some information on her. Allergies, medications, see if she has insurance," he stated as if that was the most important thing they could find out about her. "Look for contact names."

Adriana hesitantly inched toward the door. Should she be the one checking for information? That should be something Lola should cover, it was *her* first day after all.

"But . . ."

Adriana at that moment began to fear that she would never be respected by the doctors at Grady Memorial Hospital.

"Check her belongings? I want to help her," she mumbled aloud as she reluctantly stepped outside of the room.

Adriana picked up her pace toward the EMT workers who were still seated in the back of their open ambulance, right outside of the emergency room. She knew that it could be vital if the woman in fact did have medication allergies or anything of that nature.

"Hey! You guys got anything on the girl that just came in?"

"The little redbone, sprayed up like Swiss cheese?" the young worker cracked insensitively as he pulled from his cigarette. The other guy of fewer words tossed a black leather purse toward Adriana.

"There ya go. Now when we gonna hook up, Ming Lee," wise guy continued.

Adriana rolled her eyes and turned on her heels, beginning to roam through the bag in haste.

"Wit'cha flat ass!" he added in anger, but she continued to walk, no longer hearing him. She was too enthralled by the contents.

First thing she spotted was a black leather wallet. Opening it, she read the driver's license aloud.

"Penelope Daniels . . . 575 Ann Street, Newark, New Jersey? . . . You're a long way from home, Penelope," she spoke solemnly.

Adriana continued to rummage through the wallet, not coming across much else. A flight ticket, forty dollars, an old ID card to somewhere called Greystone . . . and a picture. She paused at the picture of four beautiful black girls taken at what seemed to be a nightclub. They must have been her friends. They were an array of earth-tone shades but equally stunning.

Feeling that the purse had a significant weight to it, Adriana remembered the task at hand and dug deeper. She felt all types of junk, typical woman things. Suddenly her hand ran across a ripped lining on the side and she pushed her petite fingers through it as much as possible.

"What the . . . ?" she questioned, as she grabbed something metal and pulled it out with ease.

Adriana stared down with her brows furrowed and a million thoughts racing through her mind.

A tape recorder?

"She's stabilizing, I think she's gonna make it! But we need to get her into surgery. Where's Adriana?"

Neli could hear the doctor and nurses talk amongst the room but they sounded so far away. *So, so far away . . .*

Her body felt tingly all over. She had heard them say she was losing blood but she felt no pain.

That's how it is, she could remember Kim saying one

time at Tatum's house. *Lil Pookie said you see the light and all that.*

Tatum, Sasha, and Neli had laughed at her, but now Neli wondered if Kim knew what she was talking about. Flashbacks of Kim's laugh replaced that memory. And then ones of Sasha's beauty, Tatum's smile.

Okaayyy, white bitch! she could hear them all shout as they got ready to hit the clubs.

Y'all my girls and I'll do anything for y'all, Tatum had told them seriously one day in her living room. Scenes played in her mind like a picture slideshow. Sasha's family cookout, the night they met Ree at the club . . .

That nigga look like somebody from Shottas! Kim had shouted. Neli laughed to herself at that.

He looks like a killer, she could hear herself respond.

The day they met Chauncey, her best friend's boyfriend, replayed also.

Why you so persistent? he had asked with his white smile and chocolate skin.

Because I like you.

An image of them making love entered her mind. She remembered the feel and smell of him.

Damn, you know how to make a nigga feel good.

Then it all turned sour after that.

Stop fucking calling me! You crazy bitch!

Neli, what is wrong with you? I know you've always been jealous of me, Sasha accused the time the girls all went to dinner.

Maybe you should get some help, she recalled Ray, her old boyfriend, whispering to her. Neli wanted to wake up, her demons were catching up with her and she didn't want to hear any more. She didn't want to relive these memories.

Bennie, I got something for you. Her name is Sasha. She's

got her boyfriend's money. She'll be alone. . . . That was the phone call she had made to set Sasha up.

It was Chris, it was Chris who took your money, she could see herself lying to Respect after she had been responsible for getting him robbed.

You have to kill Kim. That was another conversation with Bennie, which ended in the death of her good friend, all because Kim had known too much.

No, no . . . I'm sorry.

Now she was at Greystone, involuntarily revisiting her days in the psychiatric hospital . . . and there was her friend Emerald.

No, I wish I never met you, Emerald.

I want you to meet somebody, Emerald had introduced with a smile. *Jayde, this is Neli, Neli, this is Jayde . . .*

How do you know Sasha? she could hear Jayde ask as she had studied Neli's pictures on her bedroom wall at Greystone.

She's the bitch that has my man . . . Neli had responded to Jayde with contempt. *She also used to be my best friend.* She remembered the smirk Jayde wore after that.

I wish I could take it back, Neli thought, feeling terrible. *I wish I never met you, Jayde.*

Flashbacks of her here in Atlanta trying to warn her friends about Jayde's intentions began to play.

Sasha, please! Just listen to me.

Fuck you! Sasha had shouted after punching her down the steps.

I should've made you listen, Sasha.

I'm feeling like it's judgment day, your wicked ways have caught up with you. . . . Those were the words Jayde had cursed her with. She could envision Jayde again, standing with her gun aimed at her, which had all occurred not too long ago.

Pow! Pow! Pow! She remembered feeling the bullets.

But she wasn't dead yet. Being in this state was like being asleep, feeling emotions with no accompanying actions. She wanted to cry, she wanted to scream, and she wanted to tell someone, anyone . . . everything.

If I can only make it . . . please let me make it.

"Can someone please tell me *why* I am wasting valuable time waiting for someone to come and scrub me down when I can be saving someone's life?" the doctor questioned in a condescending tone, eyeing all three nurses.

No one moved.

"Anyone?"

Silence.

"Goddammit, you and you, let's go! . . . Damn airheads!"

Two of the nurses scattered out as the doctor trailed them, ready to begin his scrub and dress for surgery. Lola could hear them shuffle and then begin to retreat, and she seized the twenty-second moment. *It's now or never, I should have done this.*

Lola slid her hand into the pocket of her scrubs and produced the prefilled needle that she had been carrying. Stepping over to the bed, she began to switch it with the standard IV that Neli was already hooked to. Hearing the door creak open, she rammed the new needle into Neli's fresh vein, puncturing it and causing a few drops of blood to spill.

"Shit!"

She quickly wiped it with her hand and shoved the old needle into her pocket. Neli would not be making it to surgery, not with the syringe full of potassium chloride now pumping into her system.

The doctor marched in, ready to operate and bring a

now stable Neli into recovery. It wasn't but a minute into the procedure, however, when she began to go into a violent cardiac arrest.

"She's going into arrest! What the hell is happening? That's why I say every fucking second counts!" he shouted.

As the room went into panic and everyone's focus seemed to be elsewhere, Lola took the opportunity to lean into Neli's ear and whisper three sweet farewell words.

She rubbed Neli's wavy hair and smirked down at her with a wicked grin, knowing her boss would be pleased with her accomplishment. She had attained the goal that she was sent to the hospital to complete. Venom dripped from her lips as she whispered to a dying Neli with certainty and malice.

"Say Jayde, bitch . . ."

Flatline.

Chapter 1

"Sean, I'm having your baby. How is that not personal?"

—Trinity, *Still Thicker than Water*

Act I

Nine months later

"All rise fah Judge Mah-jorie! She gon' entah tha courtrum . . ."

Tatum took the deepest breath and stood slowly on shaky knees.

"Da recess ovah, court resume," the judge spat sharply, sauntering in.

Tatum's eyes stayed fixated on the large Jamaican woman as she waddled her way to her old wooden pedestal, which overlooked the courtroom. The motions were as if this woman were the Lord herself and they were all sinners and saints, impatiently waiting to learn their destiny.

"Ya be seated now," the judge then ordered.

Tatum took her seat again, thinking of the irony. In some sense, that's exactly what this was like. This woman held the key to the door that would unlock the rest of Tatum's life. All with whatever words chose to fall from her lips.

Stop it, Tatum . . . this is not about you, she had to remind herself. *This is about him. . . .*

Shifting her eyes from the judge, Tatum shot them to that beautiful man of hers . . . to Respect . . . who was only a few rows ahead of her on what would be considered the plaintiff's side of the courtroom. Tatum studied the back of him, which was as mesmerizing as his front. His broad and masculine shoulders, his sexy dreads that he regularly wore pulled back, falling long and begging Tatum to run her fingers through them, the way he filled out his $4,500 Brioni suit so effortlessly, his laid-back demeanor. His swag was inimitable, even as he sat awaiting his fate.

Tatum knew he had to be on edge, there had to be some sense of urgency running through him, but he would and could never show it. She half-smiled at his strength. Yes, it was all about him.

Feeling a set of eyes on her at that very moment, Tatum suddenly darted her gaze. *And her. It's about her, too,* she reminded herself as well.

She and Trinity made bold eye contact.

"Mr. Knights . . . Ms. Bell," the judge addressed Ree and then Trinity, who was forced to wrench her body forward and reluctantly transform her scowl at Tatum to a slight, bashful smile toward Judge Marjorie.

Tatum winced at the way Trinity had carried her aura since the moment this all began; as if she was more important than she actually was. Trinity sat with her long, tree-bark-complexioned legs crossed, hands resting lightly on her knees and her head high. As if she had been Ree's wife of ten years, instead of his beck-and-call plaything for only one.

"We now have de results of yah pah-ternity test. Ya ready ta 'ear 'em?" Judge Marjorie looked from Trinity to Ree and couldn't help the twinkle in her eyes as they landed and briefly rested on Respect. She could see why this woman so desperately wanted him to be the father of her child.

Tatum's stomach flipped repeatedly at the anticipation of the results. All the time she had been thinking of how unprofessional the court procedures in Jamaica had been compared to America, even down to the way they talked. She had been thinking of how hot it was in there, how not one single breeze had crept into the vast place and provided any kind of relief. How, unbelievably, there were no lights, only sunrays creeping through the dirty venetian blinds lightly illuminating the area. How the judge seemed to be so blasé, except for when admiring Ree; the officers seemed annoyed, the whole process just one big shenanigan. But now, she couldn't think of any of that.

"In the case of Sean Knights Jr. . . . ." Tatum fought against the sudden urge to vomit that always surfaced every time she heard the name Trinity chose to name her child.

"Mr. Knights . . ."

Tatum placed her hands together in a prayer fashion and pressed them firmly against her lips. Tears began to rim her eyes for reasons beyond her and the only thing that gave her the slightest sense of calm was Ree briefly turning to her and giving her a reassuring glance followed by a confident wink. One that said a thousand words, words that he had sung to Tatum repeatedly. *Don't worry, there's no way that's my child. We always used protection . . . there's only one woman who was meant to bear my seed.*

"Mr. Knights . . . you are ninety-nine . . . point nine percent . . ."

Tatum's hands began to shake violently and she realized it was coming from within. Her insides were actually trembling. *Please . . . please . . .*

". . . the father."

Silence.

"Ah." A slight gasp escaped Tatum's lips and tears fought brutally against her will not to cry. She stared at the judge . . . gawked, watched, waited for her to continue. To say it was a mistake. To say . . . anything.

Tatum lowered her eyes to where Ree sat, a dumbfounded look adorning her pretty face. She watched as he gradually dropped his head in a slightly defeated manner. What could she say to him? What could he possibly say to her?

She didn't want to, but she had no choice but to look to Trinity who began to yell obnoxiously.

"I told you, Sean! I told you! You only saw S.J. once! You weren't even there when he was born! You weren't even . . ." Trinity began to sob uncontrollably, unable to finish her words, and as much as Tatum wanted to be upset about it, she couldn't. Trinity had every right. She was no longer the hotel clerk that he had fucked in Jamaica while he and Tatum had been separated. She was the mother of his son. She had every . . . right.

". . . I loved you, Sean! S.J. loves you! He needs his father!" Trinity gobbled a dose of strength and continued her rant in her island-laced, broken English, as Ree seemed to be frozen. Sitting with his hands tented under his chin, deep thought, guilt, and absolute stun written all over him. "I told you!"

Tatum looked up at her and suddenly felt insignificant. As a subconscious reminder, something she didn't even realize she was doing, she began to twirl her huge engagement ring around her finger.

I'm going to be his wife . . . But I'm going to be his wife.

"Are you happy now?" Trinity questioned, abruptly turning toward Tatum. Still numb from the results, Tatum was shocked by the question, unable to respond. "You happy you kept him from his son? I know you brainwashed him!" Tatum glared at Trinity through slit eyes. Speeding up in her twirling with her tight grip on her rock was the only thing that kept her from losing it. Trinity seemed to suddenly notice the motion.

"Fuck that ring! I have his *son!*"

Tatum's natural instincts finally kicked in and she jumped up but suddenly, the two officers who should have intervened in Trinity's barrage of spewing words way before, finally began to escort Trinity out of the courtroom. Another held his hand out to subdue Tatum.

"C'mon . . . yah gon' have ta come wit us. Ya got ta go an get out of 'ere," the guard spoke to Trinity, grabbing hold of her fragile arm. As Tatum watched her be carried away, Trinity was still fixated on Ree and moving her mouth with insignificant words spewing out that Tatum couldn't possibly hear. She was too zoned.

Suddenly Trinity seemed prettier; her body seemed to fill out her skirt suit more than it had an hour ago, her long black curls seemed bouncier, her face livelier, she seemed more of a threat. Tatum knew it was her mind playing cruel tricks on her.

Still holding on to her blank stare, Tatum slowly sat back down, not ready to walk to Ree yet. Why should she? He should come to her. He should comfort her.

As if in tune with her, Ree calmly rose from his chair and turned, pushing through the small barricade and slowly walking up on Tatum. He still held his same confidence and a demanding aura. But the blow he had just taken had definitely affected him, although it was not visible in his movements.

"Come on, baby. Let's go."

He placed his hand gently on her head and Tatum looked up at him in confusion. She wanted more. She wanted him to say more.

Grabbing her small clutch that complemented her beige Ellen Tracy dress, Tatum stood and stepped out in front of him, trying to walk out of the dim courtroom as poised as she had walked in.

They made their way outside to the awaiting Maybach both looking like they'd stepped straight off the runway, but feeling like they'd stepped straight onto the highway . . . and had been hit by a tractor trailer.

"Mr. Knights! Mr. Knights, can we get a pictcha, a pictcha!"

A few local papers asked as soon as they stepped outside, as if this simple paternity hearing had been world news.

"Ya gwan give us a dollah? Please!"

"Me hungry . . . me want a water ice!"

"Me want a water ice, too! A dollah for me, too!"

Some local kids begged, scattered around him and Tatum. Tatum had almost forgotten that in Kingston, Jamaica, they were different. They were royalty.

Ree peeled off several twenties but posed for no pictures as he and Tatum slid into their awaiting ride.

The gust of chill from the blasting air-conditioning greeted them, seeming to provide a temporary relief from the sweltering heat.

"Crush, take us back to the estate, man."

He gave the order as if the whole ordeal hadn't taken place.

Tatum's body tensed.

"But I thought we were going to the plane?" Her voice was weaker than usual, its spunk seeming to be sucked dry out of it.

Ree looked to her and his gaze softened to a sympathetic one, one that said a million apologies. He couldn't control the circumstances and he knew he'd hypothetically done nothing wrong, but he recognized it had to upset her. Reaching over, he grabbed her hand.

"I know, Tatum. Look, I need you . . . I just need you to go without me. I'll be right behind you in a few days."

Tatum didn't like change. And for some reason, she felt like this was the beginning of a big one.

Tatum and Ree had been through so much to be together: from the death of one of her best friends, Kim; to the murder of her brother; to Ree going on the run from the Feds after her brother snitched on him; and finally them reuniting by fate in Jamaica, despite the fact that he had gotten involved with Trinity and evidently had gotten her pregnant. Tatum couldn't take any more hurdles and definitely any changes.

She placed her thumb and forefinger on her temples, feeling a headache coming on, and she took a deep breath.

"Okay so . . . why are you *right* behind me in a few days, Ree?"

She couldn't hide her irritation if she wanted to.

Ree studied her briefly and then looked ahead, appearing to be choosing his words carefully although Tatum was aware that he knew exactly what he wanted to say. A man like Ree *always* knew what he wanted to say.

"Look, I gotta go see him, Tatum. You should know that. And I have to figure out how I'm . . . how *we* are gonna work this shit out."

He sounded exasperated.

Tatum understood, she really did. But could she help

the fact that it sickened her? And for a man who always seemed to be so right, he had one thing majorly, drastically wrong.

"Well then I guess we'll both go back in a few days. Because I'm staying too." Tatum would be damned if she left him on this island with his new *baby mama*.

Ree knew where it was coming from. He had heard Trinity's slick comments. Had he not been so self-consumed in his sudden shocking reality, he would have responded to them.

"Tatum . . . you know you have nothing to worry about. Nothing," he repeated with certainty.

"And I thought you had a fitting for your dress tomorrow. You know Sasha's there waiting for you so you two can do all of that women stuff you've been running up the phone bills talking about."

He tried to add a little humor as he pinched her chin with a chuckle but Tatum didn't break a smile. She stared him unblinkingly in the eyes.

"Oh, that can wait, Ree . . . the wedding shit can wait. As a matter of fact, the wedding can *wait*," she added, turning her gaze to the window glumly so he wouldn't see the tears if they decided to fall. The beauty of sunny Jamaica as it all whizzed by did little to lift Tatum's solemn mood.

Ree wasted no time addressing the comment.

"You wanna tell me what that's supposed to mean?"

Tatum took a deep breath and shrugged, saying words more brave than she actually felt.

"Well, maybe we should . . . just postpone it. Given the circumstances," she added in a mumble.

Ree stared at her long and hard before replying.

"And what's that gonna do? Look at me." He lightly grabbed her face and turned it to him. Tatum reluctantly met his gaze with her own watery and beautiful, big brown doe eyes. He asked it again. "What's gonna change, Tatum?"

When she didn't answer, he continued. "Six months from now . . . a year from now, five years from now, it's still gonna be the same circumstances."

Tatum hated his rational way of thinking sometimes. It angered her that he was trying to act like there wasn't a big pink elephant in the Maybach.

"Yeah, the same circumstances but time to think," she replied. "Think about if I'm even the one you need to be marrying."

"Are you serious?" he asked her in disbelief.

"Ree, you . . . you didn't know that S.J. was your baby when you asked me to marry you in that hotel room. You didn't know that Trinity was telling the truth!" She could feel herself becoming upset and her cheeks becoming hot, the burning from a cry itching in her throat. "I just want you to be truthful with what you feel. I can handle it . . . just don't leave me in the dark."

"Tatum . . ."

Ree tried to grab her and pull her close to him, but he could feel her resistance.

"No . . ."

"No? What you mean . . . come here!" She was throwing up a wall at a time when they needed to be connected.

"Are you for real?" Tatum questioned in disbelief. "It's your baby, Ree!" she screamed suddenly, as if reminding him of the past hour and a half. It felt good to finally get that out.

"I thought there was no way that was your baby?" she whispered with pain all in her voice.

"And I thought you told me you would be fine even if it was," he calmly reminded.

Ree looked down at her and their faces were inches

apart. Tatum studied him, feeling beyond emotional. He was so handsome, so captivating. A thought of him and Trinity conceiving Sean Jr. entered her mind. She had to divert her gaze at the thought.

"Tatum, listen. Who cares if I didn't know Trinity was carrying my baby. I knew that I wanted to marry you . . . right? Ain't that the reason I put that ring on your finger?" he asked her as if she already knew the answer.

"If I wanted to marry Trinity, I would've put it on hers. Don't ever question that."

He then brought his hand up to her flawless brown face and brushed his fingertips across her cheek. "A baby won't change how I feel about her, and it definitely won't change how I feel about you. I just need to know that what we have is strong enough to get through this."

Tatum stared up at him.

"I love you, Ree. I really do," she admitted softly.

"And you know I love you more," he reminded her before meeting her lips with his. He wouldn't let her say another word.

When the kiss broke, Tatum realized they were already at the estate. Ree didn't move though. He continued to stare at her with his piercing brown eyes and then he spoke in his low Jamaican-laced voice.

"C'mon, let's go inside. I'll have Rose make us some lunch . . . and we can talk some more if you want."

Rose was the live-in keeper of the estate who had been taking care of it while Ree and Tatum divided their time between Jamaica and the States.

As Crush walked around and opened the door, the couple stepped out of the car, Tatum first of course, and planted their feet onto their vast property.

"Thanks, Crush," Tatum spoke as he closed the door behind them. She had grown fond of the big guy who had been Ree's good friend for many years and recently had turned into their driver and her occasional bodyguard. Ever since he escorted Tatum to the hospital in Atlanta the night Aubrey was poisoned, they had begun to form a bond of friendship built on very few words. She knew he had to be genuine for Ree to trust him the way he did. And his nature reminded Tatum of a giant teddy bear's.

"Yo, I'll call you when the jet's ready and she's ready to go," Ree informed him. Tatum remained silent but she found it amusing that Ree still thought she was going back to the States without him. Even if she was confident in her position, which she was, she was not going to just give Trinity any opportunity. She pursed her lips, and as Ree began to walk off, she leaned into Crush and whispered.

"You can get lost 'cause I'm not going anywhere." He smiled subtly because he had heard some of the discussion and he knew exactly what she meant.

He put his hand to his brow and bid her a farewell in the form of a salute. Tatum returned the gesture.

She began to follow behind her man and Ree stopped and stood at the front door smiling with his eyes as he watched her.

That was the woman meant to be his wife. When she reached him, Ree gently placed his hand on the small of her back, guiding her in the large arched door.

"Let's find Rose," he spoke once they stepped inside. "What you want to eat?"

"Something with shrimp," she answered evenly, knowing exactly what she'd been craving. "I guess I'm gonna go call Sasha and change. I'll be right back."

Before she could completely strut off, he grabbed her gently by the arm and pulled her into him, kissing her softly on the lips. He then released his grasp and allowed them to part ways.

That kiss set her entire body on fire, but she wouldn't let him know it. Tatum thought of everything that had just occurred as she made her way up one of the twin spiral staircases.

Reaching the bedroom, she stepped out of her brown-and-beige, zebra-striped pumps and allowed her pedicured feet to sink into the soft fur-like carpet. She found the shoes' proper resting place in the Prada shoebox and went to grab her flats, but realized she had left them at the condo in Georgia.

"Back and forth, back and forth. I'm starting to forget shit."

After unclasping her clutch with a sigh, Tatum retrieved her cell phone and dialed Sasha with FaceTime while awaiting the sound and view of her best friend. Finally she answered and Sasha's cinnamon-toned, sweat-glistened face came into view.

"What are you doing?" Tatum asked with a chuckle, still getting a kick out of being able to see people she spoke to. "Are you on the treadmill?"

Sasha giggled and smiled.

"I just got off. Gotta keep it tight, keep it right!"

Tatum gave a half eye roll and smirked.

"Yeah, whatever."

"So," Sasha started excitedly, unable to contain her anxiety. "Tell me the look on that bitch's face when they read the results!"

Tatum raised her eyebrows coolly and took a seat on her large, soft bed, suddenly feeling exhausted.

"It was . . . it was something else."

Sasha laughed, bugging out.

"Ooh . . . I know it was! Court fees, twenty-five dollars. Paternity test, one hundred fifty dollars. The look on Trinity's lying-ass face when the results are read . . .

priceless!" Sasha laughed, mocking the MasterCard commercial. "Did the bitch look hurt as hell?"

Tatum shrugged and took a deep breath before answering. She began twirling her ring again.

"This bitch did. . . ."

Sasha's smile gradually faded as she studied Tatum's relaxed demeanor, now turned solemn. Tatum had behaved too calmly for Sasha to ever assume that it had turned out to be Ree's baby. She didn't seem angry. But now, now she could see that Tatum was neither upset nor happy. Tatum was just . . . Tatum.

"But . . . how?" Sasha had to know.

"I don't know." Tatum shook her head, truly not knowing what else to say.

Tatum could tell Sasha didn't want to say it but she reluctantly asked.

"Do you . . . do you think he was . . . lying. About always using protection?"

Tatum glanced up and peered around the doorway to make sure Ree was not coming up the steps.

"Nah . . . I don't think so. I just . . . I just don't see him lying to me about something like that. I know that sounds crazy 'cause niggas lie all the time. But I don't think Ree would."

Sasha just pressed her lips together and nodded, truly not knowing what to say.

"So," she started again. "Did you tell him?"

Tatum took a deep breath and looked up again, wanting to be extra careful that he wasn't around.

"No . . . no, I couldn't. The timing, after all of that . . . it wasn't right."

"The timing is never right, Tay. You gotta tell him."

"I will. Just not now."

"Why not?"

"Why?" Tatum snapped.

"It's just . . ." Sasha paused and then continued. "Whatever, we'll talk about it at the fitting."

"Oh yeah . . ." Tatum knew that Sasha was about to be pissed. ". . . about that."

"What?" Sasha asked, sensing Tatum's trepidation.

"Look, Sash, I know a fitting with Monique is like . . . impossible. But . . . I'm gonna have to cancel it."

"Cancel it?" Sasha asked with a raised voice like Tatum had killed her dog. Sasha thought a fitting with Monique Lhuillier was like dinner with Jesus, that's how much she swore by fashion. She was more shocked by this than the paternity news. "Bitch, are you smoking crack!"

Tatum allowed a chuckle to escape through her melancholy. She had expected this.

"Sasha, have you been listening to me? It's his *baby*. I don't even know if we should go through with all of this."

Sasha remained quiet but her heavy breathing told a story of its own. She spoke calmly and slowly.

"Tatum. You cannot let this ruin everything. In two weeks you are going to be *Mrs. Sean Knights*. Nobody else." She took another breather and then proceeded. "Look, I know you didn't expect this, neither one of y'all did. But it was always a possibility. And you said you wanted to get married to him regardless. You also said how important it was for you to get married on your parents' wedding anniversary, even *after* the paternity test was scheduled and you knew it was a few weeks before. *Monique Lhuillier* stopped what she was doing, to *personally* design your dress, and you won't even go to get fitted for it? What type of person are you?" Sasha asked in shock.

"You know, I always knew you were a cold bitch . . . I knew it," she added in a slight joking manner, and

Tatum couldn't help but giggle. Her eyes squinted up and she had to laugh out loud, her same goofy, silly, loud laugh.

She looked up midlaugh and she saw Ree now standing in the doorway staring warmly at her as she continued her conversation.

"All right! All right! Fine . . . I'll see you tomorrow, bitch."

"All righttt," Sasha squealed excitedly. "I can't wait! Now . . . are you gonna tell him?" she added.

Tatum's smile faded to a faint nervous look as she glanced at Ree and then abruptly cut Sasha off.

"Girl, let me call you back."

"Tay, listen you better—" *End call.*

Tatum half-smiled at Ree and then placed her phone on the bed. He walked over and sat next to her and her heart sped up wondering how much he had heard.

"I'm glad you talked to your girl," he spoke to her. "I'm glad she made you laugh." He stared at Tatum. "You know I love seeing you laugh like that."

Tatum smiled at him realizing he hadn't caught anything but the end of the conversation.

"So what you gotta tell me?" he added.

Sasha, Tatum thought. *Big mouth.*

Tatum thought quickly on her feet.

"Um, just that I'm going back tonight. I'm gonna go to the fitting . . . you just can't cancel on Monique Lhuillier, you know," she added with a hint of sarcasm, hoping he'd buy it. He wrapped his strong arm around her waist and she knew he had.

"That's my girl."

Ree then pulled her to him, turning her face with his hand and leaning in, kissing her deeply on the mouth. Tatum's whole body trembled when she tasted his tongue. Still. He still did that to her. Breaking the kiss, he stared at her before speaking.

"So . . . I guess this means you still gonna marry me, huh?"

Tatum had to kiss him on those perfect lips once more before she answered.

"Hmm . . . maybe." Her voice was thick and sultry. "Depending on what happens in the next hour, Mr. Knights."

Moving closer, she straddled him with ferocity. She wasn't sure what had come over her. She had just found out that he fathered another woman's child and all she wanted to do was engage in baby-making acts of her own.

"Damn . . ." Ree grunted, grabbing ahold of her wide hips as her dress rose to the most upper part of her thighs and her legs wrapped around his waist. Ree pulled her closer so she could feel his vast hardness beneath her as he eyed her creaminess. He hadn't expected this, but he welcomed it as any man would.

He leaned in and ran his tongue along her collarbone.

"Mmm," Tatum moaned, circling her midsection and subtly grinding on him. She was trying her best to work this Trinity situation out of her mind. Sexing her man and reminding herself that he belonged to only her would be a sure step of progress.

Slowly unbuttoning his shirt, Tatum began reveling at his tattoo-decorated muscular upper body. She traced her fingertips along every design and every ripple in his build. Reaching below, she then ran her hand along his thick shaft through the fabric of his pants. Tatum's bedroom voice and sexual movements had Ree hard as a baseball bat.

"That's all you right there," he assured her in his sexy baritone.

"It's mine?"

"You know it."

"I know what to do with it too," she promised with a lick of her full lips.

"Show me what you know then."

Tatum couldn't contain it. The fire inside of her was ablaze and Ree was like her water, she needed him to subside it. Kissing him with fervent passion, she meticulously unbuckled his pants feeling her juices now begin to pour out of her. She was sure that her thin panty barrier was pointless and that she had well leaked onto Ree's designer slacks. But he didn't seem to mind as he assisted her, releasing his long, thick tool from his boxers.

Just like a work of art, it didn't matter how many times Tatum had seen it. Each time left her in awe. She paused her kiss to gaze at it for a moment.

Hello, she thought, eyeing her prize.

Still in a daze, Tatum felt Ree skillfully push her panties to the side as he began to run his fingers across her moist clit. Seeing that she was already dripping wet, Ree wasted no time guiding Tatum down onto his dick with ease.

"Come 'ere, baby . . ." he moaned.

Tatum closed her eyes and wrapped her arms around his neck tightly, grabbing ahold of his hair and resting her face on his shoulder in pure pleasure.

"Ree," she cried out desperately, feeling a gush of liquid instantly release onto him. She was on the brink of tears from the ecstasy she was feeling and the raw emotion of the day's events combined. It wasn't long before Ree felt the moisture on his shoulder as he stroked her.

"Why you crying, baby . . . huh? . . . don't cry," he urged softly as he thrust deeper into her, sending Tatum into an orgasm. "I love you, Tatum. You're my queen. . . ."

Ree wrapped his strong, tattooed arms around her and sucked gently on her neck and shoulder before repeating, "You're my queen, Tatum."

Tatum's pussy was like a never-ending faucet, her wetness just continued to pour and release, no halting.

"God damn, you so fucking wet, Tatum."

Hearing the pleasure in his tone sent Tatum into another concurring orgasm, which caused her inner muscles to tightly contract on Ree's dick. The feeling put him near his moment.

"Shit, Tatum, you gonna make me cum."

"Ree," she cried out, feeling so many emotions at once. "Why . . . oohhh why . . ."

She closed her eyes and held her man for dear life.

"Why'd it have to be yours?" she found herself asking as she released for the second time, another tear running down her cheek. Ree hushed her, careful not to ruin the moment.

"Sshhh, Tatum . . . Ssshh, baby . . ."

Ree hooked his strong arms through hers, grabbing ahold of the back of her neck and forcing her down completely on him, where she was unable to run from his length. Tatum bit her bottom lip in pleasurable pain. When it became too much to hold in she screamed out in desperation as her legs trembled.

"Oh God! Pleaseee . . . Oh Ree, cum, baby! Ohhh shitttt . . ."

The pressure was too much. He was going to make her explode.

She's too fucking wet, Ree thought to himself as he

continued to go all in. It had him about to lose control. Against his will, the thought of Trinity having his son entered his mind. He couldn't help but be angry about the whole situation. At a time like this, Tatum's time, his time. Then he thought of how he had handled the situation. Then he was angry with himself.

Tatum could feel him tense and begin to become more aggressive. She could literally begin to feel him taking that anger out on her and her tender pussy.

"Ree," she called out exasperated. "Please . . . oh! Please . . . easy baby . . ."

Ree was at his point of no return. He interlocked her long hair around his fingers and began to thrust his hips toward her, forcing every inch of him into her. Tatum felt his dick jump and knew he was right there. She would take the pain to grant his pleasure.

"It's okay . . . it's . . . it's okay, baby. Give it to me," she urged sexily, tears welling her eyes from the pressure.

Ree grunted, feeling what seemed to be buckets of release building from his sack up through his groin. She was gonna take it all.

At the moment of his ecstasy, Tatum brought her mouth to his and kissed him with passion. She could feel the love transfer from her to him. He recognized it and he responded. His body relaxed, his movements returned to easy ones, smooth, loving ones.

"Tatum . . ." That was it. She brought him there. They were in that moment, temporarily escaping the reality of the situation that had unfolded, escaping the preset to the obstacles that would unknowingly be coming. Tatum gripped her man, finally opening her eyes and looking at him. All tatted up, body seeming to be sculpted from a thug heaven. *He's a fucking* man!

The piercing ringing of the landline interrupted their moment.

Brrringggg!

They both tried to ignore it.

Brringgg! Brringggg!

"Fuck," Ree groaned, coming down off of his pleasure high, accepting that the best part, the very brink and after-moments of his climax had been ruined.

Kissing Tatum on the lips, he slowly lifted her off of him and stood, his large dick still hard.

He walked over to the cordless, tucking himself back into his pants as Tatum removed her wet panties, letting out a deep sigh. She wondered who it was calling them at the estate; only a handful of people knew they had to come back to Jamaica for the court date.

"Yo," Ree answered, as if his hood greeting was customary. He did little to hide the annoyance in his voice, sharing Tatum's curiosity about the call.

"Hey, it's me," the female caller greeted. "We got a little issue . . . I need to holla at you."

Ree could hear the noise on the other end—cars, wind, music. She must have been driving.

He sighed, looked over at Tatum, and then spoke. "I'll be back in a couple of days. We'll talk then, Jayde."

Tatum pursed her lips when she learned who it was. *Of course . . .*

"No need," Jayde replied confidently. "I'm pulling in now. I'm downstairs."

"Why are you not in Atlanta?" Ree questioned seriously.

The way he asked her caused Tatum's ears to perk. He sounded peeved, almost angry at the realization. Tatum wondered if Jayde was already messing up their huge "master plan."

"Like I said . . . we had an issue." Jayde's voice softened

a bit. She was a boss bitch, *the* boss bitch, but Ree was the king. She knew her place. "It can't be discussed like this."

Ree remained silent, realizing she meant over the phones. He wondered if anything was going wrong. He couldn't afford that. This was his last go in the street business. One final score and he would be set forever and done. He couldn't afford any mishaps.

"I'll be down in a minute."

He disconnected the call before she could get another word out.

"Jayde's here?" Tatum wasted no time asking.

Ree nodded as he buckled his pants.

"Why? Why is she in Jamaica?" Tatum stood up and began to fix herself.

"I'm about to find that out right now," he assured her.

"Does this have to do with that drug stuff, Ree? Is she already messing up, because you promised that everything would go—"

"Ssshh . . ." Ree stepped up quickly and placed a finger to Tatum's lips in haste. He looked her in the eyes.

"Don't ever ask about that, Tatum. Don't concern yourself with that. I mean it. I want you to know nothing about that," he added with firm authority. He meant it too. Not only was it not her place in his business, he also would never put her in harm's way. He would keep her as ignorant as possible to all of it.

Tatum swallowed hard, not knowing how to take his statements. He kissed her forehead as a softer gesture.

"You just worry about making an honest man out of me in a few weeks," he teased. "I can't be shacking up with you in sin anymore, Miss Lady." He shot her a wink as he turned and headed out of the room.

Tatum let out a half smile and took a deep breath, letting it go . . . for now. As she took a glance around the room, a thought suddenly ran through her head. She called out to him.

"Hey!"

"Yeah?" He turned abruptly.

Picking up his Dolce shirt with swiftness, she tossed it at him hard and he caught it midair with a crinkle in his brow.

"You forgetting something? Put it on," she demanded.

Ree chuckled but followed suit, sliding his arms into the dress material. That's what he loved about Tatum. She knew when to fall back but she also knew when to step up. She had a voice, and he respected it. He wasn't the only one who called the shots.

Chapter 2

"Chauncey is and will always be in the streets."

—Sasha, *Still Thicker than Water*

"Cominggg!"

Sasha looked down at her cell phone once more before making her way to the front door.

Ignore. For the tenth fucking time . . .

She placed the phone on the kitchen counter and sashayed through the house, the house that used to be just Chauncey's house when he had followed her and Aubrey here to Atlanta. Now it was also her house . . . *their* house, which they shared as a family. It felt good.

She wondered if it was her aunt at the door dropping her daughter back off. It couldn't have been Chauncey because he had keys, he wouldn't ring the bell. Reaching the foyer, she heard her cell vibrate in the distance. She knew it was probably Jayde calling again.

Can't she take a hint? Sasha wondered.

The bell chimed just as Sasha neared the peephole. Sighing, she yanked the door open.

"Impatient much?" Her brow rose cutely with the

question. "He's not here," she added, shooting Bleek a light smile.

Bleek often stopped by. He was a worker for Chauncey and Jayde and had recently become someone whom Chauncey seemed to trust. This was evident being that he was the one to help clean up the body when Sasha had murdered her husband, Mike, only after Mike had attempted to kill her and her daughter. That was a secret Sasha planned on taking to the grave and something she fought daily to forget.

Sasha turned and proceeded back inside, still in her spandex workout gear. She had just finished up her daily treadmill run and phone call with Tatum.

"You can come in and wait, though; he should be here any minute. We're supposed to go pick up my car and then go to dinner. Speaking of which . . ." Sasha turned to Bleek with narrowed eyes. "You better not be coming over here messing up our plans."

Bleek held up his hands defensively and stepped back, shooting her his charming boyish smile.

"Look, I just came over here to relay a message. Be easy, shawty."

"Well, what is it?" Sasha asked, facing him curiously.

"Had you let me get a word in you would've known it by now." Bleek smirked and his right dimple appeared on his baby face. Sasha rolled her eyes playfully.

"Well first, J-Mur . . . I mean Jayde . . . She been tryin' to get in touch with you. She said she been calling you for a few days."

Sasha tried her best to keep a straight face but her actions reflected her disinterest.

"And what's second?"

Bleek raised his brows in shock.

"Oh, word? It's like that?"

Sighing, Sasha headed to the kitchen where her cell phone was.

"Look, I was just about to call her back. I mean, c'mon, Bleek . . . I know your job is a little more important than to come all the way over to the other side of town just to ask me why I'm not taking Jayde's phone calls." Sasha's own Southern accent peaked just like Bleek's when they spoke and got excited.

Bleek shook his finger at her and pressed his lips together as he followed behind, as if he wanted to respond to her slick comments but wasn't sure how.

"Funny," he said, grabbing a red apple from the fruit bowl. After taking a bite, he proceeded, mouth full and all. "In all honesty, I could give a fuck about y'all girl shit."

He looked at her and his brows dipped low a bit before speaking.

"I also came 'cause Chaunc got held up. He asked me to swang you by the dealership so you can pick up your—"

"Oh my God, again!" Sasha exclaimed in disbelief. She couldn't believe Chauncey was canceling on her again. "First he got held up and couldn't pick me up from the airport last week. Then he got held up and couldn't take Aubrey to the doctor and you had to. Now when I finally convince him that I need a new car, he can't even take me to pick it up?"

"At least he paid for it," Bleek smirked, coming to his man's defense.

Sasha rolled her eyes.

"Yeah, Bleek, and he was supposed to take us out to eat too. What? He sent you to handle that also?"

Bleek shrugged.

"I mean I could . . ."

Sasha sucked her teeth and turned from him. Was

she being spoiled? Was she asking too much? It seemed like everything had finally started getting right. She and Chauncey could finally be a family with Aubrey and put the past behind them. She was almost over the whole him-sleeping-with-Neli deal, especially after they had learned that the poor girl had been shot dead. That had really shaken her and Tatum up for a while after they heard that. And to think, she was still in Atlanta when it happened?

The cops had also left the disappearance of her husband, Mike, alone months ago and hadn't been asking questions. And Sasha was even back in medical school.

But it seemed that recently Sasha's worries were not about any of those things. Recently, Chauncey had dived nose first into the streets and whatever concoction that he, Ree, and Jayde had brewing was leaving him with less and less time for his family. Sasha wondered if Tatum was experiencing the same thing. She made a mental note to ask her when she landed.

"You know, Bleek, can you tell me something?"

Bleek stuck his hands in the pockets of his tan Dickies shorts and just stared at her. He was dressed like a preppy schoolboy, with a short-sleeved V-neck sweater over his polo. The outfit along with his clear, Hennessey-complexioned baby face gave him the innocence of a teenager. But everyone knew he was far from innocent. That's why he had been compared to Chauncey so much. He was just as ruthless and hot-tempered.

"Can you please tell me what exactly is going on with Ree, Chauncey, and *Jayde?*" Bleek noticed that she had said Jayde's name through slightly gritted teeth. Bleek shook his head defiantly.

"Nah. I can't even tell you what I do know, shawty."

"And why is that?"

"It's not for you, that's why." He was adamant. He also

didn't mention the fact that Ree was no holds barred. Everyone in the streets knew that. Once Bleek found out that the infamous Respect was now the head of the realm, he knew everything was going to be different. They would be eating on a whole other level, which would be the lovely part. But they would also have to be on point at all times. Or you would be dead. That's how Ree ran his business.

"Now c'mon, forget all of that. Throw some clothes on. Imma wait outside. C'mon, put a smile on ya face. Act like a woman wit a man that just bought her a hundred-fifty-thousand-dollar car."

Sasha smirked a little, thinking of his words. He was right, Chauncey *did* provide for her.

"All right, I'll get dressed. Give me a few minutes."

"You might wanna take a shower though first. Seeing you *was* sweating and shit. You ain't getting into my shit all funky."

"Shut up!" Sasha spat, laughing. She went to swing at Bleek but he caught her wrist.

"Ah, I'm too sharp for you," he teased with a wink. "Remember that." Sasha giggled and he released her, and then she trotted up the stairs, getting excited about her brand-new car.

"Hi, Tatum."

"Hey, Jayde," Tatum responded, stepping into one of the family rooms where Jayde was seated on the white sofa. Ree was seated across from her. "To what do we owe this honor?" Tatum couldn't help but add.

Tatum could feel Ree's eyes on her, probably from the question she posed, but she would deal with the consequences later. She just couldn't help herself.

"Oh, it's just . . . business," Jayde replied. She wore a

green-and-black printed wrap dress that defined her artificial assets. Her jet-black mane and emerald eyes complemented the setup well, and her bright smile and feminine demeanor read more of a supermodel than a drug dealer. "I'm only stealing him for one moment. You can have him back as soon as I'm done," Jayde added with a wink.

Tatum chuckled and turned her attention to Ree, not realizing just how true the meanings of Jayde's words were.

"I'm gonna run out to the marketplace and grab some things before I leave tonight. Sasha will kill me if I don't bring her coco-water back."

Ree stood.

"Okay. And grab me some of that—"

"Black soap? In the yellow box?" Tatum questioned with a smile.

He chuckled and placed his hands on her hips.

"Yeah, that's the one. And the shea butter . . ."

"With the green lid. And a box of Vanilla Dutches," Tatum finished. "I got you," she whispered, as she pecked him on the lips and he smiled.

"Tatum, have you spoken to Sasha?" Jayde's voice was so even it could draw a straight line. That PDA shit sickened her.

Tatum turned to face her but kept her embrace with Ree.

"Yeah . . . I talked to her a few minutes ago."

"Hm . . ." Jayde's brow wrinkled. "Well, she hasn't been answering my calls," she revealed with a question in her voice.

Tatum shrugged, not knowing anything more.

"I don't know. I'll tell her to call you when I see her, though. Bye."

Tatum made her way out, holding on to Ree's hand

until the tips of their fingers were forced to part. Ree watched her the entire time. After a few seconds and when he heard the front door close, he proceeded.

"Why the fuck would you come out here?" Just like that, his whole demeanor changed as he sat back down.

"I told you. Our friend, he wants to see you sooner than we arranged," Jayde explained as if he hadn't just spoken to her like that. No one else could and still breathe, but Ree, he was the exception. She actually was turned on by it.

"So, you could've told me that shit two days from now when I got back to the States. Don't fuck up the plans, Jayde. You are supposed to do everything the way I said. You're supposed to be holding a meeting right now as we speak. Now you tell me what happened with that?"

"I let Chauncey handle it," she stated matter-of-factly. Ree jumped up abruptly and walked away from her, his anger written all over him. "Listen, I know you said for me to hold them since they're familiar with me, but seriously, I think it's better if you and I work together on the international, and let Chauncey and Bleek—"

"I don't give a fuck what you think!" He spun around furiously.

Jayde immediately silenced and had to bite her tongue. Her foot tapped, however. She narrowed her eyes at Ree as he continued.

"You are in no position to *let* Chauncey handle shit on your end. If I needed help on my end, which I don't, I'd delegate it to C before you." Ree walked over and leaned down to Jayde with cold eyes. He was so close, she could smell the cologne from his shirt, hear his breathing, and feel his overwhelming aura.

"Look, we need to get this clear, because obviously it wasn't clear for you before. I worked with your father, Jayde. Not you. I don't even know you. You and I will not work on the international because *you and I* will not work together. You handle what you're supposed to. I do what I have to. We make this money, I walk away, and you and C can go about the business as you were. Period."

Jayde swallowed hard.

"You got it?" he asked with authority, placing his index finger and thumb on her chin.

"Okay . . ." she mumbled. "But I think you're making a big mistake since—"

"There you go wit ya fucking *thinking* again, Jayde. That's what the fuck I don't need."

She could tell she had him frustrated. A part of her was excited at the thought. Jayde pressed her thighs together as she watched him pace the floor and finally stop at the bar to pour a drink. He was so sexy, so dominant. She literally wanted to get on her knees for him.

"Okay," she said breathlessly, still watching him. "You're right. I shouldn't have suggested it. I should've stayed in Atlanta and waited on you. But he wants to meet you out here. Tonight. And he wants me here. So now what?"

Ree looked at her for a while before speaking. If she didn't have her connections she would be useless to him. But for now, she was just the kind of bitch he needed on his side and the key to this working.

"Set it up."

Jayde smiled and breathed a sigh of relief, glad that the plans were panning out in her favor.

"Okay . . . I'll make the call."

Ree nodded in affirmation, and just then his cell phone began to ring.

* * *

It's about Mickel . . .
Who?
Mickel Dupree . . . Jayde's father . . .

Sasha sat in the passenger seat of Bleek's drop-top Lamborghini Murcielago reflecting on the world-rocking conversation she had shared with her mother nine months prior.

They had all been rejoicing on the closing of the drastic events over dinner—her, Chauncey, Aubrey, Jayde, Tatum, and Ree—when her mother's phone call interrupted them.

Not only had her mother dropped a bomb on her by revealing the news of Mickel and why he was relevant to Sasha, but when she had informed her mother just a few days ago that after holding in this news for nine months, she was ready to discuss it with Jayde, her mother revealed another secret.

Jayde already knows, dear. . . . She just doesn't know that you do. And trust me, it's best if she doesn't.

Now that changed everything.

Sasha had gone about the whole nine months, after learning the truth about Mickel, treating Jayde the same. She figured: why act any differently to her? Jayde was just as clueless as Sasha had been. But having found out that Jayde already knew was too much. This whole time Jayde had held on to this crucial information, and unlike her secret of being an underground drug lord that she had once also kept from Sasha, Sasha wasn't sure if she could forget this one.

"I can smell the wheels turning and burning in ya mind, shawty. You gon' have to let that go, for real. You putting a damper on the mood."

Sasha wrenched her eyes to Bleek as he drove, ready to give him a piece of her mind, but the grin on his baby face let her know he was in jest.

"Whatever," she responded, leaning down and turning up the music. Miguel's "Sure Thing" blared through the quality speakers and Sasha mellowed a bit. "It's too much to let go," she found herself adding.

Bleek remained quiet, not sure how to play it. He wasn't up for a counseling session but he could see something troubling her. He figured that was Chauncey's job to find out what it was and appease it. And the last thing he needed was for her to vent if it did have something to do with Chauncey. He wondered if it had anything to do with Jayde. He didn't want to hear about that, either, to be honest.

"You wanna talk about it?"

"No."

Good, he thought.

"But you know . . . I just don't understand people sometimes. Like what would you do if there was someone you trusted and you found out they were completely *fraudulent?*"

Bleek stared ahead through the lenses of his shades hoping that this was not about Chauncey.

I thought she said she didn't wanna talk about it.

"Uh, I mean . . . you know people make mistakes. Sometimes it ain't always what it seem. Maybe you should just holla at that person."

Bleek fed her a bunch of elusive bullshit.

"But what if you can't?" she probed.

"But I thought you ain't wanna talk about it?" he asked, before even thinking about it as he pulled into the lot. He was young, he was blunt, and he didn't really understand women.

"I didn't."

"Yet here you are talking . . ."

Sasha glared at him and he chuckled.

"C'mon, shawty, let's go get your car so you can do all that contemplating in the privacy of your own vehicle."

"Bleek, you are such a gentleman. Shayla must adore your sensitivity," Sasha stated with sarcasm, speaking of his daughter's mother and current girl-friend. She stepped out of the car along with him, and they began to walk inside. Sasha admired the sunny, beautiful Georgia day. "Don't worry, with age will come compassion," she added.

"Hey." Bleek reached his hand out and stopped her, his hand lightly pressing her stomach to prevent her from walking forward.

"I'm compassionate . . . I just don't know what the fuck you talking about so I can't speak on it. And last I checked I was only one year younger than you."

Sasha, now twenty-four years old, knew if she hadn't already known Bleek's age, it would be hard to believe. He didn't look a day over eighteen. She moved his hand out of the way and lightly rolled her eyes.

"Don't worry about it."

Sasha walked ahead of him and Bleek didn't even glance at her apple-shaped ass, which sat up high in her tan linen romper. That was out of respect. Her long legs were on display and accentuated by brown Carlos Santana sandals. Brown shades, brown Ferragamo purse, and a long brown mane complemented by caramel sun-kissed highlights.

Sasha was a stunner, that was for sure.

"Hi, we're here for the Mercedes, the cream CL600."

She was anxious and excited. She prayed her car was finally done.

The young white girl punched a few keys into the computer but seemed lost. Then she smiled.

"Oh, with the pink interior?"

Sasha grinned.

"Yes! Is she ready?"

"She is." The girl reached under the desk and magically appeared with a key chain with a small remote. "And she's gorgeousss. You're lucky." The white girl smiled from her to Bleek, likely assuming that he was her man and the one who had purchased the car. She kept her eyes on him for longer than she should have and Sasha shook her head because if it had been Chauncey, the girl's ass would have been introduced to Carlos Santana by her foot.

"Right this way."

She led them to the car and Sasha almost jumped out of her skin when she saw it. Snatching the key, she ran to her car in pure euphoria.

"How 'bout I slide through later . . . feed you and fuck you proper, shawty," Bleek boldly suggested, having caught her prior look.

The girl glanced from Bleek to a smiling Sasha in the distance, and back to Bleek while running her hand through her blond hair.

"What about your girlfriend?" she asked smiling, revealing she couldn't care less.

"What about her?" Bleek shot her the dimpled smile and she was putty. After giving him her number, she made her way back inside and Bleek went over to Sasha.

"You happy now that you got your country-ass car?" He looked at the baby pink leather and shook his head.

"You happy now that you bagged that country-ass bunny?" Sasha retorted, familiarizing with the interior.

"I owe it all to you," Bleek smiled at her. "For some reason women want you more when they think you got a girl."

"And when they think you buying that girl a custom-laced Benz," Sasha added. Bleek chuckled, knowing she was right.

Just then they heard a voice in the distance.

"God damn, that bitch pretty as hell!"

Both looked up and Sasha beamed when she saw him strolling in like he owned the place. His smooth, dark skin, jet-black waves and goatee, black V-neck, sparkling diamonds, crisp jeans, and fresh Pradas gave him the look of a celebrity. He was *so* fine.

"Ain't she tho'?" Sasha asked, standing up to greet Chauncey.

"Wasn't talking 'bout the car, kid." He licked his lips, grabbing her hips, and Sasha blushed, playfully punching him.

"Ain't no bitches over here, homie." She pecked him on the lips. "Yay, you came! Now we can go to dinner."

Chauncey sighed and Sasha knew it before he said it.

"Look, don't be mad. . . ."

"Then why did you come?" she asked, loosening out of his grip with attitude.

"I was just swinging by real quick, wanted to see how you looked in ya shit. Plus I had to drop a few more bills on the embroidering you added. But I gotta go handle something."

"Chauncey, you always gotta go handle something. I can't believe you!"

Chauncey found it ironic that Sasha was arguing about the time that he couldn't spend with her because he was out making money, money that had bought the very customized car that she was drooling over at that moment.

"I'ma make it up to you kid, I promise."

"Oh yeah? What day should I mark my calendar?"

He grinned at the way her lips puckered out when she was mad. Kissing her, he turned to Bleek.

"Good looking, yo. I'm jetting over to meet with them Southside boys. I'll fill you in later. If you speak to J,

you tell her it went smooth. Tell her hit me up at ten."
Chauncey looked over and saw Sasha was still pouting.
He had something for her spoiled ass. "Yo Bleek, make
sure you take care of that bitch."

Sasha punched him hard with all of her might, biting
her bottom lip in anger. Bleek had to laugh.

"Yo relax, I meant the car, baby . . . I meant the car,"
Chauncey shot with a grin, knowing he had gotten
under her skin. He grabbed her up and gave her a big
sloppy kiss even though her lips were still pressed in
anger.

"Hey," he said, holding her hips. "Cut that shit out.
I'll see you later."

Before she could reply he slipped his designer shades
back on and strolled away. The same girl who had helped
Sasha before watched Chauncey in lust, even after she
had just given her number to Bleek. Sasha pursed her
lips and gave the girl a once-over. Now she was really
considering the Carlos Santana introduction.

Ree wrapped up his phone call and Jayde could see
the deliberation all in his face. He had talked so intensely since the time he received the call from inside of
the estate, to the time they departed. Something had
happened.

"Everything all right?"

They were now riding in the back of a bulletproof
Expedition. Jayde's driver behind the wheel since Crush
had taken Tatum to town.

There was a pause before Ree answered, his gaze set
on the outside through the tinted windows.

"We have to make a stop. Head east, Saint Andrews,"
Ree ordered calmly to the driver. He ignored Jayde's

question. Obeying instantly, the driver took the first right to turn around.

"Shall I tell my friend that we're running behind?" she asked, not wanting to probe too much.

"We won't be long," he assured.

Jayde nodded and then reached into her bag, pulling out her phone.

"Okay, well just excuse me while I make another call." She uncrossed and crossed her legs again, letting off a faint scent of her Dior perfume, which was sprayed between her thighs.

Scrolling through her contacts, she placed a familiar call.

"Where are you?" she wasted no time asking.

There was a delay and then: "I'm leaving the dealership now. I just spoke to C."

Jayde looked over at Ree, who still seemed deep in thought. She figured she'd jolt his attention.

"Are you still with Sasha?"

Bleek glanced over at Sasha, who was sitting in the passenger side of her car while he programmed her navigation. He knew what she had told him when his phone first started to ring.

"Nah . . . nah, she left."

Sasha mouthed the words *thank you* to him.

Disappointed, Jayde changed the subject.

"Did you handle everything?"

"Yeah. And C said to call him at ten."

"That's a good boy," Jayde whispered sultrily. "Mama's gonna reward you good for that."

Ree continued to stare ahead but Jayde smirked because she knew he was listening. He was always listening, that's how a nigga like him moved and stayed in tune with his surroundings.

Bleek seemed unaffected.

"Yeah, a'ight, J. I ain't up for ya games right now."

Sasha looked over, wondering what he was talking about.

"This is no game, baby. And I ain't just talking tongue action. When I get back I'm gonna fuck you all up and down that bed."

The most Ree gave to that was a shift in his seat and a glance at his watch, but she knew she had his attention.

"Yeah well, we'll see about that. You been singing that tune for months and I felt no walls yet. Got me thinking you scared."

Sasha rolled her eyes and twisted her face in disgust. She knew whatever Jayde was saying on the other end was sure to be nauseating.

Jayde giggled at his cockiness.

"Oh trust, ain't no timid pussy this way. Tasty maybe, but not timid."

"Yeah, I hear ya talking," Bleek stated nonchalantly. He already had said a mouthful with Sasha in the car, and for some reason it was uncomfortable.

"Hear me now, feel me later," Jayde said, as they pulled up to the pit-stop destination Ree had requested. It was someone's home.

"I'll be in touch."

Pressing the END button, she dropped the phone into her Valentino purse. Ree opened the door and stepped out. Before he closed the door he turned to Jayde.

"Ay yo, next time have that conversation in private. Business is business. Personal is personal. And I don't like it mixing . . . I'll be back."

He slammed the door and Jayde's pussy jumped with the vibration. She smirked, knowing he had heard every seductive word.

"He's a fucking god," Jayde bellowed, throwing her

head back. The driver looked at her through the rearview and she caught his eye.

"What? Mind ya fucking business!"

Knocking twice on the door, Ree adjusted the waist of his pants so that his Smith & Wesson .45 ACP sat comfortably. He carried a gun at all times so the weight was nonexistent; sometimes he had to shift it to make sure it was still there.

He could hear footsteps approaching on the inside so he was able to anticipate her way before the door even creaked open.

"Hi, Sean."

Trinity stood before him with her short, black silk robe clinging to her damp body. A smile adorned her natural face, which bore no traces of the makeup she had worn earlier. She had obviously just gotten done showering.

"Come in." She stepped aside and opened the door wider. "S.J. just woke up."

Ree stepped into the front foyer, closing the door behind him. The house was dim; most of the curtains were drawn. It was small, but it was neat and clean; a major step up from Trinity's prior dwellings in Tivoli Gardens, the roughest projects in Kingston.

Following her into the modest living room, Ree saw the bassinet set up in the corner and sighed. Instead of immediately walking over, he placed his hands in his pockets and stared from a distance. Trinity found it amusing.

"You can go and pick him up, you know? He won't bite ya, Sean." Her voice was island laced as she giggled, much thicker accented than his since she had never been to or known anywhere but Jamaica.

Ree took heavy and slow steps toward the child, never taking his eyes away. Finally reaching him, Ree leaned over and studied the small bundle. The baby was dressed in a mere onesie since the house was warm with only a few fans going. Little fingers, little toes, a small nose, innocent eyes . . . he was perfect.

As Ree stared at S.J., Trinity couldn't help but study him. She was infatuated with him and sure that it was love. She used to believe it was because he was so powerful, so important, so rich, and so *respected*. But the truth was that the short time she had been in Ree's world, it had been the happiest time of her life. He was always honest with her, whether she wanted to hear it or not. He was attentive and satisfying in bed, he was attractive, and he was dominant. What more could anyone ask for in a man?

"He's beautiful, isn't he?" Trinity beamed, walking closer to them . . . to him.

". . . He is." Ree's voice was low, almost in a whisper. As if he was thinking deeply on something. Trinity hoped he was thinking on giving them another shot and shipping his American project princess back to the States.

"He's got your eyes," Ree acknowledged, still looking at the baby. "And your nose . . ."

Trinity smiled, knowing that he did take after her greatly.

"Yeah, he does."

Ree looked up at her and stared intently for a while. Then he let out a small smile. Reaching his hand up he ran it across Trinity's cheek and brought it down, cupping her chin. He could see her eyes lower in lust.

"Can I tell you something?" he asked her.

"Anything, Sean." She was breathy, full of hope.

Ree looked down at S.J. and then up at Trinity, whom

he had spent a year of his life with. Had Tatum not come back into his world, she probably would still be in his life. He made unflinching eye contact.

"He looks nothing like me."

Trinity's eyes widened and she crinkled her brow in hurt.

"Sean . . . he looks like me."

Ree looked down at the child again and chuckled.

"Yeah, he does. But he looks *nothing* like me."

"Sean," Trinity started with devastation in her voice, as she nervously tightened the belt on her robe. "That . . . that doesn't mean anything! You got your test. You know the answer! Why are you coming over here with this shit? You got your damn test!"

Both were so focused on each other, they had no idea that they were no longer alone.

"That was *your* test, Trini. Not mine." Ree's tone was so cold Trinity was surprised his words didn't freeze before they reached her ears.

"W-what?" she stuttered in disbelief.

"W-what?" he repeated, mocking her as he stepped closer with a deadly glare in his eye. "So . . . who helped you?"

Trinity's breaths became faster, shorter, harder.

"What are you . . . what are you talking about, Sean?"

Ree knew that Trinity had no pull, no money, and no connections. He knew everyone in the legal system in Jamaica and was almost certain no one would conspire against him. He had to know how she'd done it.

Reaching in his waist, he calmly asked the question once again.

"Trinity. One more time. Who . . . the fuck . . . helped . . ."

Trinity's eyes shot wide open and she grabbed her throat with both hands instinctively. Blood began pouring profusely from her neck.

She locked eyes with the person behind Ree as she began to gargle and choke.

What the fuck? Ree thought as he turned around.

Jayde stood with her smoking gun in her left hand, a visible silencer attached to it. Ree looked back to Trinity as she slid to the ground, hanging on to her last breaths. Her eyes revealed a glimmer of recognition as they stayed fixed on her attacker, Jayde. Ree caught the look. He cut his eyes to Jayde when she walked up closer.

"I thought I told you to wait in the fucking car. . . . Why the fuck would you do that before she could answer me?"

"You were taking too long," Jayde replied nonchalantly. "I told you—"

"I don't give a fuck what you told me. I told you to wait in the . . ." Trinity's gargling blood and torturous sounds annoyed Ree. He no longer wanted to hear them or see her struggle with her life. He pulled out his own gun and sent a bullet straight into her skull, killing her instantly. Then he focused back on Jayde like nothing had occurred.

"I told you to *wait*. Stop trying to be a boss, Jayde. You're not my fucking Co-D."

Jayde smirked as she stepped around Trinity, careful not to get blood on her new Giuseppe heels.

"And here I was thinking I was doing you a favor. We have to meet our friend in twenty minutes, and we can't be late." Raising her gun once again, she aimed for the bassinet, but Ree stopped her.

"You see, you're too messy. We don't do anything that's unnecessary. Killing the kid is not necessary."

He grabbed her arm, lowering her gun with strength. After that he leaned down and picked up a surprisingly still quiet S.J.

"Let's go."

They headed for the door, Jayde on Ree's heels. Wiping off her gun, she stepped outside behind him as if she hadn't just committed murder. She had a question.

"How'd you know?"

He looked over at her and just then an old Dodge minivan pulled up. An older, very modest-looking Jamaican man emerged and stepped hesitantly toward Ree. Ree looked away from Jayde and walked over to the man, handing him the baby.

"Rodney."

Rodney smiled; glad that he could help Respect, glad his life had been spared, and glad that he was finally holding his child. He was sure Ree would kill him for having waited so long to tell him about the time Trinity forced him to sex her unprotected in the closet.

Rodney was a bellhop at Ree's hotel who Trinity had used as her pawn to get pregnant. When Rodney had approached Trinity after she gave birth and asked to be in his son's life, she had told him that the baby was not his, and that it was Ree's. When he threatened to reveal to Ree that they had been intimate and that he himself wanted a blood test, she confessed her plans that she was passing the baby off as Ree's in hopes that Rodney would work with her to keep their secret.

She told him in confidence that she had someone on the inside who would pass the judge fraudulent results if it turned out not to be Ree's baby. She told Rodney he would not be able to see S.J. but that she would pay him hefty for his help. She was sure Rodney was convinced. However, Rodney, being the stand-up family man that he was, could not see himself not being a father to his child even after secretly considering her offer. Then, after she confirmed to him that her source had told her the results were in fact negative and that Ree was not the father, Rodney knew he had to get in contact with Respect. He had to do the right thing for S.J., for his son.

Trinity was wrong for thinking that Rodney's motives were impure and money-oriented like hers. She figured she would pay him with the money that Ree would surely be freely giving her, and Rodney could go on his merry way with his family, not caring about his biological son with her. She didn't realize that she could not play Rodney when it came to his family. And she certainly couldn't play Ree when it came to his.

Chapter 3

"My father, Mickel, as you probably know . . . ran arguably one of the tightest, longest, and best drug empires for almost three decades straight."

—Jayde, *Still Thicker than Water*

"You nervous?"

The question caused Tatum to lift her eyes up from her phone. The last-minute wedding details had held her attention since they had left the estate, that and a few of her lone thoughts. She was surprised that Crush had blurted that out, especially since he was usually extremely quiet.

Tatum shrugged, really giving it thought. *Am I nervous?*

"I don't know, I guess a little." She thought about the recent events and added, "Yeah, I probably am."

Crush nodded as he continued to focus on the road, leaving Tatum with a new deliberation on her mind.

If she was nervous, why was she? Was it because of Trinity and the baby? Was it because of Ree going back into the streets this one last time? Was she really unsure if he was the one she was meant to spend the rest of her life with?

She literally shook her head at the last thought as she picked up the note and read it again.

Something came up. Meet you in the States. Love you.

When she had returned from the market and found it lying next to her shrimp scampi, she was sure that her husband-to-be had left on some occupational mission with his new business associate, Jayde. To say that she was completely comfortable with it would be a lie. But Tatum felt like this, along with so many other things, was one of the many tests of their relationship.

"You wanna know something?"

Okay, now he was starting to scare her.

"Um . . . I guess so," Tatum chuckled lightly. She had changed into jeans, loafers, and a designer T-shirt for the flight. Her hair was pulled back and she was comfortably chic and fabulous. "Does it have anything to do with you suddenly becoming so verbal?"

Crush had to laugh at that, his three-hundred-plus-pound frame shaking with each roar.

"Nah, ma, I just figured . . . we been around each other. I know you probably wanna know how me and Respect know each other. And why he trusts me with you."

Crush said the last part as if Tatum were a million-dollar bill. She looked at him with a smile because she truly had been curious.

"Yeah," she responded. "I *do* wanna know about that. That time we came to Atlanta was the first time I heard your name."

"Wasn't the first time I heard yours," he answered with

a grin. Tatum crinkled her brow as he proceeded with the story in an unhurried drawl.

"Dig, ma, I met Respect back in Brooklyn, right. He was just building his shit up over in the States and the nigga I used to work for, well, Respect . . ." He paused and looked at Tatum through the rearview and then buffered what he was going to say. "Respect let's just say . . . put him out of business."

Tatum figured that meant he had killed him and she tried not to show it on her face.

"Anyway, I ended up being the last nigga to come on board with Respect, and at first you know, I'm like who the fuck is this Jamaican nigga? 'Cause where I'm from we ain't really trust them muhfuckas. Half the time, ain't know what the fuck these niggas is sayin'." Tatum shared a laugh with him as he spoke.

"But I got down, and I saw that he was a real dude. He took care of people. We made so much fucking money. I mean yo, niggas hadn't seen money up there like that since . . . I don't even know. You woulda thought we were Rich Porter, Alpo, and them niggas. Respect had it locked . . . Brooklyn, Harlem, Jersey." Crush seemed to have stars in his eyes reminiscing.

"Well back in . . . I think it was '03, '04 . . . nah it was '03. I got knocked. I got caught up in some crazy shit, took a bid for my man. Respect took care of me. He took care of my lawyers, my family, he bought my moms and my girl a crib down in Atlanta, made sure they were good; made sure my kids were good. I mean he was a *good* dude. When I came home I told him I was out and he was cool on that. He told me fuck the money, I didn't owe him shit. He appreciated my loyalty and the way I handled the situation. I told him I'd always have him on anything. Anything he needed me for."

Tatum thought about the way he was praising Ree.

It made her feel conflicted. He was a drug lord, he killed people, but he was nice? Caring? Hospitable? She continued to listen.

"He'd call me and fill me in on shit, and we got kinda tight. When he would come to Atlanta for business, we'd link up. Anytime he needed a hand with shit, one-shot deals, I'd be there. He always took care of me, too. And anytime something important would happen, he'd put me up on it. I wouldn't hear from him for like a year, but when something happened, he'd hit me up," he chuckled. "Like when he moved the base from New York to Jersey, I knew about it. And when all that shit happened in Jersey, I know you know about that . . . when he had to jet, I knew about it." He looked at Tatum seriously through the rearview and continued. "When he met you . . . I knew about it."

Tatum's ears perked.

"Seriously?" she questioned.

"Yo, I'll never forget. When I told Respect I was going to propose to my girl, he clowned me. I told him it'd be him one day and he told me 'Yea all right, I'll let you know when that happens.' One night he calls my crib like four in the morning talking 'bout 'I found her.' My girl's about to flip 'cause she ain't know who the fuck it was. I'm trippin' 'cause I ain't know what this nigga talkin' about. I'm like 'Who you find, and what you gonna do to her?' He's like 'I found her. I found my wife.' He was gone off of you."

Tatum smiled, thinking of the first time she'd met Ree.

She figured since Crush was being so open and honest with her, she'd go for the gusto. Ask him what was really on her mind.

"Can I ask you a question?"

"What up?" he replied, pulling into Respect's private airport. Tatum looked down before finally spilling it.

"Do you really think this is it, honestly? This . . . *one* last time."

Crush pulled up to the jet and put the gearshift in park, thinking hard before responding.

"To tell you the truth, ma . . . yeah, I do. The shit he putting together now is almost too sweet to resist. But once it's done, the way he set it up from what I know . . . he's done. I think Respect knows he can't do this forever."

Tatum prayed his answer was more truth than not.

"And what about Jayde?" Tatum found herself asking. "How important is she in all of this?"

Crush smirked and then replied.

"Not as important as she'd like to think. See she doesn't get it. Ree is a strategist. She's a pawn. She has her use and that's it. Respect doesn't have partners. Never has . . . never will."

Tatum took a deep breath, for some reason slightly pleased with that answer.

"Well, it's been real, Crush. Thanks for the heart to heart." Tatum winked and then opened the door, stepping out as the pilot came and started to load her luggage.

Crush bid her farewell in his signature salute and she returned it with a smile, and just as she was about to close the door she doubled back with one last question.

"Hey Crush."

"What up?" he replied quickly.

"You said that Ree always told you the important stuff, right?"

He nodded and stared on at Tatum, waiting for her to continue.

Tatum looked him in the eyes curiously.

"Did he ever tell you about Trinity?"

Crush let out a small smirk before shaking his head.

"Nah. Never."

Tatum nodded. And with that, she closed the door and boarded her plane.

They had ridden the entire way in silence, neither of them thinking twice of the murder that was just committed. Murder to the both of them was as natural as everyday conversation. It was another element to the interaction process; meet people, know people, love people, kill people. Both Jayde and Respect were street-born, street-raised, street products.

"We're here," she spoke with a slight excitement, as the car pulled up to a small brick house.

They had ventured through forests, trails, and many twists and turns to arrive at this destination on the very outskirts of Jamaica. If seclusion was his goal, he had achieved it.

"He's in there?" Ree's eyes scanned the small country home, which appeared to be desolate. He tried to take in as much as he could in the seconds before the truck powered off and they began to exit. He visibly reached into his waist, produced his weapon, and double-checked that the clip was loaded and ready.

"You don't trust anyone, huh?"

Ree's blank stare was Jayde's response. She tried to lighten the mood.

"Maybe after this we can head down to Moe's for some seafood. Murder always makes me hungry—"

"I just want to have this meeting and get back to the States to Tatum." Ree was dead serious and business-oriented the whole time, just as Jayde had been told he would be.

She tried to disguise the revulsion on her face with a smile.

"Of course, fair enough. Follow me."

Trailing up the stone walkway, they reached a wooden door and Jayde knocked with the heavy brass hanger.

"This is his?" Ree questioned.

"It belongs to someone he trusts," she replied, a little irritated with his earlier rejection. A beautiful woman like Jayde never met rejection. Ree figured so and found it amusing. Before he forgot, he had a question for her.

"How did you know Trinity?"

Jayde's heart rate sped up but her face kept its cool.

"I didn't."

Ree stood a step or two behind her and studied her out of the corner of his eye, looking for signs of dishonesty. Jayde didn't break a sweat, however.

"Right before she went, she looked at you. She recognized you." He wasn't asking her, he was telling her.

Jayde could hear footsteps approaching the door and replied coolly.

"Of course. She probably remembered me from when I stayed at the hotel with Sasha and Tatum." Just then an older, skinny black man pulled back the heavy door and Jayde smiled as if her previous words had been truthful. What? Tell Ree that she was in fact the person who had assisted Trinity with the fake test results in hopes that it would help scare Tatum away? She didn't have a death wish. And to think that little bitch was about to actually tell Respect who had helped her. Jayde had seen it in her eyes. *That's why I shot the bitch in the throat,* Jayde thought. *I hate a vocal bitch.*

"Hello. He's expecting us," she then addressed the man.

Ree shifted his gaze from Jayde to the butler, assuming

that she was candid in her response. There were no signs
that she wasn't.

"Follow me," the old man ordered.

Ree and Jayde stepped inside and tailed the man
down a set of steps that set off to the left. It was dark,
and the only light came from the illumination of the
lantern the man carried. The place was old and damp,
resembling a dungeon.

"What the fuck is this shit?" Ree mumbled, not liking
the setup. In the position he was in, he reckoned he
could kill Jayde with a bullet to the back of her head, hit
the butler immediately after, and start busting at anyone
else in this chamber if something should pop off.

"Why are you so nervous? You know he would never
bring harm to you," Jayde assured.

Ree in fact wanted to let her know that he wasn't even
sure if *he* existed. A large part of him was skeptical of her
revelation.

"Sweetheart, your bullshit choice of words insults me.
I'm cautious, not nervous."

"My apologies." Jayde grinned, still strutting ahead
of him.

Finally stepping into the dim basement of stone-
covered walls, Ree could see a round table in the
distance, a frail man's silhouette in one of the chairs.

This shit is wild.

Approaching, Ree would hate to admit that he actually felt some type of emotion. He was happy, happy
that it was true. He knew it before he could see his
features; he felt his presence.

"And time has brought us here. This is a moment of
champions."

Jayde smiled wide, all of her tough exterior evaporating
into the damp basement air. She walked hastily to him as
he enveloped her in a warm hug.

"Daddy!"

"Jayde . . ." he replied. ". . . and Respect." He extended his hand to Ree as Jayde stepped to the side and he and Ree shared a manly embrace, both with a mutual amount of love for each other that you could sense.

"You were so right, Daddy. He's very cautious. I don't think he believed you were here."

Mickel grinned as his aged and handsome features became more visible. He looked to Ree with an unspoken understanding.

"Well, it's a creed of great men, Jayde. Exercise caution in your business affairs, for the world is full of trickery. But let this not blind you—"

"—To what virtue there is," Ree finished for him.

Jayde looked on back and forth between what she felt were two of the greatest men to walk the earth. Her daddy . . . and the man designed for her.

"What is this, that desiderata stuff?"

"Oh Jayde, please. Don't disrespect the creed," Mickel warned. It was a doctrine, almost an oath that Mickel had lived by and also instilled in Respect when they had worked closely together. Ree had it tattooed onto him as a daily reminder.

Mickel Dupree, Jayde's father, was one of the most prominent gangsters of Respect's generation. He ran a large and lucrative empire and was someone whom Ree had learned from and respected. He was also supposed to be dead.

"Those simple words will guide you into a life of peace and prosperity," Mickel added.

Ree silently agreed. So far it had worked for him.

"You look well, old man," Ree spoke with a smirk, examining him. Mickel wore linen pants and a linen shirt over his slim frame. His curly black hair was cropped short and his tanned Trinidadian skin was wrinkle-free.

Ree thought of Tatum being that she also had family from Trinidad.

"And you look rich," Mickel shot back. "But oh, I'm going to make you so much richer." A surge of electricity went through Ree as if someone had plugged him into a socket. To have once known Mickel's master plan was one thing. To learn that he was still alive and it was about to unfold was another. He and Tatum, and their kids, and their kids' kids, and their kids' kids' kids, would never have to worry about money . . . ever. The same with Chauncey and Jayde. He would no longer be rich, he would be wealthy.

"And you owe it all to me," Jayde intervened, shooting Ree a glance. Ree darted his eyes to her and then back to Mickel.

"Yes, my beautiful daughter, I am so glad you were able to come in contact with him. And to think, it all happened in coincidence, no? Jayde was friends with your fiancée. Speaking of which!"

Ree knew it was coming.

"There is a woman you are going to marry? *Just one?*" Mickel joked as he took a seat at the table. Ree and Jayde followed suit.

"I hope she is worthy of your lifelong commitment," Mickel added more seriously. Ree would never know, but he held him close to his heart, almost like a son.

"I hope I'm worthy of hers," Ree responded.

"I see, I see," Mickel smiled. "Well in that case, congratulations. I can't wait to meet her. I bet the stars fight her to shine."

"Most definitely," Ree assured.

"I knew a woman like her once, but it never worked out."

Jayde became secretly infuriated because she knew just whom he was speaking of, and it wasn't her mother.

"Shall we get down to business," she intervened.

"My daughter gets envious if the topic strays away from her or money for too long. Her green eyes become even greener," Mickel stated with a raised brow. He knew Jayde inside out.

"I see," Ree observed, as if taking note.

"Okay so the business. Everything is in order. It is your job to execute it. Make sure everyone does everything with perfection, Respect. If they don't, kill them." Ree nodded but found it interesting that Mickel spoke the words so freely, especially being that his daughter was one of the people whom he would be executing orders to.

"Use your judgment. If anyone seems scared or wary, kill them. If they talk too much or deviate, kill them. If they bring any type of attention to us during this short time of the operation . . ."

"Yeah," Ree responded, already knowing what he would have to and most definitely would do.

"Okay, so the world tour. The Gonzales family is ready to come on board with you. I met with them, I gave the okay. As soon as everything is set up with all cartels, they are ready to move the black tar by naval ships." Black tar was a very addictive form of heroin that was slowly being pumped into the U.S. from Mexico. With Mickel's connections, and him being alive, he was able to plug Ree into this.

"You will have to handle the Segovias from Ecuador. They are wary, I cannot lie. They want to meet with you in person. I will be there, we'll get it squared. Once that is done, they will be ready to move the cocaine wherever you need it. They are the most strategic. They have man-built submarines that transport between their border with Colombia. You will have very easy and plentiful access to quality product. This is also the way the marijuana will come from Colombia. Have you decided how all of this will be run being that you are . . . departing?" Mickel smirked in his question almost as if he couldn't believe it. However, he understood.

"Yes, once I do the initial deal, I will purchase enough for my people to supply the five major cities. Instead of breaking off cities, we decided to delegate with product. My man C has people that will handle the heroin; Jayde will be in charge of distributing the coke and cannabis. Once I'm paid, the operation will be handled by them. Chaunc will deal with Mr. Gonzales; Jayde will deal with the Segovias."

Mickel nodded.

"Sounds good. I promise you, Respect, your first billion will be made very shortly, and as quick as it comes, you will be tempted to stay and make another," he warned.

"I'm sure," Ree agreed. "But a billion will do me solid. I can't get greedy, I'm already rocking the boat. Besides, I have a wife now."

"And a son? Jayde tells me of your child here in Jamaica." Ree glanced at Jayde and then answered.

"No. That was a misunderstanding."

Mickel shook his head.

"Women," he answered. "One minute it's yours, the next, it's not." Jayde once again knew what he was talking about and chose to change the subject.

"I'm so glad that we were able to convince you, Respect, to come on board with this." Jayde knew that Ree was the only man who could execute the drug empire version of the money pyramid. Mickel was unable to operate due to his low, almost nonexistent status, plus he had no connection to the city heads, the smaller people. Jayde had some connection to the smaller folks, but she also had static with many. Plus she was comfortable with money, but not as comfortable as Ree. She also didn't have the character and skill to deal with people on such a large scale; she was best at running the lower end and Mickel knew that.

Respect had the money, the power, and the respect to literally be the guy, the sole guy to supply the three most profiting drugs into the five star points of America— New York, Los Angeles, Chicago, Atlanta, and Miami. But he would only do it for a limited amount of time and then break up his role and divide it amongst Jayde and Chauncey. He hoped they could handle it, but once he was out, he would be out. And whether they sunk or not, would not fall on his shoulders.

"You got any questions for me?" Mickel asked, as Ree leaned back in his chair, seeming to be deep in thought.

Ree stared at him and then gave a quick nod.

"Yeah, I do. What happened with the explosion? I thought you were gone . . . everyone did. How'd you get out? You set it up?"

Mickel raised his eyebrows and let out a chuckle. He looked at Jayde and seemed to be biting his tongue in her presence.

"That's a story for another time, my friend. But I will say, no. I did not set it up. I was meant to be killed. Someone wanted me dead."

Ree thought for a second of the people who could want him dead. He thought of the ones who *would* want him dead once this operation went into play and if they ever caught wind of the man behind it.

"The way I escaped those circumstances is the same way you will escape your current ones. That is also set up. Once that is cleared you will be able to move freely country to country. No more looking over your shoulder."

Ree was glad to hear that part. No more fugitive

status, no more lying low in his condo while he and Tatum were in Atlanta, back to living a normal life.

He thought back to the day all of this came into play. That day in Chauncey's basement when he realized he would be stepping back into the game briefly. He knew Tatum would be angry, and she had given him hell for it for months, almost to the point of threatening to leave. But he swore to her on his and Trinity's unborn child that this was it, and, Tatum being the woman she was, she somehow understood he had to get this out of his blood. He knew she secretly blamed Jayde for it, and in a way, she had a right to. Because Ree had gotten sucked in the moment Jayde leaned into him that day in the basement and whispered those four little words. "The rumors are true," she had teased.

And he knew what it meant. He knew that her father, Mickel Dupree, was alive.

"Why don't you be a gentleman and get the door for us?" Sasha asked in a true Southern belle fashion.

Bleek smirked and assisted Tatum with her rollaway luggage, pausing to grab the handle and pull the door open.

"See, that wasn't so bad. You're learning," Sasha joked.

Tatum chuckled as she slid inside.

"Hey, Bleek."

"What's up, Tatum?" He popped the trunk on Sasha's new Benz and glided the luggage inside.

As Sasha slid in the back with her, Tatum took the time to feed her curiosity.

"Um, why is Bleek driving your car?"

Sasha rolled her eyes briefly before speaking.

"Oh gosh, girl. Chauncey had Bleek take me to the dealership to get my car because something *came up* . . ." Tatum briefly thought of Ree's note about something *coming up* and related. "Anyway, I took him for a ride once we got it, we went to get a bite to eat, and before I knew it, it was time to come and get you."

Tatum wondered if Chauncey had asked Bleek to go for a ride with Sasha and take her to get a bite to eat as well, but she left it alone . . . for now.

"Anyway, do you like it? Ain't she a dream?"

Tatum looked around and nodded.

"Yeah, it's nice, Sash. And . . . pink."

Sasha playfully punched her and laughed.

"It's just the inside. You know I love pink, girl." Just then Bleek leaned his head in.

"Oh hell no, I ain't no muhfuckin' chauffeur, my dear. This ain't *Driving Miss Daisy*," he teased to Sasha, who seemed comfortable in the back with Tatum.

"Please, Bleek," she pouted with Bambi eyes. "We need to have girl talk, wedding talk!"

Bleek closed their door in response and slid in the driver's seat. Sasha winked at Tatum and giggled.

Tatum stared at her with a plastered smile and a confused mind. Sasha's pout and baby voice was always used on men to get her way, especially Chauncey. Now she was using it on this poor kid?

Sure, Bleek was a grown man and Tatum knew he was heavy in the streets and known for being a wild one, like Chauncey. But he was also a smooth, baby-faced young boy whom Tatum was sure Sasha could work magic on. Tatum knew Sasha loved Chauncey dearly; she had gone through a lot to be with him. She knew Chauncey had also not been the perfect man to Sasha, breaking up with her with no explanation at one time, cheating on her with her friend, and now neglecting her for the streets. Sasha needed attention, just like when Mike didn't deliver what Sasha needed and she found a way to get it elsewhere. Tatum just hoped, no, prayed, Sasha didn't get herself into any shit.

"So, where's Chauncey now?" Tatum asked aloud, sort of to both Sasha and Bleek.

Sasha shrugged.

"Girl, I don't know. He came by the dealership to see me and said he had to go."

"Oh, so he *did* come by the dealership?" Tatum asked. "Well, that was nice. At least he tried to squeeze some time in."

"Yeah, but he couldn't stay. He had to *handle something*," Sasha mocked, and Tatum nodded.

"You know how it goes, Sash. You *always* knew how it went." She was reminding her that just like herself, they knew they hadn't gotten with corporate nine-to-five guys. Faulting Chauncey for being in the streets would be like faulting a fish for being in water. *Where else could they survive?*

"I know, Tay. I just don't know when things are ever gonna be perfect for us. It's like one minute it's something, then when that's over, another hurdle. He's never been in the streets this much and it's all because of this *master plan*."

Tatum shifted in her seat because the last thing she wanted was to talk about the master plan. Plus, Ree had been so adamant on her never discussing it. She would honor his wishes.

"What do you think about it? I know Ree is all wrapped up in it, how do you deal with it?"

"It is what it is," Tatum replied, blasé.

Sasha dropped her head.

"Yeah, you're right. At least Ree has a plan, though.

At least he's not staying in it . . . at least you're worth him giving it up. And that's just for you," Sasha smiled. "He doesn't even know," she added, placing her hand on Tatum's stomach.

Tatum smiled lightly because she did feel bad for Sasha. But Sasha knew what type of man Chauncey was before she got pregnant by him, before she decided to have the baby, before she decided to get married to and then cheat on Mike with him, and before she decided to get back with him this final time.

"Chauncey won't even make a plan of when he will give it up, for me *or* Aubrey."

On that cue, Bleek turned up the music, no longer wanting to hear any more.

"You know, I really thought he was considering it after the cops questioned him when Neli died. I guess since he had beaten her in that hotel room, he was one of the first people they wanted to talk to when she got murdered. Then with the disappearance of Mike and all of that drama, I thought he was considering laying low. But as soon as the heat died down, he was right back out there," Sasha said, lips pursed with her Southern drawl.

"It'll be okay," Tatum assured her. "No matter what . . . you just gotta see what you can deal with."

Tatum changed the subject.

"So, what time do we have to be to Monique?"

"Oh my Goddd!" Sasha squealed with a big grin on her face. "We have to be there at eight in the morning."

She smiled at her best friend with tears of joy in her eyes and Tatum returned it. The love between them was so genuine.

"Tay!" she yelled excitedly, clapping her hands together. "Bitch! You're getting married!"

* * *

"APD, please hold."

Adriana sat at her kitchen table tapping her foot as the hold music of the day, Gene Pitney's "Town Without Pity," poured through the speakers of the phone.

Adriana found herself humming on the verge of nodding off.

"Hello!"

Adriana jumped up, unaware that the operator was back on the line.

Did she hear me?

"Uh yes, Detective Murphy please."

There was a slight pause and then a click followed by two long rings.

"Homicide!"

"Detective Murphy?"

"Who the hell is this?"

Adriana, true to her timid form, took a moment to gather her words at his abrasive greeting.

"Uhm . . . sir, it's Adriana. Adriana Lin. We spoke a few times. Last time, a few months ago. I just wanted to see if you found anything . . . with that tape I gave you?"

She could hear the detective's aggravation in his silence.

"What tape?"

"Oh, uhm . . . the tape from the tape recorder, of the girl . . . Penelope Daniels, who was shot. Remember, I'm a nurse at the hospital, I found it. The tape has her and the woman . . . the woman who shot her . . . talking."

There was a brief pause as if he was recollecting, followed by a sound of recognition.

"Ah, yes," Murphy bellowed. "Nope. Nothing, kid."

Adriana wrinkled her brow.

"I don't understand? The tape has her killer on it. She even said her name. It was J—"

"What was the name on the tape again?" the detective questioned peculiarly. For some reason Adriana's antennas went up. Call it woman's intuition or her good old gut, but she lied.

"I-I don't really remember. But it's on the tape."

There was another long silence and Adriana listened closely. It sounded as if the detective had closed the door because the previous minuscule noise had completely vanished.

"And you said that was the only copy of the tape you had, correct?"

Adriana swallowed hard and began to fiddle with the objects on her table, one of which was the duplicate copy of the tape she had made.

"Yeah . . . yes. That was the only one."

Another pause.

"Well, yeah, kid. Like I said, no luck. You can try back in a couple of months. Or better yet, let the girl rest in peace . . . you didn't know her anyway."

Before Adriana could get another word in, the call was disconnected.

Detective Murphy wasted no time dialing the numbers that he knew all too well. He leaned back and put his hand into the tight waistband of his pants as his oversized belly spilled over.

"It's not the first, so what do you want?" she greeted rudely.

"Aw, don't be like that, Big J. Can't an old pal just call his chum buddy?"

"What do you want, Murphy?" Jayde inquired, restless. She had just wrapped up the meeting with her father and Ree and was tired and hungry.

"Look, just wanted to let you know. That little girl from the hospital is calling about that tape again. She wants to know if we made progress."

Jayde was annoyed, but not worried. She knew Murphy was on her side. Atlanta's police department, better known as APD, was on her side as well. She still couldn't believe Neli was sharp enough to bring a tape recorder to their meeting.

"What's with this bitch? She out for law-abiding citizen of the year award or something?" Jayde spat, thinking about putting this young girl to rest depending on how annoying she continued to be.

Murphy shrugged before responding through heavy breathing.

"Who knows? I think she's harmless. But I do remember telling you every phone call that I deter pertaining to your dirt will be another ten grand. I want it in big bills, please. Oh, and throw in some of those Omaha steaks."

"You're a fat-ass glutton fuck, Murphy, and I hope your arteries clog up with lard and you die a slow death. . . . You'll have it by eight A.M."

With no more words to speak, Jayde disconnected the call.

"Everything cool?" Ree questioned, sliding into the car and catching the tail end of her conversation. Jayde was glad that he was making conversation with her.

"Of course, just more pigs wanting more money. But you know I got you covered."

Jayde smiled and Ree nodded. She had killed two birds with one stone. Covered the true meaning of the call and convinced Ree that the payoff pertained to the work she was doing to clear his fugitive status. Slowly but surely she would win the one thing that mattered to him the most . . . Respect.

Chapter 4

"It's just food, Ms. Lady, not marriage . . . not yet."

—Respect, *Thicker than Water*

The next day

Tatum stood in front of the large oval mirror with her hands on her head in despair.

What was I thinking!

"This is not the measurements that were given to me by my assistant. I'm so sorry, Ms. Mosley. She will be fired for a mistake like this."

"No, no, Ms. Lhuillier, it's not . . . it's not her fault. It's mine."

Tatum studied the beautiful gown in the mirror, its pearl color contrasting gorgeously with her mocha-esque shade. Monique Lhuillier was a hot designer hailing from Switzerland who had created some of the most exclusive and modern wedding dresses, one of which was Reese Witherspoon's signature blush beauty. Tatum's dress was gorgeous enough to rival that. The only problem was the busted seams around her midsection.

"What do you mean?" Monique questioned.

"I should've known. I should've known to give a few inches just in case," Tatum confessed, letting out a breath of air.

Monique Lhuillier remained silent as she pulled at the threads on Tatum's gown, but she was secretly wondering what type of binge eating Tatum was doing.

"The wedding has you nervous, I see. Are you a comfort eater?"

Sasha busted out laughing at the notion, and Tatum had to giggle herself through her despair.

"Actually, Ms. Lhuillier, she's a comfort sexer. The wedding has her so nervous she just up and got pregnant in the middle of it."

Tatum shot Sasha a middle finger knowing that she was tipsy from the complimentary champagne, and Monique looked from Sasha to Tatum for a clue that she was joking. When she realized she was not, she smiled wide.

"Congratulations. This is wonderful! Don't worry, the dress will be fine, you haven't gained much."

Monique's vibe was so relaxed, so comforting, it reminded Tatum of her mother for some reason. She wished desperately that her mother could be there for moments like this and her father could walk her down the aisle. Both of Tatum's parents had died years ago in a car accident.

She thought of her brother and couldn't help but conclude how he would have never been one of Ree's groomsmen. Him probably showing up at all would have been a heated debate between her and Ree in itself.

It didn't matter now . . . he was gone, too. Dead.

"Thank you, Ms. Lhuillier. I'm so sorry for the inconvenience."

Monique smiled and her olive skin tone glowed with warmth. She was a thin woman with hair that graced her shoulders. She was dressed in a stylish kimono and sipped herbal tea while she provided Tatum and Sasha with champagne and chocolate-covered strawberries.

"No inconvenience. This is why we do a fitting. To make sure it . . . fits." She yanked a thread on her final word with emphasis.

"How far along are you?"

"Um, about eleven weeks," Tatum confessed nervously, on the verge of tears.

Her voice was so shaky.

"What is wrong, my love? These are happy times. Marriage, baby . . . rejoice."

Tatum didn't want to reveal her fear of bringing a child into the world with a man who was about to implement one of the largest criminal structures ever. Not to mention the fact that she had just discovered that he had fathered another woman's child. Rejoice? Please. If she was rejoicing, she wouldn't be hiding her tiny bump through flowy clothing. She wasn't really showing, but she knew Ree would catch on soon. She was sure he probably already figured out that she had gained a few pounds.

"Yeah."

Just then, Monique's assistant tapped on the door with a wide smile.

"Excuse me, ladies, I'd hate to interrupt. But there is an *extremely* handsome and well-mannered gentleman here and I believe he is the groom-to-be."

Tatum's face lit up without her breaking an expression

and Monique smiled naturally. She could see the love written all over Tatum. She recognized love like that.

Tatum started to the door but stopped short when all three ladies shrieked, "No! No! God no! He can't see the dress!"

Tatum remembered and quickly changed into the fluffy robe Monique provided for her.

Making her way down the marble staircase of the private store, she laid eyes on Ree, who stood at the door on his cell phone. Once he saw her, he deaded the call.

"What are you doing here?" She beamed walking to him. He looked so good in his crisp black shirt and jeans. His facial hair was sharp, his wrist on glare, he was even more handsome than he was when she left him yesterday. "I thought you weren't coming until Thursday?"

"It's not Thursday?" he questioned seriously, wrapping his arms around her waist. Tatum giggled.

"Nooo, it's Tuesday."

He leaned down and put his lips to her ear, speaking in an alluring whisper.

"Oh well, then I guess I just couldn't make it til then, Ms. Mosley."

Tatum blushed as he nestled his face in between her chin and shoulder, tickling her neck with his fuzz. "I got something to tell you," he added.

"Oh yeah?"

"Yeah," he assured.

"Well I got something to tell you, too," she said, resting her hand below his waist. Pregnancy made Tatum horny as hell.

"Hey, cut that out, bad girl," he ordered sexily. "For real. Let's have a seat."

Tatum let him lead her to the peach 1920s-style couch once she saw that he was serious. She sat beside him, looking into his eyes, and a million thoughts went through her head in about ten seconds.

He's not ready. How could a man like him be ready for marriage? He wants to wait? No, he doesn't want to do it at all.

He's gonna work it out with Trinity? He saw her and the baby and had second thoughts.

No, I know what it is. He's not leaving the game, this is no one-shot deal. He's in it for good.

Ree interlocked her fingers with his and stared in her eyes unflinchingly. His expression was neutral and Tatum's breathing sped up.

"Tatum, first let me say that I know this hasn't been easy on you. With me putting a foot back into the streets, I know you're worried. I know I told you I was done before this and you're probably thinking why should you believe me now, but trust me . . . this is the last time. I just had to tell you that again."

Tatum nodded because that was one argument she had beat to death, she didn't even want to touch it again. He continued.

"Then . . . with this whole Trinity situation." Tatum inhaled. "I know I'm asking a lot by expecting you to be okay with all of this. Sit back and watch me raise a child with a woman that's not you. I appreciate you trying to be understanding through this and I know it's not easy to deal with. That's why . . . I'm glad you won't have to."

Tatum wasn't sure if she had heard him right and the wrinkle in her brow showed that.

"What? Ree, what are you talking about?"

Ree sighed and then he used his thumbs to massage her hands, which he was still holding.

"S.J. is not my son, Tatum. He's not mine."

Tatum wanted to believe him, but getting her hopes up would be cruel. She had heard the results herself.

"But . . . the hearing . . ."

"It was . . . it was set up. It was a lie," he summed up the best he could. "I just had to let you know."

"She lied?" Tatum questioned, anger now consuming her. How dare that crazy bitch put them through this?

"What, was she working with the judge?" she continued her questioning.

Ree shrugged.

"I don't know. I doubt it. Maybe someone in the lab, maybe a clerk. Who knows? It doesn't matter."

Tatum jumped up, her body trembling in rage.

"Oh yes the hell it does! Wait til I see that bitch! Oh my God, Ree. How could she do this? I'm gonna fuck her up."

Ree ran his hand over his mouth and maintained an even expression.

"No . . . no you're not."

"Yes the hell I am!" she insisted. Ree had another thing coming.

"Tatum, you can't do that."

She thought about the baby that she was carrying and took a deep breath, reconsidering.

"Fine," she agreed as she held her hand out to him. "Give me your phone then. I'm gonna call that bitch. I'm about to go HAM on her ass!"

Ree stood slowly but did not hand her his phone.

"Tatum, you can't call her."

"Why not, Ree? What, you still care about this bitch? After what she did? You feel sorry for her or something?"

Ree chuckled and shook his head.

"No."

"Then what? Boy, you better give me the phone! I want to know why she would do this! I *want* to call her, Ree."

Ree grabbed her by the shoulders gently and looked her in the eyes.

"Tatum. You can't . . . call her." He ran his hand through her hair and shrugged. "You just . . . can't."

The way he said it brought a new awareness to Tatum that she hadn't considered and a chill went through her body. And the reason she didn't consider it was beyond her. She was dead. Trinity was dead.

Tatum briefly thought about the way Ree handled disloyalty and deceit. Would he kill her if she was disloyal? *Could* he kill her? The thought shook her to the bone.

In all actuality, she understood. Trinity had done something so foul. But was it that easy for Ree to just kill a woman whom he had once had a relationship with? The reality hit Tatum like a blow and she had to sit.

"You all right?" he asked with concern.

". . . Yeah."

"You sure?"

"Uh . . . yeah. Look, Ree . . . there's something I need to—"

The buzzing of Ree's cell in his hand interrupted her statement. Ree held his finger up to her and brought the phone to his ear.

"Hold up, baby." He then addressed the caller. "Yo . . . Yeah, I'm here. I need to see you."

Tatum could hear a deep voice coming through the phone and she was almost positive that it was Chauncey.

"All right, that's good news, that's very good news. I'm on my way." He disconnected the call and focused back on Tatum.

"So what were you saying?" He brushed his fingers across Tatum's chin and she smiled up at him.

"Nothing . . . it's not important. It—it can wait."

Ree narrowed his eyes at her but didn't speak on it. *When the time is right,* Tatum figured. They said their good-byes and parted ways, and Tatum finished her fitting, trying her best not to think about anything else.

Later that day

"Mommy! Mommy!"

Sasha used her knuckles, the only part of her hand that wasn't covered in marinara sauce, to wipe a bead of sweat from her eyebrow.

"Mommy . . . I want more! I want more!"

"Okay, Bri-Bri, just give Mommy a minute, okay? Mommy's hands are dirty."

"Mommy, I want more!" Aubrey continued to yell in her squeaky voice as she sat at the kitchen table. Evidence of her recent doing, spilled tomato sauce, all over the floor and her clothes.

Sasha shook her head at the mess. "Why did you do this?" Reaching for a new roll of paper towels and trying not to dirty them, she held the roll between her chest and wrist and broke the seal. The paper towels immediately rolled to the floor, landing right in the pile of sauce, and getting soiled.

"I want more cheese! More cheese!"

Sasha let out a breath of exasperated air and kneeled down. *Father, help me.*

"Aubrey, you have to wait. You spilled this sauce everywhere and Mommy has to clean it!"

Aubrey soaked in her mother's words.

"Sowwy," she mumbled dramatically, poking out her lip.

As Sasha attempted to clean the floor and her hands, she thought aloud.

"Daddy sure better appreciate this shit."

It was Sasha and Chauncey's anniversary. The day

they always used to celebrate when they became an "official" couple. For Chauncey it was the day he cut off his other broads. It also was the day Chauncey had proposed to her, before the madness.

Sasha reached up and cleaned off Aubrey as best she could, then turned and disposed of the dirty towels in the trash. It wasn't long before Aubrey started up again, the request that caused her to reach across the table and knock over the sauce in the first place.

"Mommy, I want cheeesee," she whined as the phone began to ring.

"Aubrey . . ." Sasha said through clenched teeth. The last thing she was trying to raise was a whiner like herself. It was a trait she was hoping to break the cycle with. She answered the cordless and reached over and handed Aubrey a small piece of mozzarella, hoping to quiet her. "Hello . . ."

"What's up, kid?"

Sasha let a smile through at the sound of Chauncey's voice. All of this was, in the end, for him. She was looking forward to her and Aubrey surprising him with his "favorite" lasagna, and looking even more forward to the surprise she had once Aubrey went to bed.

"Nothing muchhh, what's up with you?"

Sasha figured that Chauncey's not mentioning their anniversary was a way for him to add to the suspense of whatever he had for her. *Jewelry,* Sasha concluded. It was always jewelry.

"Shit," Chauncey answered, blasé. "Hold up a minute . . ." He then addressed someone else. "Nah, put more ketchup on that for me, my man."

"Chauncey!"

"What?"

"What are you doing?" She couldn't help the urgency

in her voice. She wanted to scream, *Put that back!* He was ruining her surprise.

"I'm getting a cheesesteak from Vinny's," he responded nonchalantly.

"Why?"

"'Cause I'm hungry."

"Look, don't eat that, babe . . . I cooked," she confessed.

There was a brief silence.

". . . That's what's up," Chauncey told her. "I'll eat that, too . . . when I get in."

There's a feeling a woman gets. It has to be her sixth sense. The feeling of knowing exactly what is going on with a man before he even says a word. The feeling of knowing devastation and knowing they are about to fuck up, but you can't stop them. You can't save them from themselves.

"And what time will that be?" Sasha's voice let on that she already knew. *Fed up* was written all through it and around it.

"Uh . . . later on. Kinda late," he admitted. "So don't even wait up."

"Don't wait up? Is that what you have to say? Seriously, Chauncey! On our anniversary?"

Silence. *Shit,* Chauncey thought to himself.

"Damn, Sash, my bad. I forgot about that . . . Look, I'll make it up to you this weekend. I promise."

Sasha rolled her eyes. She was still waiting on him to make up dinner from the other day.

"You didn't even remember, Chaunc?" She sounded hurt. "You always used to remember."

She thought of everything he had said to her after she had found out about him and Neli, after she had married Mike and then made the decision to give her and Chauncey another go. How he would never hurt her again. How things would be different. But the saying "The more things change, the more things stay the same" had never rung more true for Sasha. The first few months were sweet but nine months had passed and Chauncey was comfortable. This was 2007 all over again and once again, the streets were his main bitch and his family was the mistress.

"C'mon, Sash, don't start that whining, ma. That anniversary shit was back in the day, before Bri. You acting like we married or something? It's not even a real anniversary . . . it's boyfriend-girlfriend shit," he chuckled, unaware of how hurtful his words were, like most men. "That shit is junior high. We bigger than that, baby."

Sasha was about to bring up the fact that he hadn't even mentioned marriage since they'd been back together, even though they were once upon a time engaged. She shook her head feeling the tears caught in her throat.

"Boyfriend-girlfriend, huh? Junior high? Whatever! Okay, so if that's what it is, we'll do it *just* like junior high. You know what that means? None of this! 'Cause ain't no fucking in junior high. You can beat off. Matter of fact, sleep in the guest room! And the damn air-conditioning is broke. Did you forget you were supposed to fix that, asshole!"

"Yo, who you talking to like that?"

"Mommy!" Aubrey screamed, intervening. "No bad word! . . . And more cheese!"

"You talking around my daughter like that?" Chauncey bassed, clearly upset. "Watch ya fuckin' mouth."

"You watch your fuckin' mouth, Chauncey!"

"Don't curse at my daddy!" Aubrey intervened again.

"Aubrey, be quiet!" Sasha snapped, silencing Aubrey instantly. Her daughter's defense of Chauncey angered her. She was the one who was always with her. She did everything for her. But Aubrey remained a daddy's girl.

"Yo, stop yelling at her!" Chauncey barked. "And I'll send somebody to fix it, so calm down! I got shit to do. Why you don't understand that is crazy. But you understand how to spend this money. Where you think it come from, Sasha?"

"I'm over this conversation, Chauncey. So what if I know how to spend money. I'm always by myself, so what else is left to do *but* spend money? You know what . . ." Sasha could hear Chauncey suck his teeth and she was not in the mood for any more arguing. She wanted to wrap it up calm and end as the bigger person. "You just better think real hard about what's important, Chauncey. And if this thing with Jayde and R—"

"Chill!" Chauncey yelled, cutting her off. Talking about any of that, or saying Ree's name on the phone, was a major no-no.

Sasha sighed and shook her head, trying not to lose her cool in front of Aubrey.

"I just hope this ends soon, Chauncey . . . or we won't last."

Chauncey was quiet, taking in her words but trying not to let them penetrate. Once everything was set in motion, he would be able to spend more time with his family. Plus they were leaving for Jamaica in a few weeks for Tatum and Ree's wedding. He knew the vacation would do them well.

"It'll be all right, kid. Just . . . chill. I love you. Kiss Bri for me."

Chauncey was about to end the call but right before he did, he added a solemn ". . . Happy anniversary, princess."

He hung up and Sasha listened to the dial tone for a while before doing the same. She looked over at the sauce and cheese, and all of her ingredients to her precious dinner, and felt like hurling them across the wall. Then she looked at her beautiful daughter with her big pom-pom puff on top of her head and she smiled at her.

"Mommy . . . more cheeeseee pleaseee," Aubrey requested cutely with her hands pressed together in prayer fashion. Sasha smiled through her thoughts and went and gave her a big hug.

"Mommy's sorry for saying that bad word, baby." She handed her another piece of cheese and kissed her on the head. "But you gotta take Mommy's side sometimes, too, Bri-Bri."

She stared at her pretty baby and felt the need to warn her prematurely.

"And don't *ever* let a man put anything above you, baby . . ."

Just then the doorbell chimed and Sasha looked up, and then looked at Aubrey with a growing smile.

"Who's that, Bri-Bri? Is that Daddy?"

She began making her way to the door in haste.

Maybe Chauncey had reconsidered. Maybe he was going to surprise her. Maybe the whole thing was one big ploy. Reaching the door, Sasha opened it with a wide grin plastered on her gorgeous face. When she saw who it was, her smile deflated.

"What's up? Where the air unit at?"

Sasha opened the door wider and let him walk in. It was Bleek.

Chapter 5

"Girl, you better had did ya thing. CBP!"

—Kim, *Thicker than Water*

"In local news, everyone is greatly excited of the celebration coming our way tomorrow! Sean Knights, owner of the Knights estate and the Botanical Bay hotel and resort, who also happens to be the son of Leroy Knights, prominent figure in Jamaica's social and political scene, will be married this week. The ceremony will be held at the historical Negril lighthouse. You know, rumor has it that Knights had the historical building, which as we natives are aware, overlooks the beaches of Negril and has been mostly used for tours and films, renovated for his lavish reception. The beach will also be closed off and secured by law enforcement for up to *ten* miles for the private nuptials. In case you've been living under a rock for these past months, Knights's fiancée is American-born Tatum Mosley, who we've been calling the 'street girl' for non-obvious reasons. Yes, she has the new downtown row conveniently named Tatum Street, which holds the fine shops, apartments, and the new Kimberly museum being built. Of course, Knights funded all. Lucky, lucky . . ."

"Lucky, lucky," Tatum repeated mockingly, drowning out the car radio by powering on Marsha Ambrosius's latest. "Of course, Knights funded it all," she repeated, making fun of the Jamaican-accented radio host. "Of course the street girl can't afford that. Of course."

Ree chuckled as he drove through the busy streets, cloaked behind the tints of the Rolls Royce. He had allowed Crush to return to Atlanta and he would be bringing his family back to Jamaica for the wedding.

"I can tell them to stop calling you that if you want," he suggested, never taking his eyes off the road.

"Yeah, yeah, yeah . . . Then who knows what they'll call me," she joked, laying her head back.

Tatum looked out of the window at the recognizable poverty of Jamaica.

Frail old women walking with no shoes and shopping carts. Shirtless children laughing and playing, covered in sweat and filth. And here she sat watching them from the comfort of her Rolls Royce like it was a movie. No matter how much they donated, or built, or helped, they'd always be on the other end of the spectrum. She thought of Ree's status and how she was so clueless to it when she had first met him.

"How can you be so open here?" she questioned out of nowhere as she turned her head toward the man of hers. "I mean, look at this. Pictures in the paper . . . radio announcements . . . back in America you practically have to stay cramped up in the condo. And as soon as your business is handled, it's right back to Jamaica. Why are you not private here?"

Ree shrugged.

"I don't have to be. These are my people. They take care of me." He looked over at Tatum. "Plus, when's the last time you heard American news talk about Jamaica, or any other poor black country for that matter, if it's not about an earthquake, some natural catastrophe, or some shit? They only care about us when something bad happens. Homes built, schools, museums, weddings, 'street girls' with their own blocks named after them"— he shot her a wink—"they could care less, baby."

Tatum smiled lightly and looked away from him.

"You teach me something new every day," she spoke.

Ree picked up her hand and brought it to his lips in a quick kiss.

"So do you."

He looked over at her and thought she looked beautiful. Her long hair was brought up into a bun atop her perfectly round head; her natural, soft baby hair flying loosely around her edges. There was no makeup on her face, but her deep brown skin glowed like she had on hundred-dollar foundation. She wore no jewelry besides her massive engagement ring, and a short black chiffon sundress adorned her frame. The hem stopped below her bust, and then flowed out masking the small waist he knew she possessed but hadn't seen recently.

They drove another ten or so minutes in silence, as they neared the private airport. Seeing that she was deep in thought, Ree pulled a little distance from the landing strip and turned off the car.

"Tatum Mosley is awfully quiet," he noted, dragging the words in his low baritone.

She giggled and looked over at him.

"Knights."

"What up?" he shot.

"Nooo, Tatum Knights is quiet."

"Why is she?" he asked, staring at her. They kept a good amount of space between them, both leaning their backs on their own doors, but you could tell they wanted to be close by the smirks they wore. They were magnetic, drawn to each other.

"We're getting married," Tatum spoke in revelation.

"Evidently," Ree replied. Tatum grinned at his laid-back approach to the whole thing. He had to be . . .

"Nervous?" she asked.

"Why would I be?" He shrugged. "I know you," he added with a wink.

"But you'll have to be with one girl. Only one. Forever," she added with a raised brow.

"I already am."

Tatum squinted, probing to see him break a sweat.

"You'll have to deal with all of those little things that get on your nerves about me," Tatum warned him in a cute voice. "Forever," she added again.

Ree nodded.

"Yeah . . . Hair in the sink. Stealing my razors. Chocolate chip cookies in the bed . . . I think I'll live," he said, shrugging like it was a light sentencing. Tatum laughed her laugh, loud and vibrant.

"Smart-ass."

"Silly-ass."

They could see the plane descending in the distance and knew their friends had arrived safely. The festivities could officially begin.

"Fuck kinda shit is this, boss?"

"What? Fuck you mean?"

The group of friends was all seated outside of the estate, a long table set up for them to dine on what would traditionally be the rehearsal dinner. Bellies full of lobster, shrimp, crab, and champagne, the jokes and laughter began to go into effect.

"Fuck you mean, fuck I mean?" Chauncey laughed. "What kinda rehearsal dinner is this? Niggas ain't rehearse shit!"

Sasha had to crack a smirk at that one although she had seemed to be a little stiff since they de-boarded the plane. The champagne seemed to be loosening her up, though.

"Fuck is there to rehearse?" Ree asked seriously as everyone giggled, including Tatum. "I know how to walk down a fucking aisle." He cracked a grin.

"It's a little more to it than that, Ree," Sasha chimed with a smile. She was dressed in a white jeweled tunic and her hair hung long and free, giving her an island vibe. She was doing everything in her power to get into vacation mode and enjoy herself in spite of her slight discomfort with Jayde. She sat next to Chauncey and held his hand and as a slight breeze blew, she nestled close to him. The late nights alone, the arguments, she wanted to forget that this weekend.

Bleek sat across from Sasha and Chauncey, next to Tatum, and he couldn't help but take a quick look at them before he picked up his glass and downed the rest of his Ace.

"Thank you, Sasha!" Tatum yelled with a big laugh as she slapped Ree playfully on the arm. "Now when we fuck everything up, he gonna wish we woulda rehearsed."

"We got this," Ree stated confidently.

"Yeah, a'ight, nigga," Crush joked, seated next to his wife. "This cool-ass nigga gonna be sweating bullets come tomorrow! Be careful, Tatum. He might pull a runaway groom on ya ass."

"Yeah okay!" Tatum said, shooting Ree a daring look.

"He ain't going nowhere, not with that small country sitting on your finger, girl," Crush's wife threw in.

"Word, shawty . . . that shit is *ill*. What kinda stone is that?" Bleek spoke up, refilling his champagne glass.

"It's a natural Russian Alexandrite," Tatum answered proudly.

"Fuck outta here!" Crush's wife exclaimed with wide eyes in astonishment. You would've thought Tatum said it was made in heaven itself.

"Yo, I heard about them shits. They said most people will never see one in they *life*. The three-karat joints run up in the cool mils," Bleek spoke smoothly, almost causing Tatum to giggle because he sounded like T.I. or somebody with his country drawl. "They said the ones that change colors worth ten times a diamond of its same size."

Tatum smiled and touched her ring slightly before shooting Ree a loving glance. She knew all about the rich and precious history of her stone.

"Yeah . . . I have one of the rarest. I think . . . Queen Elizabeth had one. Princess Di. Not too many after her," she added modestly. "It changes from bright green to magenta in an instant."

Tatum's heart raced as she pondered on it for a minute. A regular girl from Newark who used to club with her friends, do hair, and go to community college was sitting on the beaches of Jamaica, with her own street, and one of the rarest stones in the world in her possession. And the man she loved dearly had given it all to her. That was why she had given Ree this last deal in the game even though she had put up a fight. He had given her so much in return.

"Sash, what time your parents coming in tomorrow?" Tatum asked, changing the subject.

Sasha sipped her champagne and shrugged.

"I don't know girl, you know Queen Terri and her grand entrances," Sasha spoke, mocking her mother. "She's meeting my aunt in Atlanta so she and Aubrey can fly down with them. Was Nikki able to bring the girls?" Sasha added, speaking of Tatum's nieces and their recovering cocaine-addicted mother.

"Yeah, she said they'd be here in the morning."

Just then Jayde leaned over and whispered something in Bleek's ear as everyone's chatter continued. Bleek swallowed hard but kept a straight face and Sasha looked back and forth between them.

"You straight, J. You over there awfully quiet for the pit bull in a skirt," Chauncey teased.

"Maybe she's got something on her mind," Sasha added with a raised brow.

Jayde shot her eyes to Sasha and smirked. Something was up with her, Jayde didn't know what, though. However, she was determined to get to the bottom of it. Sasha had avoided her and gave her minimal conversation on the plane and once they landed. And for the few people in the world whom Jayde actually gave a fuck about, she didn't appreciate being given the cold shoulder by them. She'd straighten Sash out, or add her to the list of disposables. "Or maybe she's proposing marriage to Bleek," Sasha continued, gulping the rest of her alcohol and darting her eyes away.

"Nooo! Absolutely not," Jayde professed, raising her hands in protest. "Nothing against you tho', cutie," she said, winking at Bleek. "But people like *me*, and . . . marriage. Disaster," she concluded with a shake of her head. "I wouldn't do that to someone."

Her last statement grabbed everyone's attention, including Respect's. So much so that he spoke on it.

"What you mean?"

She leaned forward and looked to her left, her eyes

passing by Bleek and Tatum and focusing right on the man who had posed the question, the king of the court.

"Well, with all due respect to you and Tatum . . . I just don't see it for me. I mean . . . the life I lead. The type of person that I am, the type of person that I will *always* be, the things that I will *always* do . . . I couldn't put that on another individual. My lifestyle is not for matrimony," she told him seriously. "I would only bring a person more pain than love, and that would be selfish. If I ever loved a person enough to want to marry them, the best thing I could ever do for them . . . is let them go."

Her words hit like a twenty-ton bowling ball knocking down metal pins. You could hear a feather drop on the white beachy sands, that's how mute it was. Those words went to Ree's core, but he wasn't the only one. Everyone had heard it and was in reflection.

"Who the fuck wanna marry your crazy ass anyway?" Chauncey quipped, and everyone busted out laughing, happy he had lightened the mood. Jayde smirked and gave a Kanye shrug, but she smiled on the inside because she felt a set of eyes on her and she knew whom they belonged to. As everyone began their frivolous conversations again, Jayde slowly panned her gaze over to Respect who already had his stare on her when she reached him. She sighed when he looked away but he remained straight-faced and in thought. *Mission accomplished,* she supposed. She had gotten in his head.

As the evening began to wind down, the girls retreated to one of the guest rooms as the men went to talk in the study.

"Can you believe it?" Sasha asked as she lay on her side, spread out across the king mattress. Tatum sat Indian-style at the head of the bed, large fluffy pillows behind her, and Jayde was perched on a corner, legs crossed. Crush's wife, feeling comfortable, but not too familiar, opted for the chaise lounge chair close by.

"I know," Tatum spoke low with a faint smile as she played with her hands. "It's crazy. It all happened so fast. It seems like he was just proposing . . . now it's here. They were even talking about it on the radio. Ain't that some shit?" Tatum couldn't help but laugh. Sasha giggled and Jayde and Megan chuckled.

"I went to the market the other day and the lady was like 'Yu street girl! Yu Tatum, yu marry Sean Knights!'" she mocked in an island accent. "It's all everyone seems to be talking about." Tatum sounded like she was in a state of disbelief and overwhelmed. Jayde wanted so desperately to shout *Oh, shut the fuck up!*

"Well at least you're getting a break and get to hear about other shit," Sasha spat. "All I hear about is the master pl—"

Sasha cut herself off and shot a glance at Jayde. She had forgotten that Jayde was there and very much a part of the street blueprint. "Anyway, it's just nice they're talking about you, that's all. I'd be happy as hell if all these people were talking about me!" Sasha declared as she flipped over on her back and stared at the ceiling.

"We know!" Tatum cracked, and they all laughed. Everyone was familiar with Sasha's narcissistic behavior, even Megan, and she had just met her eight hours ago.

"So Tatum," Jayde started with a grin, ready to get the party going. "You gotta be honest, girl . . . can you *really* be with one man . . . for the rest of your life!"

Everyone giggled and Tatum did, too, just a little less.

"I mean, don't get me wrong," Jayde continued. "I see your character, and you're not out there. And I know you love Ree. But girllll, one dick? Forever and ever? Whew! More power to you."

Tatum chuckled and shook her head as everyone continued to laugh.

"Girl, when that dick belongs to a man like Ree . . . trust me. I'm looking forward to waking up to that for the rest of my life. I'm good," she replied confidently. The others could have even picked up on a hint of challenge in Tatum's voice, if they wanted to. Jayde laughed and nodded, but inside she was on fire with desire. *Silly Tatum,* she thought. *Don't you know not to brag to women about your man's blessings?*

"I hear ya, girl . . . I hear ya."

Crush's wife spoke up.

"Well, Curtis . . . I mean *Crush* . . . was my first, last, and only. I've never been with anyone else."

Everyone looked to her with wide eyes.

"Really?" Sasha asked, sitting up. "You've never stepped out? Never?"

"Nope."

"Shit, have you?" Jayde butted in, noticing the way Sasha had asked, like it was impossible not to.

Sasha crinkled her brow at her, one for the open question, and two for her own hidden displeasure with Jayde.

"What . . . ? On Chauncey? No! Why would you ask me that?"

Jayde shrugged nonchalantly and Tatum looked on. Jayde was an instigator. She noted that. She also noticed Sasha's reaction.

Tatum figured to herself that if Sasha ever did decide to cheat on Chauncey, she would probably feel justified by his prior indiscretions and the current lack of attention. But Tatum was a firm believer in if you forgive, then you forgive. Clean slate.

"Anyway," Sasha snapped, rolling her eyes and directing her attention back to Megan. "That's wild! But that's kinda sweet, too. My first was nothing I could hold on to for the rest of my life, though. He was terrible!"

"No, *mine* was terrible," Jayde challenged as Sasha rolled over on her back again and cut her eyes for Jayde's interruption. "His name was Rich. He was so wack. It was the smallest . . . Oh no," Jayde said, stopping short. "He wasn't first . . . Damn, who was first? Oh! Eric . . . yeah, Eric. He was good. I take that back. I could've married that." They all laughed, hard.

"What about you, Tatum?" Jayde added. "Who was yours?"

Megan and Jayde looked on as Sasha checked to see if her ends were split. After a few seconds of delay, Sasha turned her head and looked on as well.

Tatum was caught off guard by the question. It was a little too personal to her and she wasn't expecting it.

"What? Um . . . I . . . I don't know . . . ?" She chuckled. "I don't . . . *Why?*"

"You don't *know?*" Jayde repeated in disbelief, holding on to a laugh. Everyone else remained quiet, including Tatum who stared Jayde right in the eyes. After a few seconds, Tatum swallowed hard and looked around the room.

Finally she spoke.

". . . My ex. Ty . . . He was my first."

"Wowww," Jayde responded with a raised eyebrow. "That was *intense*. What, you still got feelings for him or something?"

Tatum sucked her teeth.

"Hell no!" She shook her head and flung her legs across the bed, preparing to stand up. "Girl, you an instigator like a mothafucka," Tatum added with a laugh. "I need to take my ass to bed, though. We all do."

Tatum made her way to the door while the other girls stayed behind. Sasha and Megan would wait for their men so they could separate into two of the six available guest bedrooms. Jayde would stay in this one.

"'Night, Pocahontas," Jayde said, winking at her. Something in the wink, it was almost sinister. But Tatum brushed it off.

"'Night, guys," she responded generally.

"'Night, Tay," Sasha yelled back. "Good night, Tatum," Megan added.

Once the door was closed, the girls gradually began their chatter after a minute or so.

"I hope she didn't leave because of the question I asked?" Jayde feigned concern. "I didn't think it would be so personal."

Megan pressed her lips together, a little uncomfortable with speaking on it, especially as she wasn't in their circle.

"Well . . . maybe something happened to her when she was younger. Maybe it wasn't a good experience."

Jayde turned and looked with a smirk at Sasha, who was still staring at the ceiling but was noticeably quiet.

"Well, *bestie*," Jayde posed a little sarcastically. "Did something happen to her? Is that what's wrong?"

Sasha zoned out, truly hoping that wasn't what it was. But to be honest, she had no idea why the question affected Tatum the way it did. She did know that Jayde was getting on her last nerve, though.

"I don't know. And to tell the truth . . . it ain't none of our business."

Tatum sat in her bed thinking, towel still wrapped around her from her evening shower. She would be married by this time tomorrow. But that wasn't what was on her mind. It was the conversation with the girls she had just escaped from the middle of.

She saw the handle of the door turn. It gradually opened, and in stepped a king.

"Niceee," Ree spoke smoothly, finding Tatum in her barely-there attire. He smiled deviously, an unlit blunt in his hand.

Tatum smiled back.

"Unh-unh, don't even think about it. Not before the wedding day. We're already breaking all of the rules. I'm not even supposed to be *seeing* you right now. So definitely, absolutely, no sex."

Ree jerked his head back.

"That's some bullshit . . . I never heard of that," he lied with a smirk.

"Yes you did," Tatum challenged, standing up and walking over to her ivory bone dresser and pulling out a silk nightgown. The towel barely covered her large ass, which poked out like two melons.

"You heard of 'why buy the cow when you can get the milk for free.'"

"But I already had the milk," Ree told her playfully, grabbing a throw pillow off one of the couches they had on the side of their bed and tossing it on the ground. "You buy the cow so no one else gets the milk."

Tatum smiled at his witty charm and dropped her towel. Then she wiggled into her short gown, knowing Ree's eyes were on her the whole time.

"Well no one's getting the milk tonight," Tatum let him know as she walked over and sat on the edge of the bed. Ree took a seat on the pillow on the floor, between her legs.

He rubbed her thigh and turned his face toward the place he wanted to visit tonight.

"What about the cookie?" he whispered in his deep baritone, nibbling on her thigh.

Tatum bit her bottom lip and shivered but then placed her two hands on the sides of his head and turned him face-front abruptly against her desire.

"No milk. No cookie. Nothing!"

She reached over, grabbed the honey oil from her nightstand, and handed it to Ree.

"Hold this."

This was normal. This was their life. Tightening his dreads while he puffed something and they shared stimulating conversation. A million-dollar wedding in less than twenty-four hours wouldn't change anything. They hadn't even had bachelor and bachelorette parties, that's how untraditional they were doing things.

Ree thought it was all bullshit, a lot of that stuff, plus he had so much going on with the business, eradicating his fugitive status, and the paternity test at the time. He would give Tatum the wedding of her dreams though before he made any of his personal moves. That was important to him. That's what she deserved.

"You know what I was thinking about before you came in here?" she asked out of the blue.

"I know what I was thinking about before I came in here," he responded suggestively, and she giggled. "But you shut that shit down. Promptly."

Tatum laughed her laugh.

"Shut up! I'm serious."

"What's on your mind, Miss Lady?"

Tatum smiled and closed her eyes. He called her *that* . . . and it was like déjà vu to when she had met him outside of Mars 2112 in the city years back.

"Mm . . . Well, I was thinking about . . . how much . . . how much I love you. For like . . . little things. You know?"

Ree rubbed her legs lovingly and thought about how Tatum had to always fight for words when expressing her emotions. He thought he was foreign to love, but his baby was way worse. He hated the things that made her so scared of her emotions. He wished he could erase them.

"There's a lot you don't know about me . . . that we don't know about each other, Ree. But you never . . . you never asked certain things. You know, about the past . . . other guys, stuff like that. It's like the future is what matters with you." Tatum thought of the conversation she had just had with the girls.

"Because the future *is* all that matters." Ree took a pull from his weed-laced cigar and stared ahead. "Why . . . is there something I need to know? Something I should be asking?"

"No . . ."

"Okay," he replied with no question in his voice.

A few more peaceful moments passed and in between they could hear laughter in the distance. It was obvious Chauncey, Sasha, Bleek, Jayde, Crush, and Megan were still up and lively. However, Tatum and Ree were content in their sanctuary.

"What's this mean?" Tatum asked, touching his exposed shoulder. Ree wore only a black wifebeater and his sweats.

"Which one is that?" He had so many tattoos, tattoos that intertwined with others—it was hard to know which one she was talking about.

"The lion. With the crown and the . . . I don't what that is," she admitted, and Ree chuckled.

"The lion . . . *that* lion . . . is a symbol Haile Selassie, who some people believe was the reincarnation of Jesus. He was an Ethiopian emperor. The Rastafarians believe that he was a king chosen by God, thus the reason for the crown. The snake represents Babylon, Western society, and all things not of us, forced on us."

"And the ganja?" she joked, knowing already what it meant.

Ree laughed.

"And the ganja, well . . . it was put here by Haile himself. The ganja is the second love of my life, baby." Tatum smacked him on the head and he laughed some more. After a pause she pointed at a scroll on his forearm.

"And that?"

Ree didn't have to look. He knew that one by heart.

"That's the desiderata."

"What's the desiderata?" Tatum could tell he was serious about it.

"It's a creed of men," he answered truthfully. "Of great men, real men."

Tatum continued to wet her fingertips in the oil, grabbing another lock and twisting.

"What's the creed about?"

Ree took a pull of his cigar and spoke smoothly.

"It's about honesty . . . loyalty . . . honor . . . love . . . it's about the way you should aspire to live life."

There was a brief silence.

"Sounds deep," Tatum confessed.

Ree turned his head slightly.

"Yeah?"

Tatum nodded.

"I can go deeper," he let her know.

Tatum laughed again. It would be hard to resist him with all of his innuendos tonight, but she had to.

"Boy, I'm serious. Leave me alone," she giggled. "We have a wedding tomorrow and I have so much to do. And you know I can barely get out of bed when you do ya thing at night," Tatum confessed in a soft sexy voice. "I need to be rejuvenated."

Ree bit his lip and nodded.

"Okay, you got that. I know you got a lot to do. But tomorrow night . . ." He turned and looked at her seriously. "I'ma tear ya ass up." He winked and she smiled.

"I'll look forward to it."

Chapter 6

"Tatum, what if I told you that I would do anything to be the kind of man that's right for you?"

—Respect, *Thicker than Water*

The Big Day

"Okay, seriously! These orchids are limp. I want these cut out and there *better* not be any more like this. I know you were paid damn good money to make sure these flowers were up to par!"

Jayde stood with her hand on her hip, barking at the Jamaican florist who had three vans full of white flowers that he was delivering to the lighthouse. As he stared blankly back at her, groups of caterers, waiters, band members, and photographers scurried back and forth.

"Let's get it together, people!" Jayde shouted, playing the take-charge friend role well. Although Jayde enjoyed having control of all situations, she couldn't care less about the wedding. It was just another ploy to keep heat off of her, one more way to get close like a cobra and then strike.

"Excuse me, miss," said one of the band members,

politely tapping Jayde on the shoulder. He had seen her barking all the orders and figured she was a wedding planner.

"Yes!" Jayde spun around, irritated. She hated when someone interrupted her conversation.

"I'm sorry. It's just . . . the singer is here . . . and he needs to be directed."

Jayde scrunched up her face in frustration.

"What do you mean he needs to be directed? Don't he got eyes like everyone else? Can't he see all the musicians are set up outside? Take him outside with you!"

Just then the man stepped to the side and the singer he was speaking of came into view.

"Hello," he spoke with a smile.

"Holy shit," Jayde whispered wide-eyed, ready to eat her words.

Even for a bad bitch like herself, she was jealous. Ree had gone all out for Tatum.

At the top of the lighthouse, in a large spacious room with tri-folding mirrors, stood a beautiful princess like Rapunzel with long tresses, awaiting the moment she would see her prince.

"Oh my God. Oh my God, oh my God, oh my God, oh my God . . ."

Tatum studied herself in the mirror and repeated the phrase over and over, appearing to be having a small panic attack.

"Oh my God . . . Can I do this? *Should* I do this?"

Tatum's stomach flipped repeatedly and she thought she was going to be sick any minute. She had never in her life felt nerves like this.

"Oh my God . . . oh my God." Just then a thought

went through her head and she cracked a small smile. "Damn, Kim. Where are you when I need you to smack some sense into me?"

She thought of how bad she wished she was there, Kim and also her parents. They were greatly missed on this special day.

A knock on the door diverted her attention, and she turned her head anxiously as the door creaked open.

Sasha stepped in with a warm smile.

"Oh my God, Tay," she whispered in awe. "I swear I can't believe how beautiful you look."

Tatum's strapless off-white gown was completely embellished with beading and crystals that sparkled when she moved. Her long train flowed for five feet and gradually faded from off-white to a champagne color, which matched Sasha, Tangee, and Chanel's bridesmaid dresses. Her hair was long and curled loosely, with a small diamond tiara atop her head. She looked absolutely breathtaking.

"Really Sash? It's not too much? I was thinking I should lose the tiara. Should I lose the tiara? Imma lose it," Tatum decided, reaching for the beautiful accessory.

"No, Tay! It's perfect. Everything . . . is perfect."

Tatum smiled with tears in her eyes and turned back to face the mirror. Staring at herself she couldn't help but feel overwhelmed with happiness and joy. She loved Ree, Respect, Sean Knights, all aspects of him, so much. And after all of the madness with Neli, Kim, Sasha, her brother, her nieces, and Trinity, and even Ree himself . . . Tatum would finally be able to have her day. It was always about everyone else. Now it could finally be about *her*. Alicia Keys's "Un-thinkable" came to mind when Tatum wondered, *Do I deserve this? I think I deserve this . . .*

She let out another smile and at that same moment

she glanced at Sasha through the mirror to share the joy, but noticed the lost look in her eye.

"Sash . . . you okay?"

Tatum took her in. Even when she was singing the praises of Tatum's beauty something seemed to be weighing on her mind. Tatum needed her best friend there with her, completely, sharing this moment with her.

Sasha looked up at Tatum and now Tatum could see her eyes becoming wet as if tears were forming. Tatum spun around in worry.

"Oh my God, Sasha. What's wrong?"

"Was it Chauncey?"

Tatum crinkled her brow, looking at her best friend in confusion. She didn't get it.

"What?"

"Tatum . . ." Sasha swallowed hard and more tears made their way to her eyes. She had just gotten her makeup done to match her silk champagne–colored, long, fitted gown but was bound to fuck it up. "Was it . . . Chauncey?" Her voice cracked on the last word of the question, on his name.

Tatum let out a nervous laugh of disbelief, never breaking eye contact with her friend. There was a long silence between them . . . too long.

"Sasha, no. What are you—"

"Tay, please don't lie to me . . . Please!" Sasha begged, her tears on the brink. At this time Tatum now had her own cry coming on.

Tatum looked down and sighed, her bottom lip trembling as the tears burned the back of her eyes. She shook her head from side to side.

"Sash . . . Sasha . . . I'm . . . I'm so sorry. We were so young. . . ."

"I fucking knew it!" Sasha screamed at her uncontrollably. "How could you? I knew it!" Sasha balled her hands into fists angrily. "He was your first. That's why you tripped like that!"

Tatum shut her eyes and pressed her lips together, wanting this to all be a nightmare. She felt so bad, worse than bad, and she couldn't believe this was happening . . . *now.*

"Sasha, I swear . . . It was nothing. I was fourteen years old! He was my brother's friend. It . . . it was one time! Oh my God . . ." she added in a desperate whisper. *Not this shit.* Tatum had all but forgotten the memory.

Sure, she had thought of telling Sasha, from the moment that Sasha and Chauncey started getting serious. But she never wanted it to be weird with her. She never wanted Sasha to think Chauncey was something more to Tatum than he was. She felt absolutely no sexual feelings for him, and she knew Sasha was head over heels for him. Tatum felt like some things were better left unsaid. To tell her would've been pointless. Tatum loved Sasha, she didn't want to hurt her. And she knew no matter how much she drilled to her that it was a one-time, young, teenage, let's-see-what-sex-is-all-about kinda thing, Sasha would always see it for more. She was protecting her feelings, sparing her that hurt and unnecessary worry.

"One time? Does that make it right? You were supposed to be my best friend! You fucked *Chauncey!*"

Tatum shook her head and at this time both girls were full-on crying. This was the worst thing that could happen.

"Sasha, I swear I am sooo sorry! I don't have any type of feelings for Chauncey. It was one time. We were kids! I swear. We never even thought about it after that. Chauncey loves you. I love you! I'm sorry . . ." Tatum sobbed irrepressibly. "You're my best friend, Sash! You gotta forgive me."

"Whatever! How could you, Tay? First Chauncey, then Neli, then Mike, then Jayde, now you! Who the fuck is real anymore? Everyone has it out for me, huh? Joke's always on me!" Sasha yelled, while the tears poured and she paced the floor.

Tatum wondered why she had said Jayde's name but then she figured she was speaking of the whole lying-about-hustling thing. Tatum went to apologize again as she continued to cry, but then a thought went through her head. A thought that, had she not been such a good friend, would have been her first thought.

"You know what. Hold up . . . are you serious? Everyone has it out for you? Sasha, you should know me better than that—"

"I thought I knew you."

"No, you know me, bitch!" Tatum boomed. "I have *always* had your back, more than anyone. I love you with *everything* in me. I've put your feelings above my own! Now was I wrong for not telling you? Absolutely. But I *know* that you know it meant nothing. You *know* that. But you're coming to me with this, going on and on, today? Of all days? Sasha, this is my wedding day! You couldn't wait?"

"No, I couldn't! I needed to know—"

"Yes, *you* needed to know, Sasha! But what about what *I* needed?" Tatum cried hard in deep pain. "You couldn't put my feelings above yours for one day? You *know* I don't want Chauncey. He's grown to be like a fucking brother to me! You know exactly why I didn't tell you, because you would act like this, overdramatic! We were fucking *fourteen,* Sasha. But you had to make it about you, right? Somehow, it just *has* to be about Sasha, huh? You want this day? Is that want you want?"

"Fuck you, Tay!"

"Take it!" Tatum snatched off the tiara and threw it

at her while her tears poured like a faucet. "Take this fucking tiara, take this dress, take my ring . . . take the whole fucking day, Sash! What do I have to do to let you know that I'm sorry! Huh? You want my man, too? Take him! You know I'd give you anything!"

"I don't want your fucking man, Tatum!" Sasha spat with disgust. "But apparently you wanted mine."

Tatum looked at her with a hurt and dumbfounded expression. Sasha knew that wasn't true, and Tatum couldn't believe this was happening. Was she wrong? Yes. She felt awful. But would she have done this to Sasha? Not in a million years. Not to her sister. She would have let her have her day.

"What's going on? Y'all okay?"

Tatum wasn't sure exactly when Jayde had entered, but she couldn't care less. She continued to stare at Sasha as she sniffled one last time.

"I'm sorry, Sasha. I really am."

"That's all you got to say?" Sasha narrowed her eyes, furious.

Tatum chuckled and shook her head.

"Nope. But that's all I'm *going* to say. 'Cause that's all I can give you today. *Today* . . . I'm keeping everything else for myself." She finally looked from Sasha to Jayde and she looked drained, tired, and just devastated. Not like she was about to get married in thirty minutes.

"Excuse me . . . I'm going to the restroom."

Sasha watched her walk away, and as bad as she wanted to go after her, her selfishness got in the way. She was the victim here, not Tatum. Tatum was dead wrong. She didn't care. They were supposed to be best friends, tell each other everything, even though she did have a secret or two of her own. One of which was that Tatum still didn't know that it was Sasha who had pulled the trigger and killed Mike, not Chauncey. The other, well the other was the one from her mother that she was holding on to. But Tatum had fucked Chauncey. And that was different.

"What the hell happened?" Jayde asked in shock. When she had left they were sickeningly BFFs, now they looked like they were about to go twelve rounds.

"Why did you ask me that last night?" Sasha asked Jayde suspiciously.

"Ask you what?"

"When Tatum went to sleep, and when Megan left . . . you asked me how close Tatum and Chauncey were before I met Chauncey. Why did you ask me that?"

Jayde had to fight hard against her urge to smile. When she had seen Tatum's reaction to the "first time" question, she thought she would fuck with Sasha and plant a bug in her head about Chauncey and Tatum maybe having messed around or liked each other at one time. Never in a million years did she think there would actually be truth to it or result in this. It was almost too brilliant.

Jayde shrugged nonchalantly.

"I don't know. I remembered you told me they knew each other before, and we were talking about maybe if something had happened to Tatum when she was younger. You said you didn't know, so I figured if Chauncey knew her before you and if they were close, then maybe he would know. Why do you ask?" Jayde questioned, but happily had a feeling already what the answer was.

Sasha pursed her lips and looked from Jayde to the now closed bathroom door where Tatum was, on the other side of the large room.

"Well, to answer your question . . . apparently they were close. *Too* fucking close. Excuse me," Sasha added solemnly after a pause, and then left the room.

Jayde smirked wickedly and then strutted over to the bathroom door in her red Alexander McQueen dress. She tapped faintly.

"Tatum, sweetie . . . Can you let me in? I'm sure whatever it is, it's not that bad. . . ." After a moment of silence, Jayde continued. "I'm sorry if someone upset you, Tatum. I don't know why anyone would do that to you on your wedding day. Lord knows you don't deserve that. But you can't let that get to you today, mama. This is *your* day. You can't let anyone else ruin it."

There was another silence and Jayde figured she'd just leave her alone. But as she turned to walk away she heard the lock on the door click and the knob turned. Jayde smiled lovingly like she was the most genuine friend ever, and Tatum let her inside.

The twinkle from the star lights that graced the ceiling of the lighthouse instantly caught the entering guests' attention. Vines of ivy intertwined with white gardenias curved up the walls and stairwells leading up to them and created a divine ambiance. "Oh my goodness . . . this is simply breathtaking."

"Hors d'oeuvre, madam?"

Terri brought her eyes from the angelic setup to the tall and slim server in front of her. His Jamaican accent produced intriguing English dialect.

"Certainly . . . what's in this?"

"This is a watermelon-wrapped citrus shrimp," he said with a smile, taking in the elegant and mature beauty of Sasha's mother.

Terri gasped lightly in intrigue and charmingly took a napkin and appetizer.

"That just sounds delicious."

"Oh it is," the server insisted. "And sweet."

"What's in that one?" Sasha's father interjected with a challenge, pointing at a tray a young woman not too far away was holding.

The server darted his eyes to him off guard, not realizing they were together.

"My apologies, sir. That tray has the cucumber lobster tart I believe."

"And that table. What about that table over there?"

"Cut it out, Bill," Terri whispered so that the server couldn't hear.

"That table has the avocado sushi and wasabi crab cakes."

"That sounds good. Why don't you go and get me some of that," Sasha's father suggested with authority.

"Certainly." He scurried away.

"Oh my, Bill, don't make a scene."

"He was flirting with you right in front of my face, Terri. 'And sweet,'" Sasha's father said, mocking the server's accent.

"He was in no such way," Terri replied with an eye roll.

"Yeah, okay. I know how these island guys operate," Bill said. "So do you," he added in a low voice.

"And what's that supposed to mean?" Sasha's mother snapped knowing just what he was talking about, and who. But why was he bringing him up after so long?

"Daddy!" Sasha beamed, making her way to them. Bill smiled at his gorgeous daughter. Her long, silk champagne–colored gown scooped high around her neck and left her entire back exposed. It fit snugly and then cascaded to a small mermaid pool around her feet. Her hair was upswept into a classy bun and she looked timeless.

"Sasha," he said, smiling proudly.

"Ma," she stated way less affectionately, addressing her mother. Not out of the norm for this mother-daughter pair, Bill paid it no mind. However, there was slightly more disdain in Sasha's voice for her mother than usual and it had everything to do with the news she had revealed to Sasha.

Terri paid it no mind.

"Sasha, this is something else. I mean, I've never seen anything like this before. This place is just . . . oh my God. And the pond out front, with the pink lighting and the beautifullll white geese. This is already the most gorgeous wedding, and it hasn't even begun. And we've been to some lavish weddings. Bill, remember that mayor's wedding we got invited to, with the horse and carriage?"

"You tell the same name-dropping stories, Ma," Sasha accused, visibly annoyed as she led them to the back. "Where's Aubrey?"

"She's somewhere around here with your aunt Betty," her father responded. Her mother stayed on the name-dropping comment.

"Well, I may tell them all the time but it's true . . . I mean, how much money does Tatum's husband *actually have?*" Terri leaned in and whispered to Sasha.

Sasha shook her head.

"You know, for a woman with such bourgeois characteristics, you really have no class."

"Sasha, don't talk to your mother like that!"

"Let her be, Bill."

However, as tasteless as it seemed, Terri was telling the truth. If Steve Wynn could blow $10 million on an antique vase and Bradgelina could drop hundreds of thousands on art for their children's bedrooms, Ree could give Tatum the wedding that she never even dreamed of. A wedding that had to cost at least . . .

"A million. At least! Has to be a million he spent."

Sasha sighed as they neared the exit of the light-house, which led to the beach area where the wedding would take place. Soft violins played by dozens of men in tuxedos greeted them.

"You don't know that, Ma."

"For goodness' sake, Sasha. He flew us all first class and had Bentleys greet us at the airport. Dom Perignon champagne in the car, three-day suites for all of the guests. C'mon, don't be naïve. *This* is a wedding. Look at that view!" she exclaimed, pointing to where the area was set up for the nuptials to take place. "I'm sure you and Chauncey's wedding will be wonderful, but it won't possibly top this. You'll just have to give it to Tatum; she'll have the best wedding."

"Jesus Christ, Mother, what the hell is wrong with you? I don't have to give anything to Tatum! We're not in competition! And what wedding? Do you see a ring on this finger?" Sasha snapped, holding up her bare hand. "Do you!"

Sasha's mother looked shocked for a moment but then just waved her hand at her daughter's dramatics.

"Oh hush, Sasha. Chauncey will ask you to marry him again. You're such a drama queen."

Terri strutted off in her baby pink Chanel skirt suit, smoothing the sides of her cropped hair. Sasha rolled her eyes because she knew all the years of people com-paring her to Vanessa Williams had gotten to her head.

"Daddy, how do you deal with her?" Sasha whined with a stomp of her foot.

"I ask myself the same question sometimes."

* * *

"This is like a dream."

"Yeah."

"This is like a fairy tale."

"Shut up, Tangee. There are no real fairy tales," Chanel spat, and Tangee rolled her eyes. They both looked around in awe as they took the three small steps onto the white marble gazebo that had been built onto the beach for the nuptials. Chairs lined both sides with a long row down the middle. White flowers were decorated all around with tiny lights embedded in them. It would probably be twice as beautiful when they started and the sun began to set.

"Y'all just don't touch anything. Don't be breaking shit, don't be messing shit up," Nikki barked with a sniff of her nose.

"Ma, I'm thirteen years old. I ain't no *damn* kid," Chanel snapped back.

"Well, you act like one. You ain't no *damn* kid then get a *damn* job and help out with the bills, instead of ya fast ass chasing behind boys."

"I gotta be fourteen to get my working papers in Virginia, remember?" Chanel snapped back, pursing her lips.

Nikki pursed hers right back and rolled her neck.

"Well when I was thirteen I found a way to work. Marinate on that, little kid. And you only two years behind her, so you start thinking on it too," Nikki addressed to Tangee.

"Hey, girls," Jayde interjected, stepping up and shooting Nikki a condescending look. "You guys must be Chanel and Tangee. I've heard so much about you from your aunt Tatum and your uncle Ree. Tatum's waiting for you guys upstairs so you can change into your dresses. Let's go! Follow me," Jayde said, smiling.

"'Scuse me," Nikki said, tapping her shoulder as she

started to walk away with Tatum's nieces. "Can you tell me where the bathroom is?" Nikki gave another long sniff and Jayde studied her with a long stare before she let go of a slow nod. "Yeah . . . it's that way."

"Thank you."

Clutching her purse firmly, Nikki hurried away. And Jayde knew what it was, she saw it every day, just from the other side of the game.

"Oh my God, look at you two!" Tatum exclaimed with wide arms.

"Auntie Tatum!" Tangee screamed, running into them excitedly.

Chanel tried to remain mature but the kid in her smiled wide and ran to her aunt as well, holding her close and fighting back tears.

"You look so pretty," Chanel said softly, both of them holding her so tight.

"You guys look so pretty, too. Nikki got your hair done? It looks good," Tatum said, smiling and stepping back. She didn't care if they were close on time, nothing came before her nieces. She would chop it up with them.

"I did it," Chanel stated, proudly running her hands through her own curls before looking at Tangee's.

"Hold up now! Let me find out you gonna be nice with hair like your auntie? You gonna open up a shop with me?"

Chanel laughed.

"Yeah."

"All right, cool, but let me ask you something else," Tatum stated nonchalantly.

"What?"

"Where are the rest of your clothes?" She looked at her thirteen-year-old niece dressed in short tight shorts with a tank top that was cut too low and showed her abdomen. It even revealed . . . *oh Lord is that a belly ring?*

"These *are* my clothes, Auntie Tatum. Don't trip." Tatum pressed her lips together and made an urgent brain note to address this issue when the wedding was over. She meant, start of the reception when the wedding was over, not next week.

"All right, y'all get changed. C'mon, we got a show to get on the road!" Tatum clapped her hands together like she wasn't as nervous as a hoe in Bible study.

"You want me to tell them we starting?"

Tatum looked up at Sasha, who stood with attitude written all over her face as she asked the question. She couldn't believe she was going to do this without Sasha's 100 percent support, but she was.

"Yeah . . . yeah, you can do that."

"Ladies and gentlemen, if you would all take your seats. We're about to begin," Sasha announced. Everyone began to grab their last hors d'oeuvre and find their child or spouse to sit.

Ree's father patted him on the back with a strong hand as they stood under the gazebo.

"Well, it's time."

Ree only nodded but remained deep in thought. Nervous wasn't in his band of emotions. But he was feeling something in that family.

"You're really doing it."

"That I am," he assured confidently. There was a pause and then his father spoke.

"You know with all these people, there's a strong possibility this can get back to the States. You're not exactly low-key with this thing here."

Ree shrugged nonchalantly.

"That's not important. Like I told you before, Pop, we got that situation under control. They can come and take me right now, it wouldn't matter . . . they just better let me finish my vows or they'd have to deal with Tatum." He shot his father a self-assured wink and his father laughed lightly.

"And they don't want to deal with Tatum. She's a piece of work!" Leroy Knights noted.

Ree chuckled. "Yeah . . . this is her day." Ree had a far-away look and smile in his eyes. "It belongs to her."

Ree's father smiled and nodded, happy that his son in the midst of his dark world had found genuine love.

"You ready to do this, playboy?"

Chauncey interrupted, stepping up in his white suit and champagne-colored tie, and slapping Ree on the shoulder.

"Born ready. Me first, you next," Ree retorted.

Chauncey whistled jokingly.

"Mannn, I don't know . . ." he laughed. "But you right. I'm probably next up to bat. I'm just holding out a lil longer." The truth was Chauncey couldn't see past all the money he was about to be making, but he knew giving Sasha her ring and wedding was his priority after that.

"A'ight, my nigga, just don't hold out too long," Ree warned.

"I won't . . . I won't. But this all you right now. So let's go."

"Let's do it."

Tatum could hear the band begin to play and it made her knees buckle.

"Oh my God! You all right?" Jayde asked as she reached

and caught her. Jayde planned to stand on the sidelines and watch the nuptials from a distance and then make sure everything was situated for the reception.

"Yeah . . . yeah, I'm fine."

Sasha looked on stubbornly, wanting so bad to console her best friend and tell her how beautiful she looked, how perfect her wedding was, and how she had nothing to be nervous about. But the resentment in her wouldn't allow it. She patted Aubrey on the head and faced forward.

"I guess . . . I guess it just hit me, you know," Tatum spoke with a shaky voice and watery eyes. "Like, I'm really about to marry him. He's about to marry me. Am I ready to be married? Is *he* ready to be married?"

"Sweetie, Ree's been married for years . . . to the game, that is. This is his second marriage," Jayde stated with a chuckle. Sasha turned and looked at her with narrowed eyes not sure if what she said was intended to console Tatum, but Sasha thought it was inappropriate for a nervous girl on the verge of anxiety.

Sasha pushed Tangee out lightly on her cue to start the line. The wedding march would be just for the women, no traditional male escorts. Tatum would walk alone, leaving the empty space for her father's spirit.

"Oh my God," Tatum whispered. "You're right. I never thought I'd say this, but you're right, Jayde. I mean . . . what was I thinking? Can I marry someone who's already married to something else? I'm not his top priority. Look how he went back to the streets again after he *knew* how I felt. Who's to say he won't do it again? Who's to say he'll even leave this time like he says?" Tatum was rambling hysterically as Chanel reluctantly walked out, looking back at her distressed aunt. *Oohs* and *aahs* could be heard in admiration of her nieces' dresses but Tatum paid it no mind. She knew the people were probably impressed with them as well as the setup of the women emerging from the fifth floor, walking down the outside spiral steps of the lighthouse and across the beach to the gazebo.

"Is he gonna leave the game alone, Jayde? . . . For real?"

Jayde wanted to laugh hysterically but she just looked at a pitiful Tatum blankly, giving the impression that she knew something that Tatum didn't. This is why Jayde had all of these little plans in motion. Playing with Tatum and bringing Ree to herself in a calculated way was so much more fun than just killing the girl.

"Sweetie, I'm sure he will. I really think so."

Sasha couldn't take anymore. Jayde using words like *I'm sure* and *I think* was putting more doubt in Tatum's mind. Sasha knew she was supposed to walk now but she didn't.

"Of course he will," Sasha spoke up. "He loves you. Look at this!" Sasha waved her hands around at all that was around them. "He'd do anything for you."

Those words put a sense of calm over Tatum, one that would vanish with the next ones spoken.

"Tatum, you don't have to do anything you're not ready for. Marriage is a big step," Jayde stressed. "I'm sure Ree would understand if you don't want—"

"Shut up, Jayde!" Sasha yelled out of nowhere, causing Jayde to snap her neck and Tatum to open her eyes wide.

"Tatum, you love him and he loves you. And even though I can hardly *stand* to look at you right now . . . you look amazing, and everybody here needs to see that. So follow me down the damn aisle."

And with that, Sasha stepped out to the beat of the music, before Tatum could even close her dropped jaw to respond.

Aubrey stepped out right on Sasha's tail, tossing flowers on the ground as instructed.

Tatum knew that Sasha was still upset with her but she was glad that she had intervened. And even though she thought she was still being a selfish bitch, Sasha was right. A minute passed and the band stopped and Tatum heard the sounds of them beginning to play her walking music, so she went to step out. Step out to love. But she just . . . couldn't.

The band stopped, and the people stood, and the music started again and the crowd waited . . . and the crowd waited . . . and the crowd waited . . .

"What the fuck is going on?" Chauncey whispered as he and Crush stood on the sides, but he didn't get a response.

Ree stood with his eyes fixed on the door, having a feeling, no, almost so in sync with Tatum that he knew . . . he knew what she was thinking . . . he knew what she was scared of and he knew she wasn't walking out of that door.

The band looked to him a little confused as they continued to play.

Sasha breathed a deep and shaky breath wondering what Jayde had said to fuck up Tatum's head.

I should've dragged the whore down the aisle with me.

"She's not coming," Chanel whispered to Tangee, but it was loud enough for some to hear. "She was all scared."

Ree looked to the thirteen-year-old girl and tried to remain straight-faced, but it was a shot to the heart. Ree dropped his head after a few more moments and gave a small nod. What would happen now? This wasn't in the plans. . . .

"Oh my God, she looks beautiful!"

Everyone including Ree looked to Sasha's mother, Terri, who had made the statement, then up to where her eyes landed.

It was Tatum, emerged and glowing, standing on the steps of the lighthouse. She seemed to be looking directly at Ree as she mouthed something to him and smiled. He wasn't sure what it was, but it was a simple *I'm sorry* for her delay. Ree couldn't move. He couldn't even think. All he could do was stare at her. That's how radiant she was.

The bandleader smiled lightly, then raised his finger and circled it, indicating to loop the song and restart it. And as they began to play the instrumental to Stevie Wonder's "Ribbon in the Sky," Tatum took her first steps toward the aisle.

Tatum stepped rhythmically down the aisle, her heart swollen with love. The sun setting against the ocean waves, the star lights and flowers, everyone's smiling faces, it was all so beautiful. But nothing more beautiful than the man who looked at her like she was the only woman in the world walking to him. Just from the way he looked at her made this day the most precious in her life. Never had she felt so adored.

Tatum reached the beach and allowed the words of the song to guide her. They were so beautiful. It was at that moment when she realized she was supposed to be walking to an instrumental.

Those gasps she had heard before she exited, right before she exited, now she knew why.

Tatum glanced to her right as *the* Mr. Wonder himself sat with his piano positioned on the beach next to the band, serenading her with her wedding song. The tears that were held captive on the brink of her lashes overflowed and dropped to her cheeks. She looked at

Ree in awe. He had done that for her. How could he do this?

Stevie belted the last words out so powerfully, so movingly as Tatum neared the edge of the gazebo, that there wasn't a dry eye on the beach. The way she looked, the way she and Ree stared at each other as she neared him, the words, the aura of the moment, it embodied love.

The song faded and Tatum stepped up the single step that put her, Ree, and the reverend on a raised level. She handed her blood-red, rounded rose bouquet to Sasha and faced Ree, taking his awaiting hands.

"Good evening, all . . . We are gathered here today . . ."

Tatum and Ree stared unblinkingly into each other's eyes as the reverend spoke. Hers were steadily pouring out tears, his fighting hard not to.

I love you, he mouthed to her, looking at her tears that fell. Tatum could only nod in response as her bottom lip trembled.

". . . the union of Mr. Sean Knights and Ms. Tatum Mosley will be that of a pure one . . . of a Godly one . . . blessed by the heavens. In nontraditional form but in the tradition of love . . . the couple has decided to share their own vows this evening . . . Mr. Knights . . ."

Ree held Tatum's hands a little tighter and cleared his throat. Never in his life had he felt such a rush of these types of emotions. He knew from the first day he saw her that this woman would bring him exceptional experiences. He just never knew this exceptional. Taking a deep breath, he spoke.

". . . You know . . . they say a man chooses his bride. But I'm the proof that it's not quite true. Because Tatum, *you* chose *me*. The first time I saw you smile, I said *damn* . . . no woman's supposed to stop a man's heart like that . . . I knew that whoever was lucky enough to wake up to that smile every day would be the luckiest man alive. I wanted that man to be me." He paused. "So I pursued you. Persistently. I spent long days . . . and many nights . . . trying to convince you that I deserved you. That you should choose me. In all actuality, Tatum, I knew the whole time that I was just as undeserving of you as the next man . . . And I say this because it's no secret that I've been less than a saint. So how'd I get to spend it with an angel by my side . . . ?" He let the question marinate and then shrugged coolly. "But . . . whether I'm worthy or not, it doesn't matter. Like you say, you're stuck with me," he joked with a grin, and the crowd followed with light chuckles. "And I swear I'll spend my life, every single day of it . . . making sure I keep that beautiful smile on your face. You're all that matters, Tatum . . . Aliya . . . Mosley. And in addition to loving, honoring, and cherishing you, I promise to never let you forget that."

If a round of applause wasn't completely inappropriate, every single person would have erupted into one. Sniffles could be heard all around as Tatum stared at Ree with love and prepared to say her own vows.

"Wow . . ." she spoke shakily, wiping her eyes. "How do you top that?"

There was another light giggle as she took a deep breath and then began.

"Sean . . . as I stand here . . . I can't help but to be *so* thankful. I am not just thankful for this moment, for our friends and family sharing this with us. Not just thankful for this dress . . . for this beautiful, *beautiful* dress," she stressed, looking down at herself, and there was light laughter. She then held up her right hand. "And for this ring! I mean this breathtaking . . . and very *big* ring." More laughter erupted and then her tone turned serious as the laughter subsided. "But I am actually thankful . . . for me. I am thankful for my being, and all of it that has made this possible. You see, I am thankful for my hands . . . because they allow me to hold yours and feel your comfort and strength. I am thankful . . . for my feet, because they allowed me to walk to you down this very aisle. I am thankful for my eyes . . . for they let me stare into the face of my beautiful king every day. And I am *so* very thankful for my heart, because it allows me to feel the most indescribable, deep, and immeasurable love. Love that I didn't know could exist." Tatum took a deep breath and swallowed some tears before continuing. "With everything that has happened . . . so much I have lost—family, friends. It's you that has truly made my life so much better. It's like no matter what happens, what I have to face, or what lies ahead . . . I know that I don't have to be scared anymore . . . because I have you. And when I think of you, baby, my heart actually *smiles*. I mean . . . I just feel good all over. And as I stand here, all I can wonder is how in a million years, I could have ever thought . . . that I could *possibly* live without you." Her tears poured consistently and she thought of the time she'd spent fighting his love, then she gathered the strength to finish. "Sean, we were two souls predestined to spend eternity together way before we laid eyes on each other on that warm summer night. You are everything that I could ever need. And I promise, for the rest of our lives, with all of me to always be whatever you need too. . . ."

If anyone had dried their tears at the end of Ree's vows, they were steadily reflowing by the conclusion of Tatum's.

"The rings, please," the reverend requested with a choked up tone.

Ree's father handed him the platinum wedding band

set, which, contrary to the entire wedding, was simple. The couple exchanged rings and people used the opportunity to snap out of their teary-eyed emotional trance and snap pictures.

"By the power that is vested in me . . . I now pronounce you . . ."

Ree pulled Tatum into a close embrace and pressed his lips to hers passionately, and Tatum released herself to him. She kissed him back like they were the only two people on the beach.

". . . man and wife . . ." the reverend added with a smile and a chuckle. He had been flown in from the States to speak at this wedding and it was by far the best he had ever had the pleasure of blessing.

Everyone stood, applauded, and cheered. Breaking the kiss, Tatum and Ree smiled and looked back to the reverend, then to their guests.

The sky was dark by now and night had fallen. Tangee slid the broom at the bottom of the leveled step and Tatum looked to Ree with a smirk. He had surprised her with Stevie and she surprised him with the broom. She knew he would have protested.

"C'mon, man . . . you serious?" he asked her, looking from the broom to her with raised eyebrows.

"On a count of three?" she said with a grin.

". . . One! . . . Two! . . . Three!" the crowd chanted, and the couple jumped. Another round of applause.

"All right! All right! That shit was real sweet," Chauncey spoke up coolly. "But yo, it's time to go all the way in!" He grabbed Sasha up and everyone cheered, heading for the lighthouse and the reception in good spirits.

Chapter 7

"Trust and love are two different things . . . I love Chauncey, but I don't trust him."

—Sasha, *Still Thicker than Water*

The premium open bar was in full effect, the servers had begun to pass out the delectable five star meals, and the sounds of Beyoncé's "Single Ladies" vibrated the walls of the lighthouse as the grandest reception Jamaica had ever witnessed came to life.

The pink lights transitioned to red and reflected off the white satin draped around the room, connecting from the ceilings to the walls in an intricate design. Aubrey sat at the round table flipping her tiny hand back and forth, mimicking Beyoncé's dance moves.

Normally Sasha would have been thoroughly entertained by her daughter's regularly adorable behavior, but her mind was elsewhere.

"What's wrong, kid . . . you don't like your lobster? I thought that's what you wanted to order?"

Tatum had provided everyone with a small menu accompanying their invitation. Guests could choose from stuffed lobster tail and filet mignon, chicken française, prime rib, or pecan-encrusted salmon, all of which looked divine. The dinner wasn't the key, though.

Tatum being a girl with a weakness for sweets had Ree go all out for the dessert portion. There was a long table with exotic fruits of every kind and chocolate fondue, red velvet cupcakes, chocolate-covered strawberries, cannolis, Tartufo, éclairs, mini cheesecakes, and an ice cream sundae station, all in addition to the five-layer white chocolate truffle wedding cake. Everything looked incredibly mouthwatering.

"Well, I love the lobster!" Terri spoke up. "It's so fresh, too. And did you see the wedding cake? That looks amazing. The little groom even has dreads!"

Chauncey had to chuckle at that but turned his attention on Sasha, who hadn't quite seemed herself since this morning.

"Hey . . . Earth to you. What's up?" he probed, snapping his finger in front of her face.

Sasha finally looked at him.

"Oh . . . nothing. I just . . . I just, yeah, probably should've ordered the chicken or something. Excuse me."

Sasha jumped up and headed to the restroom, feeling herself becoming emotional all over again. Finally reaching the sink after what seemed like the never-ending path of the trying-not-to cry trail, she let the tears fall.

What she wanted so badly was to get over it, to not think about it, to know that it wasn't true, and to have had Tatum look at her like she was crazy and scream at her for even suggesting something like that.

But that was not the case. The reality was that Tatum had slept with Chauncey a long, long time ago.

Could they ever be the same after this? Was their friendship thick enough?

A banging on the bathroom door reminded Sasha that she had put on the deadbolt and she decided she had better get back out there before someone complained about it. There were three stalls in the ladies' room and no reason for the door to be locked.

Splashing some cold water on her now bright red and puffy face, Sasha tried her best to restore her appearance. Reaching in her clutch, Sasha pulled out and applied her Laura Mercier blotting powder.

Boom! Boom! Boom!

More banging.

"I'm coming!"

She took a deep breath and decided it was best to speak with Chauncey about her feelings when they returned home. He would just have to put some time aside for that talk, no excuses.

"I'm sorry . . ."

Sasha snatched the door open, ready to apologize to whoever was waiting on the other side. However, there was no one. She caught a glimpse of Nikki, the mother of Tatum's nieces, now heading inside of the men's restroom. She assumed it was she who had been banging.

"Wait . . . Nikki! That's the men's room! I'm out!" But Nikki was gone and inside.

Sasha shrugged. Refastening her clutch, she held her head down and began to walk.

"Whatever," she mumbled, but was caught off guard when she crashed into someone.

"Oh my God! I'm sorry . . . I should've been watching where I was going."

Sasha looked up and caught the man staring at her unblinkingly, almost in a trance. It scared Sasha slightly.

He was an attractive older man with keen features and a distinguished presence.

"No . . . *I'm* sorry. I'm so, so sorry," he finally spoke zealously.

He looked like he was becoming a bit emotional and Sasha was confused by his still, strong stare.

"Okay. Well . . . bye." Sasha stepped off with an eye roll, sure that the man was just entranced by her beauty, like most were. "Weirdo," she mumbled, and made her way back to her table.

Back at the restrooms, Bleek barged through the door ready to relieve the first round of his liquor indulgence.

"Damn a nigga gotta piss like a wino."

Reaching the urinal, he pulled out his main vein and adjusted his stance, ready to let it all out.

"Ooohh weeee!" he called, feeling that relief that comes with a borderline drunken piss. The sniffing sounds from behind him interrupted his short-lived "me time" with his soldier. He knew that sound, he knew it well.

"Somebody powdering that nose," he sang low.

"I'm sorry, I didn't mean to interrupt." A woman's voice caught him off guard as he shook off his last drops and spun around while stuffing his dick away abruptly.

"Oh shit! Yo, what you doin' in here, shawty?"

The question had to be rhetorical because Bleek could see the white still caked on the tip of her nose and in her nostrils.

"Just . . . getting the party started," Nikki quipped with a smile. "But my party's all over, apparently," she added, holding up an empty baggie.

Bleek raised his brows and nodded, fastening back his Gucci slacks and moving to the sink.

"Well, you know what they say . . . all good things must come to an end," he drawled in his country drawl. "Pardon me, darling, I need to wash my hands."

Nikki licked her lips and adjusted her purple spandex dress. She knew she was attractive, despite her once again rapid weight loss.

"But that don't mean another good thing can't begin." She spoke the words as she reached around him and fondled his package through his pants.

"Whoa! You type aggressive, baby. It ain't even *that* type of party."

"But you cute as shit," she confessed, noticing the holes in his cheeks she was sure were dimples when he chose to smile. He had smooth brown skin, a calm, gentleman quality, and undeniable boyish good looks. "And I know who you are . . . you Chauncey boy . . . I know you got what I need."

Besides the fact that they were at a wedding, Bleek didn't do hand-to-hands and never had anything on him.

"Nah, I ain't got that . . . *girl*," he spoke, coding the word for coke.

"What about that boy?" Bleek knew then that she was into everything. A true fiend.

He whistled and moved past her, heading for the door. He took a good look at the chocolate little thing and knew she could be gorgeous if she wasn't strung out, even somebody's arm candy.

"You take care of yourself, shawty. You might make a man real happy one day."

Nikki rolled her eyes and began cleaning herself in the mirror, disappointment all over her.

"Yeah, yeah. Whatever. Don't nobody want me . . ."

She didn't realize Bleek was already gone and she was talking to herself. The reality caused her to utter the words again as tears came to her eyes.

"Don't nobody want me."

"Lord, what is that woman doing coming out of the men's room?" Terri questioned to herself as she headed into the adjoining door for the ladies' stalls. "Just trifling, trifling . . . even at this *beautiful* wedding. Ghetto folk for you." She pulled out her lipstick and applied a fresh coat because Terri knew that a true lady never applied makeup in public. Even if it were obvious that you did not naturally have stained lips and blackened eyelashes, you should never let a man see you "fixing" yourself up.

"These young girls these days," she whispered, reflecting on one who had just applied lip gloss at the banquet table and the other who had just been in the men's bathroom. Someone coming through the door caught her attention. She looked to see who it was and was appalled.

"Excuse me! But this is a woman's bath . . ." Her last word was left hanging in the air as her bottom lip hit the floor along with the tube of lipstick that had slipped out of her hand.

He smiled.

"Hello, Terri. You look amazing."

Her heart pounded out of her chest. He was supposed to be *dead*. It couldn't . . . it just couldn't be . . .

"Mi . . . Mick . . . Mickel," she whispered. And before she could get another word out, her body felt heavy and she up and fainted. Good thing Mickel reacted quickly . . . he never let her head hit the floor.

* * *

"You were crying? Fuck was you crying for?"

"Just leave me alone, Chauncey."

"Leave you alone? What's wrong with you, Sash?"

When Sasha had returned, Chauncey had found a way to swap out her lobster for the chicken she said she wished she had. He knew he had been putting her through a lot with his street dedication and he figured this vacation would be used best to show her how important she actually was to him. He was trying to do every little thing to make her happy, but she was making it difficult.

"Nothing's wrong . . ."

"Then eat your food."

"I don't want the food! I don't want the stupid chicken, Chauncey!" Sasha had to look away from him because she imagined his beautiful face buried between Tatum's thighs, even though the probability of their young teenage selves doing much beyond the basics was very low.

Chauncey, on the other hand, had no idea what was wrong with her, and for her to be screaming at him in a room full of people caused him to breathe deep in an attempt to calm his known rampant temper.

"Yo . . . you need to calm . . . the fuck . . . down," he warned through clenched teeth.

"Then leave me alone!" she spat, on the verge of tears.

Bleek tried to eat his food and stay out of it, but it was hard to do being that everyone else but him had left their table.

"Yo . . ." Chauncey felt a rage coming on. He couldn't believe Sasha's antics at the wrong times. "You so fucking spoiled! For real, yo, I can't even believe you sometimes."

Sasha looked at him with her jaw dropped in disbelief.

"Are you serious?"

"Yeah, I'm serious! I'm not even gonna ask you what's wrong because I already know. Shit ain't all about you! It ain't all about Sasha! It ain't ya wedding day and Tatum ain't chasing you around catering to your every need like she always do! It's the other way around and you can't handle it!"

Bleek looked up and could see the tears in Sasha's eyes and he felt for her at that moment.

"Fuck you, Chauncey! You are such a piece of shit! I wish I never even got back with ya ass! You think you can talk to me like that 'cause your shit don't stink? Well it stinks! What, you got your fancy cars, big house, you the man again, and I'm the trophy chick who just supposed to keep taking and taking your shit and all you put me through!" She was crying full fledged now. "I mean, how much more am I supposed to take, Chauncey? You're no saint! You put your family second to drugs and this stupid master plan! You sell drugs, Chauncey!"

Chauncey ran his tongue along the inside of his jawline and glanced around. Most were oblivious but a few had eyes on them. Ree, who was not too far away at his and Tatum's table, shot Chauncey a warning look. *Control Sasha,* because now she was getting too vocal about the wrong shit, his shit.

"Bitch, are you fucking crazy?" Chauncey grabbed Sasha's arm angrily, almost yanking her out of her seat, and she was in shock. But why, why would she be? He loved her, so that's what she got when he was mad. He hadn't loved Neli, and she had gotten a lot worse.

"Get off of me!"

"Yo C, chill!" Bleek spoke up.

"Bleek . . . this ain't yours, homie. I got this," Chauncey told him, even though he already regretted his actions. Sasha snatched her arm away with her mouth agape in pure pain. Her body trembled and her tears were frozen. She couldn't believe Chauncey had spoken to her like that. She jumped up and ran back to the restrooms, where Tatum was now coming out.

"Sasha!" Tatum called, truly worried. She loved her friend like a sister, more than a sister. They weren't blood, but they weren't water either.

"Leave me alone!" Sasha could barely get out as she pushed by her.

"Sasha, I'm sooo sorry," Tatum pleaded with pain in her voice. "Please, talk to me, mama."

"Get ya hoe ass away from me!" Sasha screamed, storming to the bathroom.

Tatum took a deep breath and it took everything in her not to follow her and wipe the floor with her, mostly because she was truly sorry about what happened.

"Just . . . just leave her alone, Tatum. I'll talk to her," Jayde soothed, rubbing Tatum on the back. "Go enjoy your wedding day. Stevie's about to sing again for you guys, don't ruin it."

Tatum debated, hard. She wanted to chase behind Sasha but that's what she had always done. Always chased behind Sasha and couldn't truly be happy unless she was sure that Sasha was happy first. Not today, though, not on the single most important day of her life. Tatum nodded.

"You're right. I will." She stepped toward her table and noticed Nikki sliding an extra favor in her purse. She knew it was extra because Nikki was already wearing one. The favors were simple, classic, his and hers Audemars watches positioned at each place setting, one for

each guest. The inscription read *love passes time.* Tatum
wondered which guest was getting ripped off. She made
a note to address it later as she then spun around to
Jayde. "Hey . . . you're gonna talk to her, right? Make
sure she's okay?" Tatum tried not to care but the nur-
turer in her had to make sure that the people she loved
were fine. Jayde nodded assuringly and Tatum felt a
little better, but she didn't catch the wicked grin Jayde
gave when she turned back around. Things were
unraveling just the way Jayde wanted them to and she
had no plans to mend them. Just then, Jayde looked
outside and swore she caught a glimpse of her father
carrying someone toward the direction of the beach.
She had an idea who it was and it turned her smile
upside down.

"Oh my God! Just leave me alone!"

Sasha had her head down nestled in her hands as she
sat on the lid of the toilet in the stall. She saw the black
pants and designer men's shoes and she knew Chauncey
had come to check on her, yell at her, apologize, something.

He knocked, not so aggressively, and she figured
apologize was the answer.

She jumped up, ready to just go off and tell him
exactly why she was mad. Snatching the door open,
her face tear-streaked, Sasha got the surprise of her life.

"What the . . . ? What are you do—"

Bleek grabbed her by the back of her head and
brought his face to hers, pressing his lips firmly against
her soft ones. Sasha's natural reaction was to resist, so
she did. She pushed him hard, with anger, and her body
went rigid with resistance. But he was strong, and his kiss
was so passionate, it was impossible to fight. So after a

few seconds, she gave up, and it was like the perfect remedy. Sasha then found herself hesitantly allowing her mouth to open and his tongue to have access. She was kissing him back, she was holding his much-needed strength tightly, and she was losing herself in him. His hand moved from the back of her head and his other one found the nape of her neck, as he kissed her tenderly, carefully, but with enough yearning to let her know he knew exactly what he was doing and he wanted to do it. Her perfume tickled his nostrils, her fancy style and undeniable beauty appealed to him. Yeah, she was high maintenance but he knew there was depth to her, she had been hinting at it when they had moments alone. He wanted to know what was troubling her.

The kiss finally broke, and he was the breaker. Sasha's lips, although knowing they were wrong for doing so, remained puckered and ready for more.

"Wha . . . What . . . happened?" she asked breathily. "Why'd you stop? I mean . . . why'd you start?"

Bleek pressed his forehead to hers and closed his eyes. Sasha realized the severity then of what they had done.

"Chauncey . . ." she whispered sadly. Although he was a jerk, he was her jerk.

"That's my man," Bleek finally spoke. "But . . ." There was a small pause and then . . .

". . . What about your girlfriend? Why didn't you bring her?" Sasha asked, wanting to know this since he had boarded the plane solo.

Bleek stepped back and stared at her intensely.

". . . I didn't want to. We ain't like . . . I mean she ain't like . . ."

"She ain't like what?" Sasha chuckled through her despair.

"She ain't like you."

Inhaling a shaky breath, Sasha leaned her head back against the stall. If she could rewind this whole weekend and do it over again she would.

"Bleek . . ." she spoke sweetly. "When . . . when did this happen? I mean we've been . . ."

"What? Spending mad time . . . eating, laughing, talking . . ." he reminded her with a smirk. "How could it not? You know you're beautiful. You know you can make a nigga weak, Sasha."

Sasha swallowed hard. Her mouth was dry.

"I didn't know," she confessed softly in a voice that drove Bleek crazy.

"You knew . . ." he told her, looking at her with adoring eyes. He stepped close to her again and put his hands up against the stall walls, leaning into her.

"You knew." And then he kissed her again.

Chapter 8

"This is it, right . . . No more street stuff?"

—Tatum, *Still Thicker than Water*

<u>Act II</u>

The rain poured profusely, so much so that even with the wipers on full speed, a blanket of water completely sheeted the windshield of Tatum's Range Rover at all times. She thanked God that she was parked.

"So . . ." she started, shifting in her seat. "I guess this is it, huh? You sure you gotta do this?"

Ree reached over and gently took her hand.

"You know I do, Tatum. But you know I'm coming right back as well." He brought his hand to her face and cupped her chin. "In and out . . . we talked about it, Miss Lady."

Tatum sighed and nodded when she really wanted to shake her head in protest. *He* had talked about it, and it didn't matter how many times *he* had talked about this moment, actually having it here was nothing like those talks. She didn't care how much he had gone over every detail to make sure that Jayde was efficient with the process, she didn't completely trust her with his freedom.

"How long again?" she asked, already knowing but just wanting to be reassured.

"A week, maybe two. I promise."

Tatum bit her lip and blinked back tears. She was stronger than this.

"I'm gonna miss you . . . especially at night," she confessed.

Ree sighed and looked out the window, up at the building that was barely visible through the thunderstorm and gray skies.

"I know," he said lowly. "Me too . . . but it'll be that much sweeter when I come home to you."

"In a week," Tatum repeated.

"Or two . . ." he reminded.

"Well . . . go by the supermarket and bring home some paper towels on your way home because I'm sure we'll be out by then." Tatum faced forward and her tough exterior hid the pain and fear inside of her.

Ree chuckled.

"Paper towels?" he questioned in confusion. "Why don't you go and pick some up now? The supermarket is right around the—"

"No!" Tatum interrupted him. "I want *you* to bring the paper towels home. And I better not be waiting more than two weeks for them." He could hear the tremor in her cracking voice, see the tears forming, and he now understood. It wasn't about paper towels. It was her insurance that he was coming back to her. He stared at her with honest eyes.

"Okay. I'll bring home the paper towels . . . so don't buy any."

Tatum swallowed hard and nodded, feeling for some reason a good amount of relief.

"All right, good. So . . . I'll see you soon." She wouldn't dare say good-bye.

"Yup," he confirmed.

Ree took another long look at her and then shot her one of his confident winks, opening up the passenger door. They wouldn't make the departure any harder than it was.

"Hey!" Tatum called as she grabbed his arm before he could get out. "You . . . you come home to us, Mr. Knights."

Us? Ree had a feeling. But hearing her confirmation blew his mind. His seed, his real seed . . . with his wife. It changed everything. He was more anxious than ever to get this over with.

He nodded and, with no more words between them, he shut the door.

As much as Ree wanted to bask in the elation of hearing the news of his first child being created, he knew that his focus needed to be elsewhere. So with the strength of only a man of his stature, he pushed those thoughts to the back of his mind. Dodging raindrops with a cool, confident walk, Ree made his way up the ten stone steps to the building with only one thought in his mind, executing the first step to this plan with expertise. This was it.

He reached the top of the steps and just before approaching the entrance, he went into his pocket and pulled out a rolled blunt and lighter. Placing the cigar to his lips and using his hand to assist in his firing against the raindrops, Ree took a long and deep pull, inhaling and allowing the smoke to caress his insides and set a calm over him. After another two pulls, Ree opened up the heavy glass door while still balancing the blunt between his lips and stepped inside.

Everything was exactly as he had expected.

One officer sat behind a heavy glass partition munching on a doughnut while another poured a cup of coffee from a Dunkin' Donuts Box O' Joe. The cops' jokes and laughs came to a gradual halt as the dominant man with the dreads approached them with confidence. There was a heavy silence as they anticipated what he would say. Ree smirked, walking up to the first officer and leaning into the glass.

"Good afternoon. My name is Sean Knights," he introduced politely. "And I hear you boys are looking for me."

The officer's hand stopped midair before the doughnut could ever reach his dropped-jaw mouth, while the other apparently had a loss of memory as his steaming hot coffee slipped from his hand and landed in his lap.

"Holy fucking shit! Goddammit!" he screamed, jumping up. "Han-hands above y-y-your head, motherfucker!" The officer shifted his eyes from Ree to the back of the precinct quickly.

"Roberts, we got a live one!" he shouted anxiously, still looking at Ree as if he would disappear.

"And you're not gonna believe who the fuck it is!" he added.

The other officer remained frozen as his eyes stayed fixed on the man they knew as Respect. *Turn himself in? What the fuck is this nigger up to?*

Ree smirked and put his weed out on the countertop after his last toke. And then he slowly lifted his hands and placed them on his head.

The arrogance in his motions showed that he knew exactly what he was doing. And within seconds a dozen officers surrounded him and had him cuffed. Phase one was in full effect.

* * *

Bleek lay back with his hands crossed behind his head. The feel of the red satin sheets against his skin felt good, but not as good as the warm tongue that traced the shaft of his dick and now was trailing from his washboard stomach up his slim and cut-up torso.

> . . . *And when we're done, I don't wanna*
> *feel my . . . legssss . . .*

The sounds of the sex music combined with the scented candle and her perfect, oiled-up naked body should've been enough to have his full attention . . . but it was not.

"Mmm . . . I told you I was gonna take good care of you, didn't I? Mama gon' make you an addict tonight, baby . . ." Jayde brought her red lips up to Bleek's left ear and used the tip of her tongue to tickle his lobe but Bleek continued to stare at the ceiling, lost. After a few seconds of silence, Jayde's mouth dropped in a frown and she grabbed his face with her red-stained nails.

"Hey!"

He shifted his baby browns to her face but kept his blank expression.

"You know . . . I don't believe this shit," she chuckled. "You got a wet pussy staring you in the face and you thinking about your girlfriend like a little *bitch?*"

Bleek stared at her but didn't respond. If he could get his dick past the semihard phase, he planned on shoving it down her throat so hard it bruised her tonsils, just for her slick-ass mouth. But his mind . . . his mind was on pause.

"I mean . . . I wanna *fuck* tonight. And you should be thrilled. Don't disappoint me, Bleek. That bitch'll still be there when you get home."

"Hey. Chill on the bitches," he warned, still having a

good amount of respect for his baby's mother. ". . . And I'm not thinking about her."

"Yeah right," Jayde tittered, having no idea that he was speaking the truth.

Just then, his phone rang and Jayde picked it up from the nightstand.

"Yo . . . mind ya business," he told her, snatching it from her hand. Jayde smirked.

After taking a long look and a thoughtful moment, Bleek answered.

"Yo . . ."

There was a brief silence. And then . . .

"Hey."

Bleek took a deep breath, for some reason feeling guilty at the sound of her voice.

"Hey . . . what's up?"

He stood up and walked away from Jayde toward the bathroom as he tried to ignore the scowl she wore. Jayde was not used to being ignored, and she didn't like it.

"We need to talk," Sasha blurted out, feeling like the courage may dwindle if she didn't just go all in. "You know . . . about what happened. Did you get my text?"

"Yeah . . ." he answered nonchalantly.

"So . . . why didn't you answer? Can you meet me?"

Bleek took a deep breath.

"It depends."

"On what?"

"On what you wanna meet about," he answered truthfully. "If it's about that bullshit you wrote, about it being a mistake and all that . . . then nah . . . I'm good. You said that already. You don't need to say that no more."

He tried to speak low so Jayde couldn't ear hustle. "But if you wanna talk about the truth . . . how you liked it just as much as I did. How you can't stop thinking about it . . . that's why you wanna see me in person . . . then we can do that."

The silence couldn't reveal it but Sasha had dropped her jaw on the other line. Bleek was bona fide crazy with a death wish.

"Bleek! *Liked* it?" she asked him. "Are you crazy? I couldn't like it if I wanted to. Look . . . I'm with Chauncey. That shit that happened . . . it was . . . you just caught me at a weak moment. I mean . . . I *love* Chauncey."

"I know," he told her boldly. "But right now, my man ain't really got the time for you that I do. And we both know a chick like *you* require time like a muhfucka. So I figure, why not spend it with me . . . and I use that time to convince you that it just may be something here."

Sasha took a deep breath. When did Bleek get so bold about this? She just wanted to clean up her mistake before anyone got hurt, more specifically her and Bleek. She knew Chauncey would kill them both if he found out they'd slipped up.

"Bleek . . . I don't . . . I mean, I thought that was ya man?"

Bleek having respect for Chauncey, but also not denying the things he was feeling for Sasha, decided to keep it 100 percent real.

"Nah, shawty . . . that's *your* man. I respect C, I do. But business is business. This here is something else. Trust me, ma . . ."

Bleek ran his hand over his smooth face and peeked over at Jayde to make sure she was clueless to his conversation. When he saw her lying back playing with herself in another world, he continued in a hushed whisper.

"I'm feeling you. And the shit keeps going. I don't know how to stop it. I tried . . . but I can't."

Sasha, who was now starting to walk into the hospital

where she was dropping off a résumé, had to halt in her steps in shock. What had she done?

"Bleek . . . don't . . . don't get me wrong . . ." She pulled back the heavy door to the entrance and started down the corridor, her heels clicking against the hardwood floor. "You're . . . you're attractive. And you're funny, and I have fun with you . . ."

"Then what's the problem?"

"My *man* is the problem."

"That's right . . . now what's the solution?"

Bleek was just like Chauncey in some ways . . . relentless. The way he was playing it reminded Sasha so much of Chauncey's arrogance. Maybe that's what attracted her. But she knew he couldn't compare to the history she and Chauncey had.

"And here I was thinkin' you was so big on loyalty," she quipped, remembering all that he preached when he looked out for her at Chauncey's request.

"I am," he stated confidently. "I'd never cross anybody on the levels that we deal. Me and C deal on this get-money level, and I'd be loyal to him on that. But I'm also big on going after what I want . . . and taking what's yours."

"And I'm yours?" Sasha asked sarcastically. Bleek's chuckle was his response.

"Bleek, we had a moment. We made a mistake. Let's just leave it at that." She wanted to tell him not to end his young life so soon. Messing with Chauncey was like suicide.

"Oh you know it was more than that, ma . . ." Before Bleek could say any more he saw Jayde standing in the doorway.

"Bleek, let's wrap it up. Tell your sweetheart you've got work to do." Jayde spoke loud enough for whoever it was to hear her clearly as she shot him a seductive wink.

"Ha! I should've *known* you were with Jayde. Well, go ahead. I'm sure she has a lot of *work* for you to do!" Sasha teased sarcastically as she neared the reception desk.

"But see, why you sounding jealous, tho'?" Bleek questioned as he watched Jayde strut back to the bed.

"I'm not! Trust me. Besides, I have to go; I'm meeting Chauncey for dinner. So go ahead! Tell Jayde I said hello . . . I'm sure she's gonna work the hell out of you," Sasha tittered.

"Yeah, a'ight . . ." Bleek shot as Sasha disconnected the call. He couldn't front, the thought of her and Chauncey having an evening alone had him a little jealous. And he never was the jealous type. He had dealt with chicks in the past and watched them be with other dudes after, and it wouldn't faze him. His first love had even broken his heart and skated on him for another dude, and he'd let it go. He even ended up being cool with dude after because he knew he still slid her the pipe occasionally. That's how little stuff like that used to be to him. But now . . . now was different.

"Was your girlfriend mad?" Jayde asked, snapping him out of his thoughts as he made his way back over to her. He knew she didn't give a fuck.

"Uh . . . nah. Nah, she was straight."

Jayde watched him take a seat on the edge of the bed and light up a blunt as if he hadn't just lied to her face. At that moment she knew something was up but she didn't show it. If it wasn't his demeanor that gave it away, or the fifteen-minute-long conversation, it was the fact that Jayde knew the number she had seen on his screen when she handed him the phone. And if he had to lie about it being Sasha who had called him, then the two of them had something to hide. And Jayde was determined to find out what it was.

"I'm sorry I missed Dr. Grant. The traffic out there is insane. I guess from the rain." Sasha smiled at the young girl and handed over her detailed and professional résumé enclosed in a plastic case.

Sasha looked sharp in her three-quarter Chanel raincoat and pumps, even though her damp hair had began to stick to her face slightly.

The girl smiled at her shyly, admiring Sasha's beauty.

"It's fine. He said to just leave it and he'll give you a call . . . *Sasha*," the girl read the résumé slowly.

"That's right. Okay, thanks!" Sasha waved, turning and beginning to strut off. Just then, pieces of what she'd just heard began to come back to the young nurse.

"Um . . . excuse me! Sasha! Sasha, wait . . ."

She jogged after her anxiously and Sasha turned, hearing the last call and footsteps.

"Yes?"

"I'm . . . I'm sorry," the nurse started, a little out of breath. "It's just . . . your name is Sasha."

Sasha looked at her like she was crazy.

"Um . . . yeah . . ."

"And . . . and you said . . . on the phone. You . . . you know a man named Chauncey?"

Sasha took a deep breath and rolled her eyes. If Chauncey was messing around with this Chinese-looking chick, she was going to kill him. He better had not started his cheating shit again.

"Yeah, and?" Sasha shot with a little attitude.

"And uhm . . . I'm sorry . . . but you also said you know . . . someone named Jayde?"

Sasha wrinkled her brows and threw her hand on her hip.

"Were you spying on my conversation?"

"No . . . I mean, yes . . . I mean . . . please. Do you know someone named Jayde? I *swear* it's important." The girl seemed distressed, desperate even. Sasha sighed.

"Yeah. She's my frien . . . I mean, she's my sist—" Sasha cut herself short, wanting nothing to do with anything Jayde may have gotten into. "Look . . . sweetie . . . If she did something to you . . . or to someone you know . . . just, trust me. Leave it alone. Leave *her* alone."

Sasha turned to walk but the girl grabbed her arm.

"No! Please . . . I have . . . I have something I think you should hear." The way she leaned in and whispered piqued Sasha's interest, but if it had to do with Jayde, she really wanted no part.

"Adriana! I need those charts, please," another nurse called out and interrupted. Adriana looked down at the clipboard in her hand and then up at Sasha who she was sure was someone from the tape she had heard. The more she looked at her, she kinda looked like one of the girls from the picture, even though Adriana thought all black girls looked alike. Still, it was all too much of a coincidence. *Sasha, Chauncey, Jayde . . .*

"Now, Adriana!" the nurse yelled.

"Please . . . just wait here. I'll be right back!"

Adriana ran rapid speed down the hall and handed the nurse her clipboards in haste, anxious to get back to Sasha and finally try to do some justice for the young girl who had lost her life.

Don't worry, Penelope . . . I think we've got something . . . she'll pay for what she did . . . Adriana said to herself hopefully as she jogged back.

But when she returned, Sasha was nowhere in sight.

* * *

"And this right here . . . this is the Romano cheese. If you mix it with your Parmesan, it makes the taste sharper."

"A'ight, bet . . . so give me some of that Romano, too."

"Sure thing," the woman behind the deli table smiled as she walked away from Chauncey. Chauncey had every female's attention as he stood in the middle of Whole Foods with a shopper's basket containing all of the ingredients for the romantic dinner he planned on cooking for Sasha.

He knew he was wrong for snapping on her the way he did at the wedding, and since they returned she had been letting him know it too. She'd been throwing him straight shade. Instead of apologizing the old-fashioned way, Chauncey figured he'd do things the way he did them best, the nigga way, doing something to make her smile and hope she'd forget about it.

"I see nothing's changed. Still driving the girls crazy . . . even the cheese lady done got her panties wet, huh?"

Chauncey shifted his eyes over to where the voice came from and couldn't believe what he saw.

"Lizette?"

She smiled bright, showing a white set of teeth surrounded by pink glossed lips. Lizette was a girl from Newark who used to strip at the Cherry Bar with Kim. E had even told Chauncey she was a sure freak and had done some shit with him and Kim. Chauncey never knew whether to know if that nigga was exaggerating or not though. Just thinking of E caused him to chuckle slightly.

"Yeah, it's me . . . what brings you to the A?" she asked in her Puerto Rican–dipped voice. Being in the South, anyone from up North really paid attention to each other's accents on the rare occasions they got to hear it.

"Can ask you the same thing," Chauncey shot, never being one to reveal too much.

She shrugged.

"Long story. But the synopsis. Met a ballplayer, jumped state, didn't work out. Here I am. Your turn."

"Change of scenery," he responded, keeping it simple.

Lizette studied Chauncey in his jeans, designer flannel shirt, Prada sneakers, and signature ice. Dark skin, waves, and goatee always was on point. He was the man in Brick City and he seemed to be the man here too.

"Cooking dinner?" She smiled, placing her thumb on the pocket of her short denim shorts. They covered little, just like the white wifebeater she wore over her visible leopard-print bra and matching stilettos. Her long blond dyed hair was wet and wavy in the way those Hispanic girls could do it. She looked good, but not in the classic sense. "Lucky lady," she added.

"You know her," he stated smoothly.

Lizette's eyes widened but she hid her jealousy. She hated Sasha, always had. Tatum was also a second runner-up on her *fuck that bitch* list.

"No!" she exclaimed in shock. "So she still putting up with ya ass, huh? Glad y'all made it through all that."

Chauncey knew what she meant. There weren't many who didn't know about the whole Chauncey-almost-killing-Neli-in-the-hotel-room-after-she-set-him-up-to-reveal-their-affair-to-Sasha shebang.

"Yeah . . . thanks."

Chauncey stepped up and took his packaged cheese from the grinning cheese lady.

"Wish I was the one you were cooking for," the chubby deli lady said with a grin. Lizette smirked.

"Guess I gotta take a number, huh?" she spoke as she

walked over and took a number from the red machine, but Chauncey had a feeling she wasn't talking about the line for the cold cuts.

He chuckled.

"A'ight, ladies . . . y'all be easy." They all smiled and waved, even the eighty-year-old woman standing behind him in her church clothes. With that he turned and bopped his smooth self through the aisles and out of sight.

"Chauncey, wait!" He heard the voice calling as he made his way to his midnight blue drop-top Aston Martin in the parking lot.

"Hold up, damn. You got a bitch running a marathon," Lizette joked as she trotted up to him in her heels. Chauncey threw his bags in the backseat and slid in the front.

"What's up, ma? What you want from me?" Chauncey kept it blunt. Always. He slid on his Versace shades as Rick Ross's latest began to blast from the custom speakers as he started his car.

"You in a rush?" she asked, leaning over and giving ample view of the cleavage. Chauncey played it cool but wondered who had paid for those; they weren't there in Newark. *Sucka-ass ballplayer,* he thought.

"I always got somewhere I need to be," he told her.

"Good, well then I'll keep it brief." Lizette smiled wide and her eyes slanted. She was a cute girl, more sexy than anything. "I wanna fuck you, Chauncey. Always wanted to. Never got the chance but didn't wanna pass up on it twice."

Chauncey laughed.

"What makes you think you ever had a chance, ma? . . . What makes you think you got one now?"

She shrugged.

"Wishful thinking, I guess. And for the simple fact . . . a leopard don't usually change his spots." She used her index finger to trace his jawline with a wicked laugh, knowing Chauncey's dog reputation. "I heard you was a sucker for good pussy."

"I ain't a sucker for shit."

"Well then let me be the sucker for you," she shot back. "And I'm a *good* sucker."

Chauncey sighed. And this was the shit that happened to him.

"Nah . . . I'm good, ma." He was really trying to be too. Good.

"Well, you call me if you change your mind."

She pulled out a receipt with her number already scribbled on it and tossed it in his lap. "And I'm sure you heard about me . . . the more the merrier."

She threw him another smile and strolled away.

The real reason Lizette hated Sasha was because she could never have her and she always wanted her. She was a chick that liked to go both ways. Maybe now, she could have her chance. Or maybe she could have them both . . . or maybe she could just have Chauncey. But either way, she was gonna have something.

"It's funny we meet again under these circumstances. You look good."

"And when exactly is the hearing?"

Johnny smirked at the way Tatum diverted his compliment. She was a stickler at ignoring his advances. The same way she had ignored them when he invited her to lunch after he defended her in her custody battle with Nikki.

Now with him being the most prominent, well-known,

high-paid black lawyer on the East Coast, it was no surprise that he was the one Jayde had reached out to for Ree's case. He was the best, after all.

"The hearing is in the morning. Nine A.M.," Johnny revealed as he took a sip from his coffee. He was seated on the couch of Tatum and Ree's Atlanta condo in his designer suit, legs crossed revealing his Ferragamo leather shoes. "Like I said, they will deny him bail. It's standard for a flight risk. If they don't do it, it will all look suspicious. At that time I will push for a separate arraignment with the requested judge. One week from now, he'll be home."

Tatum stared at him and her heart raced in anxiety. She prayed he was right.

"Just that simple, huh?"

Johnny smiled his handsome smile and his eyes twinkled as they took in Tatum's simple beauty in her velour sweat suit. Her body was amazing and she was gorgeous to him. He'd always thought so.

"Just that simple. Look, Tatum, that's why we went this route. They have no witnesses, drugs were never found at his home, and he can't be connected to any murders. Respect will be free to move when and how he chooses after this. Without your brother . . . they have nothing."

Tatum narrowed her eyes at him. She hated the revelation that the death of her brother was the savior to Ree's freedom. She couldn't be happy about that even if she wanted to and she wanted to let him know the comment was tasteless. Before she could get a word out, Jayde stepped into the room and played referee.

"Don't worry, Tatum. We have them all in the pocket. Money talks for these people . . . even for our *friend* Johnny here. We'll have the right judge for this. It'll be over before you know it."

Tatum let out a sigh as she nodded slowly. Picking up her vanilla chai tea, she took a light sip. She placed the cup back down on the coffee table and before she knew it, Johnny had placed his hands gently on top of hers and whispered to her smoothly.

"Don't you worry your pretty little head with all of this. Let me do my job, baby. Respect is lucky to have a woman so devoted in his corner."

Tatum looked up and stared at him in astonishment as her chest heaved. This man was flirting with her blatantly.

Johnny was very attractive. Tatum had even briefly entertained lunch with him before she and Ree were officially back together. He had that debonair, young Billy Dee Williams thing going on. But he couldn't touch Ree.

"Excuse me," Tatum said, taking her hands away. "He knows that." She subtly waved her left hand so he could catch the blinding glimpse of her ring. Johnny smirked. Jayde looked on.

Just over the brim of her coffee cup filled with Bailey's she witnessed the small yet visible exchange. It delighted her and she wondered what she could do with it.

"Johnny's right, Tatum. You should trust him," Jayde spoke up. "Everything will go as smooth as Respect promised you . . . just like he wanted."

Tatum shot her eyes up to Jayde with a raised eyebrow and a heavy promise in her glare. This was her man they were talking about here.

"Yeah, well, for your sake, Jayde . . . you better hope so."

Sasha played with the phone in her hand but still hadn't made a decision if she was actually going to do anything with it. She had rushed out of the hospital, ready to meet Chauncey and not caring too much about the nurse or anything she had to tell her pertaining to Jayde. Her mind was already on a million other things.

She felt like she wanted to burst. She needed to talk to someone about her feelings regarding the Tatum and Chauncey situation. She still hadn't decided if she would, or how she would approach Chauncey with the information. She already wanted to talk to him about her other worries, about her feeling neglected, about how he had embarrassed her at the wedding and dis-respected her, but the kiss with Bleek put her on the defense.

Another thing eating at Sasha was that she genuinely missed her friend. In her heart she knew Tatum loved her and didn't have feelings for Chauncey, it was more of the secret that crushed her. She didn't know if they could ever be the same and that scared her.

Could she trust Tatum?

However, she felt kind of messed up carrying on a regular day-to-day norm with Chauncey, but basically cutting Tatum off. They hadn't spoken in weeks, not since the wedding. Her girl was pregnant, newly married, and from what she had heard from Chauncey, dealing with Ree turning himself in. Yet, Sasha still was sitting here debating reaching out. But on the contrary, she lay down night after night with Chauncey as if he had done nothing wrong. Wasn't he just as foul for keeping the secret?

Last, but certainly not least, Sasha couldn't get the whole situation with her mother, Mickel, and Jayde out of her mind. When did life become so complicated? Where did all of these secrets come from, and were they all better off when the secrets were buried?

"People always say they want the truth . . . but the

truth is shot to shit! Give me a damn lie and my old life back," Sasha mumbled as she heard the keys jingle in the door.

"Ah, check you out . . . let me find out you just hung up wit some nigga when you heard me coming," Chauncey joked as he stepped inside with a grocery bag and a bouquet of pink roses. Sasha knew he was trying to get in her good graces.

"Yup . . . told my sidepiece I'd have to call him back," she replied blasé, nestling the cordless back on the charger. Guess she wouldn't be calling Tatum this evening either.

"Ah, you a slick one, huh?"

"Learned from the best," Sasha quipped.

Chauncey ignored the comment and placed the bag down, then handed her the flowers.

"C'mon . . . truce, princess. I love you. I'm sorry . . ."

Sasha narrowed her eyes at him.

"Sorry for what?"

The question threw Chauncey off. He had to think. He was always used to being sorry but never remembering too much why.

"What . . . What you mean? For everything."

Sasha laughed and took the flowers.

"You don't even know." She started to walk away but he came up behind her, wrapping his arms around her and holding her close. Damn he felt so good and smelled so good, she wanted to stay mad at him but he made it hard.

"Hold on, hold on, hold on, baby . . . Of course, I know . . ." He brought his lips to her ear and spoke in his deep baritone. "I'm sorry for not being around more. I'm sorry for these nights I've been out in the streets . . . not being here with my family." He turned her around and looked at her sincerely, cupping her sweet face in his hands. "I'm sorry for forgetting the anniversary and the broken promises. And I'm sorry for the way I treated you at the wedding. I was dead wrong for that shit. I'm sorry for all that . . . I love you, kid."

Sasha looked into his eyes and saw all of that love too. She knew Chauncey had the fuck-up gene in him. But she knew he loved the shit out of her. She thought about Bleek and she instantly felt guilty.

"I love you, too," she whispered.

A slow smile crept on Chauncey's face as he hugged her tight and kissed her on the forehead.

"Let me grab the rest of these bags. I'm cooking up a lil sumthin' for my baby tonight," he said, winking. "Chef Boy-Ar-C . . ."

Sasha rolled her eyes playfully as she followed him out to the car. The sweet smell of the grass and the peacefulness of the neighborhood made Sasha smile slightly.

"What you making . . . chicken?"

"No, not *chicken*," Chauncey laughed, mimicking Sasha's Southern accent.

He opened up the doors and leaned down to get one of the bags off of the floor that had toppled over.

"Damn . . . Sash, get those cans over on that side." She walked around and bent over to grab the canned vegetables.

"You know . . . heating up cans ain't cooking, Chaunc," she joked. "Everything better not be in a ca . . ."

Her words trailed off as Chauncey gathered the things and began to make his way in the house. He turned as a result of the silence.

"Yo, Sash . . . you com—" The sight of Sasha standing there, holding the receipt with Lizette's number scribbled in pink marker, halted his words. "Yo, that ain't even . . ."

"That ain't even *what,* Chauncey? What is it then? 'Cause it looks like a bitch's number on a fucking grocery receipt! What the fuck do you have it for?"

Chauncey blew out air in annoyance.

"I tossed that shit on the floor, Sash. I ain't care about that shit."

"Then what the fuck do you have it for? That don't answer nothing! How did you get it?"

"She came up to the car bumping her gums and gave it to me! That bitch Lizette from Jersey down here . . . I saw her at Whole Foods and she followed me out—"

"Oh! How convenient! Lizette from Jersey just *happened* to bump into you? The same Lizette that always wanted to fuck you and can't stand my ass. Don't you get it, Chauncey? You be giving them bitches what they want! Why the fuck did you take her number if you don't want it!"

"I didn't take the shit, Sasha!" he screamed, getting angry. A few neighbors had started peeking their heads out. "She tossed the shit in the car."

"Then you should've tossed it back at her trifling ass!"

"Sasha . . . I'm not arguing out here about this. I didn't take that girl's fucking number. Now bring yo' ass in the house."

"Fuck you, Chauncey!"

"Daddy! Mommy!" Aubrey cried, standing at the doorway. She had obviously awakened from her nap and was now distraught at the sight of her parents fighting.

"Don't worry, baby. Daddy and Mommy coming. Go back inside," Chauncey tried to coax.

"No! Daddy's coming," Sasha spoke up. "Mommy's taking a little ride, and she'll be back!"

Chauncey had made the mistake of leaving the key to the car in the seat and that was all the opportunity Sasha needed. With everything that was already on her mind, this was the last straw . . . she needed to get away!

"Sasha," Chauncey half-chuckled, about to call her bluff. "C'mon, yo, you got on slippers and shit. Bring yo' ass in here."

Sasha didn't care if she was barefoot. She hopped in the driver's seat of the Aston Martin and started the car quickly.

Chauncey dropped the bags and started toward her, forcing Sasha to throw the car in reverse out of the driveway. Slamming on the gas she powered the car in full gear, smashing into the garbage cans hard.

"What the . . . yo, chill!" Chauncey yelled, throwing his hands on his head in despair. The Aston was his baby.

"Don't worry about where I'm going either!" Sasha shouted, making a sharp left and knocking over the mailbox on the curb. That was sure to leave a dent or at least scrape the paint.

"Sasha! What the fuck! Stop, yo! Please!"

Sasha laughed like a madwoman.

"*Stop yo! Please!* Look at you, crying like a little bitch. Why, Chauncey? 'Cause I'm hurting your car? Abusing it? Treating it like shit? Now you know how it feels!" Sasha pedaled the gas hard just as Chauncey was reaching her at top speed. Angry she was, but stupid she was not. She knew he was pissed.

"Don't wait up, princess!" she shouted as she sped down the street, waving her ringless left hand. As hurt as she was, it felt damn good.

Boom! Boom! Boom!
"What the . . ."
Boom! Boom! Boom! Boom! Boom!

Bleek placed the weight bar on the bench and sat up. Someone was banging on his door like the fucking Feds.

He tried to think . . . quickly. He had nothing there, no weed, no nothing in case it was the police.

Boom! Boom! Boom!

Bleek slipped to the door quietly more than curious about his visitor. Few knew about this apartment, not even his baby mother. Just Ree, Jayde, Chauncey, and . . .

". . . Wow." He pulled the door open after looking through the peephole.

"Can I come in?" Sasha's nose was red, her face was wet, and she looked like a fine-ass Bambi, even if she had on fluffy pink slippers with her blue sundress.

"Uh . . . yeah." Bleek stepped aside and let her pass. The space was small so the motion had them close, which built the already palpable tension. Sasha tried not to focus on his exposed abs and his slim yet muscular frame. He was shirtless, with basketball shorts that hung loose just under his deep V. A doo-rag adorned his usual low cut.

"Working out?" Sasha asked casually.

"Trying to . . . til you started banging on the door like the damn boys. What's good witcha tho', shawty? You straight?"

Bleek knew she wasn't, but in a way he was glad. It was what had gotten her here. He closed the door and motioned for her to have a seat on the couch.

Sasha took a deep breath and walked over to the sofa. For a bachelor pad, the loft-style apartment was pretty neat. It wasn't huge, but it had all of the necessary amenities—flat-screen TV, stereo, weights, couch, and big-ass bed. She took a seat.

"Yeah . . . I'm fine. I just needed . . . I needed to get away for a minute. And I remember you let me come here before," she said, smiling lightly. "Plus . . . we needed to talk anyway."

Bleek remembered the time a few months ago when she and Chauncey had an argument. He told her she could chill at his extra spot and relax until she was cool to go back. He had no hidden intention then, but he figured that it was still obvious he had cared about her feelings in some way.

"What if I had . . . company?" He smirked at her with his baby face. *Those dimples.* Sasha rolled her eyes.

"I didn't see her car." Jayde's car was the first thing she had looked for when she pulled up. "And I wasn't worried about your other numerous dust bunnies. Look, if it's a bad time . . ." She started to get up.

"Nah . . . I'm glad you came. Relax." He grabbed her by the arm and pulled her back down. "You want something to drink?"

"No, I don't want Heineken or tap water. No thanks," she cracked.

"You sooo bougie," he chuckled. "I got wine. What? I can't have wine?"

"You cannn," Sasha said, pursing her lips. "But why would you?"

Bleek stood up and smirked.

"For those numerous dust bunnies you speak of," he replied, winking. He turned to walk away and Sasha sucked her teeth.

"Them bitches do not drink wine," she mumbled. "Hey! I don't want no boxed wine!" she shouted. She could hear him laugh in the distance.

When he returned with a glass of Merlot, Sasha smiled.

"Thanks." Bleek took a seat next to her on the couch at a respectful distance and propped his arm up on the cushions behind her.

"Wanna talk about it?"

"Nope."

"Good," he shot back. "'Cause I *don't* wanna hear about it."

Sasha punched him playfully and he laughed. She shrugged.

"Regular Chauncey. Found some bitch's number in his car."

Bleek shrugged.

"Probably wasn't shit. C ain't that dumb . . . Don't nobody write down numbers no more anyway," he quipped. Even though he wanted her, he wasn't a hater. And he really ain't have shit against Chaunc. He actually liked him. He just liked Sasha more.

"Yeah well, I'm still sick of it. I'm sick of the fuck-ups. After all that he put me through, he needs to be a fucking saint from now on," she spat seriously.

"Yeah, but that's impossible. Shit gonna get rocky sometime, shawty," Bleek told her with a slight laugh. "And if you forgive somebody, then you can't hold on to the old shit and pile it on top of the new shit. That's fucked up."

Sasha squinted at him.

"And whose side are you on?" she asked with attitude.

He sat up, took the glass out of her hand, and sat it on the table.

"My side." Leaning in, he kissed her lips softly and Sasha's body creamed.

"Bleek," she spoke softly, pulling back. "I shouldn't be here . . . This ain't even what I came here for."

"Then what you come here for?" he asked her seriously. Sasha thought of Chauncey and then she thought of him smiling up in Lizette's face as she gave him her number. She leaned in and kissed Bleek this time by her own will. This time she let him taste her tongue.

"I parked the car down the street . . . don't worry," she felt the need to say.

He grabbed the back of her head and kissed her deeply once more, then brought his lips to her cheek and kissed it up to her ear, where he rested and ran his tongue along it.

"I'm glad you volunteered that information . . . but I'm not worried."

He moved his body in front of hers, pushing her back against his couch pillows as he groped her body. Chauncey was a great lover, he was always in control, but Bleek made Sasha feel so sexy, like he couldn't wait to get her clothes off, like she was giving him an opportunity of a lifetime. Maybe it was his youth.

"Damn, Sasha. You smell good as hell," he mumbled, licking and sucking on her neck. Sasha had been fresh out of the tub when Chauncey had come home, and she knew he smelled her signature Rice Flower and Shea–scented skin.

"Bleek," she cried as he maneuvered his fingers up her inner thigh and toward her panties. He used his other hand to pull the top of her dress down as he began to suck and nibble on her breasts.

"Damn this pussy so wet and hot, Sasha. I just wanna suck on yo' shit all night. You gonna let me?" he asked her through mouthfuls of her titties. Sasha closed her eyes as he fingered her clit and waited for her answer like a true gentleman. He liked that shit talking, and Sasha already felt guilty, but not guilty enough to stop. But telling him to do some shit was way worse than just letting him do some shit.

"Um . . ." That's all she could give him. Bleek slid down to his knees and pushed the table back a little. Then he sat her legs up on his shoulders and slowly lifted her panties off.

Sasha didn't protest, she was completely silent.

"I'ma show you what I can make this pussy do." He said the words so sensual, Sasha let out a gasp. Bleek kept his eyes on hers as he dove in and wrapped his thick lips around her jewel.

"Oh!" Sasha cried out as he gently slurped on her pearl, then moved his wide tongue in slow circles, embarking her on a one-way trip to ecstasy.

"Bleek," she called as he steadied his pace, lapping at her like she was on a plate. Bleek spread her wider and went lower, tickling her rear hole with the tip of his tongue.

"Ohhh shittt," she called out as he began to alternate. He found his rhythm as he went back and forth, front to back, licking her ass and sucking on her clit. He had Sasha grinding on his face. The young boy definitely knew what he was doing; she remembered Jayde bragging on how he'd eaten her until she had passed out. Sasha couldn't believe it. Her pussy was jumping in his mouth like Pop Rocks. Three minutes in and she was already . . .

"Cumminggg. . . . Ooooh Bleekkkk, I'm cummmminggggggggg . . ."

"Well come the fuck on . . . gimme that nut," he barked as he continued to slurp. Sasha jerked her body up like she was having convulsions as she pumped his face with a vengeance. She couldn't believe she was doing this, but just like a dude letting a girl get his shit off, she felt no guilt at that moment.

"Fuck! Oohhhh eatttt itttt . . . oooh suckkkk ittttt! Ohhh Bleeekkkkk!"

Sasha's legs shook violently and her orgasm roared through her entire body. She curled her toes so hard that her foot caught an instant cramp. Bleek could really eat some pussy.

"Ah!" she screamed.

He stood up with a wicked grin and a dick pointing straight out through his basketball shorts.

"I told you I was gonna show you what that pussy could do. Now I'ma show you what this dick can do too."

Sasha trembled and ran her hands over his cut-up body. Was she ready for this?

"Bleek . . . I don't know . . ."

"Ssshhh . . ." he told her smoothly as he silenced her with a kiss, letting her taste herself. "Why you acting like it's our first time?"

Chapter 9

*"It was the thrill that kept you . . . the allure of the game.
You were a gangster like myself because you were good at it.
Now that you aren't . . . you don't know what else to be."*

—Leroy Knights, *Still Thicker than Water*

Two weeks later

"Did I, or did I not tell you! Oh my God! Did you see
those punk-ass prosecutors' faces when the judge said
it?" Jayde screamed, lifting the bottle of champagne
straight to her lips with a cocky laugh.

"Case dismissed!" Johnny repeated, mocking the
white judge's tone.

Tatum smiled and just shook her head in disbelief.
All had gone exactly how they said. But she still couldn't
celebrate . . . wouldn't celebrate . . . until he was home.

True to her word, Jayde had gotten the right judge
on the case. And the prosecutors had huffed and
puffed, scrambled and scattered trying to piece together any type of case when the judge moved for a
speedy hearing. When they didn't have evidence,

Johnny moved for an immediate dismissal. And it worked!

"Ssh! Ssh! Ssshh! It's on!" Jayde hushed everyone. Tatum looked at her side-eyed; Jayde was acting as if Ree was *her* man. They all turned to the television where anchorwoman Blake Gibson was giving the latest.

"Well, today's hearing of alleged mega gangster Sean Knights, also known as Respect, ended rather quickly and for some, unexpectedly. Knights was cleared on all charges of drug trafficking, racketeering, and conspiracy, all due to insufficient evidence on the prosecutor's part. Jamaican-born Knights was warranted back in 2007 but then proclaimed a fugitive when authorities could not locate him. However, Knights's attorney, well-known self-proclaimed big shot Johnny Carson simply stated today that Knights was not in hiding, nor running, just on vacation and 'laying low.' I'm not too sure what that means, but what I do know is that he is now . . . innocent, as Judge Sparks quoted, and free to live his life. Judge Sparks also warned prosecutors to tread a thin line being that there is talk the warrant that was used to raid Knights's West Orange, New Jersey, home years ago, was not signed until *after* the search took place. He said everything but the word *countersuit*, which I am sure will keep authorities from *harassing* Knights anymore, as Sparks also quoted. *How* exactly that would be, not to mention why the hearing took place here in Atlanta and not in New Jersey where Knights's warrant was originally produced, are some of the major questions surrounding this case. Questions that I guess will probably not be answered . . ."

"What the hell is a mega gangster?" Johnny asked as he let out a chuckle.

"Respect . . . is a muthafuckin' mega gangsta!" Jayde boasted, as she flicked off the television and laughed.

"I mean, did you see that circus? Those cameras? They ate him up. And he handled it so well. It was just . . . perfect."

Tatum could've sworn she saw stars in Jayde's eyes.

"We should celebrate! Let's go out to dinner! Take Ree out when he gets home tonight," Jayde suggested excitedly. Tatum sighed and stood up, walking over to the dining room table and thumbing through the mail.

"Um . . . no. I . . . I really don't feel like going out. I'd rather cook a nice dinner."

"That sounds perfect! When do you want to make it, like eightish? We can cook his favorites."

Tatum crinkled her brow at Jayde.

"His *favorites*? How do you . . . Look, Jayde," Tatum chuckled. "Just . . . just let me handle that." She wanted to also say that she'd rather the dinner be for just them two. But Johnny was already rubbing his hands together and they *had* been responsible for concocting the whole plan that led to his freedom.

Jayde smirked.

"No problem."

"Eight sounds perfect," Johnny interrupted. "That way I can go home, shower, change, go over the last of the paperwork, and get back here to celebrate." He shot Tatum a wink. She wasn't quite sure why.

"What time should I go and get him?" Tatum asked.

"He should be released between six and seven P.M." Johnny knew all the details.

"I can go and get him while you cook," Jayde volunteered.

"I can cook before then and still go and get him," Tatum told her. "Don't worry, Jayde. You've done enough." Tatum smiled her bright plastered smile and turned back to her mail. Jayde didn't know, but Tatum didn't play certain shit.

"Gotcha, Pocahontas."

"Okay . . . well. I'll see you ladies tonight. Oh and um . . ." Johnny turned around and smiled at them. "Victory is ours."

Jayde smiled back at him but Tatum just continued to concentrate on her task. She didn't care about victory. She just wanted him home.

"Yo, Sash!" She heard her name being called.

"I'm in the shower!" she shouted back over the noise of the running water.

"Ay yo, Sash!"

Sasha sighed deep, reaching down and twisting the knobs of the central-headed shower stall. Her quiet time had come to an end.

"Chauncey! I said I was in the shower!"

She stepped out and reached for her towel but it was nowhere in sight.

"Did I leave it in the room?"

Sasha let out a huff of air, mad as hell. She hated running across a floor with wet feet. She also hated when she had to open up the bathroom door fresh out of the shower and not dry. She knew the air would be on. She knew the gust of freezing air was waiting for her on the other side.

"Ay yo, Sasha! Come here!"

"Ughhh!" Sasha huffed, bracing herself and snatching the door open.

"Chauncey! Wait, dammit! I'm not dresseddd!"

Sasha screamed the words as she jogged from the master bath to her bed butt naked and soaking wet.

"Hurry up, come here!" Chauncey yelled again.

Sasha spotted her towel and snatched it up with much attitude.

"If he don't shut the fuck uppp," she mumbled through gritted teeth as she flung the towel around her and sent something falling to the ground. Déjà vu overtook her completely.

"I said hurry up," Chauncey said again. But this time, he was closer, really close, and his voice was low.

Sasha kneeled down slowly, her shaky breath coming in short gasps.

He had done it again. A black velvet box lay opened on the ground, the glare from a ten-karat princess-cut diamond hypnotizing her before she could even pick it up.

"Oh my God . . . Chauncey . . ."

"So . . . how 'bout it?" he asked her. It was the same words he had said when he proposed to her the first time, and he had pulled it off in the same manner. That meant something to her.

But that time, when he had proposed years ago, Sasha was perfect, and he was perfect, they were perfect. It was before everything. Now, they were both flawed.

An image of Bleek fucking her doggy-style on his couch popped in her head as she answered.

"Yes . . . Of-of course, Chauncey."

Her eyes were filled with tears. She seemed a bit sad. *But maybe she's just mad emotional,* Chauncey figured. Women were funny like that. But the first time . . . the first time she was jumping up and down.

She picked up the ring and slipped it out of the box, brought it to him, and held her hand out.

"Put it on me," she said, smiling lightly, looking at him with teary eyes.

"No doubt . . . this the only thing you want me to put on you?" He grinned as he slipped the ring on her finger.

Sasha chuckled, but showed no more reaction to

his innuendo as she looked away. Chauncey noted it but didn't push.

"I love you, princess . . . always have . . . always will . . ."

Sasha matched his intense stare after he spoke the words.

"I know . . . I love you, too."

This time was different.

"Tay . . . I got kinda bad news."

Tatum glanced at the clock on the wall and the time read 5:46 P.M. She was on her way out to pick Ree up and the call had stopped her dead in her tracks. She dreaded whatever Jayde was about to say to her.

"What . . . what is it? I'm on my way to pick up Ree."

"Yeah, well . . . about that . . ." Tatum could tell Jayde was driving, and she was talking loud over her music. "Just spoke with the prison . . . they not releasing him til the morning."

"What!" Tatum snapped, pissed, hurt, and devastated at the same time.

"Yeah . . . I know, love. These jails are the worst! But they promise, first thing in the morning. Eight A.M. sharp!"

Tatum sucked her teeth and blew out air. Long days and cold nights without her man, it had been torture. She didn't even have her best friend to comfort her or to talk to. All she had was a few short conversations with Crush when he called or stopped by. He was like her only friend at the moment. Tatum couldn't consider Jayde a friend.

She missed Ree terribly. She had cooked his favorite dish, her oxtails, and she had dressed in a new dress, a smoke-colored number with a bustier top that sat her melons up like they were on display at a farmers' market. The back also accentuated her ample behind and distinguished hips. Her hair was loose and wavy, the way he liked, and she was wearing his favorite Escada scent. She had gone all out in her excitement.

"Shit!" Tatum couldn't help but spit out. "I cooked this dinner. I got my hopes up . . . I didn't want to sleep alone again," she found herself speaking her thoughts aloud.

"I'm sorry, sweetie."

Before Jayde apologized, Tatum had forgotten she was on the phone. They ended the call with little conversation and Tatum stepped out of her stilettos and took a seat at her dining room table with a sorrowful look on her face.

"Don't worry," she whispered, placing her hand on her stomach and her head on the table. "I know it sucks. But daddy will be home tomorrow."

Seven fifty-eight P.M.

The doorbell to the condo sounded twice in a row.

Ding. Dong . . . Ding. Dong . . .

Tatum lifted her head, the imprint of her arm making slight lines on her face. She had fallen asleep.

Ding. Dong . . . Ding. Dong . . .

Standing up slowly, Tatum made her way through the large dining area, to the living room and toward the door.

"Who is it?"

Ding. Dong . . .

"I said who is it?" Tatum snapped, with a little more annoyance. She peeked through the peephole and then let out a sigh. *Should I open it?*

She cracked the door and stood in the space.

"He's not coming home tonight . . . didn't Jayde tell you?"

Her eyes were heavy, still being tempted by the sleep she had recently departed from. She was anxious to peel off her dress, wash off her makeup, and climb into bed.

"No!" Johnny gasped, sounding surprised. "Are you serious? She didn't tell me."

Tatum folded her arms across her chest.

"Yeah . . . they're gonna release him in the morning. So . . . party's over."

"Damn." Johnny shook his head. He was dressed leisurely, in tan slacks and a cream short-sleeved polo shirt. "So party's over?"

His smirk would have been charming had it not repulsed Tatum slightly.

"It is . . . good night."

She went to close the door.

"Wait!" he yelled out, sticking his foot in the space slightly. Tatum arched an eyebrow at him and he chuckled.

"No . . . look . . . I was just gonna ask if I could go to the bathroom. I been holding it since the exit," he said, grinning. "Pretty please," he added, pressing his hands together.

Tatum rolled her eyes and had an inner debate, a quick one being that he was waiting on her answer. The bathroom was right through the kitchen, really was no harm although she'd be wrong if she said she felt entirely comfortable.

"All right, whatever . . . just make it quick."

"I should call Tatum . . . let her know I'm on the way—"

"No!" Jayde yelled out, glancing from the road quickly

and wrapping her hand around his, which was holding his cell.

"You should . . . surprise her," Jayde said, smiling sweetly at him. "She thinks you're not coming home until tomorrow. You coming home tonight to put her to bed will be a present in itself," Jayde said, winking.

Ree cut his eyes from her to the passenger window, not taking any of her snide comments seriously. Ree was no dummy, he knew Jayde had a thing for him. He figured it had no real merit though, just another notch on her belt.

"Why would she think I'm not coming home until tomorrow?"

"Because that's what the jail said earlier," Jayde lied.

Ree thought about it and reasoned that was why Jayde had been there to pick him up instead of his wife.

"I'm telling you . . . she's gonna flip when she sees you," Jayde assured, licking her thick lips and flooring the gas.

"Yeah . . . a'ight."

Ree ran his hand over his face and leaned back. He didn't give a fuck about nothing Jayde was talking. He was just ready to see his wife.

"So you like living here? In Atlanta?"

Tatum stood against the counter, her arms crossed and covering her cleavage. Johnny had emerged from the bathroom, drying his hands on a small towel and started a conversation. A conversation Tatum was not interested in.

She wanted to tell him that the idea of living in Atlanta was all fun when she and her bestie were on good terms. But now, it was purposeless.

"It's fine."

Johnny grinned and nodded slightly.

"What about Respect? He likes it . . . ? Or he likes what you like . . . ?"

Tatum rolled her eyes subtly.

"Look, Johnny . . . not to be rude or anything. But . . . it's late. And I'm tired." She wanted to say that she was pregnant, but it was none of his business.

"I understand . . . my apologies." He started out of the kitchen and Tatum followed to walk him out. When she was close behind him, he turned around and smiled a white, charming smile at her. His dark eyes sparkled at her beauty and his handsome features hid his desire and intentions.

"You know . . . just for the record, Tatum. If I was Respect, I'd like whatever you liked as well. You are a truly . . . beautiful and amazing woman . . . I wish I had a chance with you."

His words caught Tatum off guard but the last thing she wanted was to reveal her nervousness and give him the upper hand.

"Look . . . Johnn—"

"No . . . wait . . ." He leaned in to her. "I'm not . . . I'm not trying to disrespect you in any way . . . it's just . . ."

"Johnny, you need to go."

"Tatum . . . listen . . . Just hear me out. You're special. And to be honest, this whole gangster's-wife lifestyle isn't for a woman like you. You're better than this." His voice was smooth, dripping charm, but it was giving Tatum the creeps. A chill crept up her spine.

"Johnny, you need to get the fuck out of my house!" Tatum had been calm, but Newark, New Jersey, had just emerged from her.

He grinned at her and then took a step, closing the space between them.

"Do I?" he asked, leaning down so close that she

could smell his Gucci cologne and Scotch on his breath. Maybe he had a drink before he arrived, Tatum didn't know and didn't care. "Goddamn, Tatum, that's what I'm talking about. I love your spunk," he cooed, towering over her and backing her up to the wall. "You're so fucking sexy."

"Johnny, if I gotta tell yo ass one more time!" Tatum pushed her hands into his chest with anger and she briefly had thought of Crush saying to call him if she needed him. She wished the phone wasn't on the other side of the living room. Because she needed him.

Johnny grabbed her wrists, restraining them as he chuckled at her.

"You feisty, huh? I like that."

Tatum's heart began to pound out of her chest and a cold sweat broke on her forehead. She looked into his eyes and wasn't sure if he would take it there. Was he just not getting it or did he not care? Either way, she had enough.

All right, nigga, c'mon. I got something for you. Tatum was ready to knee him in the nuts and reach the bookstand that held one of the many guns in the condo.

Johnny felt her body relax and he leaned down again.

"That's right, baby. I know you been lonely. Let me keep you company tonight . . ." Tatum was just ready to bring her knee up and make contact, when . . .

"Yo, what the fuck is going on?"

A sigh escaped Tatum's lips. There was an instant feeling of safety. She didn't have to be scared or worried or do anything, because he was here. He would protect her. Johnny took a step back and she looked around him and laid eyes on her man and she felt happy. Happy that he was home. But then she saw the darkness in his eyes. Something she was unfamiliar with. Not even when he had pistol-whipped her ex, Ty, or held a gun to her brother's head had she seen this look. It was a look . . . of death. And it scared her.

"Heyyy, Respect . . . you made it, man!" Johnny tried to state, masking his nervousness, as if he were thrilled. As if being this close to Tatum in their home at this time of night was normal. He quickly took a few steps away from Tatum. "How about that trial, brother? I told you everything would go smooth. Good to see you. We weren't expecting you til the morning."

Ree stood there, indecipherable and intimidating. He placed a calm stare on Johnny. There was no emotion on his face, not even in his body language. Ree shifted his gaze from Johnny to Tatum, who stood and now seemed nervous, scared. Ree tried to rationalize in his mind and submerge any emotions that tried to consume him—anger being the most dominant, rage, in fact.

"Is that right?" he finally responded as he walked over to a nearby bookshelf. "You weren't expecting me, Johnny? What about my wife? Come here. Come over to me, Tatum . . . where you belong," he demanded to her seriously.

Tatum swallowed hard, a knot in her stomach from the whole situation. Besides the fact that she was still shaken up by Johnny's harassment, she had never seen a murder. And she didn't want to start tonight. But she could feel it in the air. She was terrified. Someone may very well die tonight, if she didn't prevent it.

"Hey, baby . . ." she spoke as she began to walk, trying to play it off. "I thought . . . I thought you weren't coming until the morning. I mean, at first . . . I thought you were . . . tonight. That's why you know. . . . I cooked . . . and this . . ." She motioned her hands over her tight dress and appearance trying to mask her anxiety. Ree could see she was visibly shaken up. "But then, *Jayde* said . . ." Tatum shifted her eyes to Jayde quickly and cut them before bringing them back to Ree. ". . . that you weren't. I'm so glad you're here," she said wearily, fighting tears. "I'm glad you're home."

She wouldn't say that she was scared of Ree at that moment, but she was scared of his potential. Tatum wanted to tell him she was glad that he had stopped Johnny from possibly taking things too far, but she knew he'd kill him, no questions asked. She didn't know if she wanted to be responsible for that.

"And everything's okay?" he asked her seriously, as if they were the only two people in the room. Tatum finally looked him in the eyes and they held long eye contact, Ree searching for the truth and Tatum trying to hide it. She sighed, just wanting to cut the intensity, take him and go to bed, and never see Johnny again and stop anyone and everyone from getting hurt from the potential rage of Ree. Johnny was a jerk, but Tatum didn't want anyone dead.

"Yeah," she lied. "Everything's fine . . . I'm straight."

Ree stared at her long and hard, once again unreadable. Tatum tilted her head to the side and forced a tired smile. Her heart was racing though. What the fuck was happening? And why hadn't Jayde told her that she was going to get him and they were going to let him come home?

Johnny used the opportunity of the moment between the couple to try his escape. He was seconds away from shitting on himself and he just wanted to make it past Jayde who stood statuesque by the door.

"I'm just gonna head—"

"Mothafucka give me one reason why I shouldn't shoot your fucking head off, you needle-dick, pussy-ass, square mothafucka," Ree hissed, now aiming a chrome

Magnum .45 at Johnny with precision. No one but Tatum knew where the gun had come from. And when he had walked over to the bookshelf, she knew why he was going there. That was why she was so nervous and trying to diffuse the situation. She knew he would kill Johnny for sure. She realized now she couldn't lie to Ree, he saw right through her and it made it worse.

"Ree . . . please . . ." Tatum begged with tears in her eyes. He had just escaped the law, she was in no rush for him to go back, and this time it would be forever. Especially if he killed big shot Johnny Carson. "*Please,* baby . . ."

Johnny's heart caught in his throat and his whole body went numb. The only thing that brought him back to the moment was the feeling of his warm piss running down his right leg, soiling his khakis.

"R-Respect. Th-th-think a-about this, man. L-l-let's just calm down . . . T-T-Tatum. Tell him! I-I didn't do anything. She was upset. I-I was just t-t-telling her you'd be home s-s-soon. Not to worry. That's all, Respect. I-I swear."

Tatum thought the nigga was auditioning for a script by the way he was putting on the acting performance. Did he convince himself that bullshit is the truth? she wondered.

"That's true, Tatum?" Ree asked, sounding like he was already unconvinced, never taking his eyes or gun off Johnny. "Tell me if that's true."

Tatum looked back and forth between Johnny and Ree. *Lie or murder? Lie or murder?*

"Y-yeah . . ."

"You're lying," Ree dismissed, cocking the loaded weapon. "You're fucking lying. You were trying my wife, mothafucka? *My* wife . . . ?"

Johnny shook his head from side to side, tears pooling in his eyes in fear.

"Respect, please," Jayde finally intervened, after having enjoyed the drama from the sidelines. "Think about what we're doing. It's not worth it. We gotta stick to the plan."

She walked toward him.

"Stay the fuck over there, Jayde," Ree barked.

"No," she spat. "Don't be dumb." She got close to him. Close to where only he and Tatum could hear her, but Ree's glare and steady aim was on Johnny, his finger on the trigger.

"Not here . . . this is messy," she whispered lowly. "I'm sure someone probably knows where he is and you just came home. Think about what we're doing," she reminded him as she reached up and wrapped her hand around the gun. "It's not worth it."

Jayde held her grip on Ree's hand and the weapon and Tatum's chest heaved in nervousness for whether Ree would pull the trigger, and also in anger for Jayde being the one coaxing him. Jayde's whisper sounded like the art of seduction to Tatum and she wanted to snatch the gun from Ree's hand and knock Jayde across the jaw with it.

No matter how upset Tatum was, though, she was happy when Ree suddenly brought his arm down and tucked the gun in his waist.

"Fuck outta my house you pussy-clot, bitch-ass nigga," he demanded. Johnny wasted no time tripping over his feet to the door.

"Yo, Johnny," Ree called out coolly. The bass in his voice caused Johnny to turn around for some reason. Ree stared at him for a while, no words spoken. And then he smirked.

"I'll be seeing you."

A chill went up Johnny's spine but he quickly turned to exit. He didn't even close the door behind him, he just scurried his pissy self out, all of that smoothness vanishing.

"I'm sorry, Tatum," Jayde apologized solemnly after Johnny was well gone. "After I spoke to you, the jail called me back and said they made a mistake. I figured we'd surprise you. Guess it was a bad idea," she chuckled. "I'm . . . I'm sorry," she repeated with a shrug.

Tatum was infuriated at the apology.

"Why are you sorry? I'm not. I didn't do anything *wrong*, Jayde." Tatum felt like that was her implication. "He had to use the bathroom, I let him in, I was walking him out, and you two came in." She caught Ree's cold glare at her when she said that and she turned her head to him. Her eyes looked into his face, hoping, and almost daring him not to believe her. But she couldn't read him.

"And why wouldn't you tell me that my husband was coming home after you knew what I was planning. And you *knew* I wanted to go get him?"

Tatum was heated.

"Like I said . . . I wanted to surprise you," Jayde reiterated, not backing down.

"You still should've told me."

"Why?" Ree asked calmly, interrupting the spat. Tatum looked over at him in disbelief. Her mouth slightly agape at first then pressed tightly into a frown. They stared at each other, Tatum wearing her emotions on her sleeve, Ree not wearing any at all. Jayde chuckled.

"I mean . . . that's what I was about to s—"

"See yourself out, Jayde," Ree ordered with his eyes on Tatum, cutting Jayde off. Tatum shot her eyes to her, not too happy that he had done so. She wanted her to finish that statement, so she could punch her in the fucking mouth.

Jayde smirked.

"Sure. We just need to talk quickly about the trip—"

"Get. Out. Jayde." She looked at Ree and saw that he was serious this time, so she started for the door.

"Fine. Good night."

Remembering one last thing, she went to turn and speak, but this time Tatum was right there.

"*S'il vous plaît partir,* Jayde . . ." Tatum spoke, asking her to please leave. "I know you speak French and all . . . just in case you didn't catch him in *English.*"

Jayde tittered, remembering bragging to Tatum how she spoke French and Spanish fluently. The little bitch thought she was cute.

"Of course, mademoiselle," Jayde smiled. "You know, your dinner smells amazing, Tatum. So sorry it was ruined."

With that Jayde turned and headed out. This time she closed the door behind her and the couple was left alone.

After a few moments of silence, Tatum sighed and ran her hands through her hair. She closed her eyes and wanted when she opened them for none of this bull-shit to have happened. But when she opened them, she saw Ree starting for the stairs.

"Where are you going?" she asked him, breaking the silence with her brashness.

Ree halted but didn't turn around.

"Shower. Bed." He was so blasé. He started walking again and Tatum dropped her jaw.

"*Excuse me?* You're not even gonna eat dinner? We're not . . . we're not even gonna talk about any of this?"

"Talk about what?" he asked seriously, placing his hands in his pockets, turning and looking at her. "I asked you if everything was okay, and you lied. I asked you if what he said was true, and you lied. So what are we gonna talk about, Tatum? *Why* you lied?

Why you felt the need to protect that faggot-ass lawyer. So you can lie again."

Tatum crinkled her brow at him in disbelief.

"Are you serious? Do you think I'm interested in him . . . ? You think I would do some shit like that to you? In our home! You must be crazy."

Ree stared at her and chuckled at her animation.

"Nah . . . I don't think that. But I also never thought you would lie to me. And that shit ain't really sitting right wit me. So no. I don't want your dinner. And I don't want to talk."

Tatum was hurt and Ree was livid. Deep down he understood why Tatum had tried to downplay the situation, but her ability to lie to his face, and also just the thought of someone trying to touch her, infuriated him beyond recognition. Ree was still getting familiar with letting someone control a huge part of him, and the love he had for Tatum allowed her that leisure, and allowed him that vulnerability. He turned to walk away again; this time she let him.

All those days and nights without her man and Tatum hadn't imagined this type of homecoming.

She sucked her teeth and sat down at the dining room table, blowing out air in frustration.

I should've just told Ree the asshole was trying to fuck and let him kill his dumb ass, she thought. *Nah, and then see my man locked up for murder over that dumb shit . . . it ain't worth it. Maybe I should just go apologize,* Tatum thought. *No . . . that would look guilty, like I did something wrong. And I didn't. He's tripping! I'll just let him sleep it off.*

Tatum placed her face in her hands. This whole situation was stressful as hell. And who did she need at a time like this . . . her best friend. Sasha would know what to do, and it would probably be to go upstairs and talk to her man. Sasha was always way less stubborn than

Tatum. Tears came to Tatum's eyes thinking of the situation with her and Sasha right now. She missed her terribly. Although she was upset at Sasha for bringing the issue up on her wedding day, she felt terrible about what she had done and the secret she had kept. She needed to tell Sasha a million times over how sorry she was and how little it meant to her. She knew they were thicker than this and they could get through it. She decided to give her a call.

Ree lay back on top of the bedspread staring off deep in thought. He had executed the greatest amount of self-control and he was wondering if it was the right thing to do. Because all he could think about was blasting Johnny Carson's head off and he wondered how long the visions would play in his mind. He wasn't sure exactly what had happened, but he just knew whatever it was, he didn't like it. The nigga shouldn't have been in his house, period, especially with Tatum alone. And then all up close to her, and her wearing that little-ass dress, nah. The scene replaying caused the veins in Ree's temples to pulsate. The vibrating of a text coming through on his cell kept him from thinking too much more on it and doing something stupid.

"Who the fuck . . ." Ree reached over and unlocked his touch screen. He clicked on the MESSAGE icon, recognizing it was coming from Jayde. He figured it was something about the trip.

Human nature, natural male instincts, whatever one would blame the next ten or so seconds on, caused Ree to stare at his phone. After that, judgment kicked in and Ree deleted the message. Already upset, Jayde was now pushing him over the edge. Just when he was about to call and curse her dumb ass out, he saw an incoming call from her number. Perfect, she'd made it easier for him.

"Yo—"

"Oh my God! Ree, I'm sooo sorry!" she started. "That was . . . that was for someone else," Jayde lied. "I must've sent it to you by accident. Soon as I hit SEND I saw your name, and it was too fucking late! Oh my God, this is *so* fucking embarrassing. Please tell me you didn't see much . . . ? Please!"

Jayde was smiling wide on the other end, thinking of the full frontal naked picture she had just sent to him, knowing he and Tatum were in a time of distress and he was a week-plus off of sex.

Ree took a deep breath having a feeling Jayde was full of shit. She was another one. He was ready to do this business and cut his ties with this bitch. She wasn't cut from the same cloth as her father. He knew how to deal with a bitch like her in the meantime though.

"Nah . . . I don't even know what you talking about. But I'll delete whatever you sent. I won't even open it."

With that he clicked on her. No good-bye. No nothing. She was a real calculating chick. At that moment, Ree was happy he had someone more genuine . . . like Tatum. Although it was a sight many niggas would appreciate, Ree pushed the picture of Jayde out of his mind. He stood up and made his way out of the room.

Tatum was at the stove wrapping up the food. Sasha hadn't answered her call or the one after it, and as much as she wasn't sure what would face her when she went upstairs, she just wanted to curl up next to her husband and go to bed.

Just as she was opening the fridge, she heard a throat clear behind her.

"Damn . . . and I was just about to make me a plate."

Tatum kept her back turned and tried to fight the smile that grew on her face.

"Well . . . I didn't put it away yet. So . . ." Tatum closed the fridge and before she spun around, she lost the grin and slid the pan back onto the stove. "You can put it away after you eat."

She started toward the doorway, trying her best not to look at him, but that didn't work. She knew it wouldn't. Ree grabbed her arm and brought her to him. He walked over to the table, sat down, and pulled her onto his lap.

"Let's talk, Miss Lady."

"Why? Because now you want to?" Tatum asked seriously with an arched eyebrow.

"No . . . because *you* want to."

"Like you said . . . *nothing to talk about.*" Tatum tried to remain stone-faced, but it was hard. Ree looked her in her eyes.

"I'm sorry. I was upset. I don't like when you lie."

Tatum shook her head and her eyes became a little watery thinking of the whole ordeal.

"It's not that I *lied*, Ree. I just . . . I just didn't want you to get in trouble."

"So something did happen?" he asked calmly, although his insides were on fire. He could feel his adrenaline coming alive.

Tatum looked down thinking about it. Johnny was gone now, and if he were smart he'd stay far away from Ree. But she still didn't want Ree to react crazy. She also didn't want to lie to her man.

"You promise you won't hurt anyone and get into any trouble, Ree?"

"I promise I won't get into trouble," he repeated the

last part of the statement, trying to keep his tone even. "What happened?"

Tatum sighed and blinked back tears.

"The truth," he added with a stern gaze.

Tatum swallowed hard.

"Well, I told him you weren't coming home tonight when he came for the dinner. And then he asked to use the bathroom. After that, he started trying to talk but . . . I told him I was tired and to leave. But . . . he kept talking . . ."

"Talking about what?" he asked sharply.

"About me . . . and you. About you know . . . I deserve this and he wish he had a chance and all this dumb shit. I don't know . . . I think he was a lil drunk, Ree," Tatum added quickly when she felt his body tense up. Ree tried to control his temper as he took a deep breath.

"Okay. And then what happened?"

Tatum picked up one of his dreads nervously and began twirling it around her finger as she talked.

"Ree . . . does it really matter?"

The stern look he gave her answered her question, so she continued.

"Well . . . I told him to leave. I told him to get the fuck out. Then you came in." Tatum told the truth, but also left out a lot. She didn't want to say she was scared he was going to rape her.

"That's not all. What else . . ." Ree was telling her, not asking.

"What do you mean?"

"Why was he all in your face and shit, holding your arms?"

Damn, Tatum thought. *This nigga don't miss a beat.*

"I tried to push him and he grabbed my wrists. But Ree, seriously. I had it under control. He was leaving. He was going to leave." Tatum thought of how she was moments from kneeing him in the nuts and grabbing that gun. Oh, he was going to leave all right.

"So *please*, baby . . . can we leave it alone? You promised you wouldn't do anything stupid and you already scared the piss out of him . . . literally." They both shared a chuckle at that. "I told you what happened, and it's over, right?"

Tatum noticed that look on Ree's face again and her heart rate sped up.

"*Right*, Ree?"

She looked him in the eyes and it seemed it broke him from a trance. He smiled at her through his thoughts.

"Right," he agreed. He ran his hand through her hair and brought his lips to her face, kissing her.

"Good," Tatum sighed, feeling relieved. "I'm tired, baby. Let's just go to bed."

Ree rubbed her back softly and nodded.

"No doubt. You go on up, I got something to do. I'll be right there."

Tatum looked at him warily and stood up.

"Something like what, Ree? Unh-unh, you coming to bed . . . with me."

He chuckled at her.

"Relax . . . it'll only take me a minute."

"A minute to do what? What you gotta do?"

He stood and walked over to the counter, taking out a glass plate and holding it up with a grin.

"I gotta eat."

Tatum smiled and he shot a wink at her.

Tatum was glad that it was over. And she was glad that he was home.

* * *

Interlude

The air of the L.A. night was warm and muggy, and although the bright lights danced on the street, there were very few people out.

"Yo, did you see the bodies on them Hollywood bitches! Oh my God these bitches so bad, I'd drink they fucking piss!"

"Yo, you'se a nasty mothafucka, Dirk," Gunna chuckled as he walked up to the curb.

D.Gunna was one of the most popular rappers currently out. He had blown up over the last couple of years, topping the charts with two number-one albums and had toured the world, sampling some of the finest women the globe had to offer. One of those women happened to be Tatum and Sasha's late friend, Kim. That being said, it took a little more than the average stripper chick to impress him.

"Bitches all right . . . but they ain't got enough ass for me," D.Gunna dismissed, looking down the block for a sign of the valet pulling around his limo.

"Yeah, but they got titties for days!" his right-hand man since the sand, Dirk, commented.

"And them shit's faker than ya chain, lil nigga," Brick, D.Gunna's bodyguard, spoke up, as he stepped away from the high-profile strip club they had just exited and moved closer to the curb with them.

"Fuck outta here, man. My shit real! Tell him, Gunna . . . my shit real, ain't it?"

D.Gunna kept his eyes on the street but smiled slightly.

"Yeah . . . yeah, it's real, Dirk."

"See," Dirk continued, highly offended. "So fuck you, fake-ass Ving Rhames, Melvin, Baby Boy–looking mothafucka! That's why I'm calling that bitch soon as we get back to the telly. She getting off her shift, she gonna come blazeee me," he sang. "So fuck you," he taunted the huge, bald-headed bodyguard.

"Fuck who?" Brick bassed, taking a step to Dirk.

Dirk swallowed hard.

"Yeah, fuck who?" he asked, looking around scarily, and Gunna chuckled.

"Yeah, I thought so . . . *Dork.*"

Gunna shook his head from side to side.

"Can both of y'all niggas cut it the fuck out." He laughed. "And where the fuck is the driver with my shit?"

D.Gunna turned his head to the left and looked down the empty street once more, but then focused in on something peculiar to him.

A black Expedition sat a few feet away from them and had long ago pulled up and powered off its engine, killing the soft humming sound around the time that the fellas had exited. However, no one had gotten out of the car yet. Gunna narrowed his eyes but there was no way in hell he could see through the dark tints.

"Yo, Brick."

"What up." Brick stepped up quickly.

"Call the driver. See what's taking so long . . . I'm ready to get the fuck outta here."

Meanwhile, on the other side of the glass, Bennie sat with his two cousins loading up their automatic weapons and smoking a joint.

"Yo, primos . . . you see this bitch-ass nigga *D.Gunna* right here," Bennie crooned in his West Coast Mexican accent. "This nigga thinks he can just come to our city, make it rain in the fucking clubs on the hoes, walk around with fucking diamond *chains, watches, bracelets*

and shit, and nobody supposed to touch his soft ass," he
chuckled. "Like we won't just take all that shit. Dumb
mothafucka. This is the fucking jungle. Got that fucking
bodyguard with him like that's all he needs. And this
little pussy next to him. This shit gonna be too fucking
easy, homes."

"Yo, Bennie," one of his cousins spoke. "That is a
big mothafucker though, *ese.*" He eyed the bodyguard
warily.

"Yo, Raul, I know you not fucking scared. What, you
a fucking pussy now? As much as we done did this shit?"

Bennie and his cousins were professionals. They
made their living out of robbing folks, and they were
damn good at it. One of their biggest allies had been
Neli: she had often given them major leads on who to
hit and where and when, including the hit on Ree's
stash house and the false robbery in Sasha's apartment.
She even had Bennie kill Kim after she convinced him
that Kim was a mole with too much information. He did
it with no remorse, willing to return such a simple favor
to his good friend Neli. He stabbed Kim ten times to the
chest, and then raped her dying and bleeding body
before strangling her to her last breath.

After chewing out Raul, Bennie and his family decided it was time to make their move, especially before
the valet showed.

"Let's do this shit."

"Yo! Is that my nigga D.Gunna!" Bennie yelled excitedly, stumbling as if he were wasted out of his mind and
smiling wide like he was his biggest fan. "Yo, I can't believe this shit, man!" Bennie cheesed, tapping his
cousin's shoulder with so much force and excitement, it
caused Raul to rub it in relief.

"Yo, I got all your fucking songs, man! Your albums, your fucking mixtapes! *Move back, move back, or my niggas will react!*" Bennie sang the well-known lyrics.

The three men approached the rapper with ease, smiles on their deceiving faces. Although D.Gunna was a bit apprehensive, he was never one to shun a fan.

"No doubt, no doubt. Appreciate the love, baby."

"That's what's up!" Bennie squealed, throwing his hands in the air stepping up closer on him. "You cool as shit, homes. Can I get an autograph for my son? He loves your shit too!"

D.Gunna nodded and reached in his pocket for the pen he always kept handy. He wasn't feeling son's closeness, but he figured the sooner he'd sign it, the sooner son would back up off of him. Brick and Dirk watched from the sidelines, Brick a little more alert than Dirk.

"Yo, let me get . . . something . . ."

"Oh yeah, my bad, homes. Here, take this to sign it on," Bennie offered, handing him a dollar bill. "Gotta have dollar bills, right? For the bitches?"

He laughed and Gunna chuckled, and as Gunna looked down to sign he asked, "A'ight, who you want me to make it out to?"

"Make it out to my Beretta, *ese.*"

Before Gunna put it together, Bennie sprung out his gun and had it to his gut, but not before Brick stepped up ready to break his neck.

"I don't suggest it, you black gorilla motherfucker," Raul spoke, pressing his cold 9 to the back of Brick's bald head. The other cousin also had his weapon on Dirk. They were so fast with it, so quick, no one had a chance to react.

"What you want, pussy?"

For the slick comment, Bennie punched Gunna hard

the first one in the direction, as Gunna and Brick stood over a dazed Bennie.

"You thought I was soft, nigga?" Gunna questioned with venom in his voice, picking up Bennie's gun, which lay a few feet from him. He leaned over and cracked the weapon hard against Bennie's face.

"Nigga, I'm from the Bricks!"

Bennie's mouth instantly filled with blood as he watched Brick urge Gunna to the car.

"Let's get the fuck outta here, D," Brick warned, looking at the skinny white limo driver who was exiting but still ignorant to what was happening.

D.Gunna stalled, but nodded in agreement, and just as they turned, Bennie let out a cocky laugh coated in blood.

"I'm coming back for that chain, D.Gunna," he taunted. "And your album was *garbage,* homes."

D.Gunna turned around quickly, still holding Bennie's gun, and fired two rounds straight to Bennie's chest. With satisfaction, he watched Bennie take his last struggling breath. Although he was a high-paid rapper, he was from the streets first. And in the streets, respect was everything.

Brick pushed Gunna to the limo more anxious than ever for them to get out of there, and as the limo driver walked around the car, he sighed in disappointment.

"Shit."

"Holy shit, D.Gunna, is that you?" the white boy screamed. "What the fuck happened . . . yo, d-did you shoot someone?"

Gunna and Brick looked at each other and knew what had to happen. Gunna hated to do it, he had turned his life around, but it was either his life on the line, or the life of the nosy limo driver.

Before another word could be uttered from his lips,

Brick took out his own pistol and sent a bullet straight to the young boy's head, killing him instantly.

"Now let's get the fuck outta here!"

Brick jumped behind the wheel and Gunna joined an awaiting Dirk in the back. He knew Dirk was a punk, so he didn't even mention his lack of involvement in the altercation.

The purring of the limo's engine was all that could be heard as the trio sped down Sunset. Minutes passed with no words spoken.

"Shit . . ." Dirk finally cursed, breaking the silence and feeling a little guilty for not doing more. "After all of that, a nigga don't even know if I should call Kim now!"

"Who?" D.Gunna snapped, a strange feeling suddenly coming over him at the sound of that name.

"Kim," Dirk repeated with a cracked voice. "The white bitch from the strip club! The one I was holla'n at."

D.Gunna swallowed hard and nodded, the crease in his eyebrows relaxing a bit as he wondered why the name had given him a sudden flashback to his past. Shaking his head in an attempt to start to put the last twenty minutes behind him, he rolled down the window and let some fresh air in.

The sweet summer night air crept in and swept across his face, caressing his cheek and putting a sudden calm over him. D.Gunna released a smile and didn't even know why.

Little did he know, Kim had just given him a sweet kiss for taking the life of her killer. Now she could rest in peace.

Chapter 10

"Oh, it's always about money, shawty . . . and lots of it."
—Bleek, *Still Thicker than Water*

Three months later

"Welcome! Welcome, my friend!"

Ree stepped first off the helicopter and was immediately greeted by the friendly family of the Segovias, one of Ecuador's largest and most dangerous drug and crime cartels.

"Can we take your bag? Pedro, take his bag."

Ree handed over his duffel, which held his basic amenities for the next couple of days. He then turned and helped a very big and pregnant Tatum down the eight small steps.

"Your wife? My God, Señor Respect, she is breathtaking," Manuel Segovia complimented, putting the wrong emphasis on the English syllables but still getting the accolade across.

"Thank you," Tatum beamed, her glow illuminating even through the night.

"Welcome to Ecuador, Senor Respect," Manuel's wife,

Veronica, spoke up. She was a petite and beautiful
woman, with long hair that grazed her buttocks, olive
skin, and a deadly reputation. "We hope you find your
stay comfortable . . . and easy." She then turned to
Tatum. "Mrs. . . ."

"Tatum," Tatum announced, smiling and shaking her
waiting hand.

"And I'm Jayde."

Jayde descended gracefully down the steps of the helicopter with Chauncey in tow behind her. Not only was
she annoyed by the Segovias' prior blatant disregard for
her in business, but they were now gushing over Tatum
like she was the head bitch. Just because she was married
to the king didn't make her the queen . . . not in
Jayde's eyes.

"This is one of . . . this is my daughter," Mickel corrected, stepping closer to the chopper.

Jayde's face tried not to sour at his near word slip and
Ree turned to him.

"You made it, old man," Ree chuckled, shaking his
hand and stepping into a loose embrace. He hardly had
seen them among the twenty-plus Segovias who stood
around. Mickel's island features caused him to blend
right in.

"I did. And you are Tatum." Mickel's eyes danced and
he smiled genuinely. Not in a sensual sense but in pure
admiration of Tatum's beauty. "An angel," he said, smiling. "You look even more beautiful up close. I only saw
you from a distance on your wedding day."

Tatum crinkled her brow.

"You were there? Oh my God. There were so many
people, I could hardly keep up," she spoke with a beam.

Mickel shook his head.

"It's not your fault. I, um . . . I met up with an old
friend . . . I'm sorry I didn't get to introduce myself

then. Now's a better time. You were much busier last time I saw you," he joked.

"Yeah, and a lot smaller," Tatum quipped.

"Oh please, don't say that," Mickel said seriously. "Pregnancy is when a woman is the most radiant, and you wear it well. I should stop with my praise."

"You should," Ree interrupted, and Mickel cracked a smile.

"Ah, the test. My young friend is indeed in love. He will slit my throat before I get to utter another compliment to his lovely wife."

Tatum chuckled but looked to Ree, wondering if it was true.

"And you must be Chauncey. Good to put a face to the name." Mickel extended his hand and looked behind him, as if he were expecting someone else to emerge from the helicopter.

"Is this all? Wasn't there someone else?" he asked.

"Who, Bleek?" Chauncey questioned.

"Bleek's staying behind to start on the street-level situations," Ree summed up.

"No," Mickel spoke quickly. "With you," he said, pointing to Chauncey. "Your wife, no?"

Jayde took a deep breath but wanted to scream at her father at the top of her lungs.

"Oh, Sasha," Chauncey spoke with a grin. "Yeah, she just started a new job at the hospital. She had to stay."

Mickel was notably disappointed and Jayde was infuriated.

"Let's go inside," Manuel Segovia suggested.

While everyone sat by the pool enjoying a light midnight meal, Respect and Manuel took it inside to the bar area, which was so huge and had so many half-naked women walking around, it reminded Ree of some type of brothel.

"I'm glad we came to this understanding so smoothly," Ree let him know, inhaling his daily choice of herbs.

"Me too, Mr. Respect. I'm sure Mickel told you, I was not anxious to work with any new Americans. But when I heard that you would be the link in the equation, I knew we could see eye to eye. Your reputation precedes you . . . you are a businessman . . . a very smart man. I just wish it could be more long-term for us."

"Yeah well, like you said. I'm a smart man," Ree quipped.

"Exactly. That's why I hope the people that I deal with after you, can make things happen . . . so smoothly. I would hate for this to go off track."

"I believe so but then again, I make no promises," Ree let him know. "Business involves risk. In the event that there is backlash, don't bring that to my door. I cannot guarantee our conversation will be as civil as this," Ree warned. Once he was done, he would take no one bringing any street nonsense to him or his family.

"You will bring me war, I know. Like I said, your reputation precedes you. You are a dangerous man . . . like myself." Manuel and Ree looked at each other wordlessly after that last statement. After a few seconds, Manuel smiled.

"These women are intrigued by you. Look at them," he said, pointing. "They are usually my girls, but they are fascinated by you." His accent crooned. "I swear they are like bloodhounds. These whores *smell* money. They can sniff the king out of the crowd."

Ree continued to puff and did little to acknowledge the subjects of Manuel's speech. Manuel, however, shot them a smile and they made their way to the bar, surrounding them.

"You are American?" one asked in broken English, her DD breasts barely covered by the triangles of her bikini top. Her long brown hair and bronze skin gave her the look of an exotic Victoria's Secret model.

"I love a black American," another sang, running her hands through her short, bleach-blond bob. "I will surrender to you," she admitted with no shame, attempting to pick up one of Ree's dreads.

This was not new to Ree, nor intriguing. He simply involuntarily blew smoke in their direction.

"Let us please you," the exotic one begged as Manuel looked on with a grin.

Bloodhounds, he mouthed before stepping away.

"I'm sorry, ladies, I'm gonna have to pass," Ree let them know, respectively taking their roaming hands off him.

"Ohhh," she whimpered. "But I *love* chocolate," she cooed, her English hardly audible.

"Yeah, well this candy bar is allll mine. Sorry girls."

Tatum smiled flaccidly and wrapped her arms around Ree's neck as she stepped in between him and the black-dick-and-money vampires.

Ree smirked and the girls were a bit disappointed but smiled back.

"De nada." They retreated.

"Hmm, and just think . . . I almost didn't come on this trip. How would that have played out if I didn't?" she asked with a raised eyebrow.

"Different words. Same results," Ree calmly told her, and Tatum chuckled.

"Yeah, whatever. I saw that Adriana Lima–looking chick all over you."

"Yeah well I'm trying to be all over you, Miss Lady," he sang, moving close to her and bringing his face to hers. "So how can we make that happen?"

"All over *all* of me," Tatum cracked.

"Yes, all of you. Every inch," he told her. "'Cause every single inch is *sexy* as hell."

Tatum smiled.

"That's sweet, even though I'm *big* as hell. You can call me big sexy."

"Cut that shit out," Ree told her, laughing.

Tatum knew she was big, though, but she didn't care. She knew for a while that she would most likely go from not showing to huge as hell in just a few months.

"So Tatum, you say Mr. Knights finally wants to know the sex?" her doctor had asked a few days before they left for Ecuador. Tatum had been holding off the big surprise from him since she'd found out on her prior visit. It was the only visit Ree hadn't accompanied her to.

"Yes," Tatum had said anxiously with Ree on the side, quiet and calm. Inside he was eager.

Dr. Patel, Tatum's doctor, smiled at the young couple as she looked at the monitor.

"Okay, sure . . . so Sean, which one would you like to know first?"

Ree crinkled his brow and it took a moment to process.

Dr. Patel spun the monitor around slowly with a wide smile.

"Twins," she beamed widely. "A healthy baby boy and girl."

He was thrilled.

"So, you tired? You wanna go to bed?" Ree knew Tatum must've been worn out with the late flight and in her condition.

"Actually," Tatum started. "My back is killing me. Veronica said the jet sets in their Jacuzzi would be good, as long as we put them on low and the water isn't too warm. I might wanna hit that up."

Ree stood up off the bar stool and put out his blunt.

"All right, let's go."

* * *

Tatum took her time and Ree assisted her as she lowered herself into the high-set Jacuzzi, which had a beautiful waterfall attached.

Tatum had changed into her black bikini and sheer full cover that made her look sexy even in her pregnant state.

"Okay . . . okay, I got it," she told him as he climbed in after her. "I hope you can fit, with the whale in here," she laughed.

"I think I'll manage, Shamu."

Tatum took a gush of water and pushed it to him, splashing him with force.

"Hey! Contest my fat jokes, don't feed into them, Mr. Knights."

"Okay, I got you."

He grabbed her by the waist and brought her to him, while his back was pressed against the wall of the hot tub. Tatum had to lean in a little to kiss his lips, as her protruding belly put a small gap between them. The sight of one of the women who had been talking to Ree, the blond one, slowed her kiss.

"Oh hell no."

The girl was walking, smiling seductively and following Chauncey to the guesthouse. He didn't seem enthralled or too into her but he also didn't seem to mind. Tatum jumped up, ready to push herself out of the water.

"Where are you . . ." Ree turned his head and saw where Tatum's eyes rested. "Oh no. Nah, Tatum. That has nothing to do with you."

Tatum looked at him like he was crazy.

"Nothing to do with me? Ree, Sasha's my best friend!"

Tatum yelled the words, even though she had only spoken to Sasha twice since her wedding. Both times Sasha was short, she let Tatum speak to Aubrey for a while and then ended the call first. She told Tatum she had forgiven her, but her actions didn't completely show it. Things were definitely different between them.

"She's your best friend and that's a grown-ass man right there, Tatum. What do you think you even see? He's just going to the guesthouse . . . everyone's there."

"Yeah, everyone's there including half-naked hoes. And did you see how she was all up on him? Unh-unh, Ree, no. Chauncey ain't got no damn business being in there, oh!"

Tatum yelped as a sharp pain went through her stomach. Ree tensed up, alert.

"What? What's wrong?"

It took a few seconds and some heavy breathing for the pain to subside and for Tatum to respond.

"I'm . . . I'm fine. I just need to go talk to Chauncey . . ."

"No, you need to calm the fuck down. Come on, we're going up to bed."

"No, Ree . . . I'm, I'm fine." But her face told differently.

"Tatum . . . you need to go to the hospital? C'mon, we're going to the—"

"Ree! Calm down," Tatum told him. "I don't need to go to no hospital. The doctor said I'd get these. They're cramps . . . that's all, remember?"

"And she said you'd get them when you're stressed. So you need to calm the fuck down. I'm taking you to bed."

"Tatum, are you okay?"

Tatum looked up and saw Veronica, Manuel's wife, making her way to them. Something about her Tatum liked. She felt like she was a genuine person and Tatum was not very trusting. But some people had an air.

"Mm, I'm just getting a little cramping," Tatum told her, rubbing her side.

"Oh, I know all about this. I had the worst contractions from my fifth month on. C'mon. We'll get some herbal tea and you will rest on the most comfortable mattress we have."

Tatum nodded, still wanting to swing by the guesthouse and peep in at Chauncey. Ree stood and helped her out and began to get out as well. She knew she could get Veronica to walk her past the guesthouse, but Ree would ruin her plan.

"Baby, I'm fine," Tatum told him. "I'm gonna go have tea with Veronica, then I'm going to bed. I'm okay," Tatum coaxed with a smile.

Ree looked from her to Veronica.

"I'll take good care of her, Mr. Respect, I promise."

He half-nodded and kissed Tatum on the forehead. "You sure?"

"Yeah . . . yeah," Tatum urged. "I'll see you when you come to bed. I know you got one last blunt to smoke," she said, winking.

Ree smirked and lowered himself back into the Jacuzzi as the ladies walked off. Tatum was right.

Moments passed, a good amount of time, as tranquility took over the estate and the faint sounds of giggles could be heard from the distance. The large landscaping of the trees, the ponds, the pool, the Jacuzzi, the huge mansion, had Ree thinking of where he and Tatum would settle when this was all over. Picking up the rolled cigar he'd placed on the side of the Jacuzzi when they arrived, Ree also grabbed the lighter and blazed it up. Thirty seconds into his remedy and he was interrupted.

"May we join you?"

Jayde stood before him in a white two-piece that showed off all of her assets, and the tropical beauty from inside who had flirted with Ree began to lower herself into the water.

Ree knew then he would have to depart. He would just toke a little more and then bounce.

Jayde stepped inside behind her.

"So everything went smooth with Manuel?" Jayde spoke, moving toward the waterfall and allowing the water to cascade and soak her black tresses.

Ree didn't answer and Jayde should've known why. He didn't discuss business in front of anyone who wasn't a part of it.

"I love your tattoos," the exotic modelesque vixen purred, leaning back, wetting her own hair, and eyeing Ree's exposed upper body decorated in ink. "Can I touch?"

She went to move toward him but Jayde grabbed her by the hair and pulled her back with a little force.

"No, you can't have him," she told her, bringing her lips to the girl's ear. "He's off limits."

Jayde smirked, more with her eyes than her mouth.

Ree observed as Jayde turned the girl around and shoved her own tongue down her throat without warning. When the kiss broke, the girl huffed in anxiety.

"But I want him," she begged in a whisper. Ree took another pull of his blunt, squinting in their direction, but gave no response. At the end of the day, he was a man. He knew he would never give her, or them, what they wanted. But he did look on.

Jayde paid the girl little mind as she lowered her head and untied the girl's top. She took the Ecuadorian beauty's black cherry nipple into her mouth and then bit it. Jayde was dominant, almost dominatrix-dominant. As

Jayde toyed with the girl's nipples with her tongue, the woman kept her yearning stare on Ree. She was begging him with her eyes to join them. Ree could tell she wanted him to be the one touching and licking on her.

"Ven, papi. Venga aqui," she begged in a sultry whisper as Jayde slurped on her breasts.

Ree put out his blunt and wet his lips unknowingly.

And as Jayde continued to dance her tongue over the girl's body, she looked up at Ree, wondering if he was taking the bait. He sat up and began to move toward them and Jayde's clit jumped in anxiety. And just as the girl parted her lips, ready to taste what she had her eye on all evening, Ree turned and stepped out of the water.

He made his way toward the double doors and headed inside the mansion. As soon as he was out of sight, Jayde pushed the girl away in annoyance. She was done playing with her.

"Reee," Tatum moaned, the feeling of his thick tongue massaging away at her now swollen pearl, awakening her out of her just-entered sleep. She smiled as her eyes remained closed, enjoying this moment of bliss.

"Ooh shittt . . ." she purred, as he grabbed her ass and dug his fingers into her softness, burying his face deep into her and sucking on her like she was one of his cigars.

Tatum brought her fingers to his head and grabbed his dreads, for some reason it turned her on even more.

"Oh! Oh, daddy. Don't stoppp."

After swinging by the guesthouse and not being able to locate Chauncey, Tatum had an unsettling feeling in her stomach. She debated on what to say to Sasha since she actually hadn't seen anything, but she did decide to call her to at least let her know of the atmosphere. However, that call went unsurprisingly unanswered.

Tatum then had decided to come to bed after her comforting cup of tea with Veronica, and this, this was a wonderful way to come . . . to bed.

"Ohhhh! Reeee!"

Tatum's legs began to shake as she clutched his hair with strength and then she stretched her arms out as if she had grown wings, and gripped the finely threaded cotton sheets. Ree's head game always blew Tatum away but tonight . . . tonight was one of the best orgasms she'd ever had.

"Damn, baby," she panted after she released all over his goatee. "What got into you?"

Ree wiped his mouth, brought himself up to her, and kissed her in a way that made her body respond to only him.

"Let's just focus on what's about to get into you."

Sasha placed the setting on DELICATES and pressed the button to start the wash. That was the last load of laundry for the night and Sasha felt damn good.

"See, I'm not that bougie . . . I can be a housewife. Not like those Bravo bitches with like ten maids," she quipped. "I'm doing *all* the laundry. Wait til Chauncey gets home and sees," she giggled.

The chiming of the doorbell broke her out of her crazy, talking-to-herself moment.

Who the hell is it at my door this late?

An instant feeling of trepidation overtook Sasha. Not only was she in the big house alone with Aubrey, but Chauncey was also in another country, and Sasha, let's just say, hadn't had the most normal history.

Two people precisely, Neli and Mike, whom she had

trusted, stalked her and tried to ruin her life at one point.

"Who is it?" Sasha asked, trying to sound more confident than she was.

Sasha peeked out of the peephole as she neared the door and a feeling of relief and uneasiness overtook her. Relief because it was only Bleek. Uneasiness . . . because it was Bleek.

"Bleek . . ." she started, pulling the door open. "What are you doing here?"

"Bleek!" Aubrey called, running to him from behind Sasha. "Is my daddy with you?"

Bleek pressed his lips together and gave a light smile as he picked Aubrey up.

"Nah, baby girl. But he'll be back soon. Until then, I'm here to check up on y'all." He shot his eyes to Sasha, who stood before him in a pair of pink mesh shorts and a tank top.

"Bri-Bri, you're supposed to be in the bed," Sasha spoke evenly. "Go."

Aubrey, knowing when her mother was serious, heeded the advice.

"Bye, Uncle Bleek."

Bouncing up the stairs after Bleek placed her down, Aubrey made her way out of their vision.

"Damn, I love that little girl right there," Bleek said, smiling.

Sasha sighed.

"Bleek . . . what are you doing here?"

He shrugged.

"Checking on you."

Sasha rolled her eyes subtly and crossed her arms in front of her chest.

"Bleek . . . *what* are you *doing* here?"

After Chauncey had proposed to Sasha, Sasha told

Bleek they seriously had to end whatever they had before it even got started. He agreed but seemed to be having an issue with that, being that he was now here.

Bleek stared at her yearningly and smiled.

"I just had to . . . I don't know . . . make sure you was good before I laid my head down tonight."

Sasha darted her eyes, trying not to get caught up in any of that.

"I don't understand . . . you said you agreed."

"I did," he told her. "I still do. You know, you tough on a mothafucka that wanna make sure you safe," he told her with a chuckle.

Sasha shook her head in disbelief.

"Bleek, c'mon."

"I miss you," he admitted quickly. Bleek had never expressed his emotions to a girl in his young life. He didn't even know he could genuinely feel them. He cared about his daughter's mother. He liked fucking around with Jayde because she was sexy as hell. But being around Sasha felt like something else, and since they had agreed not to take it there anymore, they'd seen way less of each other.

"Where . . . where did this come from?" Sasha questioned with her brows crinkled in confusion. "I mean, we've been fine all of this time and then all of a sudden, you just started going hard body when there were no feelings there before—"

"There were always feelings there."

"Bleek . . . Stop it!"

Bleek could see her frustration as tears pooled in her eyes. Sasha was fearful, with Bleek acting like this, that it would be harder to resume back to normal than she thought.

He stepped closer to her and spoke in a deep whisper.

"Listen, ma, I ain't tryin' to upset you. And I'll respect what you got with C, I'll fall back if that's what you really want . . . for real. I did it before, I know I can do it again. Just know, I'm always gon' have love for you, shawty. And you can't stop a nigga from checking on you . . . especially when you in this big house by yaself," he added with his boyish grin. He brought his hand to her head and brushed her hair with his fingers. Bringing his face to hers, he spoke yearningly.

"I been trying since we talked, you know. Months, ma. And all I been thinking about is touching you . . . and tasting you . . . and fucking you . . ."

Sasha shut her eyes. He was so abrupt, still so rough around the edges.

"I been keeping my distance . . . tryin' to shake it. But tonight . . . tonight I had to . . . I don't know . . ."

"Bleek, you gotta—"

Bleek silenced her by pressing his lips to hers and Sasha whimpered, feeling their softness and thinking of how good they felt on her lower lips before. However, the weight from her heavy left hand reminded her of the man that she had loved for a long time, a man who was about to be her husband. She pushed Bleek away hard.

"Bleek, you gotta go!"

Before he could say or do anything else, Sasha slammed the door on him, right in his face.

She had fucked up, she had pussy-whipped the young boy, but she didn't plan on making a habit of it. She was done and over it. And Bleek would have to get over it too.

* * *

"Oh! Oh, yes!"

The cries of their lovemaking echoed through the walls of the Segovia mansion.

"Oh fuck! Oh yes, daddy!"

As she cried out, he grabbed her long hair and rammed all of that long dick deep into her.

"Arch your back . . . Arch your fucking back!"

"Ooohhhh, it's too big! Oh, God!"

"Ayo, shut the fuck up . . . before your husband hears."

Veronica turned around with that blissful look of being long-dicked etched on her face.

"He no care," she panted. "We have open marriage. Keep fucking me!"

Chauncey grabbed her hair again like he was riding a horse and brought his dick deep into her.

"Arch your fucking back," he demanded as Veronica's petite frame bounced up and down on him. "Ohhh shit," he grunted, feeling his release building up.

"Ooh, no fair. When you gonna fuck me, chocolate daddy," the blonde cried. "You were supposed to fuck me first!"

This was true. Chauncey had entered the bedroom on the other end of the mansion with the blonde, having the intention of getting some head. However, when Veronica had arrived and said she was looking for him, she didn't seem to shy away at his exposed dick in the girl's mouth. In fact, she had the opposite reaction, and requested to join. Chauncey had been worried about fucking with business, her being Manuel's wife and all, but she insisted he was not around. Besides, Chauncey had always been a risk taker, and two freak bitches at once was always a weakness. The fact that he now knew Manuel wouldn't even care if he found out made it that much sweeter.

"Shitttt," Chauncey groaned as he pulled his dick out of her, rolled off the condom, and released his load into the blonde's waiting mouth. Veronica turned around and kissed on his chest in the afterglow.

Chauncey had tried to be good, and in a sense he had been, but temptation had gotten the best of him. Besides, all niggas got they dick wet outside of the country, which was like international code or something to him. Sasha was still his heart.

"You are so good . . . you are too much for any one woman to handle," Veronica cooed, out of breath.

Chauncey kissed her on the top of her head and smirked as the blonde nibbled on his balls, sending chills through his body.

"That's not true. There's a woman that can handle me . . . you just ain't her."

Chapter 11

"Now what do I have to do to get you to join forces with me?"
—Jayde, *Still Thicker than Water*

The wind whistled loudly as a single thin tree branch tapped against the windowpane in an eerie sort of way. The storm was coming and Tatum kept her eyes on the effects of it, realizing that it added to the already creepy feeling she couldn't shake.

As a part of their relocation to Atlanta, whether temporary or permanent they hadn't decided, the finishing touches on their new ten-thousand-square-foot Georgia home had been placed while Tatum and Ree were in Ecuador. Coming back and finding herself in a brand new place before schedule was a bit of a shock to Tatum, especially since they had to cut the trip short on her part. She knew Ree meant it more as a surprise, but she secretly missed the modesty of the condo, there was too much space and the house seemed to hold whispers to secrets unknown already.

"Knock, knock." The fact that he said the words instead of doing the action made Tatum crack a smile as Ree stepped inside. He strolled over to the side of her bed and took his seat in the recliner he'd placed there.

"So . . . how you feeling?"

Tatum half-smiled.

"Okay, I guess. I haven't hurled in an hour," she added with a smile. "I'm sorry I ruined the trip."

"You didn't ruin the trip. Stop saying that. I accomplished what I needed to and you got to see the country for a couple of days. Besides, we needed to get back . . . niggas were having way too much fun." Ree looked off thinking of Jayde and her Jacuzzi romp and also, unknown to Tatum, Chauncey's adventures with the South American sluts, but Tatum only chuckled, not knowing how serious he was. She was sitting up, the TV was on but it was watching her and she wanted to move. But she couldn't. She had been ill for six days now, weak and vomiting nonstop.

"I don't know why they call this shit morning sickness . . . when you have it all the damn time. And I'm sick of watching TV and reading, Ree. I wanna leave this bed," Tatum whined, kicking at the covers and sounding like Sasha.

Ree shook his head.

"You're not leaving the bed, Tatum. You gonna slow ya ass down. Here, hold up. I got something for you." He stood up and walked over to a box on the floor they hadn't gotten to unpack.

"Play a game with me."

"Ree, you know we can't do that. The doctor said since I'm fatigued, sex will—"

"Chess, nasty girl." He held up the chess set and Tatum laughed at her thoughts.

"Ah, damn . . . I guess I'm just deprived."

Ree chuckled at her as he walked back over and began to set up the board and pieces on the bed.

across the jaw before pushing his Beretta deeper into Gunna's side.

"Gimme your fucking jewelry, bitch. I want that fucking chain, the watch, the bracelet, and the fucking rings."

Gunna had to have on over a million dollars in jewelry. It was so normal to him, he almost forgot how he probably looked like a full-course meal to niggas in the street. But damn, they were in *Hollywood!*

Gunna began to reluctantly remove his jewelry, knowing most was insured. Unlike stupid motherfuckers who claimed they'd die for they shit, Gunna was from the streets, and he knew niggas would kill for it, no questions asked.

Gunna removed his watch and bracelet, as well as his rings, and handed them over to Bennie with a grimace. Just as he was lifting his prized possession, his platinum chain with the huge diamond-flooded MAC-11, the lights from the limo could be seen approaching. The slight distraction caused everyone to glance for a split second and in that second everything turned around.

Brick snapped his pistol out of its holster with a subtle motion, turned it slightly to where it was aimed to the back of him, prayed he was accurate, and pulled the hairpin trigger.

It sent a bullet straight into Raul's groin and he cried out in pain at the same time that D.Gunna sent a right hook into Bennie's jaw, dropping him to the ground. Brick spun around quickly, his ten years of martial arts training coming to effect, aimed at the other cousin, and shot him dead in the face before he could pull his own trigger.

At the same time Bennie lifted his weapon to Gunna but Brick swiftly kicked it out of his hand.

"Wouldn't recommend it, bitch!" Brick spat.

The limo driver pulled up to the curb and Dirk was

"When's the last time you ate?" he asked, setting up his men as Tatum set up hers. Ree had been deep into tying up the ends on the next step of his business agenda for the past couple of hours, leaving Crush to assist Tatum.

"Jayde brought me some oatmeal and orange juice this morning before y'all left out."

Ree looked up, a blank stare directed at her.

"This morning? Tatum, you can't be serious. Those are my children, not to mention you're my wife. I need you to take care of yourself *and* them. Crush didn't bring you anything for lunch?" She could tell Ree was upset. She didn't want him to take it out on Crush, especially when it was her fault.

"He tried . . . but I wouldn't take it. Every time I eat something I fucking throw it up. I hate it."

Ree looked at her seriously.

"You gotta eat. End of discussion. If not for me, do it for them."

Tatum sighed.

"Ree, you know I want and love these babies more than anything in the world. I'll do anything for them. I *am* eating. I won't harm them."

Ree paid her little mind as he got up and walked over to the intercom. He ordered Crush to bring up a sandwich and soup.

"No, no more of that soup," Tatum contested. Ree looked at her as if she didn't have a say and Tatum breathed heavily. "Ree, I swear. I'll eat the sandwich. But if I eat any more of that soup I'm gonna go crazy. I have been eating that shit all week. I know Jayde was trying to be nice by making it but God, I need a break. I can't wait until Rose flies out here so I can eat some real food!"

"She'll be out here as soon as we decide what we're doing."

She knew what he meant, as soon as they decided if they would stay in Atlanta for good. Either way, they would keep their homes in both Jamaica and the States, but Ree was ultimately leaving it up to Tatum once his business was done as to where they would settle. Atlanta seemed like the place to be before the rift between her and Sasha formed, now Tatum wasn't sure how it would play out.

"I know . . . I'm still thinking about it."

He nodded, gave her a soft peck on the lips, retook his seat, and they began their chess game. A few minutes passed, and there was a knock at the door.

"Bring it in here, Crush," Ree ordered.

Crush stepped inside and placed the sandwich, glass of milk, and apple on the stand next to Tatum.

"Uh, yo, Respect . . . we need to rap about something," Crush calmly told him.

"All right . . . when I'm done."

Tatum used his moment of distraction to take one of his pawns. Ree threw her a smile and then they shared one.

Caught in their own little world, they hardly noticed that Crush was still standing there until he insisted, "It's a little urgent, my man."

Ree blew out air and stood up, looking down at Tatum.

"No cheating," he warned with a wink. Tatum wondered what was going on. That was one thing she loved and hated when it came to Ree, he never let her into that aspect of his life. Things could be going smooth as shit or crumbling around them, and Tatum would never know. The two men dismissed themselves.

Tatum took the opportunity to study the board and

try to think of a strategy to outsmart Ree at the game. He was a genius when it came to it, thoroughly skilled, quick thinking, and patient. She rubbed her large belly and a feeling of calm overtook her. A mother . . . the greatest gift from God. She couldn't wait to meet her babies. She wondered who they would look like, what they would smell like, how it would feel to hold them.

A quick glance at the television caused her to do a double take, so hard that she almost caught a crook in her neck. Tatum snatched up the remote and lifted the volume a few notches before glancing at the doorway, wondering if Ree would walk in. Her entire body broke out in a cold sweat as she listened to the breaking-news broadcast.

"It has been confirmed. The body remains found in the Chappaqua Woods last Thursday have been identi- fied as belonging to world-renowned attorney Johnny Carson. Carson, who has defended some of the most prominent figures in politics, music, and Hollywood, was reported missing by his mother and colleagues last month after he failed to show for several appearances. Four days ago, children playing discovered what appeared to be a head of an adult male, the eyes horrifically carved out. About a hundred feet away, a torso was dis- covered, the arms and legs detached as well as the victim's male sex organ removed and placed horrifically in his rectum, in a self-sodomizing action. Any further details of this gruesome case would be ridiculously tasteless; however, I will say this . . . this was a crime of personal vendetta. Johnny Carson had obviously made someone very, very angry. Details of a memorial service and any leads on this case will be updated as we receive them—"

The television powered off instantly.

"You should give the TV a rest."

Tatum looked over at Ree, her mouth slightly agape and her heart racing faster than she thought humanly possible. She felt faint, sick, horrified. Even though something deep down inside of her had expected this. A man like Ree? Let Johnny breathe after what he'd done to her? But somehow she felt like a little kid who had been caught snooping, although he had to know this would be well publicized. All of this must have been a story that broke while they were away in Ecuador. Tatum wished she would have stayed there, maybe never heard what she just had, although that was highly unlikely.

Ree threw the alternate remote down on the bed and came to her coolly, as if nothing had happened.

"You good?"

Tatum swallowed hard, her face becoming warm and her body ice cold simultaneously. Ree was half amazing and half monster; she didn't understand why she always failed to remember that until he drastically put it right in her face.

"I'm . . . I'm *fine.*"

"Good. Now maybe you should get some rest."

Tatum ran her hands through her hair and nodded, her breathing trying its best to stabilize.

"Um . . . I . . . I guess you're right."

She scooted down, bringing the covers up over her upper body and attempting to put the last two minutes behind her. Ree grabbed the chess set and placed it next to the bed, and the unspoken words floated, lingering in the air. He dimmed the lights and turned to make his way out, no expression adorning his handsome face. But this was not them, and this was not Tatum, she had to say something.

"Ree, did you—"

"I love you, Tatum."

He cut her off. He cut her off with those words and Tatum knew that was it. That was all he would say. He didn't even turn around, but she got it. He did what he did because he loved her.

Tatum nodded and took a deep breath as she watched him walk out and crack their bedroom door.

"I love you, too."

That's all she would say as well.

The powerfully loud sound of crashing thunder broke the silence of the peaceful bedroom. However, it wouldn't be the storm that awoke Tatum a few hours later, close to three A.M.

It was an eerie sense of loneliness that had seemed to creep up over her, in her bed, even as her eyes remained shut and her mind danced between sleep and consciousness. An instant feeling of coldness, a sense that her body was now the only one that occupied her otherwise warm bed stirred her.

Tatum's almond-shaped eyes slowly fluttered open, taking in the darkness of the bedroom, and then tempted to shut again, but she fought against it.

"Mm . . ." A soft moan escaped her lips and she attempted to roll from her right side over to her left. She wanted to face him. Even after learning what had happened, she wanted to be close to him.

She wanted to see the silhouette of his Adonis build under their covers, see the shapes of his shoulder, neck, face, nose, and lips and smell his masculine scent. Hear his heavy breathing as a soothing remedy to this now uncomfortable feeling of anxiety. Ree would make it go away. That's how dominant he was. Able to put her at ease even in his state of rest. And every night when she awoke, he was always there next to her doing just that.

Tatum shifted and turned, and smiled prematurely as she reached her arm over to connect with him. Her dainty hand was met with emptiness, bare sheet and pillows. This time, her eyes were forced open by her curiosity.

Where is he?

Tatum sat up, now aware that she was definitely alone in her massive bed. She gradually lifted up and glanced around the dim bedroom.

". . . Ree?"

As if everything else was now awakened with her sight, all of Tatum's other senses now came to life. Her damp gown clung to her body, and Tatum wondered why she was sweating so much. She ran her hands through her long hair and down over her frame, and panic struck in her heart. She smelled it. It was a distinct yet unfamiliar smell. One that she hadn't smelled often but recognized it when she did. How had she missed it before?

Tatum's heart began to thump loudly, so loud that she could hear it clearly over the violent storm. Throwing the blanket back, she frantically ran her hands over the Italian linen sheets hoping, just praying, and then . . .

"Oh God, no . . ."

Wetness. It was all over. It surrounded her. Dread completely consumed her as she took deep and short breaths of fear and her eyes rimmed with tears. Tatum's mouth remained in an O of horror as she hesitantly reached for the nightstand, completely terrified. Now she could feel the dampness all around. The bed wasn't just wet, it was soaked. As she kicked the blanket to the floor in a frenzy, Tatum's hoarse moans were caught in her throat but couldn't escape until she knew for sure. She flicked on the desk lamp and her suspicions were confirmed in the second that it took the light to travel and illuminate the bedroom. Blood was everywhere!

It was all she saw and Tatum brought her hand to her mouth in terror, but noticed that it was now red and dripping with the ghastly wetness.

"Oh God . . . oh my God," she whispered, her voice trembling.

Where was he? And as if her mind had finally registered and connected the two, Tatum shook her head at the reality of his absence and the fear she felt from it. She needed him, now, drastically and immediately.

Tatum allowed her lungs to inhale a deep and shaken breath of air that assisted her in belting out the most horrific and bloodcurdling scream that she had ever experienced in her entire life. The tears of dismay continued to streak down her face as the vibration started from the pit of her stomach and traveled up through her vocal cords in desperation.

"Rrrrrrreeeeeeeeeeeeeeeeeeeee!!!!!!!!!!!!!!!!!!!!!!!!!"

"Somebody get the doctor! Get the doctor now! This woman's bleeding way too quickly, we're losing this baby!"

"No." Tatum's cries were barely audible but the pain was etched all in and through her face as they pushed her with rapid speed through the hospital halls. Blood soaked her entire lower body, had been left in puddles in the Maybach seats, and now had the stretcher completely colored red. This couldn't be happening to her.

"Babies," she tried to mumble, but it was pointless. There was no way she could be heard over all of the commotion. "Two babies . . . save my babiessss," she wailed softly, too weak to do anything more.

"Somebody *pleaseeee!*" the paramedic screamed with

tears in her own eyes. She was a mother as well, so this was personal. Two nurses were hot on her trail leaving behind a frantic Ree who had to be subdued by three security guards. "We're losing them!"

Tatum thought she had finally gotten it right and realized there were two embryos growing inside of her, but then it hit her through her traumatic state that the "them" the woman was speaking of included herself. At that moment, she didn't care. She just wanted her babies to be healthy . . . and alive.

"Please, please, please! Where's the doctor?" she heard someone scream again.

There was a whirlwind of chaos surrounding her and at a terrifying time like this, she was walled by strangers. Tatum could hear a male's voice now, recognize the harsh demands being spewed around. He was the doctor; however, the rapid blood loss had her mind and vision clouding. Tatum wanted to cry some more but she was too weak. *What have I done? The sex? The hot tub? The tea? The hustle of the wedding? What did I do to deserve this? It has to be my fault . . . it just has to. Stress over the Sasha situation? Stress over Ree and his trial and drug bullshit? Lord, please forgive me. Please God, don't take away from me the best thing that ever happened to me. Don't take my blessing, Lord! Please don't take my babies!* Tatum silently begged.

She thought back to the ride to the hospital. She had never seen Ree so, well . . . scared.

"Floor this mothafucka, Crush! Fuck them lights!" Ree was a madman, spit spewing from his mouth, veins bulging out of his neck. She remembered Crush somberly suggesting that maybe they'd wait for the ambulance as Ree cradled Tatum in the backseat, her head in his lap, her blood filling the seats.

"I'm not waiting for them mothafuckas! This is my fucking wife and my fucking kids! I'm not waiting for no mothafucka to save them. Now floor this bitch!" In a nanosecond his voice transformed to calm and soothing vibrations.

"Tatum, baby, it's gonna be okay. You hear me? You're gonna be okay. The babies . . . the babies are gonna be fine. You hear me?"

Even in his dominant assurance, Tatum could hear something that crushed her inside—a small glimmer of doubt that he tried to conceal.

Tatum felt her breaths becoming shallow as the lighting around her changed, it was much brighter. Maybe she was being transferred to an operating room. Was the light in her face? Or was she dying? One thing she knew for sure was if her babies didn't make it, she certainly didn't want to either. Losing them would top her list of the tragedies she'd weathered. She'd certainly check out.

"Can you hear me, Mrs. Knights? Can you hear me? Do you think you can push?"

Tatum figured she wasn't dead yet. She tried to respond but she was way too weak. She gave the slightest of nods as her eyelids felt like they weighed a ton each and had no choice but to shut. *Please don't take my babies . . .*

"You wanna keep ya fucking hands, then get them the fuck off me! I ain't going nowhere!"

"Sir, you have to step—"

"You see my wife over there? Do your fucking job!"

Tatum awoke from her momentary blackout to the sounds of shouting voices, one in particular.

"My hus . . ." she tried to mumble. "R-r-r . . ."

"Bitch, go help my fucking wife!" she heard him yell again.

"Let him stay!" a deep voice bellowed, and Tatum

recognized it as the one from earlier that she had connected to the doctor. "We're in the middle of an emergency cesarean, people! Time is crucial!"

Tatum wasn't sure if she was drugged or just half conscious, but she couldn't focus, and she couldn't feel anything. Someone slipped a strong and masculine hand into hers and held a firm and semi-comforting grip, she felt that.

She fluttered her eyes over to her husband as he knelt holding her hand, and she could see the emotions that he was trying desperately to fight in his face. Was this real? Was she really here? Was this happening?

A part of her expected to wake up in her bed in her Atlanta home and realize this was all a dream. Another part of her wished to wake up in their home in Jamaica and have it had been an even bigger dream with Ree never coming back into the drug business, Sasha never discovering her secret, her never becoming pregnant with babies that she couldn't stand to possibly lose, Trinity and Johnny not being killed, none of it. Tatum even wondered if a part of her wished to wake up in her bed in her two-bedroom town house in Newark, hop on the phone, call Kim and Sasha on a three-way, and to have never even had met Ree in the first place. Him just being one huge, spell-binding and earth-shattering dream. One look at him made her realize that was not true, though, regardless of the circumstances.

"Okay!" The doctor sounded excited. "We've success-fully entered the womb. I see movement, breathing! These are good signs!"

Tatum's heart skipped although her body remained numb.

"Let's take the boy . . . no, from the position, let's remove the girl . . . the boy is . . ."

His voice trailed off. Tatum felt her hand drop, which

meant Ree had let go. She realized he was probably going to find out exactly what was happening beyond the lifted sheet that she couldn't see past, even if she had the strength to lift her head.

"The boy is what?" she heard her husband ask. Seconds later, she felt something. It was hard to explain. It was like a part of her was gone, a disconnect, a weight lifted. Tatum's heart paused. Was that her losing her baby? After an excruciating pause, she heard angels, she heard a cry. A faint, weak, and broken cry, but a cry nonetheless.

"Your son . . . your son," she heard the doctor announce. Tatum breathed a sigh of relief but then held it in again because they were only halfway there.

"Get him to the incubator, he's fighting but his breathing isn't strong!" Tatum hated those words. She heard hustle and bustle, lots of movement. She heard Ree asking questions with authority, them giving half answers. She also heard the doctor again. ". . . the girl . . . okay, she's almost . . ."

There was lots of silence, long pauses, the sound of tools being used and at work, Ree's breathing, her heart pounding, and then . . .

"Okay, she's out! She's . . ."

"She's what?" Ree demanded.

The doctor didn't respond. Or maybe Tatum just didn't hear it. From a place unknown, Tatum used every bit of strength she had and put it into her small hand, pushing down the sheet weakly. She had to see her daughter.

"Mrs. Knights, no!"

Blue.

A little brown baby should never be blue.

It should be impossible.

But she was.

If Tatum had any more power, she would have reached

for the scalpel herself and slit her own throat, but all she had the strength to do was to lose any strength she had left.

"Noooo . . ." she wailed, turning her head away from everyone. "Oh God . . . Oh God . . . Noooooooo!"

She couldn't even focus enough to lay eyes on Ree. Had she done so she would have seen the look of pure defeat, hurt, and agony in him, too strong for him to hide this time.

"I'm . . . I'm sorry . . ." the doctor must've mumbled. "For your loss."

There was a crash, a loud noise of things shattering to the floor.

"Mr. Knights! Please! P-please try to calm down." The doctor was scared.

Ree must've knocked some shit over. Tatum was in too much pain to even care.

"Your son is fighting . . . he . . . he needs you! Rebecca, p-please check on the status of the boy."

"Mr. Knights . . . please," the doctor coaxed. "I know . . . I know . . . but your wife . . . your son . . . they . . . they need you."

There were voices, movement, yelling, all types of background noise that Tatum was too distraught to decipher. Never had a pain been this dominant, nothing had ever hurt this bad, not even the death of her parents.

My son . . . I have to try to pull through for my son, she knew. And although she was in a state of complete devastation, unbearable pain, she couldn't wallow in it. Tatum was forced to put her mourning on hold. She had to pull enough of something from inside of her to say a prayer for her baby boy. *Please, Lord, don't take him, too. And if you do, my only wish is that you take me as well. Because I can't feel this twice.*

And then her eyes shut.

* * *

"Oh my God, oh my God, Chauncey! You have to drive faster! We have to get there. I have to get to Tatum . . . She needs me." Sasha looked out of the passenger window with tear-filled eyes. "She needs me," she mumbled again as the tears then fell to her cheeks.

Chauncey looked over at Sasha, upped his speed-ometer by another ten miles per hour, and took her small hand into his. He didn't know what was going on with Tatum and Sasha, and why they had been having a little distance between them, but he knew the depth and love of their friendship. He knew it stood many tests.

"They gonna be all right, princess. Stop crying."

"You don't know that, Chauncey," Sasha sobbed. "What if they won't? I'm so stupid! I should've been there for my friend. Oh my God . . ."

Chauncey stared ahead and his brows dipped low He hoped his words were true. He couldn't help but think of when Ree and Tatum were rushing to Sasha and himself at the hospital when their baby, Aubrey, had been poisoned. Aubrey had pulled through; hopefully Tatum and the twins would as well.

"They will, ma. People have babies early every day. They're gonna be all right, I'm sure . . . We're almost there." He squeezed her hand.

Sasha swallowed hard, trying to take a deep breath and calm her nerves. She thought of Chauncey's words, his demeanor, and his comfort at this time. He was the only person in the world who offered her that strength when she needed it, besides her daddy . . . the daddy she'd known all her life.

"I love you, Chauncey," she felt the need to say, never

meaning it as much as she did at that moment. "I love you so much."

Chauncey looked over at her with love in his eyes and squeezed her hand even tighter.

"I love you too, princess. Always will. You better always believe that shit."

Then he upped the speedometer by another ten miles, doing 105 all the way there.

"You look like me."

Ree paused. He never thought he'd be here. It was just him and his son, and watching him fight for his precious life, his tiny hands balling and his small body stretching with every breath being forced into him, it made Ree feel something that he wasn't used to—emotional.

He studied him. He was perfect. He was frail and still newborn-baby pale, his skin was soft with tiny wrinkles, but he was perfect, and he was fighting with all of his might, you could see it. He wanted to live.

Ree felt what he knew he should've felt with S.J. before but it had been impossible, an unbreakable, intense connection.

"I mean, you got your mother's mouth . . . those puckered lips. You know you can't be puckering those lips like that tho', little man," Ree chuckled lightly. He swallowed hard as his son just lay there with his eyes closed, seeming to be comforted by his voice, but Ree wondered if that was even possible. "But we gonna work on that. Yeah . . . we gonna work on a lot, me and you. And you gonna work on me. You gonna make me a better man . . . no doubt about it. 'Cause I give you my word, we gonna get you out of here. And bring you home. . . And spoil you like shit." He laughed lightly, with a hint of solemn in his voice. He wanted to touch him, but he couldn't. So he just ran his fingers lightly along the plastic.

"You know what else you got like your mother?" He asked the question as if the baby would answer. "You got that innocence. That purity . . . that light." It was what had made Ree fall in love with Tatum after all, thus making him fall into even deeper love with their off-spring.

"And in case you don't know . . . in case you can't feel it yet. I'll . . ." Ree paused, studying him with love and pain. "I'll do anything for you. I love you, little man. All right, get some rest . . . I'll be right back. I'm going to check on your mother . . . I'll be right back."

Ree felt the need to repeat it, not wanting his son to feel like he was abandoning him for even a second. He doubted he even knew he was there, though.

Ree turned to head out of the room, knowing he needed to go be there for Tatum. When he did, his son opened his eyes. He must've known.

First thing Sasha saw, which was the last thing she wanted to see, was Jayde pacing the waiting room floor like crazy, like she was Tatum's distraught best friend instead of her. And of course her plaything Bleek was seated not too far away, a blank stare on his face until he saw Sasha.

"Have you heard anything?" Sasha asked Jayde, know-ing her need to know what was happening was greater than her repulsion to speak to Jayde.

"She lost one . . . the little girl. The little boy is hanging on." Jayde barely looked up from the floor. She seemed uncommonly distressed, frazzled.

"They said the little boy gonna pull through," Bleek spoke up, keeping his focus on Sasha.

Sasha didn't know how to feel. Lose a child, gain a child, both at the same time. She pressed her eyes closed to fight tears as Chauncey just ran his hand over his face and then wrapped his arm around her shoulder.

"Where's Tatum? I need to see her," Sasha finally said after a brief silence. Chauncey motioned for Bleek to stand and follow him and they walked a little to talk in privacy.

"She doesn't want to see anyone," Jayde briefed.

"Oh please, it's me." Sasha waved her hand dismissively and started walking in the direction of the hall.

"No one!" Jayde spoke up. She held her hand out, stopping Sasha, and Sasha shot her the look of death.

"Bitch, if you don't get your hands off me," Sasha hissed through clenched teeth.

Jayde laughed, her regular demeanor returning.

"Wow. Either you got a death wish or you just may know how lucky you are, Sasha."

Sasha squinted at her, not taking a liking to being threatened.

"Lucky? Please. Lucky for what? That we're *friends,* Jayde?" Sasha thought it was funny because if they were really friends, Jayde would have told her about Mickel. She wouldn't be so sneaky.

Jayde snickered.

"No. Lucky that you're *family.*"

Sasha dropped her mouth slightly and then slowly pressed it into a tight scowl. Jayde must've known that she knew, she must've figured out why Sasha was throwing her shade, and now she was taunting her with it.

"Bitch!"

Sasha shoved Jayde hard and instantly a security guard stepped up, right when Jayde was reaching for her hip.

"I'm gonna have to ask y'all to leave!"

"I'm not going anywhere, make her leave!" Sasha shouted. Chauncey and Bleek hurried over.

"Yo, what the fuck is going on?" Chauncey roared. Lately, everything had been going nuts. Sasha and Tatum, Sasha and Jayde, Sasha and him. Sasha just seemed to be a ticking time bomb.

"This bitch won't tell me where Tatum is!"

"She doesn't want to see you, Sasha," Jayde stated calmly.

"Yo, kill that, Jayde. That's not your place," Chauncey dismissed, knowing Jayde was trying to hurt Sasha's feelings, and he wasn't having it.

"She did say she didn't wanna see nobody, though," Bleek spoke up, stating the honest.

"Yeah, well both of y'all mothafuckas don't know shit about they relationship, so both of y'all need to shut the fuck up," Chauncey barked.

"Yo, wit all due respect, C. You ain't gonna be chumping me like you do ya old lady in public."

Sasha dropped her jaw at Bleek's insult and Chauncey turned to him eyes ablaze.

"Nigga, fuck did you just say?"

Chauncey's jaw tightened in anger and he stepped to Bleek, fingers inching to his waistline.

The guard called for backup and another approached as he reluctantly stepped to block Chauncey.

"I'm saying you might not respect your broad, but you gonna respect me, shawty."

Chauncey chuckled and after a few seconds, he nodded and tapped his hip calmly, smiling at Bleek.

"I respect that. But yo, I got something you gonna respect too, B. Let me holla at you outside for a minute."

"No, Chauncey!"

Sasha stepped up. The absolute last thing she wanted was for Bleek and Chauncey to blow up and Bleek reveal their affair to him. She couldn't let Bleek ruin her life like that.

"I'm with that. I been meaning to holla at you anyway," Bleek stated confidently.

Sasha pressed her eyes shut and her heart pounded. This all got too real, too fast.

"No, stop. Please . . . don't kill him. Don't kill him, Chauncey!"

Chauncey looked at her like she was crazy. But she wasn't. She knew after that statement, the guards would not let them outside together at once.

"Whoa whoa listen! Before you all go to jail, let's get this under control. You and you!" The guard pointed at Jayde and Chauncey. "Leave!"

"No, please, sir, he's with me. My friend just lost her baby, I just need to see her. Please!"

The officer looked at Sasha's gorgeous face and her brick-house body in her jeans and tank top, and he had to oblige.

"Okay, Nurse, can you go see if her friend wants visitors? You and you, let's go." He motioned for Jayde and Bleek to go with him. Jayde didn't budge.

"Now! Before we call the police."

"Can you tell her it's Sasha!" Sasha screamed to the nurse.

The guard went to grab Jayde but she snatched her arm away.

"Don't do that, sweetheart," she warned. "Bleek baby, just go wait for me in the car. We got business to handle anyway. We gotta do that for Ree, and I can't disappoint him."

Sasha sneered at her, not liking how she said the last statement and Jayde returned the sneer, which proceeded with a sinister smile.

Bleek nodded. Cooling down a bit, he shot Sasha one last look and then walked out.

Chauncey had his eyes on his now-ringing phone and didn't notice. When he looked up, another nurse gave him a glower. He was not supposed to have it on. But this call was crucial and couldn't wait, it was business, in fact the business he had just discussed with Bleek a few minutes ago and he and Jayde were now going to handle. Chauncey stepped into the men's restroom to take the call, not caring about the rules. For once he'd put his issue with Bleek on the back burner and handle business first like a real boss. He'd have to spank his ass later, though, for real. Jayde used the opportunity once he was gone to say some parting words to Sasha.

"Sasha, look, I don't want to fight with you. I'm sorry if I hurt your feelings." Sasha just shot her a blank stare, not caring too much about her apology, and Jayde continued. "This is dumb, Sash! I mean look at Chauncey and Bleek. All of that nonsense, about to come to some serious shit. And what were they fighting over anyway?" Jayde gave Sasha a long up and down stare, from her head to Sasha's toes then back up to Sasha's face. "Nothing. They were fighting over . . . ab-so-lute-ly nothing."

Sasha smiled and bit her lip, knowing Jayde. She was calling her "nothing." Before she could even respond, or consider it, Chauncey emerged from the bathroom.

"Sir, where's the women's restroom?" Jayde asked

with a grin, turning her back to them. "I promise I will leave after that."

He pointed down the hall just as the nurse was approaching.

"Sasha?" the nurse called out.

"Yes!" Sasha turned, remembering the real reason she was here. Forget all of this extra stuff, she was here for her friend, her best friend.

The nurse looked at her solemnly and swallowed hard.

"I'm sorry . . . Mrs. Knights doesn't want visitors at this time."

Sasha felt her heart drop to the heels of her Giuseppe sandals.

"Not even me?" Tears rimmed her eyes.

"Told you," Jayde spat as she turned and headed to the bathroom.

"Yo, fuck her," Chauncey spoke up, before Sasha went crazy and he'd have to murder Jayde because he knew she was deadly and would react foolishly. "Let's just go. We'll come back tomorrow, princess. She'll be a little better then. Shit'll be calmer."

Sasha stood stagnated for a while, frozen . . . then reluctantly nodded and allowed herself to fall into Chauncey's embrace. She didn't even care about what Jayde had said or any of the drama. Now her heart hurt because she knew she hadn't and couldn't be there for her best friend. She'd let her pride come in between their friendship and she hoped Tatum could forgive her.

She allowed Chauncey to lead her away in sadness, his immediate focus now on mending her broken heart. And as the waiting area cleared and everyone retreated, Jayde made a detour from the bathroom . . . to the incubators.

* * *

"He's got ten little fingers . . . ten little toes. My eyes . . . my nose . . ."

"Ugh." Tatum snapped out of her grave trance to give a half joke. She smiled weakly, envisioning him, she couldn't wait until she could walk to go and see him.

"Your mouth . . . seriously, your mouth. I hope he really doesn't have your mouth though, you know? Or I'm gonna go crazy." They shared a light laugh and Tatum waved her hand with the little strength she had. Tears still steadily flowed for her ordeal, though; she couldn't stop them, even while laughing.

"I am not loud," she whispered with a hoarse voice, still staring off. Ree's face gradually turned serious. He knew she was hurting. Beyond that, he knew she was destroyed. He was too. But it was like he was with a shell of Tatum, and this person was trying its best to impersonate her, and laugh and smile like she would, but the imposter couldn't. A part of her was dead. Hopefully their son could bring her back to life. Ree wet his lips lightly before speaking.

"He's fighting, Tatum. He is. He just needs us to fight with him, baby."

Tatum stared off deep in thought on Ree's words. They hit her and she knew what they meant. She had to pull it together for her baby.

The young blond nurse entered with a smile.

"I just checked on him, your little one . . . about ten minutes ago. He's so strong. He's doing really well. Have you decided on a name yet?"

Tatum had been scared to give him a name, scared that he'd be taken too. But she was ready, especially after Ree's statement.

"Taye . . . his name is Taye," she spoke up hoarsely.

Ree smiled lightly. They had discussed giving the twins her deceased parents' names and he had told her it was up to her. Now he saw she decided to, and he was glad.

"And my daughter, can you . . . can you tell them her name was Tamia?"

That was her mother's name. And that was how they had come up with her name, the first parts of their own names, Taye and Tamia . . . Tay-Tam . . . Tatum.

The nurse smiled, seeing she decided to actually name her daughter and hold a funeral as the doctor offered.

"Of course . . . that's beautiful."

Just then the doctor stepped inside. He smiled lightly at Tatum and then turned to Ree.

"Mr. Knights . . . may I . . . may I speak to you for a minute?"

"Doctor, when will I be able to go and visit my baby?" Tatum interrupted, sounding a little excited.

"I'll be right back and . . . we can discuss it." He didn't make eye contact.

Tatum didn't notice. Ree did.

"Mr. Knights," he repeated.

Ree stood and walked out of the room, following the doctor. His calm demeanor hid his anxiety.

The doctor turned, faced him, and just stared at him for a moment.

"He's dead."

Ree said it. Ree said it because the doctor's eyes told him it. He didn't want a speech, he didn't want fancy words or other terms like they did for Tamia, like *still-born*. No, she was dead. Athough Ree said it first his heart desperately wanted the doctor to dispute it.

"He . . . he . . . he . . . just stopped . . . *breathing*."

In an instant the doctor found his thin frame pinned against the wall and Ree's hands locked around his throat. He saw the devil. He saw death. He was shaking terribly and incredibly frightened.

"Mr. . . . Knights," he gasped.

"What did you do?" Ree spewed in a rage, his grip growing tighter and his visible tattoos on his neck and arm seeming to come to life dancing on his bulging veins.

"P-please, Mr. Knnnightsss. I'm s-s-sorry," he choked out the words.

"What did you do?" Ree repeated angrily, not giving a fuck about where they were or who this was. He needed to release this demon. Someone would die tonight, like his children did.

"Mr. Knights . . . P-P-Please! I . . . I didn't do anything! I swear . . . I didn't do a-a-anything!" the doctor pleaded through borrowed breaths.

Ree saw the fear in his eyes, he saw the panic. Ree closed his own lids briefly and his grip became looser. Something else was taking over his rage . . . defeat. He'd never felt defeated, never had lost. But tonight, death had fought against him, against a man who could make any and every thing happen, and control all, but death had won.

Ree let the doctor's body fall limply to the ground as the doctor gasped for air, still visibly shaken.

"Exactly," Ree told him calmly. "You didn't do any-thing. You just cut my children out of the womb and let them fucking die. Get the fuck out of here . . . Now!"

The doctor scrambled to his feet and disappeared down the hall terrified.

Ree himself then dropped down to the ground in a

squat and put his hands on his head. He couldn't cry, for some reason, he just couldn't. Maybe it hurt so bad he went numb. But he knew he had to sit there and let it soak in, and then let it go. He had lost a daughter and a son in one night and he knew in a way he was about to lose his wife, at least for a little while. And even as a man of his stature, he couldn't do anything about it. No, he was defeated.

Chapter 12

"A nigga fucks up, a lot. All of 'em. They all fuck bitches, they all lie, they all cheat. Sometimes they stop, sometimes they don't."

—Chauncey, *Thicker than Water*

<u>Act III</u>

"Yeah, a'ight. Set up the last meeting for the schedules. Get the wheels rolling on this mothafucka."

And with that last demand, Chauncey disconnected the call. He was glad this shit was coming to an end, the planning and setting-up end. Now it was time to get money, and for Respect, time to almost be done.

Since the hospital incident Chauncey had been dealing with Bleek strictly on a business level. Bleek shot him a "my bad" after that and Chauncey blew it off, but he definitely saw the young boy in a new light. Had it been a couple of years ago, he'd be covered in dirt. But the new Chauncey saw the bigger picture, especially after Ree painted it for him. Just from the conversation they'd just shared, one could tell Chauncey didn't fuck with him too tough.

"Clown-ass country mothafucka," Chauncey mumbled as he twisted up something in his swishers. It was dark out and he was parked outside of his home in his Range Rover, something he rarely drove.

He was gonna blow this one and then go blow Sasha's back out, that was the plan at least.

"Mr. Mills? Mr. Mills, is that you in there?"

Chauncey stared blankly out of his tinted windows at his little old white neighbor, Mrs. Pearl, as she tapped on his vehicle. She could barely see him but he could see her.

"You gotta be fucking kidding me," he mumbled. Mrs. Pearl looked like Blanche from *The Golden Girls*.

"Yeah, Mrs. Pearl, it's me," he said in exasperation, placing his smoke in the ashtray. He cracked the window.

"What's up?"

Why this little old lady thought they were best friends, Chauncey found amusing and confusing. The last thing her little white ass needed was a big black drug-dealer friend. But he figured she knew he had money, and she had money, so they had that in common.

"Oh," she said, smiling and giggling. "I thought so. But I haven't seen you in your truck in quite a while." Chauncey nodded while she laughed some more, trying to steal peeks at what he was doing. Mrs. Pearl was nosy as hell.

"Um, well, anyway. I just wanted to say that I baked a pie for you, Sasha, and the little one. Apple of course, with the Granny Smiths, from the backyard."

Chauncey couldn't front, that sounded type right at this moment.

"That's what's up, Mrs. Pearl. Good looking out."

He always talked to her in his slang, she got a kick out of it.

"No doubt, C, no doubt," she said, smiling back, and they both shared a hearty laugh. "You just come by and grab it when you're done . . . or tomorrow morning."

"All right, Mrs. Pearl. I'll probably swing by in the A.M. That's cool with you?"

"Cool with me, cutie pie!" She winked and then began moving her old, wrinkled butt away and toward her door.

Chauncey shook his head and chuckled, and was about to roll up the window but she doubled back.

"Oh! One more thing . . . just be careful smoking those weeds, Chauncey!" she whispered. "The popo rolled through here *twice* this evening."

Chauncey threw his head back not able to take anymore. Wait until he told Sasha, she always got a kick out of his Mrs. Pearl stories.

"All right, thanks for the heads up." The laugh was still in his voice.

She started walking again after shooting him a nod, and just as Chauncey was rolling up his window, she turned again.

"Oh! One more thing . . . wait, what was it? Oh, forgive me, Chauncey, you know I'm almost eighty years old, I'm getting up there. Oh wait . . . yes, I remember. One more thing!"

Chauncey shook his head and rolled the window all the way down. He knew when Mrs. Pearl said that, they'd be talking all night. He sparked up and prepared for it.

The knocking on her door let her know that he was there. She smiled, grabbed a bottle of Beyoncé's Heat perfume and sprayed it in her hair, at the hem of her bustier, and on the lining of her panties as she grinned wide. She strutted sexily to the door and pulled it open, standing modelesque in her black lingerie, garter belt and thigh highs, and spiked heels. Her pussy instantly creamed from the sight of him.

"Damn, you don't waste no time, huh? You did all that in twenty minutes?" Chauncey asked, stepping inside calmly but enjoying the scenery.

"Years of practice," Lizette smiled, thinking of her days at the strip club. Sometimes she literally had to get as sexy as possible in three minutes flat. "Come in, make yourself at home, Chauncey."

"I plan to . . . right in here," he told her, placing a finger to her lips. He licked his own and stared right at her, his dark eyes piercing her brown ones. "And in here," he added, palming her ass. Lizette was on fire, Chauncey clearly in control.

She closed the door and followed behind him as he stepped heavy through her apartment in his expensive thug wear and jewels. He smelled good, like Issey Miyake cologne and money.

"You know . . . I was surprised when you called. Even when you said you were coming, I still didn't believe you."

"Why is that?" he asked, blasé, flopping comfortably down on her couch. "Come here, walk to me."

"I don't know," she sang immaturely, moving to him. "Nah, slow."

She paused, and then did as she was told.

"So you the boss? You like to be in control, huh?"

Chauncey smirked as she neared him. Lizette had a body on her, something out of this world. But she was a dimwit. He didn't want to fuck her brain, though, he just wanted her to bless him with it.

"You talk too much. Come do something with all that mouth."

Lizette chuckled and then knelt down, squatting in between his knees. Chauncey picked up the remote and turned to the basketball game as she unbuckled his pants.

"So you want a quiet chick . . . like Sasha?"

Chauncey took the remote and hit her on the side of her head roughly, stunning her a bit.

"That's what the fuck I'm talking about. You talk too much."

Lizette pouted and rubbed the side of her head. She wasn't feeling too sexy now but she also didn't want him to go.

"Ow."

Chauncey softened a bit, cupping her chin.

"Come on, ma. I came here to relieve stress. Not pick up more of that shit. Just suck my dick, baby. Suck it like a pro . . . I know you can."

Lizette licked her lips and smiled, pulling out his shaft.

"You know I can."

If Chauncey was into pimping, it'd take nothing to put her on his team. She ate up all his shit.

"That's my girl," he spoke lowly as she wrapped her lips around his thick head and wet it with extra saliva. She hocked up spit and covered his dick with it, and then she used her hands and mouth to do spirals on his tool.

"Damn . . . that's what I came for!"

Chauncey leaned back and enjoyed the trip as Lebron scored a three.

He was back to his old ways.

* * *

Ree had dived nose first into wrapping up the plans and making as much money as possible, trying his best at executing his only form of therapy for something emotional occurring in his life—forgetting it. He wanted to hold on to the slight memory of his children, especially those stolen moments he had with Taye, but he also, as bad as it sounded, wanted to forget them.

He tried to be there for Tatum but she hardly let him. Their bedroom was constantly filled with flowers, mostly from Sasha, some from him, Crush, Jayde, and Chauncey. Sasha visited her and he could tell Tatum tried her best to be present during the visits but she was still lost. Often she would just sit in the dark, drapes drawn, or sleep the day away, company or no company.

But still he talked to her every day. He fed her, helped her bathe, washed her hair, and rubbed her on her back until she fell asleep in his arms every night. They were in a space, a space that shouldn't have been theirs to own for at least some years to come. No, as newlyweds, and newly multimillionaire newlyweds, they should have been living it up, sexing and spending lavishly. But tragedy had put a halt to all of that and Ree was sure they would bounce back shortly, but again he would be wrong.

"Yo, boss."

Ree looked up to the door. He was seated at his mahogany desk in his outsize office, a cigar and top-quality herb scattered strategically in front of him.

"Crush, what up . . ."

Crush stepped inside, his heavy build sliding through the door as he closed it behind him. He walked over and took a seat across from Ree.

"You decided what you gonna do yet?" Crush asked genuinely. He could see the stress on his old friend. He knew Ree, he knew he lived this lifestyle effortlessly, but he also knew that he was at his best when he wasn't living it.

"I don't know, man," Ree stated, running his hand slowly over his face and leaning back in his seat. "You know, I'm trying to see what Tatum wants, but at this point I think I'm ready to pack this shit up, throw her over my shoulder, and just carry her ass back to the island. It's been nothing but bullshit since we came to Atlanta. I think I'm cursed in the States," he chuckled.

Crush shared in the chuckle and nodded to himself.

"I think that's the best, yo. For real. And you know I'm with you the whole way."

Ree had offered Crush a job with him, whether he stayed in America or moved back to Jamaica after the deal was done. He even offered to purchase Crush and his family their own home in Jamaica as well. Crush was grateful and secretly hoping for that opportunity.

"And everything almost squared up with this thing, right? Then you really ain't got no ties here."

Ree nodded.

"Yeah. I'm ready, too. I mean this shit was easy, too easy. I couldn't pass it up. If it was just me, you know, I'd live like this to the grave. But my life is not about me anymore, Crush. And this shit is taking a toll on her."

Crush understood, and he respected Ree for thinking of Tatum. He liked Tatum a lot and he loved her for Ree.

"Yeah man, you gotta do what's best for y'all, boss. I just went up there, tried to get her to eat. But she wouldn't. She was crying and shit before I came in there, I can tell. . . . She tried to hide it, though."

Ree remained quiet at Crush's revelation. He knew Tatum tried to remain strong in appearance to people. The thought of her crying alone stung him. But he knew she would recover.

"She'll be all right." He spoke the words, thinking that'd make them true because he ordered them to be. "Once this shit is over, she'll be all right. It'll be me and her. That's it."

Crush wanted to ask, but didn't know how to . . .

"You think . . . y'all gonna try . . . like you know, for another seed?"

Ree clenched his jaw but released it, finally lighting up the cigar he'd been rolling.

"No. But whatever happens . . . happens." He shrugged. He knew Tatum wasn't ready for that yet, but he'd be ready whenever she was.

"Truthfully, I just want to finish up here and get shit back to normal. Only problem is . . ." Ree paused. He rarely discussed his business or concerns of it, but Crush was the one person he felt he could talk about that with.

". . . Man, I *have* to get Manuel on board with the program. He's down with this first run because it's me. But he's skeptical about the next, because it's Jayde. So he's at a standstill, the nigga don't wanna move at all. He doesn't trust her."

"I can see why," Crush huffed, half under his breath but Ree caught it.

"Trust me, I feel you. I feel the same exact way. But it's business," Ree summed up.

Crush shook his head before adding, "It's just something about her, boss. Like the bitch ain't wrapped too tight."

Ree shrugged.

"She's stupid. I mean she's street smart and she's very calculating, but she moves dumb. She thinks dumb." Ree laughed lightly. "I can't believe she's Mickel's daughter." He was looking forward to cutting ties with Jayde as well.

"She's not a threat, though. She talks tougher than she walks," Ree incorrectly assumed.

"But you don't trust her either, right?" Crush asked, really not caring for Jayde.

Ree took a long pull from his blunt and blew out smoke smoothly before responding.

"I don't trust anyone. But to answer your question . . . No."

A knock at the door interrupted their conversation.

"What?"

Ree considered it probably was Tatum and rephrased his words.

"Come in."

The tall and heavy wooden door creaked open and in stepped a bright red stiletto, followed by the other, long legs donned in a Herve Leger dress and those greedy, money-green eyes.

"Gentlemen."

"Who let you in?" Ree asked abruptly. Crush only turned his back to her and faced Ree.

Jayde cut her eyes at him and then addressed Ree.

"Tatum. She was heading out."

Ree crinkled a brow.

"Tatum was outside?" He couldn't believe it. Was she coming around? Why hadn't she come to him?

Jayde shrugged.

"Yeah. She said she was going to feed the horses, see them, brush their hair or some shit," Jayde informed him dismissively. If she got the chance to replace Tatum in this lavish-ass ranch-style mansion, the first thing that would go was those fucking horses. Ree and Tatum thought they'd provide the perfect American dream for their twins, both would have their own ponies. But Jayde was not the kind of woman into animals and furry things. Too much love, too much attention off her, too much upkeep. The only animal she ever owned was her six-foot yellow python, Butter. And he was deadly, just like her.

"Someone just called for you. I told them to call back in three minutes and I'd bring you the phone," she informed him, holding out the cordless.

"I didn't hear the phone ring." Ree continued to smoke and squinted at her, mind still on Tatum's decision to get out and get some air, get moving.

"Well it did. I stopped by the kitchen to grab a water and picked it up. It only rang once."

"I'm not taking calls."

"I think it's urgent."

"Why you say that?"

"The call was from Jamaica."

"So why didn't you bring it to me?"

"I knew you were talking to Crush. Didn't want to interrupt," she combated with a smile. She knew Ree was skeptical of her; she actually enjoyed it. Because the dark side of her understood the dark side of him, the kind that was a thrill seeker and attracted to dangerous and unknown situations, like the streets. It was a gamble, because you didn't know if the streets would love you back. Jayde was like the streets, she was a dangerous, unknown, and thrilling situation and she knew eventually Ree would be drawn to her.

Tatum was like the straight life, like running the hotel in Jayde's eyes. Sure, it was nice, simple, pretty, and easy, but it was a boring, guaranteed, sure thing. And bottom line, it just wasn't for him.

"Where's your water?"

"What?" Jayde laughed.

"Your water. You said you went to grab a water, where is it?"

"On the kitchen counter," she laughed some more,

showing all of her pretty whites. "Now you're fucking with me. Why don't you tell me which part you think I'm lying about so I can convince you it's the truth," she spat with confidence. After the two held eye contact for a while. Ree had to chuckle at that but Crush didn't. Just then the phone rang, an 876 area code signifying a call from Jamaica appeared.

"Yes," Ree addressed. The calm in his face, the one had just been placed there by the effects of his cannabis and the news of Tatum's progress gradually began to fade. Crush could tell it was serious.

"When did this happen?"

A long pause followed.

"How is he doing?"

Another pause.

"I'm on my way."

And then Ree disconnected without another word.

"Yo, everything cool boss?"

Ree stared blankly ahead, his thoughts racing a hundred miles an hour. Finally he spoke.

"The hotel burned down last night. Leroy was inside," he spoke evenly, talking of his father. "He was pulled out but he's in the hospital. They said about eighty people died. I have to go."

Crush couldn't believe his ears, eighty innocent people, just dead. Lucky Ree's father had survived, but still, he was shocked. Jayde was not, but she appeared to be.

"Oh my God! You want me to call the jet for you?" Jayde asked sincerely.

Ree couldn't think straight.

"Uh . . . yeah."

"I'll call it, man," Crush spoke, standing up, shooting Jayde a stiff stare and stepping out. Ree went to move out after him.

"Wait. You need me to do anything, Sean?" Jayde asked sweetly, stepping close to him and lightly grabbing his arm when it was just them two left. Ree looked down at her manicured hands gripping his bicep and then back up at her.

"Nah."

He pulled away from her, swaggering out of the office. A second later he doubled back.

"Hey, Jayde?"

"Yeah," she answered quickly, turning and staring right in his eyes.

"You can do me one favor."

She smiled at the statement. "What's that?" She was more than willing and ready. Ree looked her up and down and then ordered, "Don't ever call me Sean again."

She swallowed hard, as if drinking down her pride, smirked, and nodded.

"Got it."

Ree turned this time and kept walking. He needed to find the woman who did have the privilege to call him that name. He needed to find Tatum.

"She was here, but she left, Mr. Knights. In that direction . . . toward the trees." That's what the guy who came daily to tend to the horses had told him when he went to the stables. Now Ree walked toward the hill where a bunch of weeping willow trees shaded the land. He found Tatum standing at the cliff overlooking the long drop that led to the shallow lake and rocks below. For some reason, the sight made Ree apprehensive.

"What you doing, Tatum?"

The sound of his voice made her body jump slightly from a trance, thinking she was alone. She stumbled a bit but Ree already had his hands out, steadying her and then pulling her back.

"Why are you standing so close, anyway?" he asked seriously, his voice carrying a hint of worry.

Is she? She can't be thinking about doing anything crazy. Nah, not Tatum. She was too strong. But how much could the too strong take before they gave in and became weak?

"I just wanted to see," she spoke lowly, still gazing out at the dead air, dead air that led to the deadly hundred-foot drop.

"Well, you can see from back here, baby. That's dangerous."

No answer.

"Listen, Crush is calling the jet. We have to go to Jamaica, some shit happened. I'll explain on the plane."

"How can you just bounce back?"

"Excuse me?" Ree really hadn't understood. Her back was still to him, but he squinted at her. She was still wearing a long, purple silk robe tied tight. Her hair was dry in wild curls from when he'd washed it but didn't know how to straighten it or comb it or do any of that shit she did to it to keep it from getting like this. The wind blew through them and the scenery was so serene, but a bit eerie.

"How . . . can you . . . just bounce . . . back? You act like nothing ever happened? You act like none of this shit happened."

Ree sighed. This was her first time opening up about her feelings and he knew she questioned his method of handling things, but he couldn't discuss that now, too much was happening. Ree was not used to dealing with this magnitude of emotions, everything for him had always been black or white, life or death, kill or be killed.

"Tatum, I didn't. Look, we'll talk about this later.

Right now, the hotel has burned down, people are dead, Tatum. We have to go . . ."

"When will you be back?" she asked him. Ree blew out air.

"Tatum, you're coming with me. Pop was in the hotel . . . he's in the hospital."

That hurt Tatum. She wanted tears to come to her eyes for Pop but they couldn't. Every single tear her body could possibly produce had soaked her pillow for her babies. But she hadn't seen Ree cry one. Not one single tear from him. And that infuriated her.

"I don't care."

Ree clenched his jaw, gripped his fists, then released. She was hurting, but he swore if it was anyone else, he would have pushed them off the fucking cliff.

"You don't know what the fuck you're saying. So let's go, put on some fucking clothes, and get on the plane." He grabbed her roughly by the arm, trying to maintain his composure. Tatum snatched herself away.

"Don't fucking curse at me, Ree! I know what the fuck I'm saying. Maybe I don't give a fuck about your father the way you didn't give a fuck about our babies! You were talking about fight, and Taye fighting and us fighting for him. But you didn't fight! You got me fighting this pain, alone. I'm alone! So no, I don't care! You didn't care, why should I? You go, I'll stay. And then if he dies you can go sell more drugs and act like he never existed either—"

Ree gripped her by the back of her head so swiftly, holding the root of her hair firmly and inflicting slight pain. Tatum never saw it coming. She noticed the tightness in his face, the anger. She had gone too far. He tightened his grasp, bringing his face to hers and unblinkingly piercing his black eyes through her. He could see the slight fear in her.

"Tatum . . ." He spoke through gritted teeth. But he couldn't say anymore. He just stared at her as the seconds passed.

One second . . . breathe . . . just fucking breathe.

Two seconds . . . relax.

Two more . . . loosen your grip, she's scared.

Three more . . . don't hurt her . . . whatever you do, don't hurt her.

For that one he allowed about ten more to pass before he could feel his patience return.

Ten more seconds . . . just walk away. That's what you do, just walk the fuck away.

And after a long glance at her, he did just that.

"Now what?"

"Now what, what?" Jayde questioned with a chuckle, wiping her eyes.

Ree sighed heavily, grabbing his keys and phone off his office desk. He glanced up once at Jayde who stood by the window, seeming to try to clear her face up.

These fucking women.

"Why are you crying?" Ree feared it was something with Mickel.

"I'm not . . . *crying*," Jayde tittered.

"Why are you upset?" he rephrased. *She thinks she's so fucking tough. But she's not.*

Jayde licked her lips and put on her performance as a vulnerable woman. She thought of Sasha and mimicked her ways.

"I'm not. I mean . . . I guess so much shit is happening, you know. I'm so worried about Tatum and I feel so bad for you guys. And then . . . your dad. And then you."

"Me?" Ree didn't understand that part. He wondered

where the hell Crush was with the jet. He began to scroll through his phone for his number.

"Yeah you," Jayde countered, looking at him as he seemed focused on anything but her. "You know I only try to help sometimes. I know I may come off strong . . . but you're crazy hard on me, Mr. Knights. Or Respect . . . I don't know what you want me to call you," she added in a joke. Ree looked at her.

"I'm hard on you? I thought you were a gangster," he mocked her, placing the phone to his ear as it rang.

"I'm still a woman, Respect. You know I looked up to you for a long time. My father always praised you. I wanted to learn from you . . . to make him proud so he could boast about me the way he did about you."

Crush didn't answer the phone so Ree hung up.

"But it's like you can hardly stand me. Like you're scared to be around me. Why is that?"

"I'm not scared of shit, Jayde," Ree corrected. "I don't really have time for this. But trust me, it's not you. When it comes to business I don't believe it should entail too much interaction. The day we decided to do business together is the day you should've let all of that big-brother, looking-up-to-me shit go."

I don't want to fuck the dog shit out of my big brother, Jayde thought as she eyed his sexiness and the way he filled out his designer threads, but she reasoned with, "But you don't *like* me. You don't respect me. If I wasn't Mickel's daughter you would probably want me dead."

Ree sighed, placing his hands in his pockets, and thought about what she was saying. He gave her credit for addressing it.

"I think you're guileful, Jayde . . . very manipulative . . . and I think you're trickery at its best. And yes, I owe my life to your father, but I don't want you dead. Now I have to go. We through here?"

Jayde laughed lightly.

"Yeah, we through." Ree started out but she stopped him in his tracks with her next words.

"But you're the same exact way."

Ree spun around, a bit intrigued and challenged.

"Trust me, Jayde, we're nothing alike. Now where the fuck is Crush?" he said more to himself, starting toward the door again.

"Really? So you're honest? You're not calculating . . . 'trickery at its best'?"

"Not at all," he replied to her confidently, turning around in annoyance. He wanted her to know exactly what he was saying.

"Take E, for example, how you handled him. On some setup shit but you deal with C. See that's sideways shit. We don't move the same."

"I beg to differ," she combated, hearing footsteps in the distance. "But I'll let you go. We can finish another time."

Ree was feeling tested and he wanted to know what she thought she knew. He looked at her with a deadly stare.

"Speak on it."

She swallowed hard and then pressed her lips together. Folding her arms across her chest, she stared back at him.

"Chris," she spoke. Ree remained expressionless. "How would Tatum feel if she knew you were responsible for her brother's death?"

"Listen to me. You don't know what the fuck you're—" A loud crashing of glass in the hallway caused Ree to turn and abruptly snatch the already cracked door open, Jayde right behind him. Ree saw nothing, but looked down and saw a broken white china cup and saucer, liquid, maybe water, and a tea bag. *Her tea bag.*

He brought his head up and caught Tatum's frizzy curls bouncing away as she ran.

"Tatum!" His voice thundered and it was deep, loud, and thundered through the whole house. "Tatum, come back here!" He ran behind her, finally catching up in his swiftness in the left-wing living room. He grabbed her arm and pulled her to him but she spun around swinging with tears drenching and completely covering her face. *She knew. She fucking knew.*

"Get off of me! You fucking monsterrrr!" She punched him repeatedly and Ree didn't have to tide his temper. His guilt and fear of losing her overpowered any anger he could possibly have.

"How could you do this? How could you fucking do this to me! Why didn't you just leave me alone! How could you?" Her cries were like howls, coming from the pit of her stomach. The pain of losing the only family she had left now resurfaced. And it had been at the hands of the man she loved. She had thought Chris's street ways had caught up to him and it was some miscellaneous bastard who took his life. But she shared her bed with him, she shared her bed with her brother's murderer. And to think she was coming to apologize for what she'd said to him about his father.

"Tatum! Calm down! Listen . . ."

"Listen to what?" Just then Crush walked in on what seemed to be a disaster.

"Listen to you? You're a fucking animallll!" Tatum covered her face with her hands, just wanting to die. Visions of Ree holding a gun to her brother and pulling the trigger, and then making love to her, drove Tatum crazy. She brought her hands to her hair and began pulling it roughly, chunks falling in her hands.

"Ughhhh!!!! I hate you! I fucking hate you! I wish I never fucking met you! You ruined . . . my . . . life!" She

pointed her finger in his face and screamed it with
certainty. Ree swallowed hard and stared at her, never
had he felt bad about anything he'd ever done, any
murder he'd ever committed, or any wrongdoing he'd
ever executed. But this was the worst feeling he'd ever
felt. Hurting and betraying the person he'd loved most,
and knowing he could lose her.

"Tatum . . ."

"Stop it. Just stop it, Ree! This is it. Don't you see?
The fucking leaving me for Jamaica! Trinity and all of
her bullshit! This fucking battle I've been fighting with
the streets, hoping you'd leave them! Your fucking
master plan! Her!" she yelled, pointing at Jayde. "That
bullshit with Johnny, losing *my babies.* And now *this.* I am
done! Just stay the fuck away from me! I should've never
let you back in my life! I wish they would've locked you
the fuck up where you belong, in a cage you fucking
monster!"

Ree just stared at her solemnly, not even knowing
what to say. She was telling the truth. He was. He had
been selfish, but with the purest of intentions, to think
he could avenge Chris's deception and still be with his
sister. He looked around and saw Jayde and Crush
standing there, stunned.

"We need to be alone." They started to move.

"No! I don't wanna be alone with you," Tatum spat,
staring at him like a madwoman. "You make my fucking
skin crawl! I'm leaving you!" She dashed for the door,
but Ree grabbed her and pinned her hard against the
wall, holding all of his weight against her.

"Tatum, calm down! You're gonna hear me out. I
know you're upset. But we're gonna talk about this. And
you're not going anywhere. You're my wife, and we took
vows . . . I love you."

"Ha!" Tatum hock-spat in his face. "Talk about that.

I'm getting a fucking divorce, now get the fuck off of me! You're out of your fucking mind if you think I'm staying with you!" She went to move again but Ree grabbed her shoulders and slammed her back against the wall forcefully.

"No," he barked. He stared in her eyes and Tatum could see he was terrified for the first time ever. "Tatum . . . please," he whispered. Ree never begged for anything in his life. He stared at her with pleading eyes. "I'm not letting you leave."

She went to move again, but this time he gripped her arm with one hand and her neck tight with the other. Crush moved in.

"Boss . . . just . . . just let her cool down. C'mon, boss . . ." He could see Ree was hurting Tatum in his forceful way of preventing her from leaving.

Tatum looked at him in disdain.

"What you gonna do, huh, Sean? You gonna kill me, too?"

Ree tried to keep the eye contact, tried to connect with her in that way that only they could. But it was gone. Tatum had already left him, he could see it in her eyes. He loosened a little, but not enough for her to move, just enough to stop hurting her.

She pierced him with her glare and then she spoke slowly.

"Let . . . me . . . go."

Their eyes were locked on each other's for what seemed like an eternity. How could he expect anything different? She was gone. Ree knew he'd have to let her go. So he did, slowly.

Releasing his grip, he took a step back as silence covered the room. Tatum's body loosened limply, her chest heaving up and down in pain, hurt, anger. Pain, because the same hands that had made her body come

to life had taken the life of her brother. Hurt, because
he had betrayed her, looked in her face every day knowing
what he had done to her. And anger, anger with herself,
because even after finding this out, she still loved him. She
still couldn't believe she'd be walking out of that door
and out of her husband's life. But she had to. Tatum
lifted her right hand and was ready to smack him but
she didn't even have the strength. She just took that
same hand, reached over to her left, and pulled her ring
off, throwing it to the ground.

"I can't save you. You're the damn devil."

And with that, she walked out. And he let her.

After a few moments of silence, Jayde sighed deeply.
"Oh my God, that was crazy. Ree I am so s—"

Jayde's apology was cut short by the backhand blow
to her face that sent her flying into the wall. A stream of
blood sailed from her mouth in thin air and landed on
the white paint.

"Boss!"

"Bitch, is this what you wanted? Is that what the fuck
you wanted?" Ree hissed, lifting Jayde's body in the air
with one hand gripped around her throat. Unlike when
he held Tatum, he was trying to choke the life out of
Jayde.

"Boss! Yo, chill. This is bad . . . that's not a good idea.
This is fucking bad."

Crush hated Jayde, but she was connected. Very connected. And their business wasn't over. He could not
let Ree, a man who lived by not letting his emotions
get him into compromising situations, make a foolish
mistake.

"You killing her, Respect!"

The color drained out of Jayde's face, but she refused
to cry. She stared at Ree sternly.

"Is that what you wanted?" he repeated. She only shook her head no. Crush continued to pull Ree and plead for him to stop. As Jayde was on the brink of unconsciousness, Ree let her go. Her body fell to the ground with a thud. Jayde was weak, but she was still breathing.

The fact of the matter was he was upset at her, but it was his fault. She hadn't made him kill Chris. He had done that on his own. He also considered how he had asked her to tell him what she knew. In a way, he invited it because he knew what she was insinuating. Still, he couldn't help but let her know what he thought of her at that moment.

"Dumb cunt." He sneered down at her with venom in his eyes. She was scared, something she was not used to being. This was the Respect she had heard about and she knew he would and could kill her. Ree then looked to Crush. He was furious, moving like a panther in the jungle and no one wanted to get in his way.

"Where's the jet?"

Crush took a deep breath, knowing what was happening. Ree was about to shut down and get back to business.

"It's ready."

Ree sighed and knelt down, picking up his phone and his keys, which had fallen in the commotion; and then he picked up Tatum's ring. He held it in between his thumb and forefinger and twirled it around.

"Go after her, find out where she went. Make sure she's all right . . . and report back to me."

With nothing more said than that, he walked out. Crush knew out of everything he'd ever done for Ree, those last orders would forever be the most important. He had to find Tatum.

Chapter 13

"Fuck you, Sasha! You ain't nothing but a dumb-ass country bumpkin that thinks the fucking world revolves around you!"

—Neli, *Thicker than Water*

The jingle of the keys in the front door announced Sasha's arrival. Aubrey immediately jumped down off the couch and ran to greet her.

"Mommy's home! Mommy's home!"

Sasha stepped in, a big smile on her face. Seeing her baby so excited for her always melted her heart.

"Hey, Bri-Bri! How's Mommy's big girl? How's Mommy's girl?" she cooed.

"Mommy, me and Daddy made sketti and bread-tix!" Aubrey announced proudly.

"Sketti, huh?" Sasha asked, smiling at her and then up at Chauncey. She knew she meant spaghetti. Chauncey seemed preoccupied in between his phone and video game, but gave Sasha a half smile.

Sasha closed the door and locked it behind her, and then strolled over to him, her Dior sundress clinging to her shapely frame.

"And how's Mommy's big boy doing?" she asked, leaning down to kiss him.

"I'm straight."

She pecked his lips and caught the hint of something. She couldn't put her finger on it, the smell. Just when she was giving it good thought, her cell phone began to ring but she ignored it.

"Who's that?" Chauncey asked. Sasha sighed.

"This fucking nurse from the hospital. She keeps leaving me messages about how she needs to talk to me because it's important. It's probably about the application I dropped off there but I told them I already accepted another offer, damn!"

Sasha all but forgot about the frivolous conversation she had shared with the nurse about Jayde, especially with all that had been happening.

"Why don't you just answer it?" Chauncey questioned with a chuckle.

"Because . . . I don't feel like it." Sasha leaned down to kiss him again. Half because he looked so good, and the other half because she wanted to catch that scent again.

"Mommy, is it bathtime?"

Ever since Aubrey had gotten the new Bathtime Dora, bathtime was her favorite time.

"Yes, Bri-Bri, c'mon it's bathtime."

"Yay!"

Sasha laughed as Aubrey led the way and she followed her mini me up the spiral stairs.

"No, rubber ducky, you can't fly!" Dora shouted, but only in Aubrey's voice.

"Yes I can, Dora," the rubber ducky responded before

air sailing from one end of the tub to the other, landing in a splash.

"Aubrey, seriously? You know better. No throwing!"

"Sorry, Mommy."

Sasha smiled and lathered up the small washcloth.

"Come here, little girl. You did know that we actually had to wash you while we're in here, right?" Sasha drawled in her accent.

"Aw man!" Aubrey stated cutely. Just then she sent the duck flying again, this time out of the tub and straight to the wastebasket.

"Sorry, Mommy!" she announced simultaneously with a grin.

Sasha raised a brow at her.

"Listen, just because you say sorry while you're doing something doesn't mean you can keep doing it, Aubrey. Now try me again," Sasha laughed, still on her knees kneeling next to the tub and now reaching over to retrieve the duck. As she pulled it out of the trash, since it was wet, it caused something to stick to it.

Sasha immediately felt sick. So sick. There was only one reason, only one. And there were no excuses.

Pussy. That's what he smelled like. Pussy.

So did he pick up my daughter from my aunt's smelling like it? Because I know he ain't crazy enough to fuck somebody with Aubrey here.

Sasha's stomach churned and she wanted to die. But she was a mother.

"Let's go, Aubrey."

"Where we go, Mommy?"

"Out the tub. To . . . to your room, baby. Play with Dora in there."

Sasha tried to fight her tears. Chauncey wasn't shit. Never had been shit. She felt like stepping outside of her body, turning to herself and screaming, *Wake up, bitch! He fucked your best friend repeatedly!*

"Are you okay, Mommy? Are you gonna cry?" Aubrey seemed so concerned. Sasha didn't want to look at her or she would definitely cry. Because he would be destroying her, too; he had destroyed their family.

"No . . . no, Mommy's . . . Mommy's okay." Sasha's voice cracked. Aubrey poked out her lip.

"Mommy, if you cry, I'm gonna cry too."

Sasha was about to break.

"C'mon, baby." She scooped Aubrey up, placed her in a fluffy towel, and brought her to her room. After turning on the TV and pulling out her toys, she stood by the door. Before closing it she told her, "Aubrey, don't come out, okay? Even if Mommy's yelling and Daddy's yelling, just stay in your room, okay?"

Aubrey looked up worried, but slowly nodded. She didn't want a fight to happen but she knew it was about to.

"Promise?" Sasha asked, clutching her finding in her hand and now smelling the pussy smell so strongly, but it was all in her head. She couldn't wait to get answers.

"Promise," Aubrey mumbled.

Sasha closed the door and double stepped down the carpeted steps, moving quickly as if a fire were lit on her ass. She stormed straight to him and stood in front of the television, where Chauncey was sitting in his basketball shorts and wifebeater, playing a war game and sipping a Corona. Shit was sweet now that he had gotten some, she figured.

"Did you fuck her in my house?" Sasha roared, holding up the gold Magnum condom wrapper. Tears rimmed her eyes and her body trembled in pain. She and Chauncey didn't use condoms.

Chauncey stared blankly for a minute and then, as if

she had asked him the time, he looked around her and continued the game.

"Yeahhh . . . I got something for y'all mothafuckas," he spoke to the game. "You in my way," he then addressed her.

Sasha, feeling completely disrespected, reached down and picked up the entire PlayStation system and, without thinking twice, she hurled it across the room and it crashed loudly against the wall.

"Now maybe you didn't hear me the first time," she repeated sternly. "Did you fuck *her* . . . in my *house* . . . you dirty mothafucka!" Sasha had taken entirely too much of Chauncey's shit. She was beyond hurt, she was furious at his audacity.

Chauncey remained calm as he picked up his beer and took a long swig. He squinted at her before a slight smirk appeared on his face. His response blew Sasha's mind.

"Did you fuck him in *my* house?"

Sasha's heart came to a halt. Her golden caramel face now turned a pinkish pale.

"W-wha . . . Who?"

Chauncey chuckled and then placed the beer down. He stood slowly and just stared at her, cocking his head to the side. This was the woman he loved, the only woman he ever loved. And he knew her better than she knew herself.

"You know," he started, with his finger pointed as he stepped from around the coffee table. "I wasn't sure if you actually fucked him until this very moment. When Mrs. Pearl told me that nigga's car was in the driveway while I was away, that you was kissing him and shit, blatantly in the doorway, of the *mothafuckin'* house that I bought, I ain't know if that shit was true. I said nah, not my princess. This old lady senile. Sasha play *me* for a little nigga? A little nigga that wanna be *me* at that? But look at you. You shaking, ma," he taunted with a smile. "You scared? You scared, Sash? Oh, shit ain't fun now that it's on you, right? You fuck that nigga Bleek in this house? Huh? Yeah, I fucked Lizette, right on your side of the bed, bitch. How it feel?"

Sasha stood stagnant and she felt the vomit coming up from her throat. She couldn't stop it. She doubled over and threw up on the living room floor, right where she stood. This couldn't be happening.

"I didn't . . ." she whispered, still doubled over.

"What you say?" Chauncey held his hand to his ear dramatically.

"I said I didn't fuck him!" she screamed, tears now streaming down her face.

"You a mothafuckin' liar!" Chauncey yelled like a madman, running up on her. "Lie to me again, mothafucka!"

"I didn't!" she lied again, terrified. She was truly, truly scared. What had she done? What would Chauncey do?

"I should break your fucking face!" he screamed, the pain now hitting him. He didn't want to believe it until he saw her reaction. Just the thought of Bleek fucking her sent Chauncey's temper bubbling over as he smacked Sasha on the side of her head, causing her to stumble.

"What was in your fucking head?"

"Chauncey! I'm sorry!" Damn, her reflex scared her and made her apologize. "Oh my God, please!" she begged, seeing his veins bulge and his nostrils flare. "Aubrey's upstairs . . . please!"

"Bitch, ain't nobody gonna do nothing to ya trifling ass!" he barked. "Take off my fucking ring!"

Sasha cried hard, taking deep breaths and gasps in between her heavy sobs.

"P-p-please . . . ppplease . . ."

"Take it the fuck off, Sasha!" he demanded, leaning down and now nose to nose with her. His fists were balled, and a smart woman would have just done what he asked, but Sasha was not a smart woman.

"I-I love you, Chauncey . . . You hurt me, too!" She cried hard, trying to pull her ring off but she was too weak. She had a pounding migraine and couldn't see straight because she was crying so much. Her heart was breaking by the second. What was she thinking?

"You . . . you hurt me! You were never home!"

Chauncey slit his eyes at her and ran his tongue along the inside of his jaw.

"Never home? So that's your excuse for whoring? Bitch, I was out making money for your spoiled ass! You ungrateful . . ." He picked up a crystal vase and hurled it at her, losing his temper. It landed against the wall two inches from her face. ". . . Bitch!"

"Oh God!" Sasha was scared. Scared for her, scared for her baby. She prayed that Aubrey kept her promise and stayed in her room. Sasha knew she had to be terrified.

"Chauncey, please, you're scaring Aubrey," she begged.

"No, I'm scaring you, hoe. Take off my fucking ring!" Sasha tried, but moved too slow for him. He reached over and yanked it off her finger.

"No!" Just then, Sasha's cell phone vibrated. Chauncey stormed over to it, wishing this nigga had the balls.

"Chauncey, I swear it's the nurse from the hospital!" she pleaded. "I don't talk to Bleek! I swear, I told him to leave me alone!"

Chauncey snatched the phone out of her Marc Jacobs bag. He stared down at the number and then laughed like a madman. He answered.

"Nigga, bring yo' bitch ass over here and come get this bitch," Chauncey barked.

Sasha shut her eyes in devastation. It had to be some

sick joke, the likelihood that Bleek had chosen this time to place his weekly "we should still be friends" call.

"Bet," Bleek answered coolly.

Chauncey threw the phone down and charged at Sasha.

"So you don't talk to that nigga, huh? You fucking dirty slut!"

"I swear, I don't!"

"Tell me what you did," he demanded.

Is he serious? Sasha looked at him like he was crazy.

"Nothing!"

"Stop fucking lying!" he screamed in her face.

"What do you mean!"

"Did you fuck him!" he yelled again. "Nah, don't answer that, I know you did. Did you use a condom?"

Sasha ran her hand over her face and it filled with tears and snot.

"Mmm," she mumbled.

"Did you!"

"Yes!" she screamed back in his face.

"He ate your pussy?"

Sasha sobbed hard, leaning her head back and closing her eyes. This was the worst. She just wanted this over with but Chauncey had her cornered and captive.

"Chauncey . . . please . . ."

"Did he eat your pussy?" he asked again. Sasha looked at him and shook her head from side to side. What type of sick shit was he on?

"Yes." She didn't know why, but she didn't feel like lying anymore. Chauncey had cheated, what made her so different? Now he was feeling how she felt when she walked in on him and Neli in that hotel room.

"You liked it?"

"I don't know . . ." she whispered.

"You fucking know!"

"Yes."

Chauncey chuckled and stared at her, seeing her calm a bit. It pissed him off.

"You sucked his dick?"

"Why, Chauncey, why?" She knew this would send him over the edge, but she knew he'd know if she lied. Plus Sasha loved giving head before, during, and after sex. Especially in the sixty-nine position. He knew that.

"Did you!"

"Yes!"

Chauncey lost it, sending a blow to her cheek.

"Why?" he demanded, infuriated. He was even angrier than he was at Neli when he beat the shit out of her. The only difference with Sasha was that he actually loved her. "I gave you every fucking thing! Yeah, I did my dirt . . . but that's the street life. You get money, you dodge police, you fuck bitches, but I always held my home down. I fucking kissed the ground you walked on, bitch! So why? Answer me!"

"He listened, Chauncey! He was there," she admitted truthfully.

"So you fuck him? You suck his dick 'cause he listened? You let him eat ya pussy 'cause he was *there*? So a nigga over here buying houses, cars, wardrobes, and this nigga fucks my pussy 'cause he was there. What a fucking come up!" Chauncey laughed in the air like it was Def Comedy Jam. "You'se a dirty bitch."

"You fucked Neli! She was my best friend!"

"That bitch was never your best friend and get the fuck over it! That ain't ya fucking joker card, baby. It don't work like that."

Sasha started crying again, not believing that after all of this, she still wouldn't end up with the man she loved more than life itself. And this time it was her fault.

"You fucked Tatum!"

"What?" Chauncey looked at her like she was insane.

"You fucked Tatum, you heard me! I found out!"

"What, when I was like two? Fuck outta here, Sash!"

"Fuck you, Chauncey!" Sasha was fed up. She loved him but he would not put this all on her. She had made a mistake but he had made several. And she wouldn't be too many more dirty whores and bitches without him taking credit for his shit. She stood up.

"Yes, I fucked Bleek! And no, it may not be a *street code,* but guess what, I have needs! And you hurt me! You cheated and after you cheated, you neglected me, letting me know, you didn't even care how I felt! I fucked up once! You fucked up so many times. And then you come here and fuck her in my bed, smelling like her pussy. I'd say we're even! I should've kissed you with dick on my face after you fucked Neli!"

Chauncey charged at her like a tiger on its prey and Sasha took flight, heading for the stairs, scared as hell seeing the fury in his eyes. She tripped and he grabbed her ankle, sliding her down five steps with force, giving her rug burns on her legs.

"Ah! Get off of me! Stop!"

He smacked her in her head and Sasha screamed out.

"Don't put your fucking hands on me, Chauncey!"

She kneed him hard in the nuts and stood abruptly, running swiftly up the stairs and locking herself in the bathroom once she reached the top. Her heart was beating through her chest.

Chauncey began banging on the door with force.

"Open the fucking door!"

Boom! Boom! Boom!

"Open the mothafuckin' door, Sasha, before I break this bitch down!"

"Daddy! Stop it!" Aubrey came out of her room, tears streaming down her face.

"Aubrey get in your room, now!" he yelled. She cried harder and retreated back in her room, her heart broken from her Daddy yelling at her like that.

Sasha hated to hear that; she prayed Chauncey calmed down. Just then the doorbell rang and her heart stopped. This could only get worse.

She heard Chauncey's heavy steps leaving away from the door and a few seconds later she heard screaming.

"Oh so you just gonna walk in my mothafuckin' house, nigga! You fucked my bitch!"

"Fuck you, nigga!"

Then she heard rumbling, shit breaking, shit banging. They were fighting.

She came out and ran straight to Aubrey's room. Her heart hit the floor when she opened the door and the room was empty.

"Aubrey!" Sasha didn't care about those niggas fighting anymore, she just wanted to find her baby. She ran down the steps frantically but didn't spot her, just Chauncey and Bleek tussling.

"Where's Aubrey!"

In that second, Bleek looked up at her. That gave Chauncey enough time to do what he had to.

"She's hiding in her closet," Chauncey spoke calmly, knowing he had put her there before he went downstairs. When they looked back to Chauncey, he now held a chrome 9-millimeter pointed straight at Bleek's dome.

"So was it worth it, little nigga?" he taunted.

Bleek swallowed hard, looked to Sasha, and studied the bruises on her face, her crying, and her seeming so distraught. He felt like shit, that's why he had kept the secret. For her. Bleek looked back to Chauncey and held his chin up, seeming to show no fear. They were so much alike, they even looked alike at that moment.

"Answer me, nigga," Chauncey demanded, cocking his gun back. "You quiet now? Was you quiet when you was fucking my pussy? I bet you wasn't. Bet you was crying out like a bitch! You fucked my girl, nigga! Is you crazy?"

Bleek's jaw flinched and he felt like, *Fuck it*. He looked at Sasha.

"I'm sorry, ma."

Sasha pleaded with her eyes.

"No, Bleek. Please." Her begging was exasperated. This would just be the cherry on top of the fucking icing. Bleek looked to Chauncey and smirked.

"I fucked *your* bitch? . . . Nah, C. Let me put you up on something, my man . . . You fucked *my* bitch."

Chauncey narrowed his eyes in contemplation and, after a few seconds, busted out laughing. Looking from Sasha and then back to the country boy, he shook his head in disbelief.

"Damn nigga! You that pussy whipped? That's your bitch now, huh? So this the kinda clown niggas you rolling wit, ma?"

Bleek chuckled, staring down the barrel of the gun and figuring he had nothing to lose. He knew a nigga like Chauncey, he knew he was dead anyway. So he let it go.

"Nah, nigga, that's *been* my bitch! Back in high school, tell 'em, Sasha. I popped that cherry. Every time she came to Atlanta we would kick it. Then she met your grimy ass and she was head-sprung off your New York bullshit."

"Bleek, please!" Sasha urged, feeling the tremble in her body start from her toes moving through her legs.

"Nah, let him fucking finish!" Chauncey spat angrily, his eyes glaring at her. "So you knew this nigga, huh? Of course . . ." he spoke with a deadly calm, putting it together. "You was always coming down here, hooking up with Jayde. So you used to see this nigga when we was together?"

"And she used to cry on my fucking shoulder about all the bullshit you put her through too," Bleek added salt to the wound with a smirk. "She knew you was cheating. She just didn't know it was with her own fucking homegirl. I told her she could do better. I told her I was the one."

"Oh, so you was beasting on me for fucking Neli while you was in Atlanta. But you was in Atlanta fucking this nigga!" Chauncey laughed like it was comical.

"We were just friends!" Sasha yelled, just knowing that she was in her nightmare. "Bleek, you know we were only friends!"

Why did Bleek have to put this out after all of these years?

"Fuck that!" Chauncey screamed, feeling like his heart was ripped out of his chest and stabbed repeatedly. "Bitch, I was gonna make you my wife! You're the mother of my fucking child!"

"Actually," Bleek started with a smile, and the breath left Sasha's body. Chauncey shot him dead in his skull, a bullet going straight through his forehead and killing him instantly. Sasha screamed like a maniac.

"Oh my God! Chauncey! What did you doooo!" She dropped down next to Bleek's limp body. He had kept her secret all these years. That's how much he always loved her. And now, he was dead because of her.

Chauncey couldn't even bear what Bleek was about to say. Just the thought had him about to lose his mind.

"Is that his fucking baby, Sasha!" He waved the now smoking gun at her. "Answer me!"

"No!" she yelled, her face wet with tears. "She looks just like you!"

"Is that your only fucking defense! Your only proof!" Chauncey was now crying at the recent revelation; this was the worst. "Aw man, don't tell me this, man! What the fuck! Not my Bri!" He was pacing the floor, gun in his hand. "Not my fucking baby! Argghhhhhh, I hate you, bitch!" He charged at Sasha and she cowered lower to the ground.

"She's yours! She's yours, I swear!"

"How the fuck do you know? Did you fuck him that summer? Did you!"

Sasha cried hard and dropped her face in her hands. She was so young then. You make mistakes when you're young. Chauncey had broken up with her for those couple of weeks for no reason. She had visited Atlanta and Bleek was looking good, he was getting money with Jayde, he was showing her attention. She needed that.

But Aubrey was Chauncey's spitting image. Sasha may have questioned it when she first got pregnant, but she and Chauncey were good by then, he had proposed, things were looking up. Even though Bleek had his doubts he let her ride with her insistence that it was Chauncey's. By the time all that stuff happened with Neli and Kim died, Sasha felt in her heart it was Chauncey's. She considered an abortion, though. But when she met Mike she figured it didn't matter anyway. She had a new family.

"Sasha . . ." Chauncey started, calmer than he'd been that whole evening. She looked up at him and saw his tears falling. She felt terrible. "Sasha, did you fuck him when you got pregnant with Aubrey? Please tell me you didn't."

Sasha sniffled, her lip trembling something awful. She looked up at Chauncey and shook her head from side to side.

"She . . . she looks just like you, Chauncey!"

Chauncey knew that meant yes. He lifted the gun to her, ready to kill the source of all of his pain, but he couldn't pull the trigger. *Look at her face.*

"Freeze! Drop the fucking gun!"

Police stormed the house, weapons raised and pointed at Chauncey, ready to fire on his black ass.

"Drop the fucking gun, motherfucker!"

Chauncey held unflinching eye contact with Sasha and her world crumbled. They were at a point of no return.

"I'm so sorry, Chauncey! Oh God, please don't take him! Don't take him!"

Chauncey never took his eyes off her, even when he slowly lowered the gun to the ground and stood back up.

Fuck it, he figured. *Just fuck it.*

"Hands on your fucking head, now!" the officers yelled.

"Please!" Sasha screamed out, standing abruptly. Bleek's blood was completely covering her. "Oh God! Chauncey . . . I swear. I swear we'll fix this, baby!"

Chauncey continued to just stare at her, wondering if they were always destined for disaster. Maybe they were never meant to be. But they were drawn to each other.

"You're under arrest. You have the right to remain silent . . . anything you say or do can be and will be held against you in the court of law . . . you have the right to an attorney . . ."

Sasha ran up to him.

"No, please! Take those cuffs off! Take 'em off! Don't leave me, Chauncey! We can work it out! I forgave you, just forgive me, babe . . ."

"Step back, ma'am!" the officers yelled, and noticed the bruises on her. She was most definitely next on the list of dead bodies, at least they figured so. Sasha knew in her heart Chauncey could never kill her, though.

As they cuffed Chauncey's hands behind his back, Aubrey emerged down the steps holding the cordless phone to her small face.

"Yes, they're here now," she spoke, and Sasha's heart fell, knowing she had called 911 like Sasha had taught her a while ago. Most likely when she heard the gunshot.

"No," Aubrey cried, looking up at the sight of Chauncey being led away in handcuffs. "Daddy! Daddy! I thought somebody shot my daddy! Don't take my daddy!"

Chauncey looked at the little girl he always called his own and knew he'd never see her again. He was going to jail forever and even if he wasn't, their family was over. He looked down at Bleek and then spoke to Aubrey.

"Somebody did shoot your daddy, Bri-Bri." With that he shot one final look at Sasha.

Sasha shook her head in disbelief as Chauncey and the officers moved through the door. And as they were just about to walk through the doorway, she called out to him.

"Chauncey!"

He turned his head although the cops had his body facing forward, and Sasha mouthed the words that he had once mouthed to her as he was being sent to a jail cell years ago, ironically.

You still love me?

Chauncey stared at her long and hard and just as the officers pushed him and ordered him to keep it moving, his mouth moved and she read his lips . . . *No.*

And then he was gone. And then they were over.

Chapter 14

"If you ever do anything to my brother, I would never forgive you. Never."

—Tatum, *Thicker than Water*

"You can stay here as long as you want, dear. And you know that."

Tatum sniffled, dipping her green tea bag in the hot water repeatedly and thinking hard.

"Thank you, Mrs. Seals," she replied, a bit delayed. She was at Sasha's mother's home, the one place that she knew Ree could not and probably would not find. Not right away, anyway. She had been calling Sasha since she arrived in Jersey, thinking maybe she could fly up, but she hadn't received a response yet.

"Tatum, please . . . none of that 'Mrs. Seals' here. You call me Terri . . . or you can't stay," she joked. Tatum laughed with her as Terri took a seat on the couch opposite Tatum, her own cup of tea in hand.

It was in these wee hours of morning, the latest hours of night . . . 3:36 A.M. to be exact. This was when Tatum could see the true Terri, the one who was awakened out of her sleep so she sported not a stitch of makeup yet her skin glowed like warm honey. The one who donned a silk pajama set instead of a Chanel suit. And the one who was smiling more, laughing, joking, quite the opposite of what Sasha always complained about. Tatum wondered if Sasha ever saw her mother like this. She was always deeming her so frigid. The thought made Tatum crack a smile.

"You look like your mother when you smile," Terri told her. That made Tatum smile even more. Terri had met Tatum's parents a couple of times when the girls were younger, before the crash, obviously. She remembered how close Tatum was to them.

"Your mother always knew you'd turn out great, Tatum. . . . She'd be really proud of you." Tatum wondered if that was true. Married to a gangster? Would that make her parents proud? Something inside of her told her they would have been anyway.

"But Chris . . ." Terri started shaking her head and it made Tatum tense. "Your mother always said he couldn't avoid trouble. He was destined for it . . . God rest his soul."

Tatum pressed her lips together and chose her next words carefully.

"Mrs. Se—" She looked at Sasha's mother and smiled. "Terri. I know . . . well, I think I know what you're getting at. And yes, Chris . . . I can't make excuses for him. He did some dumb things. But he . . . he didn't deserve to die. And it shouldn't have been *my* husband to kill him, you know what I mean?"

Terri sipped her tea slowly and nodded at Tatum. Tatum had filled her in openly about everything that had happened. Unbeknownst to Tatum, she could relate more than anyone could imagine.

"Tatum, baby, I want you to do me a favor, okay? I

want you to think about Chris. Not in the way you think about him usually, you know . . . growing up together, birthdays, and brotherly talks and seeing him in diapers, those things. I want you to think of the type of life he led in those streets. The things he did out there because he was a different Chris than you knew. Tatum, those streets are not a joke. They are not a movie, and when you're out there it's a whole different ball game and new rules. Do you honestly think that the way Chris was living his life and the decisions he made in those streets wouldn't have led him to his grave sooner or later? Or better yet, think about this. If Respect would have done what he did to *anyone else* besides your brother, because of what they did to him, would you still think it was wrong? Tatum, these streets have a code. And in order to survive in them, you have to live by the code."

By the time Terri finished, Tatum was back in tears and angry. She did not agree and no matter what, she could not justify what Ree had done.

"So what? Ree had to honor the code? Snitches get stiches? Rats gotta die? Ms. Terri, with all due respect, I think Ree would have survived just fine without killing my brother. That was my brother!"

"And that is your husband, young lady! And your brother tried to put your husband in jail for a very, very long time! And how could he ever rest letting him walk the streets? Tatum, the type of man Ree is. The type of person he was bred to become . . . you don't understand. Baby, these streets birthed, raised, and sculpted him. He doesn't even *think* like normal people. And the moment you said 'til death do us part,' you accepted that about him. I know what kind of man he is because I know what kind of people created him." She thought of Mickel. "He could not survive letting your brother live. And I don't know how you ever expected him to.

Honey, I always thought you were more street smart
than that. You should have considered that was what
happened. Now I'd expect that from Sasha," she said,
smirking.

Tatum chuckled in disbelief. She half-expected Ree
to pop out from behind Terri, holding on to her strings
like she was his puppet.

"Ms. Terri, I asked him. I begged him not to . . ."

"And he said okay. And just like that he wasn't going
to touch him. Forget his reputation, forget his freedom,
risk going to jail forever because you asked him to . . .
Okay." Terri nodded sarcastically and Tatum sipped her
tea, getting pissed.

"Baby, this is no Teri Woods fable. You are not living
the real-life *Hustler's Wife* story."

"Ms. Terri, how do you know those books?" Tatum
had to laugh, her tears still falling.

"I'm serious!" Terri exclaimed. "Young lady, marrying a man like Ree comes with a price tag. And not a lot
of women can afford it. But if you love him, and I think
you do. You have to think about if you really want to
spend your life without him for something you can't
change."

Tatum sighed, taking in an abundance of air and
shaking her head no. Her mind and body was rejecting
the notion before she even gave it thought. They were
saying no, you cannot be with your brother's killer. But
her soul. Ree was all up and through her soul.

"I don't know, Ms. Terri. We have been through too
much. Too fast."

"This to me is even more of a reason to hang on to
each other. . . ." She let that marinate for a moment.
"But I won't pressure you. Honey, you have got to make
that decision for yourself. Just make the right one."
Terri's thought faded out to the choices she herself had

made. For no reason did she want Tatum to end up like her. Her thoughts were broken by Tatum chuckling and posing her next question.

"No offense, Ms. Terri . . ." Tatum couldn't do the *Terri* thing; she had too much respect for her elders, so *Ms. Terri* would have to do. "But seriously . . . you are the last person I'd expect to be lecturing me on the code of the streets. And do you understand my pain, though? Like he betrayed me. Looked in my face every day knowing he hid this secret from me."

Terri nodded.

"Oh yes. And that was wrong. And there is *nothing* like when a man you love with everything in you betrays you and breaks your heart. Only defense I can offer is that he probably loved you too much . . . and he didn't want to risk losing you. Not when he had gotten you back in his life after the first time you guys parted. Nothing's sweeter than a second chance, Tatum. And you never want to ruin that." Her own words really made her think of Mickel then. "And trust me, I know more than you think I know." Terri took another sip and grinned over her cup.

Tatum laughed but then realized she was being a tad loud.

"Oh my God, I'm sorry! I don't want to wake Mr. Seals."

Terri's face transformed from a smile to one of a solemn look, and then she raised her eyebrows slightly.

"Tatum, Bill's not here. He's moved out. He has an apartment over in Highland Park and he's purchasing a new house."

Tatum was shocked, stunned; she needed to make sure she understood. Sasha's parents were the black American dream, the Huxtables, the Obamas. Sasha would surely be devastated.

"He's moving alone?"

"Mmm-hmm," Terri responded, nodding, seeming to not be too affected.

"Did he cheat?" Tatum asked in shock, sure that was the case. *Of course he cheated, successful, attractive black man. That's what happened, probably with a white woman,* Tatum assumed.

Terri laughed, so much so she had to cover her mouth to prevent her tea from spilling out. After a pause and a clearing of her throat, she spoke.

"No . . . no, my dear. He didn't cheat." She placed her cup on the table and looked at Tatum, as if debating something. And then she nodded, affirming to herself.

"Tatum, I'm going to tell you a story."

Tatum put her own cup down and leaned forward, resting her head on her folded hands. She was intrigued and finally had someone else's drama to take her mind off her own.

"I'm going to start with Jayde."

"Jayde?" Tatum questioned harshly. *Did Jayde fuck Mr. Seals? I wouldn't put it past her.*

"Yes Jayde," Terri confirmed. She sat back and sighed. "You told me you overheard Jayde say that Ree killed your brother, correct?"

"I said that she said he was responsible," Tatum remembered, because she remembered feeling like that didn't give her enough clarity. She wanted to know if he pulled the trigger.

"Did she know you were there?"

"I mean . . . she knew I was outside."

"But she knew you were home?"

"I was . . . I was quiet when I heard their voices. I doubt she knew—"

Terri laughed, cutting her off. "Tatum, please. Do me a favor? Don't ever doubt that woman."

Tatum swallowed hard, looked down, and then looked back to her.

"It doesn't matter, though. She didn't make him do it. *He* did it." Terri stared at her for a while and then started on a different angle.

"Baby, Respect is close with a man . . . *was* close with a man . . . Mickel Dupree . . ."

"I know Mickel," Tatum stated quickly, and then realized she'd said a mouthful. Ree told her how important it was to act as if Mickel were dead. "I mean . . ."

Terri took a deep breath.

"Okay! Now that that's out of the way, we both know he is alive. But please, Tatum, don't ever say that again."

Tatum nodded and wondered why Terri cared so much about keeping Mickel's status.

"Anyway," she started again. "Let me tell you from the beginning. When I was a young girl . . . in Atlanta, I used to go out with my girlfriends every Thursday up to the skating rink. I mean, it was all the way *live*," she laughed, and Tatum laughed too. "Anybody who was anybody was there. Local basketball stars, street guys, local celebs, everyone. And there was always this group of guys that would come . . . right before closing time. They'd come in, they'd throw their money around, they'd take women, and they'd leave in their fancy cars. Everyone knew they were dope dealers, most didn't care. They were *it*. The ringleader . . . the head honcho . . . none other than Mr. Mickel Dupree himself. Everyone knew who he was." Terri smiled thinking back to it. "He had eyes for me, I mean badly. And if you think I'm something now, honey, please, I was a brick house. I had a twenty-four-inch waist, sweet hips, lips, and fingertips. I still had my hazel eyes and a perfect Farrah Fawcett hairdo." Tatum laughed at that.

"But I was something, the most wanted of the bunch.

I hardly paid him mind, but my friend Emerald, boy, was she head over heels for him. She'd always say, 'Terri, I'm gon' have his baby if it kills me!' See, Mickel had wavy hair, he had clear island skin and those eyes. The prettiest teeth. And he could sweet-talk any Southern girl right out of her underwear. But he didn't seem to be checking for her. He pursued me and pursued me and I fell eventually." This shocked Tatum, now her ears were fully perked.

"I asked Emerald if it was okay. She said it was fine, she was over Mickel. He was a *dog*. So we began courting. He took me everywhere, to California, New York City, Vegas. We saw boxing matches and sat with celebrities, he bought me chinchilla furs, draped me in diamonds, I always say he's the one that set the groundwork for the standards I live by now. He spoiled me so. And he loved to show me off. We had an apartment over in Macon, Georgia, and we'd have these crazy parties and he'd just watch me dance all night and he'd smile. And he'd tell all of his friends that I was *his* Terri. I was his star. And I'd be going with my white bell bottoms, halter top, and my Farrah Fawcett and we'd laugh and this may shock you, but we'd do a few lines because back then it was different . . . and I mean we were just crazy in love. So in love! I was so wrapped up in Mickel I didn't know what was happening in town anymore. Well, word got back to me that Emerald had birthed a baby, a girl, and that she was claiming it to be Mickel's and I just died. Apparently she claimed they were together but I later found out she had been one of the women he'd picked up after the skating rink closed one night, one of those nights before we got together and I had turned him down. People were saying she was sleeping around and they didn't think it was even Mickel's baby. Anyway, my heart was broken, it didn't matter. I left Mickel, as hard as it was. After I left, I started hearing that he always had the little girl with him, he adored her. She had pretty green eyes like her mother. I just figured and knew he had to be a family with Emerald now." Terri sipped her tea.

"That was mistake number one. . . . Some years passed and I moved away, came up north to Maryland. Then my mother had a stroke and I went back down to Atlanta to my parents. A lot was the same but some things were different. Mickel was larger than ever! His empire ran the entire city and as soon as I stepped foot in his state, honey, he knew. He was knocking on my door the very next day. He told me how he never should have let me go, he was never with Emerald. He adored his daughter, *Jayde* . . . but Emerald was too possessive. I was the one for him. And I believed him. We fell in love again and that's when it started. . . ."

"What started?" Tatum asked quickly, feeling like she was in a soap opera, watching it all up close and personal.

"Well first, it was just phone calls. Emerald felt that I took her family away from her, you know. Then it was flattened tires, busted windows. Mickel even beat her a few times but she kept at it. Then the baby. He would bring Jayde over and she was a child by then, and I wasn't all the way comfortable with it but I tried to make the best out of everything. But the child was not . . . *normal.* I would wake up and she'd be standing next to our bed, just staring at me. Those green eyes piercing me through the dark. When I would ask what she was doing, Mickel would wake and she'd change instantly, saying she had a bad dream, could they go call her mom? That's when I knew she was manipulative. Then I got pregnant, and everything spiraled out of control. I mean, it all happened so fast. . . . First, Mickel was being indicted and there was a secret government witness.

I told Mickel it was Emerald's doing but he didn't want to believe me. But I knew she would go through great lengths to know my child grew up without Mickel just like hers. Then, one day someone snatched me off the street, I was three months pregnant. They told me they'd kill me if I didn't tell Mickel that he wasn't the father of my child, end our relationship. To tell the truth, I was tired of dealing with Emerald and I knew Mickel would most likely be going to jail for a long time. My father was pressuring me to get away from him before I wound up dead and my baby as well, and I would have done anything for my child. So I ended it with Mickel. I told him I had met a man in Maryland when I moved and was still seeing him when we got back together. I told him that man was the father of my baby. The truth was I *had* met a man in Maryland, and he was Bill, my husband. But when I went home and got back together with Mickel, I ended it with him. But when I left Mickel, Bill was willing to take me back, pregnant and all."

"Just like Mike did with Sasha," Tatum noted. Terri laughed.

"Yes, but Bill's a little better than Mike. And more sane. The thing is, though, I knew Sasha was making the wrong choice then just like I had."

Tatum squinted at her.

"You think you made the wrong choice?"

Terri sighed. "I don't know. I mean, I guess you figured it out that baby was Sasha and she was raised as Bill's. After my father got sick, we ended up moving to Atlanta and I was so scared I would run into Mickel and he would see his features in Sasha. But unfortunately, one day I picked up the paper and saw that he was dead, someone blew up his boat while he and a woman were on it. Everyone knew it was Emerald. Apparently she went crazy when she found out he fathered another child, a little boy, Julez. Not too long after, Emerald was sent away to a psychiatric hospital up in East Orange, New Jersey."

"Greystone?" Tatum questioned peculiarly.

"Probably."

"That's where Neli was," Tatum gasped. "Do you think Emerald is still there?"

"Oh, Tatum, I don't know. But I did hear that she was miserable there. And now that I know everything, after a long talk with a friend, I know that she was put there as an alternative. Mickel made a promise to Jayde he wouldn't kill her when he found out about the boat and he used the situation to his advantage since he was being indicted, but he did force Jayde to sign her mother away or she would be murdered. That's why he sent her so far away. I don't know how Jayde forgave him for that but I know she was upset. To tell you the truth, to this day I don't know if Jayde is actually Mickel's."

Terri stirred her cold tea.

"Anyway, I cried for months after I learned of Mickel's death. And just when I was getting back to normal, my little girl makes friends with Jayde Dupree." Terri laughed at that. "I thought maybe Jayde was too little to remember, she was being raised by Emerald's sister at that time, the woman that Sasha and many others believe is Jayde's mother. I even thought that maybe she believed that Sasha in fact really wasn't Mickel's and I was simply an old friend of her dad's, but one day she came over when she was a teenager and she laid it out. She told me she knew everything, she told me that she knew I lied and that Emerald had sent the man to kill me if I didn't end it with her father. She claimed she knew her mother was ill and that she didn't blame me. She would keep the secret with me. She knew about Mickel's other children too. But something in her eyes still let me know the girl is not one hundred percent genuine. We moved to Jersey shortly after, wanted to start over."

"Does Sasha know?" Tatum asked curiously.

"She does now. She's still very upset at me about it and upset that Jayde knew. . . *Jayde*," Terri chuckled to herself, repeating her name. "You know I thought she was left back in my past." Terri then stared at Tatum seriously. "But somehow this woman has weaved her way into your life now, and into your home. And *so* much has happened since then."

Tatum leaned back and held Terri's eye contact.

She never trusted Jayde, she wasn't that dumb. But Jayde was the link between Ree and a billion dollars, so they tolerated her. *But what could she have really done?* Tatum thought. Besides maybe reveal the truth about Chris on purpose. So what? Ree had done it; Jayde hadn't killed Tatum's brother, he had.

"She won't be there long," Tatum spoke matter of factly.

"Well correct me if I'm wrong, but you're sounding like a woman that's still claiming that house . . . *and* that man," Terri said, smirking.

Tatum ran her hands over her face and screamed. "Ughhhh! Ms. Terri! I don't know what to do." The good thing was all of this madness had snapped Tatum out of her trance from losing her babies. She was wide awake now.

Terri shrugged, standing up and leaning against the couch. "Follow your heart. I wish I had. Very rarely do you get a third chance, Tatum, but I did. So that's what I'm going to do. Follow my heart wherever it leads me. That's why I said you can stay as long as you want. Because in a few days, I will not be here." Terri smiled wide and Tatum dropped her mouth, thinking on it heavily.

Is she serious?

"No . . . !"

Terri nodded quickly. "Oh yes! Tatum listen to me." She smiled, giddy like a schoolgirl, and she came hurriedly to Tatum, taking Tatum's hands into her own. "Only one man will ever make your heart dance and your head light and your feet lift . . . and every girl in the world won't get to experience it, I promise you! Most of these people are settling with people they have *grown* to love. But if you love someone as soon as you lay eyes on them and they make your life feel like a twenty-four-hour fantasy ride, you don't let that go. Don't! Just think about it. But in the meantime and excuse my French . . . get that bitch out of your house!"

They both laughed at that and Tatum reflected on what she said. Terri shook her head. "If that girl was raised by Emerald, I'm telling you . . ." And Terri left it at that.

Tatum took a deep breath with a heavy mind and a lot of info to digest. She felt it was impossible to go back to Ree; her brother would turn over in his grave if she did. How could she look at him every day? But was Terri right, had she been naïve to not know, or maybe she always knew? But she couldn't deal with the certainty of it. But then again, did she want to just walk away? And what about Jayde?

Tatum had a decision to make, and it was the hardest of her entire life. She figured she'd sleep on it.

Sasha's tears fell softly against her cheeks as Corrine Bailey Rae sang her life in "Till It Happens to You". Chauncey was gone, she knew it was for good. And this time hurt worse than any, because her own actions left her responsible.

Sure, he'd messed up . . . plenty of times. But she had messed up in an ultimate way. She thought of an old Chris Rock joke, men lie the most . . . women tell the biggest lies. Even the details of the joke made Sasha chuckle in disbelief. He had said a man's lie was like "I was at Tony's house . . ." instead of telling where he really was. A woman's lie was like "It's your baby . . ."

He hit that right on the nose.

Sasha glanced up at the rearview mirror and watched Aubrey stare peacefully out of the backseat window. She looked just like him, Sasha noted. Those eyes, the sharp nose, there was no doubt to Sasha that she was Chauncey's. Now, if they would have performed a blood test, would Sasha have sweated a little? Sure. She knew she had slept with Bleek. She watched Maury, she knew anything was possible.

"Mommy, why are we slowing down? Those cars behind us are getting mad."

Sasha gasped as she focused on the gas needle.

Fuck! They had ridden the entire 95 and were now at the lower exits of the New Jersey Turnpike, and she hadn't a drop of gas.

"Please . . . please . . . please. Please let me make it to the rest stop," she pleaded, on the brink of tears.

But she knew it was useless, the car was doing less than twenty miles per hour now, and the pedal was floored.

Cars began to honk at her aggressively as, with cloudy vision, she switched lanes to the shoulder, almost colliding with a tractor trailer. This would just add on to her already building aggravation.

Sasha didn't even know what she was doing. She was so used to running home when anything happened that she had packed up her and Aubrey's stuff and jumped in her Benz before even calling.

When she finally did, her mother informed her that her father had moved out and, surprisingly, Tatum was there. Although Sasha wanted to see Tatum, she didn't want to see her mother. For some reason she couldn't forgive her mother for the lies she told, even though her father told the same ones and had raised her knowing she wasn't his. Maybe it was because her mother added more insult to injury by now telling Sasha she was going to "follow her heart." Sasha knew what that meant, and she felt for her dad. She had found out that, lo and behold, Mickel was around and he had even been at Tatum's wedding. So she knew her mother was going to be the same old, selfish Terri, and only think of herself. Sasha wanted to go be with her father to console him.

She talked with Tatum a bit and made her promise they would link up when Sasha arrived in Highland Park. They each had lots to fill the other in on. She wondered how Tatum would react when she found out that she had kept the secret of Bleek hidden from her as well. Her car's putt-putting to a complete stop just as she reached the shoulder broke those thoughts.

"Oh my Goddd," she groaned, taking out her phone and trying not to panic in front of Aubrey. She didn't even have Triple A. Who needed Triple A when she had Chauncey or Bleek always around to come to her rescue? Just like typical Sasha, she relied on others to handle things like that for her.

The minute Sasha went to search the Internet for a tow truck company nearby, her iPhone powered off, dead and finished.

"Shit!"

"Ooohhh," Aubrey cooed, kicking her legs and smiling.

She always got excited when Sasha said a bad word, she thought it was highly entertaining.

"Aubrey, please."

"Call Daddy," Aubrey stated calmly.

Sasha sighed and then smiled at her baby through her fretting.

"We can't, baby. Daddy went away to school, remember?"

Aubrey poked her lip out, remembering. Her daddy was back in school, the same school he was in through the first stages of her young life.

"I we-mem-ber," she mumbled sadly, placing her head against the window. She was sad *and* sleepy.

Sasha reached in the glove compartment for her car charger but, to her dismay, it was not there.

"This cannot be happeninggg to meee!"

"It's okay, Mommy," Aubrey assured, about to prepare for a nap.

Sasha jumped out of the car, and speeding traffic almost knocked her door off the hinges. She calmed a bit before she ended up killing herself and she walked close to the car, heading to the trunk.

"If it's not in the car, it has to be in one of the suitcases. Has to be," she spoke to herself. The sun was beginning to set and she knew she didn't have much daylight left. Cursing herself for always being irresponsible, she tossed clothes around, digging and searching for something she had a feeling wasn't even there.

"What the fuck! Where is it?" Even as she demanded the answer from herself, she was almost positive it was left in the Jaguar when she had driven it home the other night. The night when it all went down. The night that changed her life.

Just thinking about it and about her current plight brought tears to her eyes and, this time, she didn't fight them. She let them pour freely as she continued to throw clothes.

"Why can't anything be where it's supposed to! Why do you see something over and over again when you don't need it and when you need it, you can't find that shit! And why is it my fault, huh? You cheated too! You lied! I hate you! I hate you!" She broke down sobbing coming to the reality that Chauncey would probably be in prison for the rest of his life. "Why did you leave me!" she screamed, throwing a pair of jeans and a silk Miss Sixty top to the back of the trunk. "Why!"

"Are you okay, ma'am?"

Sasha spun around quickly and spotted a large white man, fairly young, with a trucker's hat and steel-toe boots looking at her sincerely.

"I'm . . . I'm fine. Thank you." She wiped her face and sniffled, clearing her throat. "I . . . I ran out of gas."

He looked her up and down, looked at the scattered clothes in the trunk, and could tell she was heading somewhere, or leaving somewhere else.

"I'm sorry to hear that. You wanna ride to the gas station?"

Sasha thought for a second. Did she want to take her baby into a strange man's pickup on the brink of dusk? But what if no one else stopped? He did seem nice, but shoot, nowadays you never know.

"Do you have a phone that I can use? So I can call a tow truck?"

A few cars passed quickly, the noise causing her to have to scream over it a bit.

The man stood stagnated for a moment, blank expression and all, and then a smile appeared out of nowhere.

"Well gosh, dolly, I sure do. Just follow me over to my truck, it's just right here. Call whoever you need."

Sasha felt relieved. Finally help! She began walking to

his truck but then stopped abruptly after a few steps, about halfway. *No, stupid . . .*

"Can you . . . just bring it to me . . . ? I'm sorry," she added, not wanting to seem ungrateful. The sun was only peeking now, so his features became shadowy. The cars seemed to be zooming by at rapid speed, no one seeming to care much about them.

The man turned and looked at her, bit his lip, and shook his head in disbelief.

"My God, pretty lady, you sure are high maintenance. You treat all Good Samaritans like this?"

Sasha chuckled but didn't appreciate the comment. She crossed her arms in front of her chest.

"It's not that. I just . . ." His walking up close to her put her on the defense and cut her words off, her thoughts immediately going to Aubrey.

"Now see, all I was trying to do was be a good, red-blooded, All-American man. But you here treating me like I'm some psycho killer. I oughta leave you out on the highway."

Sasha's nostrils flared and she turned quickly to walk away.

"Don't worry about it, I'll just wait," she spoke into the wind in stride, but he grabbed her arm, preventing her from walking any more.

"So since when you Negro women get to be so unappreciative? You in my country, brown sugar!"

"Get the hell off of me!" she yelled at him, pushing him. She swung her arm to hit him in the face but he grabbed both arms tight and began pulling her to the truck.

"Get off of me! Help! . . . Are you crazy! I called the cops . . . they're on the way to help me!"

"You ain't got no phone," he laughed, still pulling her roughly. He was so strong.

Sasha's heart beat out of her chest. This couldn't be happening to her, it was unreal. She kicked and struggled but he was incredibly strong.

"Get in the truck!" he demanded, almost having her close to it. He was about ready to knock her out with one punch and really get the party started.

Just then, a black-on-black Maserati riding fast but incredibly close to them caught their attention. The passenger window was down.

"Help!"

The car rode past where they were and Sasha went back to being terrified. They didn't hear her. But then Sasha saw the bright brake lights as it pulled over quickly, a few feet in front of her car. It had stopped so fast, the dirt from the shoulder kicked up behind it.

"Yo! You all right?" the driver yelled, stepping out hastily at the same time and walking swiftly to them. Her country attacker released her suddenly and hopped into his ride. Sasha, once free, forgot how he had just dominated her and her anger took over. She kicked and punched at his truck as he rammed the gas.

"You psycho! I got your license plate!"

Her hero, now seeing that, ran to them hoping to catch the guy, but the predator's fear got him out into traffic before he could reach them.

A few seconds later, the mysterious superman was next to Sasha, breathing heavily from the quick run.

"You all right, miss? Did he hurt you?"

Sasha's chest heaved up and down in fear, relief, and shock. She shook her head no, barely able to speak.

"My . . . my baby. My daughter . . ." She pointed to her car and began walking.

"Your baby? He took your baby!" The stranger was immediately irate, standing straight up and looking toward traffic.

"No." Sasha smiled slightly to calm him. "No . . . she's in the car. Thank you. Thank you for . . . for stopping."

"No doubt," he spoke, blasé. "Something ain't look right."

Sasha began walking toward her car and he followed.

"I'm gonna make sure you get in your car and you drive away before I pull off."

Sasha smiled and sighed in relief at his kindness and at the sight of Aubrey now sleeping peacefully in her car seat. She faced the stranger.

"Thank you." She almost forgot why she pulled over in the first place. "Oh, actually . . . I *can't* drive away."

"You hurt?" He crinkled his brows, looking her up and down as best as he could in the night.

"No . . . I'm out of gas," she chuckled solemnly. For some reason, he put a sense of calm over her. He really was like a hero. "Can I . . . can I use your cell phone to call a tow truck?"

Sasha's voice began to crack and she knew what was coming but she didn't want to cry in front of this man, and then he'd think she was crazy and leave her stranded.

"Yeah, of course . . . Here."

He handed her the phone. By this time, it was completely dark. And where were the state troopers when you needed them?

Sasha found a tow truck company and they let her know they were on their way.

"How long?"

Sasha sighed. "Forty-five minutes," she mumbled.

Although she was relieved they were coming, forty-five minutes seemed like an eternity, especially since she knew her hero would probably have to leave and she'd be waiting alone.

"I mean, I can run you to a rest stop and we can get a gas can, you know . . . handle it like that."

Sasha took a deep breath and shook her head, leaning against her car.

"No offense. But after all of that . . . I'll just wait for the tow truck."

"I feel you. I'll wait with you." There was a brief silence and then . . .

"Thank you."

"No problem." Another long pause and a few serene moments passed, and then a couple of preliminary raindrops added to the mysterious events. *Of course.*

"Why don't we sit in the car, ma?" her hero asked, putting his hand out and feeling the rain coming.

Sasha looked skeptically and he could see it, even in the darkness. He chuckled.

"I mean, we can sit in yours. Or you can sit, get out the rain. I'll sit in mine. At least we know yours ain't going nowhere."

Sasha laughed. He was right. He could do less to her in a car that was out of gas than a dark field on the side of the road.

"No, you can sit in mine. Come on."

Sasha walked around to the passenger seat and got in. She then opened the driver's door for him, signaling with her hand for him to join her.

"Come on, come sit down."

He climbed inside slowly, sliding the seat back. The doors being opened caused the inside lights to come on, and even in her solemn time, Sasha noticed how attractive he was. She stared at him while he adjusted the seat. He actually reminded her of Chauncey.

"There we go," he spoke in his deep baritone, finding the right position for his tall and chocolate frame as he leaned back and looked over at her.

"Pink, huh?" he spoke about the interior. "I can dig it."

Sasha laughed lightly and looked down. Looking at

him really did remind her of Chauncey, her own tall, dark, and handsome man who was now gone.

"That's your daughter right there?" he asked lowly, looking back and seeing Aubrey sleeping. "She's a little dream."

Sasha smiled and looked back at her princess.

"Yeah, that's my love. She's my mini me."

"I can tell," he told her. When Sasha looked back to him, he was staring at her.

"Dig, ma, you look real familiar." His voice was deep but low, as he spoke a few notches down from normal, trying not to wake Aubrey.

"So do you," she replied quicker than she expected, in the matched low tone.

Sasha, for some reason, even though she knew she shouldn't have been thinking of it at this time, wondered if she looked attractive. She knew her jeans hugged her hips and her tank top showed her small waist and perky breasts. But her crying had probably ruined her mascara and her long straightened hair was probably frizzy from the tussling and fret. However, he looked dapper and clean in his crisp jeans, black Louis Vuitton sneakers, and black V-neck. She also noticed the Presidential Rolex, and the Maserati didn't miss her. Some women never met a baller in their lifetime, but Sasha was a magnet for them.

"You actually remind me of my husb . . . Well, my fianc . . . Well . . . my baby's father."

He chuckled lightly, noticing the debate over the formal title.

"Word? What's his name?"

". . . Chauncey."

Dude stared at her for a while and then snapped his finger and pointed at her.

"And you're Sasha."

She raised her eyebrows.

"How you know?" Her country accent peeked out when her voice rose an octave. He laughed smoothly.

"Calm down. I met you before . . . at a party once. My bad, I'm Gavin. But you can call me G." He put his hand out.

Sasha took a deep breath of extra relief. Now she remembered him being an acquaintance of Chauncey's and she had a new sense of calm. She remembered thinking he was fine when she met him before and now she knew why she could hardly stop looking at him.

"Okay, I remember," she said, smiling and shaking his waiting hand. "Wow, that's crazy. What a coincidence!"

He shrugged and looked out of the window at the passing cars.

"I don't really believe in coincidences though, ma. I was *supposed* to stop that crazy mothafucka from causing harm to my man C's lady. You see, that's the way the universe works."

She swallowed hard and looked down. She wanted to tell him she was no longer C's lady but she left it alone.

"So you believe in fate, then," she stated, rather than asked.

He looked over at her and smiled a little before nodding.

"Yeah . . . yeah I guess I do."

Chapter 15

"I'm not like you. I can't just be alone and be all right . . .
I need a man."

—Sasha, *Thicker than Water*

The bottle turned straight up and Ree parted his lips,
allowing the liquid poison to enter his body, hoping
he'd feel the numbing effect sooner than later. Drinking wasn't his norm, but neither were any of the events
that had occurred in the last few weeks for that matter.
Ree needed to wash away something he wasn't quite
sure could be washed. He needed to void any feeling.

So he turned to the bottle, which had always been his
father's solace. He knew it was what had been Leroy's
crutch when he was getting over his mother's death. He
wondered if it would help him get over who he needed to.

Otis Redding's soulful croon on *"Pain In My Heart"*
soundtracked the moment unintentionally, filling the
space of the office, and Ree's mind wandered as the
music played.

Ree had to chuckle at the irony of the words as he
took another swig of the premium brown liquor.

"Fuck it," he tried to mumble, tried to convince himself.

He knew there was no coming back from what he'd done. There was no sorry, no flowers, no dress fresh off the runway, or no shoe straight from the next season's catalog that could get him back right with Tatum. It had to be over, he'd destroyed someone whom Tatum loved more than him and he knew the moment he pulled the trigger this could be one of the consequences. He had made that decision consciously, as all of his decisions had always been made.

With the intention of facing the possible circumstances knowingly and readily.

But there was a feeling, one that he wasn't sure how he'd be able to live with. Even more than losing her, he never considered how it would feel knowing he had hurt her in such a powerful way.

It would be easier to let her go, knowing she was happy. But knowing she was somewhere hurting and not being able to mend it, and knowing he was the cause, was worse than Ree could have imagined. He would forever be etched in her mind not as her soul mate, or the man who loved her more than life itself, but as her brother's murderer.

"Respect." Crush's voice tuned Ree into the moment as the door slowly cracked open.

"Yeah," Ree responded, swallowing his liquor.

He looked up and Crush stood, a blank expression adorning his face. Jayde stood by his side.

"She's here," Crush informed him, as if Jayde weren't standing right there.

Ree had been expecting her. She had gone and met with the people Chauncey was initially supposed to. She had stepped up to the plate to keep the wheels moving in the operation and smooth them over even after all of the bullshit that had gone down. When Chauncey got into the trouble, the Gonzales family and even the

Segovias were on the brink of pulling out. This was why it had been so hard before to put together the master plan; they both rarely took risks.

Ree threw up his hand, motioning for Jayde to take a seat in the dimly lit room. He reached over, turned on his desk lamp, and leaned back coolly, taking another long drink. It was so quiet they could hear the crickets outside the mansion.

Crush stood for a moment, staring at Jayde who now walked up and stood across from Ree in her short, white Thierry Mugler bustier dress, but still not sitting. Her long hair was slicked up into a ponytail showing off those devious green eyes, and her shiny red lips were now curled up in a smirk. Crush didn't like the broad, there was something about the way she moved.

"That'll be all, Crush," she directed, as if reading his thoughts and feeling his eyes burning into her back.

"Yo, you cool, boss?" Crush narrowed his eyes at Respect.

Ree's glassy and low eyes traveled over Jayde and then to Crush.

"Yeah . . . yeah, I'm good."

Crush knew he was fucked up. He knew he'd been fucked up and Crush wished Tatum would walk through that door any moment. He nodded and started out but was halted by Ree's next words.

"Still nothing?"

Crush paused but didn't turn around. He had never lied to Ree a day in his life, but he had been doing it recently.

"Nah . . . We still don't know where she is. But I'm on it, boss . . . I'm sure she all right."

He knew his loyalty should have been to Ree, but he had formed a recent bond with Tatum, so when she begged him not to tell Ree where she was after he had her followed, he obliged. Not only because he thought she deserved some time alone but also because he felt it would be more beneficial to the situation. Ree loved Tatum but Ree was used to rules, *his* rules that people followed. Ree didn't know the rules of love because it was a game he was an amateur at. Crush knew if Ree found out where Tatum was, he'd drag her ass home just out of his basic need for her to be with him, and the type of person that Tatum was, that would only be the end of them. Crush knew if there was any chance that she'd forgive him, it'd have to be of her own will and in time. However, he did wish that process would speed up.

"'Sure' isn't good enough," Ree spoke seriously. "I need to know, man. You're usually on point with this type of thing, Crush . . . what's up?" Ree cocked his head to the side and studied his old friend.

Crush sighed and turned around, putting on his most sincere face. He wondered if Ree already knew he was lying.

He stared at Ree and a few seconds passed. He looked to Jayde and he immediately knew he would definitely either get Tatum home or let Ree know where she was at this point. Something changed, something didn't feel right.

"Yeah . . . you right, boss. I'll have something for you, don't worry."

He shot one final assuring look at Jayde and then made his way out.

Ree meant to thank him but ended up doing so in his head as he pressed the bottle back to his lips.

Jayde looked around the room, taking in the mood. The music was still playing and now Otis was singing about how strong his love was for someone, about how he'd be the ocean, deep and wide to catch all the tears his love cried, and Jayde gritted her teeth slightly wondering if that was how Ree felt for Tatum. The window was cracked open and a summer breeze crept in and added a tantalizing chill to the room. And even with Ree a bit more laxed and incoherent than usual due to the alcohol, leaning back in his chair, legs opened in a laid-back fashion, half of the buttons on his shirt undone, Jayde couldn't help but feel spellbound by him.

"I told you to sit . . . yet you're still standing. That's what I don't like about you," he admitted truthfully as he eyed her. "You're difficult."

Jayde chuckled, smiling wide. She knew the liquor probably had him more verbal than normal. He usually had very few words for her.

"You're right . . . I'm not easy. But you shouldn't hold it against me." She walked closer. "But for you . . . I'll sit."

She perched herself up on his desk, her legs crossed not too many inches from his face.

Ree looked up at her and frowned.

"Four other chairs in the room, Jayde. Pick one."

Jayde smiled seductively at his rejection.

"Uncomfortable?" she posed.

"Unmoved."

She pursed her lips at that one but still did not move, hoping he didn't push the issue. He didn't.

"It went okay," she started, filling him in on business. "Everyone is still on board even though they say it's real unfortunate what happened with Chauncey. But physically, I don't know if it's going to be possible. We were pushing it with only me and Chauncey. But now . . . just me? I hate to say it, but I need you. You don't think you can stick around longer? A boss always has to be ready to step up, right?"

She looked him right in the eyes and prayed that things were playing her way. She just knew getting Ree to partner up with her for good, in and out of business, would be easy; especially after having the hotel burned so he could not even have that business in Jamaica.

She knew if he really wanted to he could build a new one, but why would he do that? It'd be easier to just stay here and stay in business with her, especially with Tatum and her nagging him to quit, out of the picture. The whole thing with Chauncey had just been a bonus, luck playing on Jayde's side.

He chuckled at her juvenile logic and attempt at reverse psychology. The problem with Jayde was that she thought she was smarter than everyone.

"I'm not your boss, Jayde. And you don't need me . . . I served my purpose." Ree had formed the trinity, kind of like the pyramid scheme. He started it but was no longer crucial. As soon as all was done, he'd collect his fee for his brilliance and be on his way.

Jayde sighed, feigning defeat. He'd give in, she just needed to work a little harder.

"Okay . . . well, plan B. I told you . . . I know someone. I mean, I don't really *know* him. But Mickel can vouch for him. He worked Jersey, like yourself. Ju—"

"Julez Payne," Ree spoke, cutting her off as he picked up a pair of feng shui balls. "Central Jersey, Southern Jersey, down to Philly . . . pushed dope, coke, bud, X . . . was onto that Oxy shit back before anybody knew it was money in that. Had the suburban white boys strung out and selling his shit on the Princeton campus. Made a few mil in his ten-year run but his prime was like eh, '05 to '07. Retired in '08. Runs PMF Enterprises now . . . I know."

Jayde was impressed.

"You know him?"

"I tried to recruit him. Almost did . . . but a lot of shit went down. . . ." Ree's voice drifted off as he thought of

the whole demise of his Jersey operation with Chris as a
key to it. Ree knew that was a big reason Julez had retired. They were on the brink of doing business, and
when shit started unraveling, every major dealer in
Jersey started feeling the heat. Julez has gotten out at
the right time. The game was changed. And if you weren't
in the top five percentile of moneymakers, you were a
fool to still be doing it.

Jayde pursed her lips.

"I can see how that could have been profitable. Although from what I heard, he was a bit flashy. You
would've had to tone him like you did Chauncey," she
giggled, recrossing her legs and letting him know she
knew history as well. "I hear he's pretty arrogant too."

Ree lifted an eyebrow at her, only halfway amused.

"You? Call arrogance? Besides . . . you shouldn't
speak that way about your brother," Ree quipped.

Jayde's face became serious as she rolled her eyes.

"I don't have brothers, or sisters, or any of that bullshit. I don't know what Mickel was doing, trying to
create the *Godfather*-themed Brady Brunch, but I'm not
for it. *I'm* his daughter, that's all I know. But Julez . . . if
convinced . . . may be a business asset to us."

Ree sighed in annoyance as he threw down the balls
and they hit his cherrywood desk with a thud.

"Us? Again, stop with the us shit, Jayde! To you"—he
pointed at her aggressively—"and that's a maybe . . . if
the nigga even wants to step back into this shit. But do
that shit *after* I take my cut and walk the fuck away. Don't
bring anybody new into the equation while I'm still
here, I directly forbid it and it will most definitely be
consequences if you go against that. After I'm gone, you
do what you do, but don't speak my name." Fuck saying
his name five times like Candyman, if Jayde or anyone
even spoke his name one time after he was gone, he'd

leave them where they stood, and he wouldn't need a hook.

"So you don't trust him? He's Mickel's son."

"I trust Mickel," Ree spoke immediately and sternly. "I can't speak on his offspring."

Jayde knew that included her. She watched as Ree took another swig of the liquor. He was nearly bottomed out so she knew he had drunk a good amount. Her eyes lowered to the seat of his chair and she could see the imprint of his package lying against his right thigh. My God it wasn't even hard but it was still a creation of massiveness. Jayde licked her lips subtly as if eyeing a lemonade stand on a ninety-eight-degree summer day.

"I hope you will be able to take your cut on schedule, Ree. I really do. Hopefully the Segovias and the Gonzales family trust me enough to let this go through my hands. I must remind you this is why Mickel needed you in the first place; I could not do it."

Ree closed his eyes and leaned his head back, not worried about that. He had met with them, which was his purpose in being there. He had provided the funds. He was still there and available as insurance for this first run.

"I'm still here, Jayde. It's already in progress. Everything is coming in and going out on schedule. All you have to do is worry about how you're gonna run this after I'm gone with C out of the picture. And there's no need to discuss that with me so this conversation should've been over."

Ree let the empty bottle slip out of his hand onto the floor and the thick glass clattered against the wood but didn't break. There was another full bottle that sat on his desk and he contemplated breaking it open.

He pinched the bridge of his nose with his forefinger

and thumb, eyes still closed, and reflected on the situation with Chauncey.

After all that had happened with Tatum, he hardly could think about Chauncey getting himself into trouble . . . again. Ree now saw how love crippled a man's mind, blocking out all that was equally as crucial and important. Ree wanted to steer Chauncey to what he had been, what he had become. He knew he had it in him. However, this last stunt, Ree couldn't save him from. Not even Jayde's big judge and police friends could do much. The officers who had responded were straight cops, the body was there, and his gun was dirty. No matter what, Chauncey would have to do some time. At least with Ree's case, they were able to pull the tech-nicalities with the warrant as a way to dismiss all. There were no loopholes for Chauncey.

"You seem like you have a lot on your mind?" she noted aloud, knowing it was Tatum. "Maybe you should pick up your balls."

Ree's eyes shot open and he glared at her sensing an insult. Jayde smirked.

"These balls." She picked up the feng shui balls, which barely both fit comfortably in her dainty hand. "So these things really relieve stress?"

Ree stared at her a moment longer before looking away snidely.

"So you just rub these balls around in your hand and they take all the stress away," she continued with a giggle. "Why not just rub on your own? . . . Or get someone to do it for you?"

Ree stared at the girl, really stared at her. All of her witty talking and slick moving, grinning and chuckling, and her sexy body and attractive features, it may have worked on the average nigga, but he saw right through

it. He rubbed his goatee and looked toward the door.
It was closed.

"What do you want, Jayde?"

She pursed her lips and straightened her back.

"What do you mean?"

"You know exactly what I mean. Why are you still
here? The past fifteen minutes . . . the past weeks . . . the
past months, you've been tap dancing on me with your
passive-aggressive attempts bordering seduction and
aggravation . . . for what? You claim you've heard enough
about me, you must know the last thing I find intriguing
is bullshit. You want me to be your big brother, you
look up to me, you want to be my partner, you wanna
rub my balls. I can't keep up. So again I ask. What . . .
do . . . you . . . want?"

Jayde took in a deep and shaky breath. Not shaky out
of fear, but because she had just been turned on in a
way she wasn't sure was humanly possible for her. She was
positive that if Ree just touched her, anywhere, she
would orgasm instantly.

"No bullshit, huh?" she finally spoke. "I like that."

"Do you?"

"I do. And I'll be real." If she was to really be real she
would reveal all she had done to try to play Ree into her
hands. But she had to admit at this moment, he was far
from the average guy. She wondered if her games, while
clever and played in a way that even the smartest of men
such as Ree could not detect the most sinister of her
actions, were still not enough to reel in a fish as big as
Ree. Sure, she had come in and upswept his world from
the sidelines like a vicious tornado and it had all seemed
like things that could only occur by fate. She purposely
had moved in a way that even the biggest skeptics would
have to ask, *But how could she have been responsible for that?*
But still, he and his foundation had remained grounded

as if deep rooted in the soil of his universe. Would honesty be the best policy, or at least half-truths? Maybe she'd give it a shot.

"You, be real?" He seemed amused.

"Yes . . . Okay, I do want you. And I've never wanted a man before."

Ree stared at her unblinkingly.

"You've wanted a woman?"

"I've never wanted anyone. But you . . ." She shrugged. "I want you. That's all."

"What do you want from me . . . to be with me? To be what . . . my girl? My wife?" There were small doses of laughter in his question as if it were comical.

"You don't need a wife, Respect. The only flaw I found in you is that even while recognizing your unordinary presence . . . your overpowering effect on people . . . your almost . . . Godlike qualities . . ." Ree chuckled at her overdramatization of himself as she continued.

"Even as you recognize these things in yourself. You still try to live by the conformities of regular mortals? I don't get it. You know you needed a wife like I needed a hole in my head."

Ree narrowed his eyes, reflecting on her thinking and the possible truth in her statement. If she were accurate then she had just contradicted herself. Because if anyone needed a hole in their head, it was Jayde. Ree didn't know her full capabilities or what she had done, but he knew she was poison to the earth. And if she wasn't Mickel's daughter, he would have killed her back in Chauncey's basement when she revealed her snake-like character. He tuned her back in as she continued her declaration.

"All you need," she spoke seductively while subtly beginning to rub on her own thigh. ". . . is a woman who will be whatever you need her to be, whenever you need her to be it. Your partner. Your ally. Your soldier. And your lover. You need a woman that will bring you some-one's head and then bless you with some head in return. And then may go out and get another bitch and bring *her* home to bless you with some more head," she tittered. "You don't need structure . . . rules . . . monogamy. I can tell you're too much man for one person. I wouldn't do that to you. I would only want my share."

Ree scratched along his jawline and made bold eye contact.

"So a fuck. You just want a fuck?"

"If that's all you took from what I said, then I guess that's what I wa—"

"Yeah, that's all I took from what you said."

He stood up and stared in her sparkling green eyes and he could see her chest begin to heave up and down. Her breathing changed, she was nervous, anxious, one or both. He walked the few inches up to her that closed the space between them and studied Jayde. She was beautiful, there was no doubt about it.

Ree stared at her face and then allowed his eyes to travel down to her long, slender neck, down to her cleavage, and then along the rest of her body as he grazed her shoulders and down her arms with the tips of his fingers.

"Why didn't you just tell me, baby?" he spoke in a low voice while he eyed her thighs.

"I was . . ." Jayde could barely speak as she felt a gush of liquid burst from her canal to the seat of her thong immediately. "I was . . . playing . . ." His fingers felt like the tips of a million feathers singing on her nerve endings. "I wanted . . . I wanted . . . ooh!"

She yelped in excitement as he yanked her legs open,

roughly grabbing her knees and separating them with one forceful push.

"Yeah . . . I know what you wanted . . ." Ree brought his hands up the outside of her thighs and under her dress. "All of that shit, right? Tatum and that punk-ass lawyer. I know you wanted me to catch them in some shit." Jayde's eyes lowered in lust as he palmed her ass.

"You bring up that shit with Chris, knowing Tatum was here. Yeah . . . I asked you. But you hoped she'd hear it, didn't you?" Jayde was lucky to still be breathing for that one. Even though Ree was the one at fault, half of him believed Jayde intentionally wanted Tatum to hear that. If she wasn't Mickel's daughter . . .

"No," she whispered heavily as he pulled her head back by her hair roughly. "I swear . . . I didn't want to say it. You . . . you asked me. You made me say it." Being so close to him was better than any sex she'd ever had.

"You know I wanted to kill you, right?"

"I know," she admitted, bringing her hands to his muscular arms and rubbing them. "I'm sorry . . . I swear I didn't mean to, ooh Ree please . . . fuck me. Fuck me, please."

"Yeah? What about your sister?"

"My sister?"

Jayde's heart dropped but she didn't show it. He knew?

"Yeah. Sasha. Tatum's her best friend . . . you have no loyalty to her?" he questioned lowly as he looked her in the eye.

Jayde stared back at him and reached below, beginning to unbuckle his pants.

"No," she answered flatly. "Fuck me. I'm too hot for you right now, Ree. I can't take it."

Ree chuckled.

"Yeah, you hot. I know you hot, Jayde." She went to

reach for his dreads but he grabbed her wrists and pinned her back against the desk roughly in one swift motion, laying her whole body flat with it, unable to move. Jayde had never been dominated like that before and he was so strong, her emotions danced between lust and fear. The fear of him actually added to the attraction and sexual tension.

Oh my God, finally, Jayde thought. *Jesus Christ he is so fucking beautiful, I want to suck the blood out of his dick.*

Ree reached under her dress and ripped her panties off with one forceful tug.

"You hot?"

"Yes!" she replied, humping the air like a sex fiend anticipating that dick crack.

Ree pulled out his dick with one hand, while the other held her wrists against the desk. Jayde lifted up anxious to see it but Ree let go of her wrist and in a nanosecond later, had her pinned back down with his hand around her neck.

"Lay! The fuck . . . down, Jayde. Since you so fucking hot . . ."

Her chest continued to heave up and down and her eyes rolled in the back of her head as she waited to feel his penetration.

"Yes! This pussy is hot for you too, daddy!"

His clasp around her neck became tighter as she heard him chuckle.

"Well maybe you should cool the fuck off, then."

Jayde crinkled her brow in confusion and a second later felt wetness between her legs. But it wasn't her own. She struggled out of Ree's now lighter grasp and sat up, only to find her white one-thousand-dollar dress being soaked and stained yellow. Ree wore a smirk as he continued to piss on her entire lower body and as her jaw dropped, he aimed the remainder of his half-drunken relief wherever it would land on her body. Coming to an end, he shook the last of it on her and his face turned serious as Jayde for once was speechless. Never had she been so disrespected. She lifted her hands not knowing what to do with them and looked down at her crotch with her mouth agape.

"You so fucking hot, Jayde, that you have no loyalty to your family . . . your friends. You disrespect my wife . . . in her home," he spoke venomously as he picked up the new bottle of Hennessey. "Yeah I say you hot all right . . . you need to cool the fuck down." He then began to splash the premium liquor all over her, bathing her in it with a grimace on his face in disgust. Jayde jumped up and guarded the liquor with her hands, wiping her drenched face and screaming at the top of her lungs.

"Ree! What the fuck! Do you know who I am?" She was furious. She was a murderer as well and would have dusted any nigga who dared do this to her. Not to mention who her father was.

"I know who you are, Jayde," he affirmed with a light laugh. "But as for myself. You obviously have no clue."

"Argh!" she yelled hysterically, now smelling the stench of piss on her. Crush came crashing through the door and was perplexed at the scene. Ree's desk completely wet, his pants unbuckled. Jayde in a disarray, her short dress hiked but stained yellow and the smell of urine now perfuming the scene. Leroy came in right behind him.

"Sean, what de hell is going on!" Ree's father barked, not liking what he saw, urine or no urine. "Where is my daughter? Where is Tatum! Aren't you supposed to be looking for her? Crush, take this hussy out of here at once!"

Ree smirked and zipped up his pants, taking his seat as if nothing had happened.

"It's okay, Pop. She was just leaving."

Ree's father retreated in anger back to his guest room, where he had been staying since Ree went to get him after the fire. Crush then reached for Jayde, but she snatched away.

"I can fucking walk." She shot a glare at Ree and then him, and then made her way to the door, storming out angry and defeated. Crush wanted to ask Ree what had happened but he was afraid to know. He hoped that Ree hadn't fucked her.

"Close the door on your way out, Crush. I am not to be disturbed anymore this evening." Ree placed the half-full new bottle to his lips and swigged, eyes toward one of the walls, with thoughts of Tatum now filling his head. He could care less about how angry Jayde was, anything that had occurred with her walked out of his office when she did. Crush took a deep breath and nodded, and then retreated, closing the door behind him. He was surprised to find Jayde leaning against the wall when he stepped out of the office.

"Fuck are you still doing here?" he asked sharply.

"What, you not happy to see me?" She studied the big man with the quiet demeanor as she tried to regroup. It was only a minor setback. She had come on too strong. She had to restrategize. "You don't like me, do you, Crush?"

"I don't know you. But from what I know . . . no, I don't like you."

Jayde sucked her teeth and shook her head from side to side.

"Well . . . see, that's just too bad, Crush. Because one day, you may be getting *my* tea and soup. And how are we going to get along then?"

Crush looked at her like she was crazy. Was she insinuating she'd be taking Tatum's place? He nodded.

"Yeah, okay," Crush spoke dismissively. "I'll get your tea when Respect stops treating you like a fire hydrant."

Jayde narrowed her eyes at him, knowing that was an insult about the peeing situation.

"You know who you remind me of, Crush?" She didn't wait for an answer before finishing. "You remind me *a lot* of E."

Crush looked at her long and hard. He knew she had played a part in E's death and he wondered if she was implying something. He stepped up to her sternly.

"Well, that's too bad," he spoke evenly. "'Cause I ain't no fucking E." He spat the words so angrily that spit foamed on the sides of his mouth. He had gone from teddy bear to grizzly bear in 2.2 seconds. She saw why he was so close with Ree. Jayde ran her tongue along the inside of her cheek and then nodded. With little to no more words spoken, she turned on her heels and strutted down the hall and out of the mansion.

"Yeah . . . take your pissy ass out of here," Crush mumbled. He then picked up his cell, still eyeing the front door and reflecting on Jayde's hidden threat and the scene he had just busted in on. Shit was getting out of control. He dialed the number and waited for the person on the other line to answer. And when they did he only spoke seven simple words because that was all that was needed.

"Hello?"

"Hey . . ." He started looking from the door Jayde had just left out of to the closed office door where Ree was inside sulking. He shook his head in disbelief. "Look . . . you gotta come home, now!"

"So that's why you believe in fate?" Sasha smiled wide, soaking up the last part of G's story.

"Yeah . . . I mean . . . I don't know about *fate*. But I definitely think everything happens for a reason. Like I said, me and my girl, we got a hell of a story. One for the books, you know? But we were meant to end up together . . . I'm sure you and C got a story of your own."

Sasha swallowed hard and dashed her eyes around the car.

They were both reclined, talking for the past forty minutes about anything and everything. The conversation seemed to flow so easy. She was a little relieved when she found out that he had a girlfriend, that way her fantasies of Chauncey's friend, especially while they had just broken up, could be put on hold. *What is wrong with me? I love Chauncey to death. Maybe I always have to get over one man by getting under another?* Sasha broke her own thoughts.

"Well . . . yeah, we have a story. But it's no fairy tale like yours. Chauncey and I are no longer together," she admitted, once again feeling the sadness. She could see the dismal look in G's eyes. He felt bad for her.

"Sorry to hear that." There was an awkward silence that followed. G began to drum his fingertips on the wood-grain steering wheel and Sasha bit the inside of her cheeks. That's when the two noticed bright lights from the tow truck approaching.

"They're here," Sasha announced with relief. G looked over at her and gave a half smile and she returned it, and then they both exited the vehicle.

"Thank you for waiting . . . and for, I don't know . . . saving my life. Sounds like from your story you like to do that a lot," she quipped.

G chuckled.

"Yeah, maybe I've got that broken bird syndrome or something. You know, always wanna play Superman or some shit. Anyway, it was my pleasure."

Sasha smiled and as the tow truck driver approached, she spoke to him and G stood on the sidelines. He stepped closer when he heard the conversation raise a pitch.

"How can you not take debit?" she asked, perplexed.

"Lady . . . do I look like I have a damn ATM machine in my truck cab? You called me out here for this shit and you ain't got no money?"

G stepped up.

"Whoa, whoa, calm down on the language, my man. It can all be resolved." He dug in his pocket and peeled off hundred dollar bill after hundred dollar bill.

Sasha sighed and ran her hands through her hair.

"I can't let you . . . I can't let you do that. You've already done too much."

G laughed smoothly.

"You ain't got no choice, ma. Maybe in some ill twist of fate you'll pay me back one day."

He shot her a wink and paid the tow driver.

As the man began to hook up Sasha's car to the truck, Sasha went inside and retrieved Aubrey. G walked them both to the tow truck and helped them inside, closing the passenger door behind him. Sasha sat in the passenger seat with Aubrey on her lap and the tow driver then hopped in the driver's seat.

G smiled again and threw up his hand, bidding her farewell.

"Hey! Gavin!" Sasha called to him after he started off.

He turned and looked at her curiously.

"I was wondering . . . you know, I'm thinking of moving back to Jersey . . . and . . . I don't know . . . maybe you know some places, or some houses for sale? I'm really not going to have too many friends up here." Sasha knew she was stretching. Why did she want to see him again, even after knowing he had a girlfriend? She convinced herself that maybe she really did want to know someone if she moved back to Jersey . . . for friendly stuff.

G stood still for a moment as if thinking about something and then he walked back to her. He pulled out a card and handed it to Sasha.

Reading it, she lifted an eyebrow.

"In case I get hungry?" she joked. The card read MADELINE'S SOUTHERN CUISINE RESTAURANT. G laughed.

"Nah, that's my spot. Call me there . . . if you move back. And I'll hook you up. I'm actually selling my house and my loft."

Sasha rubbed the card between her fingers like it was money and wondered why he was selling his house and loft. Then she thought of the fact that he *had* a house and a loft. Where was he going?

She smiled.

"Thank you." He nodded and grinned, and this time she let him walk away. And the minute he did, the pain from losing Chauncey returned.

Chapter 16

"I can't let you go, Tatum. I know I should. And you should let me go too."

—Respect, *Thicker than Water*

The house felt cold. Icy. Even with it being midsummer, and the air-conditioning running low, Tatum still sensed a chill from the high, stone mansion walls. It was even colder than when she had left. She closed the front door behind her slowly and took a deep breath. She was more nervous than she could have ever imagined. She felt like a stranger to the place, as if she didn't belong. And she wondered if she did. She wasn't sure what she was doing there either. The eerie silence as the house slept seemed to ask her the same question. After Tatum received the phone call from Crush, she wondered if she was returning to get her things and finalize their separation, to get closure. Or was she being drawn back to him? All she did know was that she had to come back, that was for sure. Tatum crept across the dimness of her vast living room. It was open, huge with two sets of spiral staircases with wide steps that led up the stairs. The rubber-soled Tod's flats she wore made little to no noise on the mahogany floors. She had borrowed them from Terri, along with her drawstring linen pants and plain white tank, being that she had come to her in a silk robe and nothing more. Tatum started for the stairs guessing Ree had to be in bed at this time, but then heard a noise coming from his office. It was a thud sound, as if something had dropped onto the floor.

She took in a deep breath and nervously detoured, making her way to him in there. Tatum didn't know why she was so scared to face him. Maybe because of what he had done, maybe because she was scared of the love that would surface when she saw him. And she didn't want to feel that. She didn't want to betray her brother like that.

Stepping to the door, she knocked lightly.

"Crush . . ." he spoke with a slight slur. "No disturbance."

The sound of his voice made Tatum's heart rate speed up and tears instantly came to her eyes. She loved him so much. She wanted nothing more than to run and hug him and hold on to him forever and ever. But how could she? Tatum brought her fist from the door and took a step back, turning to walk away. She couldn't do this. She had to leave, leave while she still had a chance, before she could connect eyes with him, leave this man, this monster, leave this life. She looked to the front door and now saw Crush standing there. He simply shook his head no and pointed toward the office. Tatum sighed and rolled her eyes, knowing he was right. She wanted to go in there as bad as Crush wanted her to go in there. She put her hand on the knob and as she twisted it and pushed the door open, an image of her brother laughing entered her head.

"Crush . . . seriously . . ." Ree sat with his feet kicked up on the desk, his head thrown back and his eyelids closed. Two empty bottles now lay on the floor and the windows were wide open. Music played in the background, now Al Green's "I'm Still in Love with You" was the one to greet Tatum.

Tatum stared on at him, her tears now becoming denser. His breathing was that of him being asleep, but he wasn't. She could feel his pain, and although he was the one who hurt her, she wanted to console him. Tatum sniffed and gasped at the overwhelming emotions she felt, her sweet breath filling the room and seeming to awake Ree. She hadn't spoken, but that gasp held the softest, most acute hint of her voice that he was in tune with and picked up on. He thought he dreamed it and closed his eyes again until she spoke . . . "You look like shit."

Ree took a deep breath, his heart immediately felt heavy. He couldn't open his eyes at first because he couldn't fathom it. *How could she come back?* She was even more perfect than he had thought she was. He really didn't deserve her.

Ree opened his eyes slowly but still didn't turn his head.

How could she come back?

"Tatum . . ." He spoke her name low in his deep baritone, but that word held so much emotion, as if he had put all of his love into saying her name. He had put every *I'm sorry,* every *I missed you,* and every *I can't live without you* into that one word. And Tatum felt it.

He finally looked at her, and she stood before him, just as natural, beautiful, broken, and devastated as she was when he had last saw her. It hurt him because he wondered if this would be the last time he saw her.

"I . . . I never meant to hurt you, Tatum. I *swear.* Back then . . . I was only . . ."

"Ssshhhh." Tatum placed her finger lightly to her lips

and silenced him. She closed her eyes and tears dropped onto her brown cheeks like sun showers hitting the desert sands. She had made her choice. A decision that was never hers to make, only her heart's.

"I don't want to know, Ree. Do you understand?" She opened her eyes and stared at him with sentiment. "It was . . . it was *so* much better when I didn't know." Her voice cracked and she cried, and he stared at her feeling like his chest had caved in seeing her like this.

She slowly stepped over to him. Her legs wobbly with every step, her brother's memory fading with every step, her heart breaking for one reason and coming together for another simultaneously . . . with every step. Finally reaching him, standing in front of him, her breathing became deeper and her tears continued to fall. *How could you be with him?* she knew her mind was asking. *How could you not?* her soul replied. Ree looked up at her, really looked. Her wet face wearing her inner struggle, her small frame shaking in fear, her mouth was opened but she couldn't speak. She couldn't even look at him. Ree closed his eyes and wrapped his arms around her waist, bringing his body forward and burying his face in her stomach. He breathed in deep, soaking her in and holding her tighter than he ever had. "Tatum."

He squeezed her even tighter and Tatum felt his love. She broke down and cried even harder.

"I love you so much," he revealed so truthfully. "I couldn't live without you if I tried . . . I'd go insane, Tatum. I'd go insane," he repeated, still holding her close and nestling his face in her.

"Ah," a faint sigh of emotion escaped Tatum's lips. She grabbed his head, her fingers holding his dreads tight as her tears continued to pour and fall on his head.

"I . . . I love you, Ree," she cried hard. "I can't . . . I can't leave you . . . I love you too much."

He kissed her stomach through her shirt and held her for what seemed like forever. Finally, he stood up, still holding her as close as humanly possible. Reaching his height potential, more than a head above her, he ran his fingers through her hair and looked down at her. Their bodies pressed against each other with no space allotted, Tatum could now feel the wetness of the fabric on her midsection.

Her mouth fell open and she looked up at Ree. His eyes were red, they were glassy, and they were piercing through to her, not hiding it. He had cried on her stomach. She had never seen him cry, not even for their babies.

"Ree," she whispered, bringing her hand to his face as they stared each other in the eyes. She brushed her thumb across his right eye and felt the wetness from his lashes fall onto her finger. "Ree," she repeated.

He took the same hand, holding her wrist, and began to kiss each fingertip softly, never breaking their eye contact. He then brought his head down and kissed her palm. He brought his face to hers and kissed her forehead with passion. He kept his lips there for a while, not believing she was there, and then he moved to kiss her eyelids, one by one.

Tatum took a deep breath and held on to his shirt with strength, scared that he'd fade away. He kissed the tip of her nose and while her eyes remained closed, he stared at her unblinkingly. She was so beautiful. Ree brought his lips to hers and kissed her gently on them, and then he kissed her chin . . . her neck . . . her earlobes.

"I'd die for you," he whispered in her ear, knowing at that moment he meant it with all of his heart.

He picked her up swiftly and Tatum panted.

"Ree, what are you—"

"I'm taking you upstairs, baby."

Tatum sniffled and allowed her head to fall into his chest as he carried her like a baby. She felt his strength, smelled his natural scent that was like an aphrodisiac. Never had she felt so protected, so loved, so safe. The love she shared with Ree was unlike anything she had ever seen, felt, read, witnessed. It was almost religious, the amount of devotion and belief she had in him, to him. It was unbreakable.

Up the long stairs and finally reaching the bed, Ree gently placed her down and lowered himself on top of her. Tatum stared up at him.

"Make love to me, Ree," she whispered, tears rolling down her face and hitting the pillow. He kissed her tears.

"I plan to."

"For the rest of the night," she urged, closing her eyes and enjoying the feel of his lips on her face.

"For the rest of your life," he corrected.

He kissed her lips deeply and Tatum allowed her tongue to intertwine with his. Tasting him was like water that her body needed to survive. Ree pulled away and sat up, moving down her body and removing her shoes. He kissed her toes gently and caressed her feet. Allowing his hands and mouth to roam, he trailed kisses all up one leg to her thighs and down another. Ree brought himself up again and removed her clothes slowly, studying every curve on her body as if they were miraculously formed like the dips and valleys of the Grand Canyon. He placed each of her blackberry-flavored nipples into his mouth, one by one kissing, licking, and nibbling on them. He kissed underneath, in between, and around her breasts. His lips trailed south as he coated her stomach with sweet kisses as well and then dipped his tongue into her navel with ease. He kissed the results of the cesarean that had been performed as if it were just as beautiful as any part of her body, and then finally after separating her legs and kissing her bare pussy as if he'd missed it just as much as her lips, he slid his tongue into her sweetness and savored everything from being with Tatum in this intimate way. He loved the way she tasted, adored the way her body responded to him, he was obsessed with pleasing her. As he slid her soft clit in between his lips and sucked, Tatum's body tensed and she pressed her inner thighs on the side of Ree's face.

"Relax, Tatum. Open up . . . let me take you there."

Tatum parted her thighs farther with the assistance of his strong hands and that's what she allowed him to do. Take her there.

Ree licked, and probed, and sucked on her like eating her pussy was a class he was trying to pass with flying colors.

"Ree," she called out, feeling the moisture travel from between her legs to the crack of her ass. "Ree!"

Her body shuddered as she felt the perfect orgasm approach. It was great in intensity but superb in length. Ree's pace was steadied, and whatever he was doing now, with these gentle tongue strokes mixed with quick flickers, prolonged it for twice the normal span. Tatum closed her eyes tight and squeezed, feeling like she'd never stop cumming.

"Ohhhh!" Just as her clit began to beat like a drum, Ree gently took it between his teeth and Tatum damn near passed out.

"Ree! I can't . . . I can't . . . No more!" He sucked, slurped, and gave it one more quick kiss before coming up, obeying her orders.

Tatum squeezed her legs together, trying to subdue the throbbing as her pussy whispered for Ree to return to her. She stroked his chest with her hand as he unbuttoned his shirt and her eyes lay open half midst.

"Give it to me, Ree. Give me King. I want King."

Tatum had named Ree's dick King because it reminded her of King Kong, big, black, and destructive. And it was no secret that he was the king, so it worked.

Ree placed both hands on the side of her gorgeous face as he allowed his dick to guide itself into Tatum's tightness, a place easy for it to find since it belonged. He closed his eyes and relished the moment.

"Ahhh, shittt," he groaned, while beginning to glide in and out of her, enjoying the gushy sounds and feeling. "And if I needed one more reason why I couldn't let your ass go," he chuckled, licking his lips and feeling a chill go through his body. This pussy belonged to him. He knew it as well as it knew him. Tatum smiled and gripped his hair, throwing her hips to him regardless of the painful pleasure.

"Yesss, ooohhh I love youuu, Reee," Tatum squealed, feeling her clit swell up on the verge of another explosion.

"I love you more." The words caused Tatum to burst, soaking his thighs and the sheets with her juices. "Goddamn, I love you more."

The ringing of the cell phone awakened Sasha out of a deep sleep. She had made it to her father's apartment in Highland Park, New Jersey, found out that Tatum had returned to Atlanta from a message left with her dad, threw her phone on the charger, and passed out with Aubrey on his pullout couch.

Now it was 5:23 A.M. and some psycho was calling her back to back.

"Who is this?" she asked groggily, removing her sleeping mask, not recognizing or studying the number too much.

"Sasha? . . . Is this Sasha?"

Sasha sucked her teeth and sighed.

"Well, who did you call?"

There was a nervous giggle that followed.

"Right . . . Look, I'm sorry Sasha, but . . . this is . . . this is Adriana, the nurse from Grady Memorial Hospital. I *really* need to talk to you about your friend . . . Jayde. I know I've been missing you the last times I tried to get in contact with you."

Sasha huffed and threw her head back against the pillow, not believing this shit.

"Listen, lady. Like I told you, I really have no interest in anything that has to do with Jayde! She gets herself into shit all the time and I really want no part of her. If you were smart, you would follow my lead. I mean, I'm sorry I haven't called you back but I really just wanted nothing to do with her. Now if you'd excuse me, it's five-something in the morning and I'd like to get back to sl—"

"Did you know a girl named Penelope?"

Sasha's eyes shot open. Had she heard her right?

"Excuse me?" Sasha asked, her heartbeat speeding up rapidly.

"Penelope . . . Penelope Daniels," Adriana repeated, now in a hushed whisper. "She died at this hospital and . . . and I really think I have something you need to listen to. I think you may be in danger."

Sasha's breath caught in her throat and she quickly sat up, turning on her father's end-table lamp.

"Okay. What is it?"

* * *

Tatum's eyes fluttered open and a smile crept across her face. Ree was seated in the chair in the corner, facing her with a bunch of papers in his hand. The morning sunlight crept through the window, illuminating his rugged, handsome face.

"Mmm," she moaned sweetly. "What are you doing up so early?"

He stared at her for a while, smiling with his eyes. Finally he grinned.

"Just . . . thinking."

"Just thinking, huh?" Tatum's wavy hair was loose and wild scattered over the pillow and she was topless, the sheet covering her waist down as she lay on her stomach. "What are you thinking about?"

He shrugged.

"What are we going to do after this is over, Tatum? I'm basically done . . . like I told you I would be. Now what?"

He hoped she would say she wanted to leave here. But he would leave it to her. Tatum took a deep breath and looked off. She thought of everything that had occurred, Trinity, the trial, Johnny, Chauncey, Bleek, her babies, it had all been a genocide of death and turmoil.

"I want to go back . . . home. To the coconut trees and to being the street girl," she smiled slowly, looking at Ree. He smiled, too, and Tatum giggled.

"That's why I love you." He leaned over to kiss her and one of the papers he was holding fell to the floor. Tatum sat up, scrunching her face and holding the sheet across her chest. She bent down and picked it up in confusion.

"Ree . . . what is this?"

He stared at it and ran his hand over his mouth before replying.

"That's yours."

Tatum stared at the picture for a while and tried to fathom why this would be hers.

"Ree? A hot air balloon? Why would I . . . I mean, it's *nice* . . . but . . ."

"Tatum. Remember how you were telling me . . . you know, we can do anything. Put this money to other things. Remember you said to reach for the clouds?"

Tatum nodded reluctantly. She remembered, but she didn't mean for them to reach for the clouds by buying a hot air balloon. Ree could see the question on her face and he laughed.

"Look, hear me out. Basically, the hotel burned down and we're going to rebuild it, right? But in the meantime, I thought it would be good for you to have your own business as well. I run the hotel, and you run . . ."

"A hot air balloon? Oh, so you giving me the chump change, huh?" Tatum joked. Ree laughed again smoothly.

"Tatum. There are no hot air balloon attractions on the island, yet everyone always has been interested. So what I did is I purchased you twenty hot air balloons, starting off small. They will go up twice a day, once for a group that wants to watch the sunrise, another for the sunset." Tatum's interest became piqued once she realized he had put so much thought and planning behind it. A business of her own did sound intriguing. Ree continued. "Each balloon seats twelve but will require a minimum of ten before we lift off. The average price for a hot air balloon ride is between two hundred and four hundred fifty dollars. However, on an island like Jamaica, three hundred fifty dollars a person is easily a steal. So that's twenty balloons, ten people per balloon, at three hundred fifty dollars . . . that's . . ."

"Seventy thousand dollars a day, Ree!" Tatum exclaimed, wide-eyed. Ree shrugged.

"Not exactly. That's seventy thousand dollars that morning. Another seventy thousand dollars for sunset. As a nice little side business, which is one hundred percent your own, you should pull in at least four mil a month . . . on a slow month. Although, the way the tourists have been showing interest and flocking to the island, I doubt you'd have a slow month anytime soon. The workers are ready to be hired, insurance is already purchased, and you don't have to do anything but sign the ownership papers, baby." Ree smirked at her and shot her a wink while Tatum tried to close her mouth. "How's that for chump change?"

She jumped up and straddled him, kissing his face.

"I love you, I love you, I love you! Do you seeee what I mean, Ree," she exclaimed to him. "I told you . . . you're a genius. You don't have to hustle in the streets. You're just a hustler *period*. Your mind is out of this world."

His kiss was his response. They sat there for a minute wrapped up in each other before Ree tapped her, signaling his need to stand.

"I gotta go handle something and then I'll start getting everything ready for us to go back home. You got anything you need to do?"

Tatum stood as well.

"Yeah, Dr. Patel called while I was gone so I'm gonna make an appointment to stop in and see her. After that, I need to have a long talk with Sasha, see how she's feeling especially after all of this Chauncey nonsense."

"You haven't talked to her?"

"We talked real quick, but she was driving and all I could really do was tell her how sorry I was . . . I still can't believe Bleek is dead." Tatum stared off deep in thought. Ree put the papers in the top of the dresser and slammed it shut, then walked over and kissed Tatum on the lips.

"Yeah well, we getting the fuck outta here before any more shit happens." He headed for the door and Tatum silently agreed.

"I just don't understand why you wouldn't come to me first, Tatum? As your doctor, it looks like I didn't properly advise you of the risks and procedures, you know?"

Tatum didn't understand why the doctor was so upset. She had only been her doctor since they had moved to Atlanta. And it wasn't like Tatum and Ree were trying, so what would she come to her about? Tatum sat across from her with the desk in between them, her leg bounced in anticipation as she tried to keep up with Dr. Patel dancing in circles around what she had to say.

"Svelta, I wasn't trying to get pregnant, it just . . . happened. I don't understand."

Svelta Patel reached into the manila folder that held the results of Tatum's lab results from the hospital. She was visibly upset and continued to shake her head and sniffle. She wanted to birth those twins.

"Tatum, do you realize as a result, you . . ." Her voice trailed off and Tatum became tense, rigid immediately.

"I what?"

"I mean . . . let me rephrase. As a possible—"

"No, no rephrasing, give it to me straight, Svelta, no chaser! What?" Tatum's lip trembled as she assumed what was about to be said. She immediately regretted telling Ree not to come with her.

Dr. Patel looked Tatum square in the eyes and took a deep breath.

"Tatum, you may never be able to have children. Your uterus lining is too thin. You may never be able to carry full term."

Tatum shut her eyes and swallowed the lump in her throat. Straight, no chaser, she had asked. But she wasn't ready for that.

"I don't . . . why . . ." Tatum's voice was barely above a whisper.

Dr. Patel crinkled her brow at her and shook her head.

"Tatum . . . if you wanted to get pregnant I don't think you should have gone straight to a fertility drug. Not to mention, *that* one. It already is very controversial and given in small doses. The amount you consumed, I mean my God! Like I said, you should've come to me and I would have advised you . . ."

"Svelta, what are you talking about! I wasn't on any fertility drugs! You have my files mixed up or something." Tatum hoped that was what it was. And maybe the thin uterus lining part was wrong, too.

"Tatum . . . Aliya . . . Knights," Dr. Patel spoke, holding up her file and standing in aggravation. "You, my dear, had a ridiculously high amount of Clomid in your bloodstream. And while it does help to increase egg production it also thins the lining, which is why it is usually countered with another drug and is a last resort. Why in the world would you take so much?"

Tatum stared down at the floor and wondered what was going on. She was in a bad dream. She hadn't heard anything past the first sentence. After trying to get over this last blow with her brother, she was sure the ill fates had stopped. But now . . . this. *Clomid?* The tears poured and wouldn't stop.

* * *

Tatum had been calling Ree like crazy since she'd left the doctor's office. She cried the entire time she drove and she was amazed that she hadn't wrecked the car and had made it to the mansion in one piece. She finally decided to calm down and try to put her thoughts together. Making decisions and trying to piece together a puzzle while upset was as useless as hanging clothes to dry in a rainstorm. After the fifth call, she finally left him a message of three short words. "Get home, now."

Tatum whipped the Range Rover that she'd chosen to drive that morning into the circular driveway and hopped out before she could barely get the key out of the ignition. Her thoughts raced at top speed.

Okay, think, Tatum . . . think. When . . . Who . . . Why . . .

Although still as perplexed as she had been when she left Dr. Patel's office, Tatum immediately began looking through mantel drawers and cabinets at the house. Most of what she found was stuff from Ree's trial, cards from the loss of her children, bills.

"What the hell am I even looking for?" she questioned out loud, stopping abruptly and placing her fingers to her temples in frustration. She refused to cry anymore, she felt like she'd cried enough for a lifetime. Now, she was ready to get mad, get answers, and put the bad behind her.

She picked up her cell to see if Ree had returned her call yet. For some reason she just felt like he would have the answers. Either that or he'd be able to get them. Seeing that he had yet to call back, Tatum bit her lip ready to call him once more. The chiming of the doorbell stopped her from completing the task. Tatum marched over to the front door in haste, wondering who it could be. Crush was out with Ree and Ree had keys.

Tatum peeked through the peephole and quickly brought her face back. She swallowed hard as she looked off to the side and thought for a second. Tatum ran her now sweaty hands over her bright multicolored maxi dress and sighed, opening the door with a cool face.

"Hi, Jayde."

Jayde spun around with her mouth opened, having her back turned to the door at first. She was dressed in a black high-waist miniskirt and white top, all spandex, and black-and-white platform Louboutins, definitely dressed to impress.

"Tatum? W-wow!" Jayde exclaimed with a chuckle of disbelief, clearly thrown off as she ended a call on her cell phone. This definitely threw her for a loop; she was sure Tatum was done with Ree after the Chris situation.

Wow, the dick must be that good, Jayde concluded.

"I wasn't—I wasn't expecting for you to . . . to be here," Jayde admitted, for once telling the truth.

Tatum raised an eyebrow slightly.

"Really? Well I *do* live here, Jayde. But I wasn't expecting you."

Jayde smiled flaccidly and then pressed her lips together, evening her lipstick.

"Touché. Well, I was just coming to talk to Respect about some last-minute business details. Is he around?"

Tatum stared at Jayde for a moment and then nodded coolly.

"Come in, Jayde. He's not around but he should be shortly. You can wait."

Jayde followed Tatum inside and studied her when she was sure Tatum wasn't looking. The bitch was naturally beautiful, Jayde couldn't change that. Even with the evident sadness in Tatum's eyes they still sparkled. She thought of how Ree had pissed on her the night before and wondered if he would ever do such a thing to her. *Nope,* she figured. *Not his precious Tatum.*

"Did you want something to drink, Jayde? Maybe something to ea . . ." Tatum's words trailed off as a lost look appeared on her face and her mouth hung opened. Jayde was perplexed but Tatum had just had a sudden epiphany.

"No, I'm not hungry or thirsty. But . . . Tatum, you okay? Did you need something? You don't look too well."

Tatum shook her head, snapping herself out of her trance, and smiled lightly, fighting the tears that she knew she'd better not allow to present themselves.

"Uh . . . no. Nah, I'm good. I'm just . . . I don't know . . . a little out of it. To tell you the truth, I just came from the doctor . . . I'm just thinking of something that she told me. . . ." Tatum studied Jayde for a minute after she spoke the words and Jayde studied her right back.

"Oh . . . Well what did the doctor say?"

Tatum looked off for a minute and then strolled over to one of the vintage mantels, placing the papers and junk she had been rummaging through back. She no longer needed it.

"I'd . . . rather not talk about it . . ." Tatum continued to move slowly, restoring order to her cabinets as her mind wandered. Was it too farfetched? But weren't any of the possibilities? None of it made sense. Tatum broke the growing silence with her next choice of words.

"You know, Jayde . . . I never got the chance to thank you for all of the beautiful flowers you sent. You know . . . after we lost . . . the *babies.*" Tatum's voice changed on the word *babies* but she tried to conceal it. Jayde took a seat on the couch perpendicular to Tatum and crossed her legs confidently.

"Oh Tatum . . . no need to thank me, please. I was

only trying to help. I could only *imagine* what you went through."

Tatum licked her lips and nodded, still keeping her back turned. She felt a bolt of adrenaline go through her but she maintained a cool exterior. At that moment, she heard the buzzing of her cell phone but chose to ignore it. She would just see Ree when he got home. Tatum began twirling her ring out of habit and stared at the wall.

"And also . . . all of the help you've been, Jayde. I mean, even beyond business, you've been here for Ree . . . like a friend or *something*. Especially at times when I couldn't be . . . I mean it just seems like for all of the terrible things that have been happening . . . you've been right *there* . . . *Always* right there. I may not have commented on it, but I definitely have noticed it."

Tatum closed the small double doors to the cabinet and Jayde looked at her from the corner of her eye snidely. *Was she?*

"Well . . . of course, Tatum. I mean I hate that these things happened . . . but I am definitely glad that I was able to be here for you guys." Jayde snapped open her clutch, and rested her fingers on the edge of her small .32 handgun, wearing a smile on her face. "At the end of the day, we're like a family, you know?"

Tatum chuckled lightly and nodded.

"Yeah . . . it def seems like it. Even down to sharing family recipes," Tatum tittered. "You know, Jayde, I was thinking of making some of that soup you cooked for me when I was pregnant." Tatum spun around and looked at her seriously, her lips pressed tight together and her stare piercing through to the real Jayde. "What exactly did you put in it?"

Looking up at Tatum, Jayde locked eyes with her. No one blinked, no one moved, and Jayde had to give

it to Tatum. She wasn't as dumb as Sasha, just as Neli
had warned. She had caught on before Jayde had the
pleasure of presenting herself. A light laugh escaped
Jayde's lips as she revealed a sneer. It was definitely party
time, so she merely shrugged.

"What was in it?" Jayde repeated before looking
up at the ceiling, placing her index finger to her chin.
". . . Mmmm, I don't know. I guess just a little of *this* . . .
a little of *that*."

Tatum let out a small chuckle of disbelief as her eyes
glazed over in rage, turning up toward the ceiling. How
could somebody be so evil? All because of what . . . wanting her man?

"So you poisoned me, Jayde?" Tatum finalized with
a narrowed glare. "You killed my *children?*"

"Oh please, don't blame your rotten womb on me,
Tatum. I only saved you a lifetime of pain and hurt. Respect was not going to paint the perfect family picture
with you so get that out of your head . . . you would have
been left with not one, but *two* snotty nose kids back to
the projects of Newark faster than you can say Brick City,
baby. The man was always . . . supposed . . . to be with . . .
me. He was created for me."

Tatum gave a half smile and nodded slowly. Her cell
phone began to buzz again and she knew Ree had to be
worried, but she only began to back into the large wall
decorated by books in the opposite direction of her
phone. She kept her focus on Jayde . . . and Jayde's
purse.

"You have a lot to say, Jayde. You such a bad bitch,
right? Why didn't you tell me from the jump you wanted
him? Then the baddest bitch could've just won. Instead
of playing like a phony-ass *punk*, and pretending to be
a friend?"

Jayde stood up, not blinking once and studying Tatum's face for any kind of fear. There was none.

"I enjoyed watching every minute of it, Tatum. You were like a pawn . . . a character . . . you were something to play with, someone who was supposed to be so strong and I weakened you, and now I'm getting bored and you know what . . . Why am I even talking to you—"

Jayde quickly pulled out the .32 just as Tatum brashly reached and grabbed for one of the books.

"Ah, ah, ah, baby girl," Jayde sang with a grin, staring Tatum right in the eyes as Tatum held the book in her hand, frozen. "Drop the book . . . drop it! I know where every gun is in this house. I'll have a bullet in you before you can even get it out."

Tatum gritted her teeth and glared at Jayde venomously, but she didn't show any fear, because she had none. Jayde had taken so much from her, she didn't care anymore. But she wasn't going out alone.

Tatum breathed deep and nodded against her will. She held both hands out, still holding on to the book.

"Put it down, now!" Jayde snapped, looking like the devil herself.

Tatum reluctantly began to lower down to the ground, bringing the book lower and lower. She knew Jayde was going to kill her, she knew these were the last moments of her life, but she needed to buy time.

"Okay . . . okay . . . I'm putting it down. You win . . . okay, Jayde? I'm putting . . . it . . . down . . ." Tatum squatted and began to gently release the book, moving slow and steady.

Jayde smiled wickedly.

"Oh, I didn't win . . . not yet. But I will."

Jayde threw off the safety and in that instant, Tatum's face turned from trepid to sinister. Tatum flung the book up at Jayde hard, praying it would cause enough distraction as she dashed behind the sofa in the same instant, dodging the shot that Jayde wildly fired.

"Bitch!" Jayde cursed, as the book landed in her face, throwing her off. She quickly regained her balance and aim but was again stunned by Tatum pouncing fearlessly on her, leaping from behind the couch like a cat. Tatum tackled Jayde like a linebacker, knocking Jayde's frame to the ground easily due to the five-and-a-half-inch stilettos Jayde couldn't balance on. This also sent the small gun flying smooth across the freshly waxed wooden floor, way out of reach for either of the girls.

"Argh, you grimy bitch!" Tatum screamed, grabbing a fist full of Jayde's hair and delivering a vicious blow to her jaw. Jayde in return grabbed Tatum by the neck and jaggedly dug her nails into her throat. Forget squaring up, this was straight survival of the fittest.

"Get . . . off . . . me . . ." Tatum struggled to say as she brought her fist again to Jayde's face, connecting with her lips and splitting the bottom one in two. Blood instantly filled Jayde's mouth. Licking it playfully, Jayde giggled lightly and threw all of her weight onto Tatum, struggling but managing to roll on top of her and continue to choke Tatum with all of her might. She wanted this bitch to die! Tatum swung like a maniac, looking into the eyes of a soulless shell, feeling like she just may be taking her last breath.

Nah, I ain't going out like this . . . I ain't . . .

She brought her hands to Jayde's bloody face and held the sides of her temples, digging her thumbs into Jayde's eye sockets roughly. Tatum's long nails scratched Jayde's corneas, causing blood to now trickle into her vision.

"Argghhhh!!!" Jayde screamed, releasing her grip to pry Tatum's hands off and losing the upper hand. In that instant Tatum used all of her might to push Jayde off of her and regain control, getting up and kicking Jayde hard in the crotch.

"Oh," Jayde cried out, clutching her pussy in agony. Tatum used the opportunity to boldly head in the direction of the gun. Running at top speed, she reached it and leaned down to grasp it, but was brought back by Jayde gripping her long tresses and pulling her head backward. Tatum was contorted at an angle to where all she could do was swing wildly.

Laughing madly as her blood spilled from her face down onto her dress, Jayde wore the look of a deranged monster.

"Give it up, Tatum," she urged maliciously. "I've got twenty years tae kwon do experience. I can kill you with two fingers!" She took her two fingers and dug them roughly into the pulse points of Tatum's throat as she continued to hold Tatum backward, and Tatum continued to pull and swing at her. "Two fingers," she taunted. "That's all it took to kill your little boy. Two fingers up to his little nose and mouth . . . Say Jayde, Tatum."

"Ahhh!" Tatum's rage allowed her to pull with all of her might just an inch ahead of her and snatch up the crystal vase that sat on one of the end tables, barely holding it with the tips of her fingers and feeling like her hair had been ripped from the root. But it didn't matter, her pain was void. This bitch had killed her baby.

She brought the vase up over her and crashed it into Jayde's head behind her with fury.

"You gonna die today, bitch!" Tatum bent down, picked up a piece of shattered glass while Jayde remained dazed, then she spun around slicing the side of Jayde's face open. "I'm from Newark, hoe! Fuck your tae kwon do!" Tatum brought the glass to her again as Jayde held up her hand and sliced her palm clean open.

"Arghhh!" Jayde hollered in agony.

"Give it up, Jayde!"

Dropping instantly in a split decision, Jayde clipped Tatum with her foot and sent Tatum collapsing clumsily to the floor. She reached long, her height working for her, and grabbed the .32, standing up wobbly over Tatum even though it seemed like there were two of her. The blow from the vase had her dizzy. Jayde smiled a deadly one, aimed, and heard the click. . . .

"Drop it."

"Ah," a sigh of relief escaped Tatum's lips as she looked up.

"Drop it or I'll be more than happy to put a hole through your big-ass head, you dirty bitch."

Jayde snickered, even though she sensed defeat. She would never show it, though, it wasn't in her nature.

"Aww, isn't . . . isn't this sweet." She turned around and faced the brave soul who dared held a gun to her head. "She fucked your man and you still come to save her. Aw, well *people let me tell you 'bout my best friend!*" Jayde sang sarcastically. "So how are you, sister girl?"

Sasha bit her bottom lip and stared into the eyes of Jayde. She had already cocked the 9-millimeter, that had been the first noise. The second one would be the bullet being sent to her dome. She just wanted to make sure Jayde didn't take Tatum with her.

"Drop your fucking gun, Jayde!" Sasha demanded.

Tatum lay still on the floor, looking back and forth between Sasha and then to Jayde, who still had the gun aimed at her but her body turned toward Sasha.

Jayde stared at Sasha for a long moment and a deadly silence filled the air. Everyone knew this could go any way. It could be *Reservoir Dogs* by the time this thing was over.

And then out of nowhere, Jayde busted out in laughter, like the scene was beyond comical.

"Wait . . . wait . . . hold up, hold up . . . I think I need my camera," she hooted while still waving the gun in Tatum's direction. "I can't take it . . . ! Okay, wait, *you're* gonna kill me? Sasha, have you even held a gun before? Or let alone shot one? Hell no!" Jayde continued to crack up. "You're gonna reflex, your arm's gonna go up flying and you're probably gonna end up shooting the chandelier," she joked. Tatum inched her body up and Jayde dropped all laughter and pointed straight at her with the weapon.

"Keep it still, brown sugar, I ain't even done with you yet." Jayde turned back to Sasha.

"Sasha, you don't know what you're doing. That's a gun, not a nail file, princess."

Sasha smiled and brought the nine right to Jayde's forehead.

"You betting a thousand on being wrong, *sister.*"

She thought of how she had shot Mike, and no one knew about that except her and Chauncey. Tatum and Jayde both wondered what that meant but were in no position to ask it now.

"Drop the gun, Jayde, now . . . or we'll just have to see whose bullets fly the quickest."

Jayde's face dropped instantly. She saw that Sasha was serious. Eyeing her with sincerity, Jayde's eyes began to plead.

"Sasha . . . really? You knew me way before you knew this bitch. She fucked your man. Lied to you! . . . We're family. You would kill me over *her?* We're blood! Blood is thicker than water, Sasha!"

Tatum swallowed hard, hoping Sasha didn't listen to her but already knowing in her heart she wouldn't. Sasha shot her eyes to Tatum and then back to Jayde. She placed her finger on the trigger and shook her head.

"No . . . it's not . . ."

Sasha closed her eyes, ready to kill again, finger applying pressure on the trigger and praying that Jayde didn't pull hers first. The front door flew open, stalling her and creating a chaotic scene.

"Freeze! Drop the weapons! Everyone, drop the damn weapons!"

"Drop 'em now!" About ten men in blue uniforms swarmed the inside of the mansion with their weapons drawn. "Drop 'em or we shoot!"

Sasha immediately lowered her gun and one of the men aimed at Jayde.

"These mothafuckas here." Jayde sucked her teeth and tossed the handgun onto the couch.

A few seconds later, a woman walked through the door and Tatum wondered what the hell was going on.

"She's fine," the woman said, pointing at Sasha. They immediately took their weapons off of Sasha.

"That's her," Sasha mumbled, pointing at Jayde with disgust in her eyes.

The officers sneered at Jayde and two approached her, one roughly pulled her arms behind her back and cuffing her.

"*Jayde Dupree.* Let's see if you could wiggle out of this," he chuckled, tightening the metal bracelets.

Jayde smirked and rolled her eyes.

"Please. She had her gun on me. This was self-defense."

Another officer stepped up and smacked her across the face. He was one of the ones who had been waiting to do that forever.

"Murder isn't self-defense . . . Jayde Dupree, you are under arrest for the murder of Penelope Daniels . . . You have the right to remain silent . . . anything you say or do can be used against you in the court of law. . . ."

Tatum looked up at Sasha and the Asian girl and wondered what was going on.

Neli?

Sasha threw her a half smile.

Long story, she mouthed.

Shaking her head, Tatum chuckled in amazement. Jayde had killed Neli? Tatum sat up but didn't stand; she was so sore, weak, and exhausted. She hadn't been in a fight since Kim fucked Mamagirl from Renner's, baby father . . . and that was like five years ago.

"You have nothing on me!" Jayde shouted cockily. "I'll be out in an hour and you know it."

Adriana stepped up and pulled out a tape recorder from her purse. She glared at Jayde and hit PLAY with pride, like she'd been waiting forever to do so . . .

I'll tell her, I'll stop you, Jayde. I'll get through to Tatum! She'll listen, and then Ree won't even come near your evil ass!

Neli's voice spoke, filling the room and silencing everyone. Jayde spoke right after.

You know, Neli, I think we're done here. And I'm feeling a little like it's judgment day or something. Your wicked ways have finally caught up to you, mama.

Pop! Pop! Pop! Pop!

The sounds of gunshots echoed off of the tape.

Jayde looked at the young Inspector Gadget knockoff and laughed as Adriana pressed STOP.

"So it's you. I knew I should've dusted you, Jackie Chan." She grinned and licked her lips. "Get my lawyers," she spoke to no one directly. Jayde knew, tape or no tape, she had the courts on lock.

She allowed the officers to escort her out and her heels clicked as if she were walking the runway. *Always a bad bitch, never anything less . . .* she thought.

"I'm so sorry, Tay. Are you all right?" Sasha dropped down to the floor to her best friend, her sister, after Jayde was well out of the mansion. "All of this time I've been caught up in my shit, and she's been here . . . and I feel so fucked up!" Sasha began crying profusely.

"Adriana kept trying to tell me and I wouldn't listen. And all this time, she was after Ree . . . and after *you*."

Tatum reached up and embraced Sasha and the two hugged for longer than they ever had. The love between them almost palpable.

"Ohhh brown bitch, it's okay. You didn't know . . . no one did." The two held each other so tight, faces in each other's hair, arms providing a blanket of love and ease to each other as they cried.

"I love you, black bitch," Sasha barely managed to mumble through her weeping. "I was gonna kill her ass . . . I swear I was." Sasha giggled with tears flowing down her eyes. She pulled away and looked into Tatum's wet eyes. Tatum laughed.

"Shit, I know you were. You ran up on her like you was Salt or somebody . . . on some real Foxy Brown stuff."

Sasha laughed and continued to cry as she nodded, now giggling hysterically.

"I was gonna show her gangsta, Tay. I really was. I was gonna smoke her ass."

Tatum cracked up and the two looked like two giggly little girls. Adriana even couldn't help but laugh.

"Yo, nobody says *smoked* anymore, Sash."

"Nobody but me. Wit my corny self."

They continued to laugh and reached for another hug.

"Ah, I love you, baby," Tatum told her so sincerely. Tatum backed up after a minute or so and pointed to Sasha's chest. "You . . . are right . . . here," she spoke, pointing to her heart. "Always."

Her voice cracked and a tear trickled down her face. Leaving Sasha behind would be the hardest thing she'd ever have to do. But she had to. Sasha knew in her heart from the declaration that Tatum was going back to Jamaica, and she didn't blame her at all.

"I know," she whispered.

Just when Tatum thought she felt all the relief that she needed, Ree came rushing through the doorway, Crush in tow with him.

His face dropped when he saw the damage to the house, the police, the whole scene. His eyes darted around the room and when they laid onto Tatum, he sighed in reprieve and nodded, assuring himself he could calm down.

He rushed over to her and knelt down. Sasha smiled at the two and stood, winking at Tatum as she stepped away.

I love you, girl, she mouthed.

Ree examined Tatum with apprehension.

"Tatum, what happened? Are you okay? Huh? You all right?" His eyes scanned over her. A few bruises and bumps spotted, he became angry.

"I'm okay, Ree. I'm okay . . . Jayde . . . she . . ." Tatum wasn't sure how to sum it up. She ran her hands through her hair and shrugged. "She tried to kill me."

Ree looked around the room, spotted the officers still surveying the scene, talking, asking Adriana questions. He took a deep breath. He couldn't believe this shit.

"Where is she now?" he asked calmly.

Tatum blew out air and raised her eyebrows as if to say *you'll never believe this*.

"Well . . . they just arrested her . . . for the murder of *Neli*."

Ree squinted and jerked his head slightly in surprise. That threw him for a loop, but Neli wasn't his focus.

"Are you hurt anywhere? Did she hurt you?"

Tears that were in the process of drying relined Tatum's eyes as she thought of the reality.

"Not physically, no . . . She . . . she killed our babies, Ree. She smothered Taye in his incubator and she laced my food with Clomid, forcing the early labor. Doctor . . ." Tatum's voice cracked as Ree looked on, taking it all in and trying not to go crazy. "Doctor . . . Patel . . . said I . . . I may not be able to carry *children* . . . ever." Tatum's face twisted in pain at that revelation. A young black officer who was standing nearby overheard and interrupted.

"Don't worry, ma'am. I know it may not be a consolation, but I'm gonna make sure she dies in prison," he assured, wanting to do everything in his power to make sure Jayde got life and nothing less. She had been at the top of his list for years.

Tatum knew Jayde's connections. She wondered if that was even possible. She chuckled lightly.

"Can you make that a promise?" she asked, looking up at him.

Ree held her chin and brought her eyes to his own.

"I can."

Chapter 17

"Everything is calculated from now on . . . You're a boss, move accordingly."

—Respect, *Still Thicker than Water*

"I don't give a fuck what you have to do! As much money as I pay you people, get me a bail. And get it now!" Jayde yelled furiously into the phone at her lawyer, and then slammed it down, almost breaking it, not caring for a response.

"Hey! Dupree! Knock it off!" one of the fat female guards yelled obnoxiously, overstuffing Cheetos in her mouth. Jayde started down the corridor, shooting her a glare.

"Aw, go shave your snatch, animal bitch."

Prison was a new scene for Jayde, but the two weeks she'd been there had been smooth so far. Most people knew her from the streets, and they respected her, which is why, as she traveled back to her cell, a Mexican woman handed her a carton of cigarettes. Everyone wanted in with her, they wanted to get paid with her when and if they ever made it out.

"Gracias," Jayde mumbled, and shot her a wink. Her long hair braided in two Pippy Longstocking plaits.

"De nada."

Jayde made her way to her cell and blew out air in aggravation. All of her connections, all of her money, she didn't expect to do two hours in jail let alone two weeks. She even had gotten Ree out in less time than that. Granted, this was murder, but she was *Jayde Dupree*. They had better get to work.

With little to do in the stone walls, Jayde decided to catch up on some beauty rest. Prison would not and could not stop her bad-ass show. Plopping down on the lower cot, she pressed PLAY on her CD player and closed her eyes. Her cell had more than the mere basic amenities. Someone had anonymously sent her plenty of leisure items like a CD player, music, books, shampoo, underwear, and things of that nature along with plenty of money on her "books." She knew it somehow came from her father.

"Dupree! New cell mate!"

Jayde sucked her teeth without even opening her eyes. She was told that she would absolutely not have to share her cell. That was one thing she thought her money had at least bought her.

"You got to be fucking kidding me," she huffed aloud, hearing the barred door clink open.

"What? Ya ghat a problem wit roomates, gyal?"

Jayde opened her eyes and glared at the girl, or whatever, letting her know that she was not to be fucked with, talked to, or approached in any manner, regardless of the pretty face.

A fucking island bitch . . .

"Hey, ya ghat a problem wit me takin' de bottom bunk . . . you sleep on de top," the girl had the audacity to suggest.

Jayde looked at the big black gorilla-looking bitch like she had lost all but a bit of her mind.

"Yeah, I got a fucking problem with that! Get your ass on the top."

The girl smirked, but threw her folded sheet and pillow package on the top bunk with no contest. The guards announced lights out in five minutes.

"So . . . what cha do ta get in here, Jayde?"

Jayde rolled her eyes and scowled.

"I killed someone . . . A big gorilla-looking bitch, in fact."

The woman chuckled and began taking off her shoes, obviously preparing for bed and learning that Jayde was far from social. She stripped down to her underwear and a T-shirt and climbed up on the top bunk quietly.

"Lights out!" another guard yelled, and then disappeared out of sight.

Immediately the prison went dark. There were small lights from the hall and light illuminating from the tiny windows, but that was about it.

Jayde sighed, looking forward to some sleep. Maybe the lights out would signal a *shut the fuck up* for the big bitch with the mouth. In the morning, Jayde would chew her attorneys out so they could chew the court out so they could get her the fuck out of here.

"Good night, Jayde," the big affectionate gorilla sang to her.

The hard sucking of her teeth was Jayde's reply. She closed her eyes and seemed to have a vision in the darkness behind her lids within seconds.

Jayde . . . Jayde . . . Good night, Jayde . . . What cha do ta get in here, Jayde?

Wait . . . I never told her my name . . . ? The guard only called me Dupree . . .

Jayde's eyes shot open in alarm, immediately on the defense, and she found the girl no longer out of view on the top bunk, but now standing right next to her bed with an evil scowl. She felt like she was in a scene of a horror movie just looking at this girl's mug.

"Who the fuck sent you?" Jayde hissed, trying to sound confident while her heart pounded in fear. Her body tensed and she swallowed the smallest amount of saliva that had managed to creep into her dry mouth. She debated calling for the guards but wondered if it'd matter. If it was who she thought it was, no one would come.

Of course . . . the accent . . . how could I be so dumb?

"Did you brush ya teeth?" the girl asked calmly, giving Jayde another foretaste at her accent with a nasty smirk growing on her ugly face.

Jayde's pride went out the window at the realization that she may be at her life's end.

"Guard! Guard!" she yelled, sitting up in the bed. The girl snickered and stepped closer.

"Here, ya can use my toothbrush." Without any warning, the girl took the makeshift shank formed out of her toothbrush straight to Jayde's throat with force. She stabbed her swiftly and deeply, like she was trained for it.

"Arghhhhhhhhhh . . . !" Jayde began to gargle on her own blood as the woman repeatedly stabbed her in the neck. Jayde could only bring her hands to her throat, trying to block more punctures, trying to stop the bleeding, trying to fight for her life. There was no use.

"P-p-pl-pleaseee," Jayde whispered raspily, holding her throat with her eyes wide, trying to make her way off the bed weakly. The woman took one final look at her and, with no mercy, brought the shank down one final time, deep into her neck, pushing it in as far as it could go and twisting it until she heard Jayde gasp her last cold breath. She grimaced down at Jayde, who was obviously dead, her eyes frozen open in terror, glowing even in the dark. *They say you deserved it if you die with your eyes open . . .*

She took her bloody tool and wiped it on her T-shirt and with absolutely no remorse she spit on Jayde's corpse.

"Maybe in yah next lifetime . . . yah gwan learn tah Respect."

And then she climbed back on the top bunk and went to sleep.

Crush pulled the Maybach up to the small dock and marina in Cabbage Key, located off of the Florida Keys. The place was remote, almost seeming deserted, and Tatum looked around at the barren exterior in curiosity.

"And why are we coming here again, babe?"

Ree turned and looked at her and then let out a delayed smile. He pinched her chin with love.

"I just need to say good-bye to a friend. Then we can be on our way."

Tatum figured she knew who the friend was, but she didn't press the issue. Some things she'd rather not know; she had learned that the hard way.

"Okay," she whispered with a small smile.

Ree exited the vehicle with ease and Tatum watched him the entire time. Even as he walked toward the small boathouse in the distance, he seemed to control movement itself. She was in love with him; she knew she'd made the right decision in her heart to stay by his side.

"You ready to get back to the islands?" Crush asked,

interrupting her thoughts. Tatum smiled wide at him and nodded.

"Oh yeah . . . most definitely. What about you? You excited about living in Jamaica? . . . You know you gonna be singing the 'One Love, One Life' song from the commercial," Tatum joked and Crush cracked up laughing.

"Seriously," she started. "I used to sing that song all the time when I first moved there."

Crush chuckled some more and slowed his laugh to respond.

"Of course . . . Me, Megan, the kids . . . we can't wait. Starting over, you know what I mean? And I know it's a new start for you. What's the first thing you gonna do when you get back?"

Tatum thought about it and then grinned.

"Well . . . I'm gonna get these hot air balloons going and make that money. I know that much!"

Crush nodded with a smile.

"Yo, tell me about that shit. Respect was telling me it's some money in that but I couldn't believe it."

"Well . . . it's these hot air balloons, right? And we have twenty of them . . ." Tatum started, enthralled in telling the story exactly how Ree had told her. In the meantime, Ree had entered the boathouse.

"Respect! What a pleasant surprise. I would ask what do I owe this honor but I'm afraid I already know."

Ree smirked and nodded, studying Mickel in his white linen pants and top looking like he'd shed ten years. He was looking happy, young, alive . . . really alive. He motioned his hand for Ree to join him in the small living room, which was adorned with straw furniture. The boathouse was modest, there were few amenities, but it looked like the perfect vacation getaway. Like a little piece of paradise.

Ree followed Mickel and took a seat at the small couch perpendicular to the chair Mickel sat in. He looked him directly in the eyes and let out a small sigh.

"You know what I'm going to say, old man."

Mickel shook his head and grinned.

"You're going to say that you'll recruit all new people, get this plan going, be the head of it like I always wanted you to be, and make us a whole lot of money, correct?"

Ree chuckled and pulled out a pre-rolled blunt. He lifted it, asking if he could light it with no words spoken. Mickel nodded and Ree pulled out his lighter, putting flame to the tip. He inhaled and, after a few seconds, he released his words with the disposable smoke.

"It's not happening, old man. I'm gone. I don't want to stick around and find anyone else. I don't want to stick around and do it myself. I don't even want to do the first run. It's over. I came to tell you that in person."

Mickel seemed disappointed but in reality, he knew. After Chauncey, and then after Jayde getting arrested, he knew that it was over. Maybe the master plan was never supposed to come into play. Maybe brilliant drug schemes like that only happened in the movies and the books.

Mickel nodded at Ree and took in a deep breath.

"I understand. Not that I don't regret the way everything happened, I know we could've made a lot of money. But it is over, because I have too much to risk trying to do it myself. Plus both families are not comfortable with all of this heat . . . so much has occurred. And for what it's worth, Respect, I apologize for . . . you know . . . Jayde. And I know how you normally would have handled that. I appreciate what you did . . . for me . . . because she is my child, and I do love her, as I do all of my children. How is Tatum? Do you know if she will be able to . . . still have children?"

Ree's response was a mellow shrug as he took another pull from the blunt and put his eyes toward the floor. He didn't want to talk about that. He felt so many things at that time and he knew he had accomplished what he'd come to . . . almost. And just because one knows what he is supposed to do, it doesn't make it easier. Ree felt conflicted.

Just as Ree was on the brink of contemplation, Mickel's cell phone, which sat on the table between them, began to vibrate with an incoming call. Both men looked down, but Mickel was the one to recognize it.

"Ah, it's from the lawyers. It must be word of Jayde." He caught his excitement and looked to Ree in empathy. "I'm sorry, Respect . . . is this . . . is this uncomfortable? I can take this in the other room."

Mickel knew it had to be hard for Ree, especially the type of man that he was, to let Jayde breathe after what she had done. He knew if Respect wanted to, he could have had Jayde touched in prison.

Ree took another toke of the blunt because he knew that Mickel was about to find out that he in fact *did* have Jayde touched in prison. He hoped he would understand, but deep down, he knew he would not.

"No . . . you can take the call. I'm heading out." He gave Mickel a handshake and brought him into a manly half embrace. And when Mickel was close, Ree whispered to him.

"Hey, old man . . . one more thing."

"Yeah?" Mickel asked, seeming concerned, feeling Ree's off energy, with his cell phone still vibrating in his hand. Ree stared him right in the eyes and then brought his mouth to Mickel's ear in privacy, placing his hand behind Mickel's head.

"I'm sorry." Before Mickel's eyebrows could fully furrow, Ree brought his .45 against Mickel's cheek and sent a bullet straight through his skull, the silencer muzzling the sound but nothing preventing the blood and brain matter from splattering onto the table.

Mickel dropped to the ground instantaneously, with his face still wearing a look of confusion, hurt, and pain. Ree stepped and stood over him, emptying two more bullets into his chest, staining his white linen shirt red and putting him out of his misery. Kneeling down with his elbows on his knees, Ree then brought his hand over Mickel's face while wearing regret all in his own and he gently closed Mickel's eyes.

He had loved the man like a second father, and many would deem him heartless for what he had done, but he knew he and his family would never be at peace if he didn't kill Mickel first. Once Mickel found out about Jayde, he would war, and Ree couldn't afford that, not with Tatum in the picture. He would surely kill Respect, or try to, and Tatum, and anyone else he wished. They had the same mentality.

Ree let out a sigh and took one final look at Mickel, wishing it didn't have to end like this. He saw the vibrating start on his cell phone again and he thought of the only positive, which was that he killed Mickel before he would have to hear the heartbreaking news of his daughter's murder.

Ree turned to head out with a heavy heart but was halted by a voice.

"Respect, what are you doing here . . ."

He spun around and Sasha's mother, Terri, stood holding a white china teapot, wearing her own white linen set.

"Where is Mick . . . ?"

She scanned the area looking for her love and when

her eyes finally covered every corner of the room and
landed on his dead body, she dropped her mouth into
an O of horror and dropped the teapot, sending glass
crashing and shattering everywhere. No words would or
could come out at first. Not after all of this, after all they
had been through. Finally her thoughts met her vocal
cords and she screamed out in pain. They were wearing
white because it was their wedding day. Although it
wouldn't have been very legal since she was technically
still married, it would have had value in their hearts.

"Whyyy!!! Respect, whyyyy!!!" Terri cried out in deep
agony as she looked up at Ree with tear-filled eyes. "How
could you? How could you kill him! He loved you!" She
dropped down to Mickel's body and cradled his head in
her lap, crying abundantly, and Ree looked down at her
in remorse.

Why did she have to be here? he couldn't help but wonder.

Ree sighed, feeling terrible, and without another
thought he raised his gun and sent a bullet straight
through Terri's forehead, killing her instantly.

Callous? Maybe. Necessary? Absolutely.

Let her live and live his own life wondering and
worrying, nope, the game didn't work like that. She was
the absolute definition of wrong place, wrong time. He
took a deep breath and stepped outside, knowing in his
heart he had done what he had to do.

"So we going home now?" Tatum asked, smiling
brightly at him like a little girl on Christmas Day as Ree
slid back into the car. He was thankful that he hadn't
gotten any blood on him, but he was always careful to
try not to. He knew all about killing, down to the angles
you would shoot someone to kill them slower, faster, not
leave blood on you, not leaving blood anywhere.

Ree glanced over at her and smiled, knowing that everything he did, in some prism had been directly related to his love for, and his need to protect, his queen. Ever since he'd spotted her outside of the club in New York, she'd become a focal point in his world. He had told her he'd die for her, and he meant that. He had told himself that he'd kill for her, and he proved that.

"Yeah . . . yeah, we going home now."

Tatum leaned over and fell into his strength as he wrapped one arm around her and directed Crush to the jet. Their fingers intertwined with ease.

The two of them had been through a lot, so much, too much . . . but in the end their love had survived.

Tatum wondered if it could survive one more thing, something she thought she wanted to forget but found herself just needing one more answer to. It was now or never. Let it out or let it go. Tatum's mind danced back and forth between overindulgence and ignorance as her stomach churned and spewed up word vomit.

"Ree?" her voice sang, almost shocking herself for beginning to pose the question.

"What up?" he murmured, gazing out the window and thinking of the past ten or so minutes that had just occurred, the two murders he had just committed. He knew that, unlike the others, he'd never forget this one.

Tatum looked up at his face and made the decision that no matter what the answer was to this question, she would have to live with it. It wouldn't change any of the choices that she'd made . . . but she had to know.

"Did you . . . did you *kill* my brother?"

Ree crinkled his brows and instantly looked down at her. Crush peered through the rearview and swerved, almost hitting a curb. *What?*

Not only was Ree thrown off by her brashness, the

calmness in her voice when she asked and the eye contact she held, but he also thought she had already known the answer to that. Then he thought about the words she had overheard from Jayde.

What if Tatum knew you were responsible for her brother's death?

Responsible . . . not the one who killed him . . .

"Did you . . . did you actually . . . pull the *trigger?*" Tears filled Tatum's eyes as she held them on Ree's. "Were you the one who actually took his life? Just tell me the truth . . . I need to know . . ."

Yes. That's what Ree wanted to say. *Does it make a difference?*

But then he started to think about the reasons why he wanted to say that. Would it be for his own conscience, for his own run of karma to jot down that he'd always followed the honesty policy? Or was there, in situations when you loved someone so much that you'd do anything not to see them hurt, was there such a thing in those instances . . . as a good lie?

If there was anything that Tatum had done enough, it was hurt. Everyone knew that. He would have no more of that.

So with the straightest face and the most sincere tone, Ree brushed his fingers across her sweet cheek and answered her with what he knew was the right answer. . . .

"No."

Tatum studied him for a moment and then let out a shaky and visible sigh of relief. Ree could literally see a weight lifted off her. He would not torture her for the rest of her life, letting her know she loved a man who took her brother's life with his hands, even if she really did know the truth in her heart. He would not be so cruel to admit it. He would sacrifice his conscience for hers.

Tatum pulled in closer to him and Ree cocooned her in his arms. Crush looked through the rearview and nodded with a half smile, and everything seemed to finally be at peace.

And just as they reached the jet and Ree and Tatum shared a sweet kiss, her cell phone rang, interrupting the moment. She answered in her serene state.

"Hello . . ."

She was greeted by a woman.

"Hi . . . is this Tatum Mosley?"

Ree helped Tatum out of the car and closed the door behind her while Tatum focused on her call.

"This is Tatum . . . Tatum Knights . . . who's this?" Tatum looked to Ree wearing an expression of confusion as he stared back at her.

"Hi, Tatum, my name is Lilly . . . and I'm a nurse at Virginia Beach Hospital. I'm sorry to bother you . . . but do you know a Nichole Samuel?"

Tatum crinkled her brow, knowing that was the government name of her nieces' mother.

"Yes . . . yes, I know her. Is she all right?"

There was a brief silence followed by a deep breath.

"Well . . . no. Unfortunately, Nichole Samuel overdosed . . . on heroin . . . and she passed away this afternoon. I'm . . . I'm sorry. My sincerest condolences. We were told to call you by your nieces . . . Chanel and Tangee Samuel. They were alone in the house and the grandmother cannot be found. Is there any way that you can come here?"

Tatum glanced up at Ree, her jaw dropped in shock. She was devastated that the girls had to suffer the loss of a mother like she herself had. However, she couldn't help feel complete knowing they'd be back with her. Where she felt they always belonged.

Tatum closed her mouth and swallowed hard.

"Yes. Tell them . . . tell them we're on our way."

Tatum ended the call and looked up at Ree still in shock. She truly couldn't believe it.

"Ree, guess what . . . That was a nurse from Virginia Beach Hospital. Nikki's dead . . . she . . . she overdosed." Tatum shook her head in disbelief. "Tangee and Chanel told her to call me."

Ree looked down at her and sighed. He immediately wondered how the girls were taking it, he knew they had to get to them. He briefly wondered if anything else could happen. It seemed anything that could shake up their world, had done so. He hoped this was the end.

Ree grabbed Tatum's hand and pulled her to him, looking down into her eyes and nodding his head toward the jet.

"C'mon, Miss Lady . . . let's go get our girls."

Tatum smiled and breathed a deep sigh of reprieve, allowing him to lead the way. And she knew at that moment that they'd seen too much tragedy to ever be a happily ever after. It was damn near impossible. But her, Chanel, Tangee, and Ree, starting over and living a life in sunny beautiful Jamaica . . . man, they'd be as happily ever after as happy could be. And for everything that had led them to it, and for everything they conquered, and for everything that they knew they deserved . . . that was more than enough.

Epilogue

"I guess at least one of us gets the happy ending, huh?"
—Sasha, *Still Thicker than Water*

After the storm

Mickel and Terri's bodies were found days later by a local. There were no identification leads on the two and no one reported them missing or claimed the bodies. They were buried on the island as a John and Jane Doe next to each other . . . eternally. . . .

Chauncey is currently housed at Georgia State Prison where he was sentenced to twenty-five years to life in prison for the murder of Bleek. The possibility of his release is highly unlikely given he was in violation of his parole at the time of the incident. He accepts no mail from Sasha and declined all of her visits. After the first six months, she stopped trying. . . .

Sasha moved back to New Jersey, sharing a house with the only father she'd ever known, Bill, and her daughter, Aubrey.

Being that her mother had declared she was running away with a new lover, Sasha and Bill had no reason to ever report her missing and thus they remain clueless about her murder. After six months of no response from Chauncey with numerous attempts at apologies, she finally received a letter from him. In reality it was from Georgia State Prison stating Chauncey was requesting DNA testing of Aubrey. After persuasion from her father and Tatum, Sasha reluctantly went through with the test. Despite the fact of Aubrey being his spitting image, she was not his. Sasha now is a nurse at St. Peters Hospital in New Brunswick, New Jersey, and is currently searching the market to buy a house. She called her friend G, whom she met on the highway that memorable night. . . . They have a date for him to show her his house next week. . . .

Jayde's dead body was found in her cell the next morning. All of her accounts were seized by the state, totaling $7.2 million. She was buried by the state and after trying to locate her family, and finding out that her biological mother, Emerald, had recently suffered a severe stroke in a mental institution in New Jersey, only two people ended up attending her funeral. It was the brother she'd never met . . . Julez Payne, and his girlfriend, Jordin. . . .

Tatum and Respect moved back to Jamaica, into their old estate. After rebuilding the hotel, they now run the resort along with Tatum's profitable hot air balloon attraction. Chanel and Tangee returned with them and this time, Ree saw to it that the adoption papers were signed, legal and legit. The girls are enjoying life in Jamaica and Ree's father, Leroy, and Crush and his wife both live in homes only miles away. They sometimes all get together for dinner on Sundays.

Respect arranged for the bodies of baby Taye and baby Tamia to be flown to and buried in Jamaica, at a small private gravesite near the estate. After months of considering, Tatum and Ree finally decided to try again for another baby. After ordering her to be bedridden for the entire pregnancy, the doctors now expect Tatum to make it through the full term of her pregnancy. She is closing in on her seventh month and all seems to be well with their baby boy.

Don't miss the first book
in Saundra's Sweetest Revenge series

Her Sweetest Revenge

Available now!

Chapter 1

Sometimes I wonder how my life would've turned out if my parents had been involved in different things, like if they had regular jobs. My mother would be a social worker, and my father a lawyer or something. You know, jobs they call respectable and shit.

Supposedly these people's lives are peaches and cream. But when I think about that shit I laugh, because my life is way different. My father was a dope pusher who served the whole area of Detroit. And when I say the whole area, I mean just that. My dad served some of the wealthiest politicians all the way down to the poorest people in the hood who would do anything for a fix. Needless to say, if you were on cocaine before my father went to prison, I'm sure he served you; he was heavy in the street. Lester Bedford was his birth name, and that's what he went by in the streets of Detroit. And there was no one who would fuck with him. Everybody was in check.

All the dudes on the block were jealous of him because his pockets were laced. He had the looks, money, nice cars, and the baddest chick on the block, Marisa

Haywood. All the dudes wanted Marisa because she was a redbone with coal-black hair flowing down her back and a banging-ass body, but she was only interested in my dad. They had met one night at a friend's dice party and had been inseparable since then.

Life was good for them for a long time. Dad was able to make a lot of money with no hassle from the feds, and Mom was able to stay home with their three kids. Three beautiful kids, if I may say so. First, she had me, Mya, then my brother, Bobby, who we all call Li'l Bo, and last was my baby sister, Monica.

We were all happy kids about four years ago; we didn't need or want for nothing. My daddy made sure of that. The only thing my father wanted to give us next was a house with a backyard. Even though he was stacking good dough, we still lived in the Brewster-Douglass Projects.

All those years he'd been trying to live by the hood code. However, times were changing. The new and upcoming ballers were getting their dough and moving out of the hood. Around this time my dad decided to take us outta there too.

Before he could make a move, our good luck suddenly changed for the worse. Our apartment was raided by the feds. After sitting in jail for six months, his case finally went to court, where he received a life sentence with no possibility of parole.

My mother never told us what happened, but sometimes I would eavesdrop on her conversations when she would be crying on a friend's shoulder. That's how I overheard her saying that they had my father connected to six drug-related murders and indicted on cocaine charges. I couldn't believe my ears. My father wouldn't kill anybody. He was too nice for that. I was completely pissed off; I refused to hear any of that. It was a lie. As far as I was concerned, my father was no murderer and all that shit he was accused of was somebody's sick fantasy. He was innocent. They were just jealous of him because he was young, black, and borderline rich. True, it was drug money, but in the hood, who gave a fuck. But all that was in the past; now, my dad was on skid row. Lockdown. Three hots and a cot. And our home life reflected just that.

All of a sudden my mother started hanging out all night. She would come home just in time for us to go to school. For a while that was okay, but then her behavior also started to change. I mean, my mother looked totally different. Her once-healthy skin started to look pale and dry. She started to lose weight, and her hair was never combed. She tried to comb it, but this was a woman who was used to going to the beauty shop every week. Now her hair looked like that of a stray cat.

I noticed things missing out of the house, too, like our Alpine digital stereo. I came home from school one day and it was gone. I asked my mother about it, and she said she sold it for food. But that had to be a lie because we were on the county. Mom didn't work, so we received food stamps and cash assistance. We also received government assistance that paid the rent, but Mom was responsible for the utilities, which started to get shut off.

Before long, we looked like the streets. After my father had been locked up for two years, we had nothing. We started to outgrow our clothes because Mom couldn't afford to buy us any, so whatever secondhand clothes we could get, we wore. I'm talking about some real stinking-looking gear. Li'l Bo got suspended from school for kicking some boy's ass about teasing him about a shirt he wore to school with someone else's name on it. We had been too wrapped up in our new home life to realize it. When the lady from the Salvation Army came over with the clothes for Li'l Bo, he just ironed the shirt and put it on. He never realized the spray paint on the back of the shirt said *Alvin*. That is, until this asshole at school decided to point it out to him.

Everything of value in our house was gone. Word on the streets was my mother was a crackhead and prostitute. I tried to deny it at first, but before long, it became obvious.

Now it's been four years of this mess, and I just can't take it anymore. I don't know what to do. I'm only seventeen years old. I'm sitting here on this couch hungry with nothing to eat and my mom is lying up in her room with some nigga for a lousy few bucks. And when she's done, she's going to leave here and cop some more dope. I'm just sick of this.

"Li'l Bo, Monica," I shouted so they could hear me clearly. "Come on, let's go to the store so we can get something to eat."

"I don't want to go to the store, Mya. It's cold out there," Monica said, pouting as she came out of the room we shared.

"Look, put your shoes on. I'm not leaving you here without me or Li'l Bo. Besides, ain't nothing in that kitchen to eat so if we don't go to the store, we starve tonight."

"Well, let's go. I ain't got all night." Li'l Bo tried to rush us, shifting side to side where he stood. The only thing he cares about is that video game that he has to hide to keep Mom from selling.

On our way to the store we passed all the local wannabe dope boys on our block. As usual, they couldn't resist hitting on me. But I never pay them losers any

mind because I will never mess around with any of
them. Most of the grimy niggas been sleeping with my
mom anyway. Especially Squeeze, with his bald-headed
ass. Nasty bastard. If I had a gun I would probably shoot
all them niggas.

"Hey, Mya. Girl, you know you growing up. Why don't
you let me take you up to Roosters and buy you a burger
or something?" Squeeze asked while rubbing his bald
head and licking his nasty, hungry lips at me. "With a fat
ass like that, girl, I will let you order whatever you want
off the menu."

"Nigga, I don't need you to buy me jack. I'm good."
I rolled my eyes and kept stepping.

"Whatever, bitch, wit' yo' high and mighty ass. You
know you hungry."

Li'l Bo stopped dead in his tracks. "What you call my
sister?" He turned around and mugged Squeeze. "Can
you hear, nigga? I said, what did you call my sister?" Li'l
Bo spat the words at Squeeze.

I grabbed Li'l Bo by the arm. "Come on, don't listen
to him. He's just talkin'. Forget him anyway." I dismissed
Squeeze with a wave of my hand.

"Yeah, little man, I'm only playing." Squeeze had an
ugly scowl on his face.

Before I walked away I turned around and threw up
my middle finger to Squeeze because that nigga's time
is coming. He's got plenty of enemies out here on the
streets while he's wasting time fooling with me.

When we made it to the store I told Li'l Bo and
Monica to watch my back while I got some food. I picked
up some sandwich meat, cheese, bacon, and hot dogs.
I went to the counter and paid for a loaf of bread to
make it look legit, and then we left the store. Once outside, we hit the store right next door. I grabbed some

canned goods, a pack of Oreo cookies for dessert, and two packs of chicken wings. When we got outside, we unloaded all the food into the shopping bags we brought from home. That would get us through until next week. This is how we eat because Mom sells all the food stamps every damn month. The thought of it made me kick a single rock that was in my path while walking back to the Brewster.

When we got back to the house, Mom was in the kitchen rambling like she's looking for something. So she must be finished doing her dirty business. I walked right past her like she ain't even standing there.

"Where the hell y'all been? Don't be leavin' this house at night without telling me," she screamed, then flicked some cigarette butts into the kitchen sink.

"We went to the store to get food. There is nothin' to eat in this damn house." I rolled my eyes, giving her much attitude.

"Mya, who the hell do you think you talking to? I don't care where you went. Tell me before you leave this house," she said, while sucking her teeth.

"Yeah, whatever! If you cared so much, we would have food." I got smart again. "Monica, grab the skillet so I can fry some of this chicken," I ordered her, then slammed the freezer door shut.

Mom paused for a minute. She was staring at me so hard I thought she was about to slap me for real. But she just turned around and went to her room. Then she came right back out of her room and went into the bathroom with clothes in hand.

I knew she was going to leave when she got that money from her little trick. Normally, I want her to stay in the house. That way I know she's safe. But tonight, I'm ready for her to leave because I'm pissed at her